A Fresh Start

Cass began her writing life in Regency England, enlisted Jane Austen's help to time-travel between then and the present day and is now happily ensconced in 21st-century Cornwall. Well, in her imagination and soul; her heart and physical presence reside in northern England with her ever-patient husband and Tig and Tag, their cute but exceptionally demanding moggies.

A bit of a nomad, Cass has called three countries home, as well as six different English counties, but her aspiration is to one day reunite with her beloved West Country. In the meantime, she writes feel-good contemporary romances set in Cornwall and, in doing so, manages to live there vicariously through her characters and settings.

An Ambassador for the Jane Austen Literacy Foundation, Cass is also a member of the Jane Austen Society UK and the Society of Authors.

Also by Cass Grafton

The Austen Adventures (with Ada Bright)

The Particular Charm of Miss Jane Austen
The Unexpected Past of Miss Jane Austen

The Little Cornish Cove series

New Dreams at Polkerran Point
Escape to Polkerran Point
Christmas at Polkerran Point
A Fresh Start at Polkerran Point

A Fresh Start at Polkerran Point

Cass Grafton

CANELO

First published in the United Kingdom in 2025 by

Canelo, an imprint of
Canelo Digital Publishing Limited,
20 Vauxhall Bridge Road,
London SW1V 2SA
United Kingdom

A Penguin Random House Company

The authorised representative in the EEA is Dorling Kindersley Verlag GmbH.
Arnulfstr. 124, 80636 Munich, Germany

Copyright © Cass Grafton 2025

The moral right of Cass Grafton to be identified as the creator of this work has been asserted in accordance with the Copyright, Designs and Patents Act, 1988.

All rights reserved. No part of this publication may be reproduced or transmitted in any form or by any means, electronic or mechanical, including photocopy, recording, or any information storage and retrieval system, without permission in writing from the publisher.

No part of this book may be used or reproduced in any manner for the purpose of training artificial intelligence technologies or systems. In accordance with Article 4(3) of the DSM Directive 2019/790, Canelo expressly reserves this work from the text and data mining exception.

A CIP catalogue record for this book is available from the British Library.

Print ISBN 978 1 80436 606 6
Ebook ISBN 978 1 80436 607 3

This book is a work of fiction. Names, characters, businesses, organizations, places and events are either the product of the author's imagination or are used fictitiously. Any resemblance to actual persons, living or dead, events or locales is entirely coincidental.

Cover design by Head Design

Cover images © Shutterstock

Printed and bound in Great Britain by Clays Ltd, Elcograf S.p.A.

Look for more great books at
www.canelo.co
www.dk.com

To our gorgeous granddaughter, Ava, who came into our lives as I completed this book and will change our world forever in the most beautiful of ways.

Chapter One

The One When Kate Decides to Go West

The Point Hotel, nestled in its embrace of tall evergreens above the quaint Cornish fishing village of Polkerran Point, exuded elegance, as did the dark-haired woman emerging from the entrance with a brisk step.

Unlike the hotel, however, Kate Stretton's aura concealed a tendency towards clumsiness, which she'd tried hard to overcome since childhood, and never quite mastered.

Pausing under the striking portico of the building, she fished in her designer clutch for her keys, which fell to the floor with a clatter. Rolling her eyes, she retrieved the keyring and walked carefully down the steps, relieved to have the final interview over.

Could this – at last – be the completion of the puzzle, one she'd laboured over for more than a year? Who knew extracting oneself from a failed marriage could be more complex than planning the wedding in the first place?

Driving out of the beautifully landscaped hotel grounds, Kate eased the car down the winding hill into the village, too focused on avoiding scraping the paintwork on the cottages leaning on each other either side of the narrow lane to appreciate her surroundings. Once she'd parked up on the harbourside, however, and exited the car into the crisp January air, she took an appreciative look around.

The wintry skies over Polkerran Point were the palest of blues, dusted with gossamer wisps of cloud stretching their tendrils towards the horizon. Sea birds soared and dived in the wake of a small fishing boat as it approached the harbour, their plaintive cries mingling with the staccato hammering emanating from a nearby boatyard.

Turning around, Kate leaned against the harbour wall as a brisk breeze whipped a strand of hair from her neatly fastened chignon. She tucked it behind her ear, her keen gaze skimming over pastel-painted cottages huddled in clusters on the steep hillside, as smoke curled from various chimneys, spiralling upwards against the stark background of exposed cliffs and winter-stripped branches.

'Kate! Over here!'

Wheeling around, she waved at her friend, Anna Seymour – a Polkerran resident – and set off across the street, picking her way carefully over the uneven cobbles in her high heels.

'So, how'd it go?' Anna led the way into Karma, a smart coffee shop nearby.

'They've offered me the role.'

'Fantastic!'

Anna's hazel eyes sparkled with delight as they ordered drinks, and once they'd settled onto the squashy sofas positioned in the window, she leaned forward eagerly.

'You'll take it? You could do the job stood on your head.'

Which was precisely why Kate was dithering about whether to accept.

'Ah.' Anna picked up her mug. 'You're thinking it might not be enough of a challenge.'

'I was so enticed by the thought. Moving to this gorgeous place.' Kate waved a manicured hand at the window. 'A new beginning and a fresh perspective for Mollie – a chance for her to escape that awful school.' She picked up her own mug. 'When you showed me the ad in December, it felt as though it was meant to be.'

The two women had been good friends ever since Kate had taken Anna on as a project manager at an event co-ordination company in Yorkshire, and Kate missed her friend very much when she'd inherited a property in Cornwall and made her own fresh start four hundred miles away. When Kate finally visited Polkerran Point, for Anna's marriage to Oliver Seymour just a month ago, she'd been charmed by its quiet winter beauty.

'But you don't have to do the job for ever. It's just a means to an end, to enable you to start over, remember?'

It was true, and it wasn't as if the slightly lower salary was a problem. The marital home – an extensive property on the outskirts of Harrogate – had sold a year ago and Kate could easily afford a house when the time came, especially as she'd also leapt at the chance to take a generous package from her company when they'd been restructuring.

'When do they want you to start?'

'Yesterday!' Amusement filled Kate's attractive features. 'They're flexible, saying I can work from Yorkshire initially, but as you know, being an event manager isn't something that can be done remotely. No, if I'm going to do this, I need to get down here. The school break in February will be the best time for Molls to switch.' Kate sipped her coffee, eyeing Anna over the rim of her mug. 'It was nice staying up at the hotel last night, but I prefer your place.'

Anna ran a bed and breakfast from her home at Westerleigh Cottage – a slight misnomer. For all its charm and character, it was a substantial house, perched on an outcrop of rocks near the entrance to Polkerran's crescent-shaped bay.

With an apologetic smile, Anna nestled back into her seat. 'I'm not usually full in January, but this walking group has been coming every year. I would have asked you up there for coffee, but there's no way we'd have survived the morning without interruption.'

'How so?'

Anna looked over as the coffee shop door opened. 'One of the unanticipated charms of the cove, as people around here refer to it. Morning, Mrs Lovelace.'

An elderly lady with white curls framing a pleasant, weathered face came over, a shopping basket on her arm.

'There you be, my lovely. Jeannie said as you'm be out this mornin'.' She eyed Kate with curiosity, and she bore with the scrutiny.

'This is an old friend of mine, Mrs Lovelace: Kate.'

The lady nodded. 'You'm was at the church for the wedding, young'un. I remembers saying to my mate, Cleggie. That maid'll be regretting they heels by nightfall.'

Kate laughed. 'You were quite right. I did.'

Mrs Lovelace's bright eyes fell upon Kate's much cherished Laboutins.

'And I haven't learned my lesson.' She smiled warmly at the elderly lady as her gaze took in Kate's business attire. 'I've been for an interview, Mrs Lovelace. Otherwise, I'd probably be in my wellies.'

'Kate's been offered the job of Event Manager at the hotel,' Anna interjected.

Mrs Lovelace hitched the basket more firmly onto her arm. 'Tha's right. Those people at the posh hotel would expect no less. My Jeannie works there in the down season. Has to put her Devon clothes on, she does. Well now, my lovelies. Best be getting on. Time waits for no jam.'

The lady bid them farewell and headed to the counter, and Kate eyed Anna in confusion.

'Mrs L has her own special vocabulary.'

Grinning, Kate got to her feet. 'Fair enough. Okay, I'd best head off too.'

Anna followed Kate from the cafe, chattering about her recent honeymoon in Switzerland and speaking fondly of Oliver – who was a social historian and author – and his new book contract.

'Let me know what you decide and if you need a couple of rooms in the short term.' Anna hugged her fiercely when they reached the car and, for some reason, emotion pricked Kate's eyes. She needed to be around people like Anna, those who were genuinely good at heart. 'I wish you'd been able to stay longer. I barely saw you at the wedding, there was so much happening.'

'I know. Sorry it's short and sweet this time.' Kate opened the car door and tossed her bag onto the passenger seat, before turning back for one last look around. 'I suppose I should've brought Mollie with me, but I didn't need any teenage negativity just now.'

Anna waved her off, but as Kate drove along the harbour front and took the road uphill out of the village, she reflected on her daughter. For years, every decision she'd made had been centred around Mollie and what was best for her – even sticking it out in a long-dead marriage – until the final straw came.

The habitual anger washed over Kate as Hugo's deception flared into focus, and her grip tightened on the wheel momentarily, before she drew in a calming breath.

'Let it go, let it go,' she sang tunefully, determined to harness the refrain her daughter had sung repeatedly during her old *Frozen* obsession. 'Think of Mollie instead.'

It was the perfect distraction and, as Kate reached the main road, she turned her mind to weighing up the suitability of this move and its potential impact on her mercurial, but also extremely smart, thirteen-year-old daughter.

–

A couple of weeks later, with Mollie's private school broken up for the fortnight's break, Kate repeated the journey south, this time with her daughter's blessing and all ties severed. Neither of them had been sorry to close the door for the last time on the furnished flat they'd been renting for the last year.

Dropping Mollie and Podge – their portly, tabby rescue cat – at her parents' in Bristol, Kate hugged her daughter tightly as they said farewell.

'I'll call this evening. Are you sure you'll be okay?'

'Muuuum!' Mollie had protested, wriggling out of the embrace. 'I'm thirteen, not three. You know I love Glammie and Glamps. We've already agreed how much time I can spend on my phone. Besides, Glammie wants me to teach her how to make reels. It's only a week and they'll be bringing me down.'

'I hope I've done the right thing, love. You've never even been to Cornwall and—'

'Google images, Insta, YouTube.' Mollie ticked them off on her fingers. 'This place is a seaside town, isn't it? Water, boats, seagulls. I doubt there'll be anything exciting. Besides, you've been binge watching *Doc Martin* and *Beyond Paradise* since you came back from Anna's wedding. I get it.'

Feeling she'd got the message too, Kate started the engine. Instinctively, she glanced in the rear-view mirror as she reached the junction from her parents' street, knowing Mollie would have gone inside without a second thought.

But her daughter stood on the pavement, watching as the car moved away, and unexpected emotion caught in Kate's throat.

'Get a grip,' she silently admonished as she turned out of the road. 'You're the grown up, remember?'

—

The first morning in the new job passed in a blur, which was how Kate liked it, but after a hurried lunch, she followed her new colleagues down the marble-tiled entrance hall to a meeting of all the office-based staff, which apparently took place on the second Monday of every month.

'We use the private dining room,' one of them said to Kate as she led the way.

Private, Kate mused to herself as she took a seat, was a tad misleading. Although the room was separated from the restaurant by a thick wall, there was a large arched Georgian-style window in the centre of it, and despite the leafy plants on its sill, from where Kate sat, there was a clear view of the centre of the dining area.

Kate paid careful attention to the agenda – despite it covering many topics she had no familiarity with yet – and made notes in the margin to follow up on later, but as the next slide changed, something caught her eye in the adjacent room.

A man with dark red hair had taken a seat at a table not too far away. Kate ducked her head, staring at the page of notes, her brow furrowing. She had a feeling she'd seen him before, but he hadn't been a wedding guest, she was certain...

Surreptitiously, she raised her head. If she scooted slightly to the right, he was hidden from view behind the central arrangement on the sill. Ten seconds later, Kate eased back to the left.

The man had placed a laptop on the table and, as she watched, he paused to take a sip of water before his thoughtful gaze returned to the screen. There was an air of melancholy about him that instantly drew Kate's curiosity, and she continued to observe him discreetly as he turned his head to where the windows gave out onto a balcony.

He had a handsome profile, with a chiselled jawline, a straight nose and a layered fringe of hair which he brushed aside, and—

A sharp nudge of her arm, and Kate swung around to look at the young woman beside her.

'You're on,' she said quietly.

The hotel manager continued. 'As I was saying, it's time to introduce our new member of staff. Kate, would you like to come up front?'

Summoning her most professional smile, Kate sent a final glance towards the Georgian window as she joined the manager. It was a long time since she'd noticed a man in the way she'd admired the one in the restaurant.

Was there something about the Cornish air, and if so, would it change her for ever?

Chapter Two

The One With the Clash

By the end of her third day, Kate felt a little more engaged. The current event manager was about to finish work, her baby's birth imminent, and couldn't wait to hand over a long list of projects, from weddings and family parties to various business meetings.

It sounded promising, but Kate wasn't blind to the many gaps between these bookings and how often the meeting and function rooms would lie empty.

Once back in her lovely room at Anna's B&B, she sat at the dressing table and released her hair from the sleek up-do she favoured for work, refastening it into a more casual ponytail. Then she leaned forward, turning her head from side to side. She was forty later in the year. She didn't feel she looked much older than at thirty, aside from the slight deepening of the fine lines around her eyes and the odd grey hair. Was it optimism or the soft natural light coming in through the windows?

Kate dismissed the nonsensical thought, checking her nails for any chips in the varnish as she headed to the wardrobe. There was a beauty salon at the hotel. She'd need to book an appointment soon.

A notification pinged on her phone and she picked it up in anticipation of being it Mollie, but the day immediately spiralled downwards. Hugo.

Despite the distance, and the marriage's steady demise over several years, her temper began to simmer. Every thought of her ex-husband stirred the memory of his one big deceit, the discovery of which she wasn't sure she'd ever get over.

Kate scanned the message, then threw the phone onto the bed and slumped down beside it.

When would she *ever* be done with the moron? Kate reached for the drawer in the bedside table, extracting a small leather box.

'Time for action,' she murmured, balancing it on her palm.

Five minutes later, she found Anna in the kitchen preparing dinner. 'I'll help out when I get back. I'm in a foul mood, so I'm going walkies.'

A dog – a cockapoo-mix – curled in the basket beside the hearth sat up, and Anna laughed.

'You said the fatal "w" word.'

Amused despite her inner frustration, Kate shrugged into her coat and retrieved the lead from the boot room. 'Come on, Dougal. You can keep me company.'

Walking briskly uphill, the dog happily scampering at her heels, Kate tried to shed the disgust she felt for Hugo. The great deception was, of course, the lowest of the low, but this was still trawling unnecessary depths…

> You forgot to leave your rings. Those diamonds are worth a small fortune and as I paid for them, I'd like them back.

'Get rid of them, Mum,' Mollie had urged, sitting cross-legged on Kate's bed one morning, when Hugo first demanded the return of her engagement ring and wedding band. 'Sell them and buy that Burberry bag you keep ogling. Or get a facelift. You probably need that more.'

A pretend pillow fight had ensued, but Hugo's persistence over the rings was beyond petty. The man was rolling in wealth.

Passing a doggie waste bin, Kate suppressed a snort. Shame he wasn't rolling in something else.

Emerging onto the coast path, hand dipping into her pocket, Kate stopped by a wooden railing along the cliff edge. A gap led to some stone steps down to an expanse of beach to her left, but although the tide was out, waves pounded the outcrop of rocks to her right, spray caught by the breeze dusting her face. She opened the small box and took out two rings, tied together with a piece of thin ribbon.

Her parents agreed with Mollie, but whatever Kate did with the money, she knew it would represent the loveless marriage she'd escaped, and of that she didn't need any reminders. This was a new life, time to be rid of the past once and for all.

She called Dougal to heel, hand outstretched towards where the water continued to crash to her right, but as she took a step forward, her boot caught in the uneven stones and she stumbled. The rings tumbled merrily from her grasp, only to be caught by a hefty gust of Cornish wind sailing around the headland, diverting its catch back towards the steps instead.

'Ow! What the *hell*...'

A man appeared, sporting a dark green Barbour jacket, Hunter wellies and a noticeable mark above his right brow.

'Did *you* throw these?' His voice was cutting, his expression uncompromising as he held up the rings, which swung in torment on their ribbon.

Definitely nothing melancholy about him today, Kate mused silently, taking in the handsome features which had caught her eye the other day.

'I'm so sorry,' she began, mortified. 'I—'

'What the hell did you think you were doing? Did thought even come into it?'

The temper which had been simmering rose a few notches.

'All too much, as it happens,' she snapped back.

'This is an Area of Outstanding Natural Beauty and – in case you've had your head in the sand – we're all trying to be more environmentally friendly.' His tone was uncompromising.

'I know, but—'

'Then why are you throwing metal into the water?' His gaze narrowed as his eyes raked over her. 'You're an incomer.'

She'd soon be an outgoer, if his expression was any indication of his thoughts. Still, everything he said was true, but in Kate's present frame of mind, that didn't really help. The last thing she wanted right now was to listen to a man spouting on and – worse – being right. Especially as he was. Right.

'Fine. Here –' She held out her palm, fiery brown eyes locked with steely blue.

He didn't move for a second, then stepped forward and took her hand, placing the rings in her palm and closing her fingers over them.

'Respect the water. The sea is not a disposal unit.' His tone was less angry, but his dissatisfaction was evident.

Yes, I know. I'm sorry. Got too wrapped up in the moment...

Trying not to notice the sensation of his skin against hers, Kate stilled, but he released her hand and called to someone named Bayley.

As a black labrador scrambled up the steps onto the cliff path, Kate fastened Dougal's lead, but the man strode away without any further words, the dog at his heels. Unlike his master, however, the lab paused to look back at where she stood.

Glancing down, Kate huffed out a laugh, despite the tense few minutes. Dougal, tongue lolling as he panted, watched Bayley with bright eyes, tugging at his lead, but even as the tall figure disappeared, she shook her head.

'Sorry, Dougal. That's one local we haven't made too good a first impression on. Let's go this way instead.'

–

The next few days sped by, with Kate approaching everything with her habitual efficiency. There were things she didn't know about how the hotel worked yet, but she had an ability to recall names with ease and as the first weekend approached – one without any events she needed to work, thank goodness – she felt she'd begun to find her feet.

If only Mollie was a little more… communicative. Kate suppressed a sigh as she ended a call with her mum and got up from her desk. Her daughter was too busy to come to the phone. It wasn't the first time, and she emerged from her office reflecting on the reality. Teens these days had so many apps through which they *could* communicate, actually using their devices to speak seemed beyond them. She'd just have to take her mum's word for it, that Mollie was doing fine.

She headed to the staff cloakroom, refreshing her lipstick and pressing a tissue to the top of her nose, wishing it wouldn't shine like a beacon within hours of doing her make-up. Thickly lashed, brown eyes surveyed the reflection as she refastened her hair into a clasp. She'd had a bad night, rolling to and fro in the bed like the waves toying with the rocks below Westerleigh Cottage. Mollie had been so down – even more so this last year – and Kate felt the full burden of responsibility, determined to do all she could to bring happiness back into her daughter's life. Was this going to work, though?

'Enough,' she warned her image, tugging at the bottom of her jacket. Did it look too big on her? She'd lost way too much weight with all the stress of the last year.

Leaving the cloakroom, Kate walked briskly towards the hotel reception, heels clicking on the polished tiles.

'One of your eleven o'clock's was early, so I popped him in Dogger.'

Kate and the lady on reception exchanged an amused look at the maritime reference.

'Perfect. Thanks, Jean. Coffee?' she asked, hopefully.

'On its way.'

Jean Lovelace had what Kate's gran had always called 'handsome features', which meant whilst not pretty, exactly, she was extremely striking. Kate liked her very much.

Assuming a professional countenance, she tapped on the meeting room door and stepped inside. Her worries over Mollie would have to wait.

A silver-haired elderly gentleman stood near the window, his erect frame belying his years, and he turned to greet her.

'Ms Stretton?' The man held out a hand as he joined her by the table. 'I'm Benedict Devonshire.'

'Kate. Lovely to meet you. Please, take a seat.'

'My grandson is on his way.'

They talked trivialities until coffee arrived, and once furnished with a cup each, Kate moved the conversation to Benedict's purpose.

'I have a milestone birthday pending.'

Kate smiled warmly. 'Eightieth?'

'You flatter me, my dear.' Although Benedict's eyes twinkled, his expression sobered. 'Forgive me. I am constantly reminded that it isn't PC these days to use such a term.'

Shaking her head, Kate removed her jacket, draping it over the back of the chair. 'I refuse to believe you are about to turn ninety, Mr Devonshire.'

'Benedict, at the very least, but please call me Ryther. It has long been my family's name for me and the one I tend to go by. No, indeed. I am approaching eighty-five, and there seems to be a consensus in some parts of the family that we must make a fuss about getting half-way through another decade. I assume it's in case I am not around for the next big one.'

Kate picked up her pen, sensing the undercurrents common in many a family celebration.

'What would *you* prefer, Mr... Ryther?'

'I wish to be—' The door opened before he could expand. 'Ah, here he is. This is my grandson, Rick. My boy, this is the very lovely Kate, who's an expert at managing things.'

Heart sinking, Kate rose from her chair, pinning on a smile and reluctantly holding out her hand.

'Pleased to meet you.'

Never have I wanted to meet someone less...

Assessing eyes – more grey than blue today – met wary brown as Kate's hand was grasped in a brief but firm handshake which sent her mind straight back to his placing the rings in her palm.

'We've already met, Grandy.' The man's tone was milder than their first encounter on the cliffs, but somewhat dismissive, and he remained unsmiling as he took the seat beside his grandfather.

'Intriguing,' Ryther murmured, taking a sip of coffee, his keen eyes – so like his grandson's – darting between him and Kate. 'The froideur of your tone indicates it was not a mutually beneficial encounter.'

Rick shot a warning look at his grandfather, but Ryther's lips merely twitched as he returned his attention to Kate, who tried to ignore the tense knot forming between her shoulders.

'Now, where were we, Kate? Ah, yes. You kindly asked me what *I* would like by way of a birthday celebration.'

Once again, Ryther was not to make his point, as a tap came on the door.

'Sorry, Kate,' Jean murmured, 'but there's—'

A slender woman with a sleek bob of golden hair brushed past Jean, and Kate shot to her feet as both men stood.

The vision in Gucci placed a kiss on each of Ryther's cheeks and then looped her arm through the younger man's, lifting her face for a kiss which didn't materialise as he firmly removed her grasp.

'Why wasn't I told about this meeting, my darlings?'

She had a melodious voice, a glorious smile and such an air of glamour. Kate immediately felt as though she'd just clambered out of bed.

Rick merely shrugged. 'You clearly were. How else did you happen to be here at the same time as us?'

'Nit picking, as usual, Frederick.' She sent Ryther a condescending smile. 'How are you feeling, sweetie?'

'Like I'm in the middle of a farce,' the older man muttered.

Chapter Three

The One With the Family Affair

Kate suspected she was the only one who heard Ryther's words, because the lady busied herself reaching up to straighten Rick's tie and asking him when he'd last had a haircut.

Brushing her hands aside, he walked over to the window to stare out over the grounds.

'Would you care for some coffee, Leigh?' Ryther gestured at the pot on the table and Kate met Jean's enquiring glance.

'No, thanks.' Leigh spoke in her charming tone, looking from Ryther to Rick and back. 'I'm here to sort out whatever mess you're all in over this birthday bash. Why aren't you holding it in London, Ryther? Why this god-awful little backwater?'

The expression filling Rick's handsome features as he swung around was sufficiently dark for Kate to feel she'd got off lightly the other day.

'As you're currently detaching yourself from the family, I don't see what it's got to do with you.' His complexion paled. 'Where the hell is Theo?'

Leigh rolled her eyes so hard, Kate thought she might dislodge her false lashes. 'With his new nanny, of course.' She took Kate's vacated seat and waved a hand at the two gentlemen, who had remained standing. 'Do sit down, the pair of you. You're both far too tall to be allowed.'

'We'll leave you to have a discussion,' Kate interjected, rescuing her jacket before Leigh could lean against it. 'If you let Jean know when you want me…' Her eyes flicked to Rick's for some reason, only to find his keen gaze already on her. 'I – er, she'll let me know.'

'Bloody hell,' Kate muttered to Jean as they walked as fast as decorum allowed down the hallway to reception. 'And I thought my ex had a dysfunctional family!'

Jean resumed her position behind the reception desk. 'We see all sorts, to be honest.' Her brow furrowed. 'I don't know them personally. I've seen the elderly chap around now and again, but he doesn't live in the cove.'

'He's a darling,' Kate said, adding wryly, 'not so sure about the other two.'

The phone on the desk rang and Jean made to pick it up. 'From all I've heard, Leigh Devonshire's been leaving and coming back again ever since they returned to Polkerran from abroad. The rumours are, they're in the middle of divorcing. I'm pretty sure she's currently living in London with their little boy.'

As Jean spoke into the receiver, Kate put on her jacket and headed for her office, unsure why the news unsettled her.

—

It was late by the time Kate left the hotel, and she called Mollie as she walked down the hill into the village. There was a bitter wind blowing up from the harbour, bringing with it fishy smells and the chill of a winter that was not yet done with them.

Much to her surprise, her daughter answered, and in good spirits. Ending the call, Kate walked along the harbour, head down against the nippy breeze as it swept across the water. Mollie had said she was looking forward to coming down to Cornwall, but Kate still couldn't shake the feeling she'd made a decision to suit her own needs more than her daughter's.

Crossing the bridge, she wrinkled her nose in delight at the delicious aroma of curry drifting from an open window of the Lugger, trying to embrace Anna's advice. This was a trial. Mollie needed to escape her old school and Kate wanted a reboot, somewhere that didn't remind her of the past. It had to be a step in the right direction for them both... didn't it?

'Hey, you're late!' Anna greeted Kate with a warm smile as she entered the kitchen. 'Dinner will be on the table in ten.'

'You're a darling.' Kate dropped her things on a chair and walked over to inspect the pans on the stove. 'Today's been a bit of a grind, to be honest.'

'Go and get changed, and I'll open some wine.'

Kate didn't need telling twice. To be honest, it was nice to feel cared for.

She hurriedly donned something more casual, mulling on Ryther and his family as she removed her make-up. She hadn't been called back, and Jean had confirmed they'd departed – Leigh first, alone, then the two men together – not long after Kate gave them some space.

Curious, she would have liked to ask Anna about them, but if they were potential clients, it didn't seem right to do so.

By the time she joined Anna and her husband, Oliver, at the table in the window bay, she was ready for a drink.

'What time do your parents arrive?'

'They said lunch.' Kate took a sip of wine. 'Suppose that's anywhere from twelve until two-ish.'

'Not bad,' Oliver intoned, drily. 'Barely a week in Cornwall, and you're using "ish".'

Kate grinned. 'Dad's never been the best timekeeper.'

'It's a shame they couldn't stay for a while.'

'I think after a week of Mollie, they'll be looking forward to some alone time. They've booked a few days in Falmouth before heading back to Bristol. Mum still thinks I'm a child, and the debacle of the divorce hasn't helped any. Dad reckons she wants to stay nearby in case I need her.'

'I think that's really sweet.' Anna handed Kate a plate of pasta bake. 'Help yourself to the sides.'

Kate sent her a contrite look. Anna's parents had died when she was a baby and she'd been raised by an unfeeling older cousin. Having parents who fussed would be a delight to her friend.

Oliver offered the garlic slices and Kate took one with a smile. 'My favourite, thank you.'

Once the meal was over, Oliver left them alone at the table and went to sit in a wing-back armchair by the hearth, picking up a book as Anna's cat, Heathcliff, curled at his side and Dougal settled at his feet.

Kate scooped up the last of her cheesecake, savouring the creamy mixture. 'Delish. You'll have to let me have the recipe.'

'Gladly.' Anna cast a quick look over towards her husband, who appeared deeply engrossed in his book, then leaned forward. 'So, how's the checklist going?'

'I could ask you the same.'

Anna chuckled. Both being adept at forward planning, they were also dedicated list makers, as they'd often reflected when working together.

'Well, I've finally got a home of my own.' Once again Anna's glance flicked across the room to Oliver, her features softening. 'Found the love of my life.'

'Got married,' Kate added, raising an enquiring brow. 'And?'

An impish smile formed. 'All in good time.'

Kate attempted to quash her own bitterness. She'd never told Anna – or anyone – about Hugo's great deception. Maybe she would. One day.

'Hey?' Anna reached over to touch Kate's arm where it rested on the table. 'You okay?'

'Fine.' Kate summoned a smile. 'Sometimes the regret makes itself felt.'

Anna made a small sound. 'It's time you dug out the old you.'

'I'm not sure where she's gone. I doubt I could find her if I tried.'

'Nonsense,' Anna said briskly, picking up the cafetiere. 'Top up?'

She wouldn't sleep, but then it was a day off tomorrow. 'Yes, please.'

'Back to the list. You've ticked the first box, simply by breaking free.'

'And look how long that took me!'

Anna grinned, holding up a hand and bending down her thumb before selecting the adjacent finger. 'This is the second box, moving away from Harrogate.'

Kate inclined her head. 'Continue.'

'First day in new job – that's three off the list. Do you know what this one is?' She held onto the finger bearing her wedding ring.

'Find somewhere to live?' It was, to be fair, foremost in Kate's thoughts.

'Indeed.' Anna held up the closed fist with only the little finger sticking up. 'And what about *this* wee one?' She wiggled it, and Kate chuckled despite herself.

'I'm not sure I want to know.'

Anna laughed. 'This, my old mate, is a new man.'

'Woah!' Kate held up a hand, conscious Oliver had glanced over before returning his attention to his book. She spoke quietly, but firmly. 'I've already made one colossal mistake in my life where men are concerned.'

Anna drained her cup. 'You've forgotten what it's like to be attracted to someone. To feel attractive yourself. It's time you dug out the fun and flirty Kate.'

Huffing out a breath, Kate shook her head. 'She's long gone. The only impending "f" in my life is the looming four-o.'

'Is it… has what you've been through put you off altogether?'

Kate pursed her lips, then shook her head. 'Not really. I mean, Hugo ruined my life for a while, but not for ever. I just can't see myself falling in love again. If I ever was.'

Anna leaned forward again. 'I'm not suggesting you get serious. Just have some fun, date a little, no strings.'

'I think I've forgotten how. Dating seems a looong time ago.' Kate couldn't help but laugh at the hopeful expression on her friend's face. 'I'm not even sure how people meet each other these days.'

'We'll google it.'

Kate smiled, her gaze roaming the homely room, with its charming lamps on side tables, stacks of books on the shelves lining the far wall and soft throws draped over the comfy sofa backs. The log burner cast warm, flickering light over the scene, and she sighed.

'This is such a lovely home. I hope I find somewhere soon.'

Oliver looked up from his book again, peering over his glasses. 'It's a shame I don't have one of mine available. You'd have been welcome to it.'

In addition to his scholarly profession, Oliver had set up a not-for-profit organisation committed to purchasing local properties and renting them out at affordable rents to locals.

'I'd have felt a bit of a sham. It's such a fantastic initiative.'

'Hmm,' Anna mused. 'Except it's growing a bit too fast. Now that Oliver's been commissioned to write this new book, he needs to start researching, not chasing deals.'

Oliver pointed to his forehead. 'Most of it's in here already.'

Anna shook her head at him and turned back to Kate. 'It's compounded by a proposed injection of funds from my brother, Matt, and will get worse when Daniel goes abroad. You met him at the wedding.'

'Lauren's other half?' Kate knew Lauren Kirkham well, from when she and Anna had shared a house in Harrogate. 'He's lovely.'

'They both are, but I don't see much of them now they're in Yorkshire, or my gorgeous god-daughter, so – oh!' Anna grabbed her phone. 'Hold on, I might have an idea.'

She crossed to the kitchen to make a call, and Kate walked over to the window. There wasn't much to see in the blackness, but the lights from the house spilled over the terrace and down onto the edges of the lawn and to the dark mass of sea beyond. To the right, the illuminations of Polkerran glimmered on the waters of the harbour and, opposite, in the gothic-looking house across the bay – where Kate had attended Anna's recent wedding reception – lights could be seen emanating from several rooms.

The reminder of the occasion brought a realisation. Rick Devonshire had greeted their party briefly on arrival at his home – Harbourwatch – and that was why she'd found him familiar.

She drew in a contemplative breath. Their initial interactions hadn't been promising, but Kate felt for him, rattling around in such a large property on his own. It must emphasise the loss of his son too. Sadness shrouded Kate for a moment as she contemplated how she would feel if Mollie had been all but lost to her in the divorce…

Hearing Anna's approach, she turned around. She hoped Rick, whatever sort of man he was, didn't mind being alone. Unless the glamorous wife was staying over. After all, Jean had said she made a habit of coming and going…

'I think I've found you somewhere to live. When I saw Lauren at the wedding, she was waiting to hear whether she'd got the overseas posting she's always longed for. She confirmed she had just the other day. They won't be going to the US for a few months, but it's unlikely they can get down to Cornwall from Yorkshire in the interim. Daniel wasn't keen on leaving the house empty for so long and he's just offered it to you and Mollie.'

'Oh, wow. Is he – are they sure?'

'You'd need to see it first, check if the house works for you, but I'll be surprised if you don't love it.' Anna's face shone with enthusiasm. 'You'd be just up the hill as well.'

A momentary reflection on the few properties currently available was more than enough for Kate to almost snap the offer up, sight unseen.

'We'll go up there after breakfast. I've got a key, and you can see what you think. It might be a nice welcome gift for Mollie if you've found a home.'

A thrill of excitement rushed through Kate. She'd barely experienced life in Polkerran Point yet, but there was something inherently homely about this quaint fishing village, its cottages clinging like limpets to the steep, wooded hills around the bay and the stretch of rocks out to the lighthouse.

If only it could appeal to a thirteen-year-old girl – whose current life obsessions centred around TikTok videos, Duolingo and the musical *Six* – then maybe they would be happy here in Polkerran Point.

Chapter Four

The One With the Style Council

Perched on a rocky promontory close to the coast path, The Lookout proved to be more than Kate could ever wish for. Barely eighteen months old, it had hardly been lived in, with Daniel moving up to Yorkshire to live with Lauren and her baby daughter, Amelia, not long after its completion.

It was a dream home, fully furnished and equipped, which meant Kate could leave everything in storage, beyond the few boxes of personal things she and Mollie had ear-marked for whenever they found somewhere to rent, and the views out to sea were stunning.

Anna provided a hearty lunch for when Kate's parents arrived with Mollie, and once the former had set off for their accommodation in Falmouth, Kate had taken Mollie and Podge upstairs to settle in, the cat mewing in protest in his basket.

'This was the room Anna stayed in when she was growing up and spending her summers with her aunt Meg.' Closing the door, Kate let the cat out, and he jumped straight onto the bed and began kneading.

Heading to the window, Kate's eye was drawn instantly to the house on the opposite cliff. 'You can see why she fell in love with it.'

Mollie joined her, cuddling the cat, her bright eyes flicking from the white caps dancing out to sea to the harbour, sheltered within the embrace of the cove's arms of land.

'Can I go into town? I need some new clothes. And more loom bands.'

Reflecting on the high-end, stylish boutiques, the shop crammed with walking attire and supplies and the chandlery, Kate shook her head.

'It's not really that sort of town... village. We'll go to Truro for shopping. I'll take you on my day off.'

Mollie huffed, letting Podge go and exploring the room before leaning her elbows on the sill, her chin in her cupped hands, her gaze still fixed on the scene outside.

'Why couldn't you take the week off? It's school hols.'

'I'm sorry.' Kate put an arm across her daughter's shoulders, giving a brief squeeze. 'I've only just started the job so I can't ask for time off so soon. But we've got the weekend, and I have news.'

Swinging around, Mollie folded her arms across her chest. 'It's not about Dad, is it?' Her expression was mutinous.

'No. Nothing to do with the old life. I think I've found us somewhere to live. Or, at least, Anna has, but I wouldn't commit until you've seen it. Want to come now?'

Her features brightening, Mollie brushed her fringe from her eyes. 'Yes, please! Podge is fed up of being the product of a broken home.'

'I'm so sorry, love.' The familiar guilt descended as they left the room, but Mollie grabbed her mother's arm and tugged.

'Hey, I'm joking.'

'But you're—'

Mollie shook her head vehemently as she stepped past Kate and started down the stairs. 'It wasn't much of a home and it wasn't broken, Mum, *you* were.'

Kate's mouth opened but no words came as she stared after her daughter, who'd reached the hall and disappeared from sight.

Out of the mouths of babes...

Suitably dressed for the chilly weather, Kate borrowed the keys from Anna and led Mollie up the hill to The Lookout, unsurprised at her daughter's instant and positive reaction.

'What a bewt!' Brown eyes – so like her mother's – sparkled as she almost skipped from room to room, peering out of every window, turning taps on and off in bathrooms and bouncing on each bed in turn. 'Can I have this one?'

Kate laughed. She'd known Mollie would fall for the charmingly dressed guest suite with its stylish shower room, dressing area and a desk under one of the windows. Even on a winter's day, it was bathed in glorious light.

'Can we put stuff on the walls?'

'I'll get you a pin board, we can prop it up on that long table by the window. There's lots of drawers for your Washi tapes too.'

'I can use this for making my bracelets.' Mollie patted the desk.

'And homework,' Kate added, but this garnered no response.

Once back downstairs, Kate showed Mollie the snug with its large screen, set up for gaming or movies, the living area with its floor-to-ceiling windows affording panoramic views, and the stunning hearth housing a large log burner. The vast open-plan area also contained a dining table and chairs and incorporated a spacious kitchen with an island. Despite its proportions, however, it had been beautifully furnished, with rugs on the hardwood floors, cushions and throws on the sofas and stunning artwork on the walls.

'Yay, they've got an ice machine like ours.' Mollie's voice faltered, then she shrugged. 'Like the one we used to have. What's in here?' She opened every kitchen cupboard, inspected the boot room, downstairs cloakroom and then dragged Kate outside to explore the large terrace. This afforded more stunning views of the open sea and, to their right, the entrance to the bay, the lighthouse just visible where it crowned its run of rocks, against which the sea crashed repeatedly.

'Come on, we can get directly onto the coast path.'

With Mollie hard on her heels, Kate opened a gate and stepped out onto the path which ran along the top of the cliffs.

'Anna says you can walk all the way to Trebutwith if you go that way,' Kate waved a hand to the left, 'where there's a great beach, or back down to join the lane into Polkerran this way.'

She scanned the stretch of path. Wasn't this where she'd been caught abusing the environment last week?

Mollie had wandered further along the dirt path back towards Polkerran, and Kate's gaze swept across the expanse of sea. There were no boats to be seen today, and the sky was a leaden grey, portending the rain forecast for later.

'Mum! *Muuum!*'

Spinning around, Kate's gaze fell on Mollie, then moved to the little boy clasping her hand as they approached. Dressed in a green padded coat, he looked to be around five or six, and his eyes were darting from the girl at his side to Kate.

'Hello. Are you lost?'

The boy's eyes widened as he stared up at Kate, but he didn't speak.

'I can't get him to say anything,' Mollie explained. 'He was sitting on the edge of the path by a stile.'

Kate crouched down to the boy's height, her smile kind. 'Is it because you mustn't talk to strangers?'

The little boy gave an emphatic nod.

'Ah. Good. That's right. You shouldn't. I'm sure whoever you're with will be along soon.'

Leaving Mollie to oversee things, Kate looked around. The wind whipped over the top of the cliff, much as it had the day she'd tried to dispose of the rings, and she put a hand on her hair to stop it from splaying across her face. Whoever had lost this little boy must be distraught.

She walked a few paces further on, then peered over the railing to scan the beach and rocks below. The tide was out and there were a few people walking, but none of them looked as though they'd lost anyone.

Then, a faint sound came on the wind and Kate turned around as Mollie gave a whoop of delight.

A black dog bounded up to the child, who threw his arms around its neck.

'Hello, Bayley.' Kate joined them, patting the labrador, whose tongue was hanging out as he panted, tail wagging furiously. She was aware of Rick's approach, but for some reason she felt flustered.

'Theo! Oh, my God! How many times have I told you not to wander off!' His voice was raw with emotion and Kate felt for him, although seeing Theo's sweet face fall, she didn't hesitate. She placed a comforting arm around the little boy's shoulders as the man came to a breathless halt beside them.

'He's fine. Truly. He was being very sensible, sitting by the path, waiting. And he wouldn't talk to us because he knows not to speak to strangers.'

Rick's eyes flashed for a second, but then his countenance softened as his gaze moved to his son.

'Sorry, Teds.' He ruffled Theo's dark auburn hair and he took his dad's hand. 'Thank you,' he added to Kate. 'They have no idea, do they?'

Kate huffed, throwing a sidelong look at Mollie, who merely rolled her eyes and folded her arms.

'Mollie once got on a bus and was missing for an hour. She was only six, my parents were out of their minds trying to find her. I was at work in ignorant bliss. Thank goodness for a tolerant driver when he found his stowaway.'

An awkward silence fell between them. Then, Rick called Bayley to heel.

'We'd better get back.'

He turned away, a protective hand on his son's shoulder, the dog following in their wake, and Kate's thoughtful gaze remained on him until he was out of sight.

It looked like she wasn't the only Polkerran resident facing the challenges of single parenting.

When they arrived back at Westerleigh, Anna was in the kitchen, and Mollie rushed up to her.

'It's epic, Anna. I can't wait to move in! I've got my own shower again, and there's this room, like, where I'm gonna play all my games. With Podge there, it will be just like a home.'

Anna's gaze met Kate's across the room. 'So, it's a yes?'

'Definitely. If you let me have Daniel's number, I'll go and call him so we can sort out the details.'

When Kate returned to the kitchen from the hall, she found Anna making coffee and could see Oliver on the terrace, his phone to his ear.

'Oliver looks a bit stressed.' It was unusual, from all Kate had discerned so far. He was generally a reticent man, his emotions under good regulation but his current demeanour belied this.

'It's Alex Tremayne. The man I fell for when I first came down here?'

'Oh, yes. I remember! He's on the phone?' Kate could well recall the handsome specimen from Anna's photos a few years back. 'He looked like butter wouldn't melt.'

'No, Oliver's on with his solicitor. Alex is trying to scupper a property purchase.'

'He doesn't live here, then?'

'No, thank God! He's London-based, but his family still live in the huge manor house by the church and Tremayne Estates continues to run from Polkerran.'

They settled at the table, each cradling a mug of coffee, Anna's anxious gaze on her husband outside, his broad-shouldered back to them as his call continued. His posture was rigid, his free hand gripping the railing bordering the terrace.

Then she turned to Kate. 'Ignore me. Oliver's perfectly capable of looking after himself and his business. So, what did you agree with Daniel over moving in? I meant what I said about staying here for now, making it easier for you to focus on the job, knowing Mollie is being looked after.'

'I appreciate it. That's pretty much what I said to Daniel, and that I wanted to get Mollie settled into the new school before we moved in. He's having an AST drawn up, twelve months initially, and after that we'll take it from there.'

'I'm so pleased you decided to give Polkerran Point a chance.' Anna sent Kate a warm smile before her attention returned to the man outside the window.

Kate leaned back in her chair, metaphorically crossing her fingers. Only time would tell if it had been a wise move.

—

The remainder of Mollie's holiday – also half term for the local schools – sped by in a flash, and despite Kate's having to work every day except the Wednesday and be on hand for an evening event on the Friday, Mollie barely seemed to notice.

The locals took her under their wing in various ways. Anna taught her how to make and decorate cupcakes. Oliver showed her his man cave of antiques and she'd lost herself for hours, browsing the shelves of historical books. Nicki, Anna's friendly next-door neighbour, had included Mollie on a trip to Dobwalls with her own boys. Liam and Jason were pupils at the village school, and although they were a bit younger than Mollie (and she'd turned her nose up at the idea of going to a family theme park with them), she'd returned with sparkling eyes and full of a childish merriment Kate hadn't seen for ages.

'Hey, Mum!'

'What?'

'Where do squirrels go in a hurricane?'

Kate's brow had furrowed as she stirred a pan of spaghetti on the stove. 'No idea.'

'All over the place!' Mollie's arms flayed left and right, and Kate had stared in amazement as her daughter scooped up a souvenir carton of popcorn and headed up to her room giggling.

Jean – who, apart from working some shifts on reception at the hotel in the quieter months, ran the village ice cream shop in season – had also invited Mollie to spend the day learning how to make some, which they'd had for dessert that day. A man called Tommy the Boat had added Mollie to the list for kayak classes, which Nicki's boys already attended and would start up again as soon as the weather improved, and Kate took her to the hotel leisure centre after work twice, so they could swim and use the sauna.

The weather had closed in, with rain lashing the windows of Kate's office. It was Friday evening, and instead of finishing for the weekend, she was on duty for a retirement dinner for a prominent — as she was fast learning — local, namely Mr Tremayne senior. The aforementioned Alex's father, he was the outgoing custodian of Tremayne Manor, a castellated manor house in the centre of Polkerran Point.

By coincidence, there was also a recurring get-together in one of the smaller meeting rooms of a business consortium.

Having checked the rooms during the afternoon, agreeing the order of play with the restaurant manager — along with the sandwich order for the business forum — confirming the cake would be delivered by five, and tweaking the odd flower or two in the table arrangements, overseen by a young and anxious florist (it was her first time supplying the hotel), she'd gone outside to guide her out of a compact parking space, but despite the umbrella, she hadn't escaped the elements entirely.

To make matters worse, Kate had stopped by the entrance to adjust the signage board, moving it further back to avoid the current deluge, only to overhear someone just inside the doorway on their phone.

'No, Leigh, I am not having an affair with any woman, least of all someone I've met once for a matter of minutes.'

Rick's tone was firm, and Kate looked around for somewhere else to be, but aside from stepping out into the torrential rain, she was stuck unless she walked into the entrance hall and made her presence obvious.

'Theo is *not* lying! We bumped into her by accident on the cliff path and—' There was a pause. 'You can think what you like, you invariably do, but don't threaten me over Theo.' There was another pause, then Rick made a small sound in his throat. 'She's hardly my type. I've had my fill of know-it-all businesswomen, obsessed with designer labels.'

Hackles raised, Kate straightened her Karen Millen jacket and strode through the door into the entrance hall, conscious of Rick leaning against the wall nearby as she made her way, head held high, to the cloakroom.

Still bristling, Kate eyed her damp appearance in the full-length mirror. She'd opted for a fitted sleeveless navy shift dress and jacket, along with her favourite heels, and she refastened her hair into the usual tight bun before touching up her make-up.

So what if she liked nice clothes? And how dare he declare her a know-it-all, just because she understood her job, what to do and say...

'Ugh!' she muttered. 'Men!'

Chapter Five

The One With the Squeeze

Rick was no longer by the entrance when Kate emerged from the cloakroom, and she turned her annoyance down to a simmer, but as she approached the private dining room, she fetched up short, her tummy dipping alarmingly.

Although she could only see his back, there was something horribly familiar about the man by the doors: the thickly layered blond hair, the broad shoulders, the stylish tailoring of the suit and the tinge of arrogance to the stance.

A combination of dread and annoyance shot through Kate. *Hugo*? His name hadn't come up on any of the guest lists... She took a hasty step backwards, only for her right heel to slip from beneath her on the now wet tiles, but as she felt herself falling, two strong arms caught her around the middle and hauled her upright.

She glanced down at the hands clasped around her waist, aware of the solid body behind her own, but as she was released, she swung around.

Glaring at Rick as she adjusted her jacket, she bit out a terse 'Thank you.'

He said nothing, his eyes dropping to Kate's heels. Then his head flicked up, his expression as guarded as ever as he moved past her, and she turned around just in time to see him greet the man hovering beside the double doors into the private dining room.

'Tremayne.'

Kate almost laughed aloud at her own stupidity as the blond man turned around. This was clearly the infamous Alex, once the bane of Anna's life, now of Oliver's.

Pulling herself together, she walked past them, silently scolding her skin for continuing to tingle at Rick's touch.

'Hateful man,' she muttered through gritted teeth. This was going to be one long evening.

—

'Are you okay?' Anna greeted Kate on her return to Westerleigh.

Summoning a tired smile, she dropped her bag on the table and walked over to join her in the kitchen.

'I thought you'd have gone to bed.' Kate looked around. 'Where's Oliver?'

'Nose buried deep in some documents up in his den.' Anna gestured towards the boot room door, which led out to the garden. 'I'm just making him a coffee before I go up. Do you want one?'

Kate shook her head. 'It'll keep me awake thinking about—' She caught herself just in time. 'Work.'

Damn that man. He'd done her a favour earlier, preventing her from making a fool of herself with a full-on inelegant fall, but his overheard comment still rankled.

'How was Mollie this evening?'

'Champing at the bit over moving into The Lookout, but seems happy enough. She spent hours watching reels of cats doing cute things. Then, she went up because she wanted to spend time with Podge.'

Anna picked up the mug, from which steam rose in a spiral, the comforting aroma of coffee assailing Kate's nostrils as it passed by. 'I'll take this over. Fancy a nightcap when I come back? Of the grape variety?'

'I'm on it.' Kate headed for the cupboard where the wine glasses were kept.

Five minutes later, they settled onto the sofa in front of the log burner, whose embers continued to glow through the glass window. Kate unfastened her hair and kicked off her heels, sending them a fierce look for letting her down earlier.

'Cheers.'

The clink of glasses was followed by a small silence as they both savoured the wine. Kate leaned her head back against the comfy sofa, cradling the glass in her lap.

'Tough gig?'

Kate sent Anna a resigned look. 'Not the gig so much. Bit standard, really, as retirement dos go.'

'Was this Mr Tremayne senior?'

Kate nodded, and Anna pulled a face.

'If the rumours are true, the estate has been handed over to Alex, as the only son. Hope it doesn't bring him back to the cove.'

'I encountered him tonight.' She laughed as her eyes met Anna's. 'I can see what the attraction was. He's rather easy on the eye.'

Anna grimaced. 'Not so easy on the mind, as it happens.'

'A bit like Hugo.' Kate leaned her head back against the sofa again. 'I thought he was him at first. He looked like Hugo from the back.' Heat rushed into her cheeks as she recalled the arms catching her as she fell, and Anna spluttered on her mouthful of wine.

'Oh, my God, Kate,' she exclaimed, wiping her lips with the back of her hand. 'What did he *do*?'

'Ha! Nothing.' Kate rested a hand against her warm skin. 'It was a momentary panic, the similarity, but once I saw his profile, I realised how stupid I was being.'

Anna's expression sobered. 'He still haunts you, doesn't he? Hugo, I mean.'

'Sadly, yes. Even a year after the divorce, he can't be civil. He doesn't even ask about Mollie.'

'Do you have much contact?'

Kate shook her head. 'Not really. There's no need now all the settlements are done. He didn't contest the full custody of Mollie, as you know, and she seemed to perk up a bit when we moved out last year – well, except for the school thing.'

'I think she'll enjoy the one in Fowey.'

'I hope so. She deserves a break.'

Anna eyed her friend solemnly.

'So do you.' She leaned forward to top up their glasses. 'Now, tell me what happened earlier. You're uncharacteristically jittery.'

'Oh, you know,' Kate waved an airy hand, trying to see the funny side of it, 'just almost fell on my backside, only to be saved by the last person I'd ever want help from.'

A raised brow was Anna's only response, and Kate sighed.

'That man!' She gestured towards Harbourwatch, invisible in the darkness. 'It had to be him, didn't it?'

'Oooh.' Anna's cheeks dimpled. 'So you've met Dev. Do tell!'

'Dev?' Kate queried. 'I thought he was Rick.'

Hadn't the out-going wife called him Frederick?

'Rick Devonshire. Goes by Dev.'

Kate rolled her eyes. What was it with that family and nicknames? 'Anyway, Rick-Dev – or whatever it is – isn't the most friendly of people, is he?'

Anna's expression became pensive. 'I think he's a bit shy, to be honest. I've only got to know him lately; he's always kept himself to himself, but I think that's more about being there for his son. The wife hasn't made herself popular in the cove and she's such a high-flyer, always gadding off here and there for work. She's also walked out on the marriage several times, so I think Dev has been keen to provide the stabling influence at home. Oliver knows him better than I do.'

'I met his wife the other day too, at a meeting.'

Anna looked surprised. 'We all thought she'd gone for good this time. They're supposed to be getting divorced.'

Kate wasn't so sure. 'She may have vacated the family home, but I got the impression she's in no hurry to release her grasp on the family.' Reflecting on Leigh's behaviour towards Dev – despite his rebuttal – she wasn't at all sure the lady meant for things to be over.

'How odd. There's been all sorts of speculation in the cove, as you can imagine. The turnover in domestic staff and nannies was something else since they came back from the US. Rumour had it Leigh thought *everyone* was after Dev. Oliver believes she couldn't bear it if his attention wasn't solely on her. She replaced the nannies with ones from up country, but they didn't stay long either.'

'So,' Anna prompted, settling back in her seat. 'What happened this evening?'

'He was at a meeting – local landowners and such. Anyway, the tiled floors were wet from people traipsing in from the rain, and my heel slipped. I would have been a very inelegant goner if he hadn't caught me.'

'How exciting!' Anna's eyes sparkled, but Kate rolled hers at her friend.

'You're such a romantic. You're thinking "meet-cute", I can hear your mind going, but it wasn't our first encounter.'

Anna blinked. 'When was *that*?'

As they finished their drinks and got to their feet, Kate filled Anna in. It all sounded ridiculous when said out loud, but even though they'd laughed about it, Kate had to assume Dev's opinion of her must be rock bottom.

Does that bother you, her mind questioned.

'Of course not,' she mused as Anna took the stairs to the top floor and Kate headed to Mollie's room.

Her daughter was fast asleep, as was Podge at the foot of the bed. Turning off the lamp, Kate picked up the discarded tablet and placed it on the bedside cabinet and dropped a gentle kiss on Mollie's smooth cheek.

Two more days and term would start up again, and as Kate readied herself for bed, she begged the heavens to be kind and let Mollie find her happy place in Cornwall.

—

Delighted to have a day off on Saturday, Kate settled at the table in the bay window after breakfast, her laptop open as she caught up with social media and emails. Mollie had gone up to shower. They had plans to go over to Port Wenneth to collect Mollie's uniform and stock up on food. As she had also petitioned for a new school bag, pencil case and shoes, it was likely to be a lengthy trip.

Anna was busy cleaning the guest rooms, and Oliver had taken Dougal for a walk. It was a blustery, cold late February day, and pushing aside the laptop, Kate walked to the window to admire the view.

The sky was pale grey, overlain with darker, feathery strands of cloud. White crests adorned the waves out to sea, and ripples flowed steadily towards the harbour, nestled in the curve of the bay. Smoke curled from several chimneys, drifting up past stout, tall evergreens to the manicured grounds of the Point Hotel, just discernible beyond a bank of tall fir trees.

Kate's gaze dropped down to the centre of the village. To the right of the church spire was a large, turreted building surrounded by a surprising amount of green space – Tremayne Manor.

Recalling the previous evening, Kate turned her back. Pretentious wealthy people were not her thing. Kind ones, she could deal with. The elderly gentleman, for example, whose eighty-fifth birthday party was planned for just before Easter, had been a delight to deal with. The two couples whose weddings she was organising for the summer were warm and friendly and incredibly grateful for every bit of guidance she could offer. The Tremaynes were… an unpleasant bunch.

Kate huffed a breath. Well, Alex Tremayne had put on the charm, but she was no fool. Or rather, she wasn't about to be a fool again. She'd fallen for a similar type with Hugo: the permanent golden tan, streaked blond hair, flirtatious eyes and a smile to turn you to a pile of mush faster than a rapid thaw after a snowstorm.

How could such angelic, divine looks conceal manipulative, mind-controlling behaviour?

–

Kate and Mollie had such a busy and enjoyable time shopping, they returned to Westerleigh full of their day. Leaving her daughter to unpack her new purchases, Kate joined Anna and Oliver in the kitchen to lend a hand with dinner.

The next week flew by and Mollie – after an anxious few days – came home on the bus on Friday beaming from ear to ear, running up the lane with a long-absent energy as she raced Liam and Jason, whom Nicki had just collected from the village school.

Relieved it had gone well, Kate tried not to lament the lack of challenge in her new job. This wasn't the time to change anything. Mollie needed stability, and at least there were people on hand for when Kate was working so she had company before and after school if needed.

Kate had taken to fitting in a walk around her hours at the hotel, often following the narrow road which ran parallel to the water along the side of the harbour opposite Westerleigh.

It was the route she'd walked in those heels on Anna's wedding day, when the small party of close friends had gathered at Harbourwatch – apparently, as she'd more recently learned – an invitation extended by Dev to Oliver, as a surprise for Anna.

Down on the beach, she would pick up a coffee or hot chocolate from the cute little cafe, sitting on one of the benches to watch the waves claim their bit of sand before retreating – sometimes in gentle rolls, others in more flamboyant splashes, depending on the vagaries of the weather – and despite simply trying to enjoy the moment before heading back to Westerleigh, her thoughts occasionally turned to the man living in the Gothic-style house above the rocks.

Did he feel isolated there? It was a huge property, clearly meant to be a family home. Despite her reservations over whether Dev really was shy, as Anna claimed, or simply rude, Kate pushed her sympathies aside.

'Thank you,' she smiled at the kind-faced woman behind the counter as she returned her recyclable cup to the cafe. She turned away but then swung back. 'Why are people taking photos stood outside your door?'

She gestured to where a young couple were not only taking a selfie, but waving at something above said door.

The lady placed Kate's cup in the sink. 'It's the livestream. They go proper mad for it, those Emmets do. When they go back up country, they check in on it, and when they're here, they call up the webcam on their phones and get to tekkin' snaps, doing dance routines, blowing kisses.' She rolled her eyes. 'You've never seen the like.'

Kate laughed. 'Madness.'

'Aye, ne'er a truer word said.'

Heading home, Kate tucked her hands in her pockets. Despite the approaching spring, the skies were heavy with cloud and dusk had begun to drape its veil over Polkerran.

Soon they would be in a new home. Would it be as lonely as the last?

'At least it's here,' she said quietly, as she reached the harbour and paused briefly to survey the scene in the dimming light. 'You're free. You and Mollie. And the cove is going to heal us both. I can feel it.'

Chapter Six

The One With the Jam

Mollie had been invited to a new school friend's house on Saturday and – restless and longing for undemanding company – Kate headed out with Dougal, who was more than happy to accompany her on a walk.

The coast path was muddy from the recent rainfall, so they headed into the main part of the town, where Kate took a side street described to her by Anna. It wound uphill, as did most roads in Polkerran, but where the lane branched to the right – home to a quaint row of cottages – they passed through a wooden gate onto an open patch of ground where dogs could be exercised.

There were several people there, and Kate walked Dougal on his lead at first, but after a while, she released him, watching as he tore across the field in search of who knew what, before cornering back and rubbing friendly noses with a couple of other dogs.

Kate surveyed the open field, bordered by tall hedgerows, hints of spring at their tips. Being more exposed to the elements, it was blustery, and she refastened her ponytail more firmly, then almost stumbled as a black dog nudged her in the back of the knees.

'Hello, Bayley,' she exclaimed, getting onto her haunches and giving his ears a good rub.

'Sorry. He got away from me.'

It seemed to be an occupational habit with Dev: dogs, children... wives, even...

Kate flicked a glance upwards, then resumed her fuss of Bayley, who closed his eyes, tongue lolling in contentment and provided sufficient distraction from her wayward thoughts, which were far too appreciative of Dev's wind-tousled hair for her liking.

'I doubt he could have gone far, this is a great exercise space.'

Kate straightened, giving Bayley one final pat as Dev's gaze roamed over the expanse of long grass. Dougal was having a good run around at the far end of the field, with a smaller dog who was struggling to keep up.

'It's the one thing I lack at home,' he mused, his attention returning to Bayley, who sat patiently between them now, looking from one to the other, tail wagging in earnest. 'Paved terraces aren't particularly dog-friendly.'

'Can't you move?'

Dev made a small sound, then shook his head. 'Not that straightforward, I'm afraid. Come on, Bayley.'

'Wait!' Kate dug into her pocket for the dog biscuits she'd picked up at Westerleigh. 'Is it okay?'

She held out her hand, but perhaps it was the reminiscence of the moment he'd closed her fingers over the rings in her palm which brought the ever-ready colour to Kate's cheeks.

Had he recalled it too? Dev held her gaze as though trying to make something out. Wondering if she had a smudge on her nose, Kate resisted the urge to wrinkle it.

'Look... I...' he huffed on a breath. 'Never mind.'

Dev shoved his hands in his pockets, withdrawing his own biscuit supply.

'Trade you?'

Kate put two fingers in her mouth, releasing a piercing whistle which brought Dougal bounding across the grass to join them.

Conscious of Dev's curious attention, she held out her offering to Bayley as he gave some of his to Dougal.

'Well, I'd best get back.' He fastened Bayley's lead, but the dog got onto its haunches, paws on Kate's jacket, and she chuckled as she gave him a hug.

'You're gorgeous. And you know it.' She rested her cheek on the warm head, then stepped back as Bayley returned to Dev's side.

'Oh God, I'm sorry.' He pointed to the front of her coat, now smeared with damp, muddy paw prints, but Kate just laughed.

'It'll brush off when it's dry.'

Dev didn't respond, merely bent to fasten Bayley's lead, but as he straightened, she found it difficult to discern the conflicting expression crossing his features.

Watching them leave, Kate reached for Dougal's lead to prepare for the walk back, but she couldn't shake the feeling that – somehow – she'd surprised Dev. She just wasn't sure how or why.

—

On the last day before they moved into The Lookout, Kate had the entire morning off, as she was due to work the evening, and she watched in bemusement as Anna ferried tea and coffee pots and plates of homemade cupcakes to the large table by the window.

'Are you having a party?'

Anna laughed as she placed small plates and a pile of napkins on a tray.

'No, just the usual locals popping in for a chat. You miss it, being out at work.'

Kate's lips twitched as she watched Anna fill a cake stand with scones, small pots of jam and clotted cream.

'And a little sustenance?'

'They're all agog at the moment over what's going to happen with the ailing summer festival.'

Helping Anna unload the items from the tray onto the end of the table, Kate sent her a puzzled look.

'Why's that?'

Anna held the empty tray against her middle. 'Leigh Devonshire took it on…' She hesitated. 'Well, not so much. We hadn't had anything like it for a few years. She set up this new, shinier version, ran it like a sergeant major.'

Kate's interest was piqued but before she could ask any further questions, sounds came from the boot room, and the door opened to reveal Nicki, who stood aside as three elderly people entered, along with a young woman with red-gold curls, Jean following on her heels.

'Baptism of fire,' Anna muttered to Kate as she sent a warm smile in the direction of the newcomers. 'Morning, everyone. Come on in, take a seat.'

Heathcliff – who'd been having a leisurely preen – took one startled look at the new arrivals and shot towards the cat flap as though she'd just received a notification she was late for a meeting.

The locals all clearly had their own place around the vast table. One of the elderly ladies walked with sticks, her companion bickering with the old gentleman in their wake.

Nicki waved her over. 'Come and meet the reprobates, Kate.'

Kate's mind fizzed as Anna did a roll-call, and she logged the names as they were introduced: Jean's mum, Demelza Lovelace, she'd met briefly in the cafe after her interview. The lady with the sticks was a Mrs Clegg – known as Cleggie – and they now sat either side of Old Patrick, whose wizened face was nonetheless kind and welcoming, except when he glared at Cleggie, who used one of her sticks to rap him when he told Kate she was a proper 'bewdy'.

Both Mrs Clegg and Patrick appeared to have worked at some point for Oliver, when he rented Harbourwatch.

The woman with the red-gold curls was Phoenix – or Phee – another Polkerran local who hoped to return to the cove soon after living in Mevagissey for a few years.

Everyone happily tucked into the delights on offer, and the conversation ebbed and flowed much like the tides as cakes, biscuits and scones were consumed with rapidity – amidst only one moment of dispute, when Old Patrick slathered cream on his scone before adding a theatrical dollop of Anna's homemade jam.

'Every time,' Nicki's quiet aside to Kate was acknowledged by Anna with a small smirk.

'Patrick Penberthy!' Mrs Clegg rose to the bait, and the elderly man winked at Kate.

'Now, Cleggie. Don't you go gettin' teasy. The old tuss is just a-baiting.' Mrs Lovelace nudged Old Patrick. 'You'll be jam-firstin' on the other half, Pat.'

Kate had taken a seat beside Jean, who was listening intently to Phoenix.

'It's such a shame. I mean, we only have so many ways to earn a living, and the festival could have become as important as any.'

Jean made soothing noises, then turned to Kate. 'Years ago, there used to be an old-fashioned traditional May Fayre. The usual fodder for such village events, you know. Maypole dancing and bric-a-brac stalls—'

'Stuff shoudda'bin tossed out,' Patrick barked. 'There be a reason crap's a gurt part o' scrap.'

Mrs Lovelace sent him a stern look. 'That's enough, Pat,' she admonished, as she rummaged in her bag and withdrew knitting needles and a ball of wool. 'We'm each to our own.'

'It was lovely,' Phoenix sighed. 'The fishermen's choir on the harbourside, local folk dances.'

'And the village hall full of stalls. Homemade cakes, bottle draws, and so on, raising funds for things like the Christmas lights and the school,' Anna added as she topped up the plate of biscuits.

Kate's took in the wistful expressions around the table. 'So, what happened?'

'It stopped, backalong, my lovely,' Mrs Clegg said, sending Kate a kind look. 'People didn't bother any more, wanting bigger and better entertainment than simple village fun. Then that woman arrived, set up a new'un. All posh, it was, and she brought a helluva crowd of incomers, started chargin' fees for entry.'

'It became the *Polkerran Point Arts, Music & Literature Festival*, and Leigh moved it closer to the main season to catch more visitors.' Nicki added milk to her mug. 'There's a website now, and she roped in volunteers from all over. It was crazy busy.'

'You couldn't get a spot, though,' Phoenix muttered, folding her arms across her chest. 'Local artists didn't get a look in.'

Anna sighed. 'Sadly, the cove made no financial gain either. None of the profits were passed on to the local fund-raising initiatives.'

'Good riddles to her, I says,' Mrs Lovelace added, handing a crochet needle to Mrs Clegg. 'Lepers don't change they spots, do they? It would've been more on the same, this year.'

Anna had gone over to the kitchen to boil the kettle and refresh the tea and coffee pots, and Kate joined her.

'Couldn't you take charge of this? It's a shame to lose it, and you're such a star organiser.'

Anna leaned back against the sink as she waited for the kettle to do its thing. 'I don't have the flexibility to devote to it, the summer's my busiest time here at the B&B.' A small smile touched her mouth. 'And Oliver's asked me not to get involved. He knows I would have done it somehow, but... it's not the best timing.'

Returning to the table, Kate's mind was ticking. Mrs Clegg and Mrs Lovelace were busy with crochet and knitting respectively now, Old Patrick was on his third scone – jam first, which probably accounted for the rapprochement with his neighbours – Phoenix and Nicki were chatting about schools, and Jean's attention was on her phone, a secretive smile on her lips.

Conscious of more than a spark of interest, and aware she needed more challenge than the present job alone offered, Kate resumed her seat.

'I'll do it.'

Several pairs of eyes swivelled to Kate, then to each other before resuming their study of the newest arrival in the cove.

'Are you serious?'

Kate laughed at Anna's expression as she joined them, refilled teapot in hand. 'Yes! The job's fine, and sometimes it's manic, but there are times when it's so quiet I could weep. I need something else to do.'

How difficult could it be? Besides, surely the people involved in last year's organisation knew all about it and could soon fill her in?

'You'm a proper maid, young'un,' piped in Old Patrick, a smile creasing his weathered cheeks. 'You'm be rights, getting spondoolies outta they rich folk in town.'

'Or even better,' interjected Nicki. 'Try not to cheese off the main sponsor.'

With a frown, Kate looked from her to Anna, who'd gone to put the kettle on again. 'Who's that?'

'Ah, here he is now.'

Kate looked over as someone came through the boot room door. Everyone stared at the new arrival with undisguised interest, and she had to concede Dev's embarrassment at finding a houseful was endearing.

Not that *she* found it attractive as he walked over to where Anna stood.

Of course she didn't.

'You've met Kate, I think?'

Anna waved a hand towards the head of the table. It was clear Dev hadn't spotted her as he avoided looking at the locals, but a flash of recognition was quickly replaced with a look of discomfort.

'Yes, we've met.' He gave a swift nod in her direction, then turned back to Anna. 'Is Oliver home? I couldn't get through on his mobile.'

'He switches it off if he's writing. Is it urgent?'

' 'Fraid so.'

'He's in the den. Go on up, he won't mind. Tell him I'll bring coffee up.'

As soon as Dev left the room, Kate hurried over to where Anna was topping up the beans in the coffee machine.

'*He's* the main sponsor?' She wished her voice didn't sound so squeaky.

'Yes. Well, the only one.'

'Why can't he run it?'

'I'm not sure. Perhaps you can ask him when you meet up?'

Kate's eyes narrowed as they met Anna's amused ones. 'Why would we meet up?'

'Well, if you're the organiser and he's the only sponsor…'

Bloody hell!

'They'll be so relieved you've taken it on,' Anna continued, eyeing the locals around her table with fondness. 'Dev will be too. I don't think Leigh's old cronies are being pro-active, which is probably why it's stalled.'

The move to The Lookout went smoothly, and life there soon settled into a pattern.

On the Friday of Mollie's third week at her new school, Kate walked to work deep in thought. She had a baby shower that afternoon and a wedding on Saturday. She'd promised to take Mollie to the Lost Gardens of Heligan on Sunday, but the weather didn't look promising and she might need a back-up plan.

The official first day of spring loomed, but the weather clearly hadn't received the memo, a bitter wind scampering into the cove over the heaving seas which currently battered the rocks around the lighthouse, sending spray over the cliffs beneath Harbourwatch and whipping Kate's scarf into a frenzy as she crossed the bridge.

Immediately her gaze landed on the house, Dev popped into mind and Kate finally acknowledged the source of her disquiet. The family were coming in to finalise the arrangements for Ryther's eighty-fifth in April. Would it be a re-run of their first: rudely interrupted by Leigh Devonshire? Would Dev be any more friendly? He'd been much more approachable when walking his dog. Perhaps she ought to suggest he bring Bayley along to all their meetings?

'Morning!' Jean greeted Kate warmly as she entered the foyer from the staff quarters. 'These came for you.' She handed over a couple of envelopes.

'Thanks. I'll be in the office if I'm needed. I've got the Devonshire meeting at eleven, and the balloons for the baby shower should be here by midday, so give me a shout if I haven't emerged.'

Busy making calls to various suppliers to double-check timings for the wedding on the following day, the next few hours flew by, but then Jean put her head around the door.

'Sorry,' she mouthed silently, pointing at the phone in Kate's hand. 'Couldn't get through. Your eleven o'clock's cancelling.'

'Oh.' Kate replaced the receiver. 'I was on hold to the council. You'd better put him through.' Kate smiled as she spoke into the phone. 'Hi, Ryther.'

'It's Dev.'

Great.

'Sorry. Is there a problem?'

'My grandfather has been a little unwell, so isn't going to be able to make the meeting. I'm heading up to London now to see him.'

'I'm sorry to hear that. Please pass on my best wishes.'

There was no response, so she pressed on. 'We're a month from Ryther's party, so we were going to go through the menu choices, firm up the timings and agree a date for final numbers?'

There was a huff of breath. 'Grandy says he's happy to leave all the decisions to you.'

Ah. That might well account for the negativity fizzing down the line.

'Okay. Your grandfather indicated he'd prefer a sit-down meal to an informal buffet. I've put together a range of menu options to cater for all dietary requirements, though I'll need to know in advance of any allergies, and so on. Shall I email it to you?'

Dev reeled off his email address and the call ended, and Kate leaned back in her seat, eyeing the phone with regret.

How was she going to overcome the man's resentment, when he'd mistakenly assumed she was cut from the same cloth as his troublesome wife? Did he even realise she'd overheard his dismissive remark about her?

Chapter Seven

The One Where the Crocodile Rocks

The busy weekend left Kate little time to reflect on her impulsive offer to take over the organisation of the summer festival – or Summy-Fessy, as Mollie claimed her fellow schoolmates had dubbed it.

On Monday, however, she had a window of time after lunch and she settled at the desk determined to get to grips with rescuing what she could. A swift examination of the festival's website gave her an idea of the previous year's programme, including the venues and what Leigh had been charging for entry.

Kate sat back in her seat, her gaze drifting out of the window to the beautiful hotel gardens. There were touches of green on the bare branches of the trees and a bank of bright yellow forsythia hedging had come into bloom along one side of the terrace.

It was no surprise Leigh had been driven to charge. If her husband was the sole sponsor – and it seemed from the website he was – and she'd had to pay all the out of towners to participate…

Kate knew from experience the costs involved in booking speakers, panellists and performers from her old job. There weren't just attendance fees, but also travel and accommodation expenses to cover, along with venue hire, any necessary licences and support equipment like tents, furnishings, temporary loos, and so on. The list, as she well recalled, was endless.

'And yet...' Kate mused as she got up and walked over to stare out of the window. 'This isn't what it's meant to be about.'

A quick trawl of festival websites in the south-west had, in general, supported Phoenix's view: many of these events had become a big draw for successful writers, journalists, artists and performers, none of whom were local to the West Country, and included some very big names in their field. No wonder the costs of Polkerran Point's *Arts, Music & Literature Festival* had spiralled.

Anna had explained that Leigh – when the Devonshires returned to the cove a few years ago – had pretty much joined, and in some cases taken over, most of the clubs, societies and groups in the village. A hugely successful businesswoman, she clearly couldn't switch off in her private life.

Kate had also received a brief email from Dev, acknowledging her involvement and offering the contact details he had access to. Returning to her desk, Kate pulled up the Notes app on her phone for the email address she'd also found on the website.

'Right,' she told herself firmly. 'Let's get this show on the road.'

—

The responses to Kate's emails weren't encouraging, and she tried to work out why the reticence in sharing information from those alleged to have been the 'committee'.

In the end, Kate urged them into agreeing a date and time all four of them could meet at the hotel. She'd emailed Dev to see if he wanted to join them, but was relieved when he said he was in London that week.

Kate reflected on Ryther briefly, hoping it wasn't his health causing a concern and that visiting his son was the reason. She'd really liked the elderly gentleman and hoped they'd meet again one day.

Then, her gaze dropped to the names of those who'd been Leigh's inner cohort on last year's all new, allegedly 'bigger and better' festival. She'd run them past Anna but her friend hadn't recognised them, merely saying Leigh wasn't a respecter of keeping things local.

A half hour into the meeting, thoroughly frustrated but trying to keep a smile firmly in place, Kate looked from one to the other of the three people who'd actually turned up – one of them, whoever she was, worked in Plymouth and couldn't get time off at the last minute.

'So, just to recap...' Kate glanced at the blank page before her.

Shouldn't take long...

'The website says this year's dates are in June, but as of now, there are no artists booked, no venues confirmed and therefore no deposits paid to secure anything?'

'Don't you go blaming us,' the lady to her right bristled, folding her arms across her chest. 'Leigh always did that side of things.'

' 'S'right. We just did as we were told.'

Kate sent a genuine smile towards the older lady to her left. She had been the more engaged of the three but had absolutely nothing to offer other than constantly repeating how lovely the festival was and how the authors from London had been over the moon about sales of their books after they'd done a panel.

'I promise I'm not casting blame.' Kate sent what she hoped was an encouraging look at them. 'I'm just trying to establish facts. The first thing we'll need to do is move the date. It's too late to make June work.'

Three indignant pairs of eyes swivelled in her direction.

'But it's always been in June!' The third member of Leigh's committee was of indeterminate age, with large eyes behind equally large glasses and wearing a sweatshirt bearing the words 'hedgehogs are just prickly people', and she stared eagerly around the table as though garnering support.

Two heads nodded, but Kate sent the woman a puzzled look. 'You've only done it once.'

'She's about right, then.' They all nodded.

'There isn't enough time to organise things,' Kate protested. 'If you want a festival this year, it has to be towards the end of the season. I suggest we make it a two-day event on the August Bank Holiday weekend. We'll catch the last of the summer visitors, too.'

There was a general muttering, and Kate released a soft sigh.

'Okay, so what about volunteers?' Three pairs of eyes looked at each other blankly, then at Kate. 'On the day? We'll need marshalls for managing the traffic and car park, selling programmes, and so on, and we'll need first aiders too.'

'Leigh had them for looking after guests, as well. Inundated with help, she was, once the big names were involved.'

Thank goodness.

'So, who did it last year?'

Kate dropped her pen on the pad, trying to catch eyes that clearly did not wish to be caught.

Eventually, the older lady looked up. 'People came from all over. Couldn't wait to sign up, keen to get selfies with the celebs, they were. And Leigh was part of the am-dram scene in Port Wenneth. She roped in all the club members in exchange for using her contacts to help promote their latest production.'

'Excellent. Who should I approach about it?'

There was silence, then: 'Well, since Leigh left, the club disbanded. She set it up and ran it, see?'

–

After the committee left, each of them tasked with getting some information to Kate by the end of the week, she picked up her bag and headed outside. Thankfully, it was time to go home, and fresh air was needed, but once back at The Lookout, she settled at the kitchen island and picked up her phone.

An hour later, when Mollie came in, having been at an after-school club, Kate put the phone aside with relief.

'I thought we could go out for tea tonight. Where d'you fancy?'

Mollie gave an exaggerated sigh. 'I wish there was a Maccie D's nearby.'

Kate laughed as they headed up the stairs.

'Well, there isn't. Go and get changed and we'll walk down to the Lugger. They do a very nice burger, and that will have to do.'

Half an hour later, Mollie was tucking into her meal with relish, regaling Kate with plans at the school for a trip to Cotehele. An avid reader, Mollie was fascinated with history, especially the Tudor period.

'And there's going to be a performance of *Six* in Truro too.'

Recalling the brilliant musical they'd seen in London the previous year, Kate smiled. 'You and your six wives. You're more obsessed than Henry was.'

Kate didn't have room for a pudding, but when Mollie went over to browse the dessert menu, she reflected on the rest of the evening stretching before her.

You're lonely...

Determinedly quashing the persistent notion, Kate was thankful when Mollie resumed her seat, taking a slug of Dr Pepper. 'I've ordered.'

'What would you like to do when we get back?'

'Can we play Hogwarts Legacy?'

Lauren and Daniel's snug was perfectly set up for gaming, with a massive screen on the wall and the most up-to-date controllers.

'On one condition.' Mollie raised a brow, and Kate grinned.

'You clear out some of your gear and sell it to some of the shopkeepers first.'

'Muuum. It's no fun if you make it like real life!'

By the following weekend, Kate hadn't heard back from any of the committee or received any response to her follow-up emails and voicemails.

Her hopes of moving the date hadn't reaped any benefits yet, either. Finding venues for the Bank Holiday weekend was, unsurprisingly, impossible.

The village hall was booked out all weekend. The back room at the Lugger became overspill dining in peak season, and the upstairs room at the Three Fishes wasn't easily accessible.

The bistro's private dining room was also too busy to cede space that weekend, and the new restaurant on the quay, though keen to be supportive, was entirely open plan.

Even the Point Hotel couldn't help. They did, however, offer some spare bunting for decorating the harbour front, along with several strings of outdoor lights.

On the Tuesday morning, as soon as Mollie left for school, Kate headed over to Truro to do some long overdue shopping, which not only included buying a nice mid-season coat, a sturdier pair of walk books and a gorgeous, soft throw for one of the sofas, but also a couple of niche purchases in one of the charity shops.

A thoughtful expression settled on Kate's features as she waited to pay for her finds, studying the leaflets by the till, and she pocketed one as an idea began to form.

Back home, she tucked into a sandwich from M&S with a coffee at the kitchen island and fired up her laptop, intent on ticking off more of her to-do list, but barely had she opened her email account when the doorbell buzzed.

'Oh, hello. Do come in.'

'I do hope I'm not intruding? I called the hotel, but they said you had a day off and as I was passing…'

Kate eyed Mrs Tremayne warily as she stepped into the house. Passing? The only things that went by The Lookout were tractors, cyclists or walkers, taking the no-through lane to the fields or cliff path respectively. As the lady was dressed in a smart trouser-suit, glossy shoes and carried a designer tote, she was immediately on her guard.

'Would you like coffee?' Kate led the way into the kitchen part of the vast, open-plan living area.

'Yes, please. Flat white.' The lady stared around with avid interest. 'My nephew, Daniel, had this house built.'

'It's beautiful. I feel blessed to be able to live here.'

Kate set the machine in motion, regretting her own cooling coffee, and leaned against the counter.

'Was there something in particular you wanted to talk about?'

'Let's wait until I have coffee, shall we?'

Kate turned back to the machine, giving the coffee a vigorous and totally unnecessary stir. She wouldn't be opening the biscuit tin.

'I believe you are attempting to put some life back into the ailing summer arts festival.'

It wasn't a question, so Kate decided not to favour it with an answer.

Mrs Tremayne took her time, taking a drink from her mug, then holding it up to study the pattern. 'It never tastes quite the same, does it, unless it's in a fine china cup?'

Kate sent the extremely high-end coffee machine an apologetic look. 'I prefer mugs.'

'Hmm. Well. It's to be expected. Now, I also believe you are working full time at the hotel.'

Unsure where this was going, Kate waited.

'And I believe you have a young daughter to care for.'

Now Kate was getting annoyed. 'You believe a great deal, Mrs Tremayne, but I'm still none the wiser as to the purpose of your visit.'

The lady placed her mug on the island, releasing a girlish giggle totally unsuited to her appearance.

'Isn't it obvious? I'm here to help you. Leigh Devonshire,' Mrs Tremayne sniffed, 'would accept no assistance, despite my best endeavours. How can an incomer know what's best for the village?'

Quashing the urge to say the Tremaynes had hardly been good for the local community in recent years, Kate summoned a smile.

'That would be fantastic. Is there anything in particular you'd like to take on?'

'As I am such a local influencer, I'd be willing to introduce you to my connections. They may be instrumental in taking out advertising in the programme. I offered to do as much for Leigh, but she did not endear herself to people, you understand? Insisted on doing everything herself. You'll be too busy for that.'

Kate understood very well. She was being told, in no uncertain terms, that it would be gracious to accept the offer from the self-styled lady of the manor, though how that worked now, with the reins handed over to the absent Alex, she wasn't sure.

Still, there was no denying she needed all the help she could get, so she shook the lady's hand. As she closed the door on her back, however, Kate couldn't help but feel she was dancing with the devil.

—

During her lunch break the next day, Kate nipped down into the village, pushing open the door to the bookshop and stationers – Pen & Ink – and enjoying the tinkling of the old-fashioned bell.

'Morning,' she greeted the young woman behind the counter, before turning to browse the trolley of second-hand books under one of the windows. She soon found a Philippa Gregory Mollie hadn't read and tucked it under her arm as she flicked through the nearby stand displaying various greetings cards.

Five minutes later, with a selection of cards and the latest Marian Keyes novel added to the growing pile on the counter by the till, Kate recalled her purpose in visiting and headed to the small but well-stocked children's section.

She had her head tilted to one side, studying the spines as she sought the book Nicki had asked for, when the doorbell jingled again.

'There you are!' she exclaimed quietly, extracting the latest in the *Kid Normal* series by Greg James and Chris Smith but as she straightened, she came face to face with Dev.

'Oh, hi.'

He shuffled from foot to foot.

'Hi.'

As that appeared to be that, Kate made to move past him, but he gestured at the book in her hand.

'Isn't that a little young for your daughter?'

Kate studied the cover momentarily, then met his surprisingly intent gaze. 'You'd be surprised at her reading habits. But this is for Nicki's youngest, Jason. He's a big fan. As for me,' she sent him an impish smile, 'I'm here to find books on protecting the environment.'

She moved past Dev into the main part of the shop, uncertain why she felt flustered, and added the book to the pile.

'Nearly done,' she said to the assistant, who grinned.

'No rush. We love bulk shoppers.'

Wondering if perhaps she'd been a bit cheeky to Dev – after all, they barely knew each other – Kate continued her browsing, her senses on high alert and perfectly aware of his presence on the other side of the bookshelves.

Until, that is, he appeared at her side, hand extended.

'Is this yours?'

He held up a leather fob sporting a chrome crocodile.

Kate's brow furrowed as she studied the tag lying on his palm, and she glanced at her Lacoste tote, then picked up the offering.

'Gosh, thanks. I didn't realise it had fallen off.' Unceremoniously, Kate stuffed it into her pocket. 'Probably improves the bag anyway.'

She looked up with a smile, but the upward curve of her lips slowly halted. Why was he looking at her like that, as though she was some sort of mystery to him? Had she got lipstick on her teeth, or a smudge under her eyes?

As surreptitiously as she could, considering Dev's continued scrutiny, she ran her tongue across her teeth. The panda-eyes would have to stay. He seemed a fan of the environment, perhaps he liked the look?

'I wanted to say…' He stopped, bit his lip, gave his head a brief shake. 'Right. Okay.'

He moved past Kate to the counter, handing over a couple of children's books and a jigsaw, and reluctant to follow, she moved behind the nearest bookcase until the bell indicated he'd left the shop.

Paying for her purchases, Kate stepped outside, glancing left and right, but there was no sign of Dev's tall figure, and she retraced her steps back to the hotel deep in thought.

Chapter Eight

The One With Careless Whispers

The following Saturday, Kate and Mollie headed down the hill, but before going on into town for a mooch around the bookshop and some lunch, they called on Anna, only to find her at the large table in the window. Sunlight poured in, casting a glow over the contents spread liberally around that belied the chilly day outside.

'Have we come at a bad time?' Kate's eyes scanned the papers and photos on the table, but Anna smiled warmly as she put down the letter she held.

'Not at all. I'm torn between enjoying what I'm doing and feeling horribly voyeuristic.'

Hanging her coat over the back of a chair, Kate laughed. 'Intriguing.'

'Where's Dougal?' Mollie called from the sofa opposite the log burner, where she sat stroking Heathcliff, who rolled onto her back, stretching her black, fluffy paws out in ecstasy.

'Up in the den with Oliver. They'll be here soon, it's almost coffee time.'

Anna turned back to the table and Kate picked up a photo of a handsome man, leaning against a sleek boat, who looked to be in his mid-thirties. From the style of the image, his hairstyle and attire, she guessed it was from several decades ago. Glancing at the back, she tried to decipher the fading ink scrawl.

'Neb. Autumn '75. Polwelyn.' Kate raised an eyebrow. 'Odd name. Who is he?'

'I'm not sure, except it's definitely Aunt Meg's handwriting.' Anna reached for a polished wooden box in the centre of the table. 'This is yet another of her mysteries. My brother found it under a creaking floorboard when he stayed over Christmas, but what with that, the wedding and then going away, it was put aside. Oliver reminded me about it yesterday, so I thought I'd have a look. I feel like I shouldn't, because she'd hidden it away.'

It was generally accepted that Anna had inherited Westerleigh Cottage from elderly Meg Stratfield, who'd never married and had no family.

Aunt Meg – not a relation by blood, but someone who had become important to the orphaned Anna as she grew up and passed her summer holidays in Polkerran under the lady's care – had passed away a few years ago, suffering from Alzheimer's. She'd left behind a mystery for Anna to solve at the time, instructing her to 'follow the shells', culminating in the discovery of a similar wooden box – in effect, both were antique tea caddies.

Inside the first one had been some important documents relevant to the ownership of Westerleigh, along with a letter for Anna, a few personal photos and the ring now sitting next to the wedding band on her left hand.

Kate picked up the photo again and studied it. 'Are there any more?'

'Yes, stacks of them.' Anna handed her a couple of photos, one informal, the other clearly a studio shot, the man in a suit, his hair much more neatly styled. He had keen blue eyes, extremely handsome features and the hair was clearly auburn.

Kate narrowed her gaze, tilting one of the photos to the side. 'There's something familiar about him, but—'

She looked up as the door opened and Oliver came in, Dougal on his heels.

Mollie joined them at the table. 'What are you doing? Hey, that man looks like the one we met on the cliff path, Mum. You know, the one with the black dog and the little boy.'

Her interest piqued, Kate studied it further. 'I think that's Ryther.' She raised her gaze to Anna's before it returned to the photo, and she handed it to her friend. 'Why on earth would your Aunt Meg have photos of Dev's grandfather?'

Mollie rolled her eyes at her mother. 'They obviously knew each other.'

'Rather well, I'd say,' Oliver added as he joined them, Dougal weaving around his legs. 'Did Anna show you this?'

He retrieved some torn pages from under a letter. 'Meg kept diaries. They were stacked in boxes when Anna moved here, but a few had lines blacked out or pages removed. We never knew why until we opened this box.'

'Aunt Meg was madly in love with someone called Neb, but something kept them apart. It sounds, from what we've read so far, that she ended it. We've no idea why.' Anna sighed. 'And I'm still not sure we should pry. Who knows what secrets these letters hold?'

'Maybe that man was a wife killer!' Mollie's expression brightened at the prospect, but Kate merely rolled her eyes.

'You'll have to excuse Molls. She's obsessed with Henry and his six wives.'

With a laugh, Anna got to her feet. 'Looking at the rest will have to wait. Let's have a cuppa before you head off.'

Kate busied herself gathering the papers and photos together, placing them carefully into the caddy, but she hesitated with the last image she held. Mollie was right about it looking like Dev, aside from the dated clothing – and perhaps the smile.

He hadn't actually directed one at her, yet.

–

Kate dressed with care the following Saturday. It continued to be dry, but as it was still cool, she'd chosen a fine wool shift dress and a matching three-quarter-length coat. The moment she slid her feet into heels, however, she had a sudden hankering for shedding her business image, donning the new walk boots and coat and taking a stroll on the coast path, losing herself in her surroundings.

Was she a mismatch for Polkerran? Kate sometimes felt like that one boat in the bay facing upstream when all the others pointed out to sea.

She was in the kitchen, checking her bag, when she heard Mollie coming down the stairs. Thankfully, the teenage urge to sleep in hadn't set in yet.

A giggle came from her daughter as she reached the hall, and Kate sent her a fond look as she came into the room, the perpetual buds in her ears.

'We need to go in twenty minutes, love.' Kate pointed at the cereal and poured Mollie a glass of her favourite juice.

Removing one of the earbuds, Mollie set to, then giggled again.

'What are you listening to?'

'A podcast,' Mollie mumbled through a mouthful of coco-pops. 'They're doing "Sexy/Not Sexy".'

With a frown, Kate swept toast crumbs from the counter into her hand and dropped them in the food waste. 'I don't think it's—'

'Muuum!' Mollie rolled her eyes at Kate. 'It's not *that* sort of sexy, when – ewww.' She shuddered, and it was her mother's turn to laugh.

'Okay.'

'It's this game, where a thing, like, you know, an everyday thing is *not s*exy, but if it's a bit different, then it *is*.'

'You mean its aura?'

'Vibe. Yeah, kinda.'

Kate held out a hand for Mollie's now empty bowl and spoon. 'I've heard of it. They do it sometimes on the radio. Like, a raisin isn't sexy, but a chocolate-covered raisin is.'

Mollie slid off the stool. 'You're such a mum sometimes. Gonna brush my teeth.'

'*Going to*,' Kate corrected automatically, then frowned. Was she? What was it about raisins that made Mollie think that?

By the time they reached Anna's, where Mollie was to spend the day until Kate left work, the debate continued.

'See? Bose, not sexy.' Mollie pointed to the headphones resting on the counter. 'Puro, sexy. I'm winning.'

Anna looked over as they came into the house. 'Sounds like an intriguing game.'

'Except I'm failing miserably at it.'

Kate searched her mind desperately for something not remotely 'mumsie'. 'Peanuts,' she announced with triumph. 'Not sexy. Peanut *butter*, sexy.'

Her daughter sent her a resigned look and walked off to sit by Heathcliff in the window seat, and Kate winked at Anna. 'Depends what you're using it for, mind.'

Anna smothered her laugh as Kate said goodbye to Mollie.

There. That proved it, didn't it? She wasn't *just* a mum!

–

The wedding went smoothly, with the guests in good humour and the weather continuing dry, allowing them to spill out onto the terrace, albeit with the heaters lit to keep them warm. It was gone six by the time Kate arrived back at Westerleigh to delicious aromas filtering through the open window of the boot room.

'There you are!' Anna welcomed her in, and as soon as she'd kicked off the heels and shed her coat, her friend thrust a glass of chilled wine into her hand and told her to sit. 'You'll stay to eat with us? Mollie's up with Oliver in the den at the moment.'

Kate filled Anna in on her day as she sat at the island, watching her friend checking on a hearty-looking fish pie.

'Mollie's had a busy day. They took Dougal out for a long walk this morning, and she's been round at Nicki's too, gaming with the boys. After lunch, she watched back-to-back

Digging for Britain on YouTube, and she's been with Oliver since, pounding him with questions about archaeology.'

'Poor Oliver!'

Anna put the pie in the oven to keep warm and turned her attention to the pans on the stove top. 'He loves talking history. Besides, he needed a break. He spent all the time she was next door going through some paperwork with Dev.'

Despite herself, Kate's ears pricked up. 'I wouldn't have thought they'd have much in common.'

'We've only really got to know Dev well in the last few months. Before his wife finally moved out, he didn't really socialise or interact with the locals. I'm not saying she kept him captive,' Anna smirked. 'He's very much his own man, but I think she was away so much, he wanted to be a stabilising factor for the son. He's become interested in Oliver's property schemes lately, though, so he pops in now and again.'

'What does Dev do for a living, then?'

Anna opened the Aga door, waving her oven-mitts at the escaping heat. 'He owns a lot of land, which he manages. I'm not aware he has anything to do with the family business.'

'What's that?'

'Music. His grandfather was something big in the industry back in the day – still owns the companies, even though he's retired, along with Secret Gem Records.'

Kate raised an impressed brow. 'Even I've heard of them.'

'It's who my brother, Matt's, working with. He and Ryther somehow hit it off when Dev's grandfather was down for Christmas and now Matt's writing music for some of the label's artists.'

Anna paused to stir a saucepan on the stove. 'Anyway, the family have owned Harbourwatch for years. Decades, as far as we know. When I first started coming to Westerleigh, for my summer stays with Aunt Meg – that would be when I was about six – the house was all boarded up, derelict and neglected. Phee was one of the local kids I made friends with, they all called it the Bat House.'

'A bit different to how it is now. The interior is stunning.' Kate recollected her admiration for the room they'd had the reception in.

'Yes, according to Leigh – who is never terribly discreet – the grandfather made it over to Dev and funded its renovation to its former glory. She made no secret of how much it cost, especially the restoration of the period features.'

Kate's gaze drifted towards the window. 'I wonder why Ryther would have left the house empty, to fall into such a state? What could've happened to drive him away from the cove for such a long time?'

'I've no idea. Anyway, the completion of the renovation coincided with Dev's going to the US. Something to do with Leigh and a high-profile role she'd secured, so he rented it out. Oliver took it on for three years.' Anna released a contented sigh. 'And if none of that had happened, we'd never have met.'

Kate sent her an understanding smile. She was still none the wiser as to what Dev actually did, but more disturbing was why she desperately wished to know more about him.

Chapter Nine

The One Where Kate Doesn't Like Mondays

On Monday, Kate worked her way through her Inbox, dealt with a couple of phone calls and then reached for her laptop bag, pulling out a folder Dev had handed over. She supposed she shouldn't use work time for the festival, but she hadn't taken a lunch break and it was hardly busy.

It was clear Leigh had made use of her extensive network, none of whom were from Polkerran and Kate wasn't sure about trying to involve them. There were a couple of copies of the previous year's glossy – and no doubt expensive – programme, and she noted the advertisers, but there was no information about costs. Surely there must be a spreadsheet somewhere?

Kate put in a call to Dev, purposefully ignoring the momentary pleasure when he answered rather than it going to voicemail, but it may as well have done. He was unable to provide any clue. Wondering if she ought to invite him to meet up to talk through things – especially in the light of absolutely *nothing* happening so far – the hesitation cost her, as Dev ended the call before she could suggest it.

Despite the frustration, Kate smiled to herself as she tucked the folder back in her bag and got up. She'd started to see enough in Dev to realise Anna's perception was most likely true: this was a somewhat awkward man through shyness more than anything else.

He also probably thought Leigh had his phone tapped, if the local chat about her paranoia over other women was anything to go by.

Kate headed home, determined to move things forward – if only someone from the committee would respond to her messages! She gave Jean a quick wave as she passed the ice cream shop. It looked almost ready to re-open and soon Jean would be ending her shifts at the hotel to run it again.

Kate paused to admire the rowing boat on the harbourside, newly planted out with spring flowers. Her phone pinged and, hopeful it would be one of the committee, she pulled it from her pocket only to scowl. Hugo. She scanned the message then deleted it. A complaint about how much stuff she had left behind fell on deaf ears and didn't warrant a response.

She and Mollie had taken the only things that mattered to them, but the unexpected contact was enough to cloud Kate's day. At least it couldn't get any worse.

'You look like you're in a mood,' Mollie greeted her when she reached The Lookout, and Kate dropped her bag onto the island, releasing the clip holding her hair in place.

'I'm not,' she lied, running her hands through her tresses and flexing her shoulders, as if by doing so she could shake off Hugo's intrusion into their new life.

'Whatever,' Mollie drawled, taking the stairs two at a time.

Kate shrugged out of her jacket, swapped the heels for slippers then looked around at the empty room; she needed more air.

Out on the terrace, the night was drawing in, a cool breeze caressing Kate's skin. The muffled sound of waves crashing onto the rocks below the coast path drifted across the hedgerow bordering the grounds, and long grasses danced rhythmically; she closed her eyes, letting the sounds and salty smells fill her senses.

The sudden image of Dev in the bookshop, his blue-grey gaze – not assessing, but merely puzzled – swept into place, and Kate's eyes flew open. Where had that come from? And what had he been trying to say?

There was no denying Dev disturbed her, inexplicable though it was. Kate hugged her arms across her waist as Anna's words whispered through Kate's tired mind: 'You've forgotten what it's like to be attracted to someone. To feel attractive yourself.'

Was Anna right? Was she subconsciously looking for something she'd long lost?

'Of course not. I'm perfectly happy as I am, free from the past and *definitely* not in need of a man.' Kate returned to the house and headed upstairs. 'And certainly not *that* man!'

When she emerged from her bedroom fifteen minutes later, make-up free and in her comfiest loungers, she heard giggles coming from Mollie's room, followed by a hoot of unfamiliar laughter, and Kate tapped on the door – now sporting a sign which read '*I'll be out dreckly…*' – and opened it.

'Hey, Molls. What do you fancy for dinner? Pasta or risotto?'

Her daughter hurriedly closed her laptop, and Kate tried to quash the frisson of anxiety as Mollie turned around. Looking decidedly culpable. Hadn't that been the livestream webcam pointing at the tidal beach below Harbourwatch, along with a still-shot of it?

Unfortunately for Mollie, the phone was still on speaker, and the voices of some of her friends trilled into the silence growing between mother and daughter.

'Look, look, look! She's back!'

'She's so *old*. Take another pic!'

Ugly colour fled into Mollie's cheeks as she snatched up the phone. 'Sorry, gotta go. Catcha later.'

Kate folded her arms across her chest.

'What were you doing? And don't say "nothing".'

Her daughter leaned back in her chair, a mutinous look on her face, arms folded in defence.

'Mollie, I'm not stupid. Nor am I blind. You were clearly on a call with one or more mates and it looks to me like you're all watching the webcam at the beach like it's some sort of reality TV and saying mean things about those swimming ladies.'

'Fine,' Mollie muttered. 'We were. We share screencaps, that's all. It's only like being there and taking photos. It's just a laugh.'

'Being mean about people is never funny.'

'Didn't bother Dad,' Mollie retorted. '*He* used to find it pretty amusing.'

Hugo's second appearance in as many hours was sufficient for Kate to lose what was left of her thinning patience. She strode over to the desk, scooped up Mollie's laptop and then her phone for good measure.

'Twenty-four hours, and you can have them back if you can explain to me why I should let you. And don't quote school work.'

Kate left the room, her spoils clutched in her shaking hands, exercising the last of her restraint in not slamming the door behind her, but when she reached her own room, she sank onto the bed, wiped out.

'It's just a trying day,' she intoned as she flopped onto her back, staring at the ceiling. 'It'll be better in the morning.'

Dinner was a fairly silent meal beyond 'please can you pass the pepper', but for once, Kate didn't care, and she let Mollie stew. After she'd loaded the dishwasher and settled into the armchair by the bay window, a figure came to stand beside her, then sank into the adjacent chair.

'Sorry, Mum.'

Kate threw her daughter a keen glance. 'Are you? Or are you hoping I'll reduce your sentence?'

A huff of breath was the only response and for a minute or two they both stared out at the darkening skies. It was a clear night, and a crescent moon could be seen playing peekaboo behind passing wisps of cloud.

Kate sighed, shifting in her seat to look at her daughter. She didn't want to be too heavy-handed. She understood Mollie had been through a lot this last year or so and she'd faced a massive upheaval with this move to the other end of the country.

Getting in with new friends was important, but none of that excused what she'd been doing.

'You do understand why it's wrong, don't you? That's a livestream – a webcam – and it doesn't record images. It would be against the law. Capturing what you're seeing on it and sharing it with your friends is just plain wrong, never mind the cruel comments about people simply enjoying a hobby they love.'

Mollie's bottom lip was sticking out, which it did when she was about to enter a major sulk.

'Molls, I mean it. I'm not trying to spoil things for you. I don't want you to make any missteps, that's all.'

She didn't reply, simply got up and headed to the snug, closing the door with a decided snap, and Kate sighed.

Roll on, tomorrow.

–

Kate had handed Mollie's laptop and phone back the following evening, her daughter still sulking as she headed upstairs with them. Unwilling to dwell on whether she'd made the right decision to not take things any further, she got on with preparing dinner, relieved it was the weekend.

Mollie was due to start kayak classes on Saturday with Liam and Jason, and Nicki had offered to take her with them to the cinema in the afternoon too, and while Kate savoured the down time, she was again consumed by a hollow sense of isolation.

'Maybe we should get a rescue dog,' she mused, striding across the beach below The Lookout, trying to outpace her low mood.

There were two dogs on the beach with their owners, playing cat and mouse with the waves sliding in and out across the wet sands, and suddenly one she recognised came running to jump up on her jeans.

'Hello, Dougal,' Kate exclaimed, rubbing his ears, looking up to see Anna coming towards her.

They fell into step together for a while, Dougal enjoying the freedom of chasing up and down the beach, but soon they were the only people left, and they stopped near an outcrop of rocks, perching on its edge.

'Is it always this quiet?'

'Only until the Emmets return for Easter. Then there's a lull, with a small peak for the May Bank Holidays. The summer is off the scale, though, so make the most of it.'

'So many of the cottages along the waterfront have no lights on at night.'

'They're mostly second homes, out of the price range of the locals, especially the younger ones. They tend to move away. It's why Oliver started to buy property in Polkerran to rent out at affordable prices, giving priority to residents. He's upset the Tremaynes time and again by beating them to a deal, but now Alex is in charge, they're selling even more things off.' Anna sighed. 'I think Mr Tremayne senior thought by handing the estate to Alex – he's the only child – he'd come home and run it, but I can't see him giving up the bright lights and city wage of London.'

'So instead, he's selling the estate off, bit by bit? Isn't that good for Oliver, though?'

'It would be, but I think I mentioned Alex refuses to sell to him? Oliver's even had others try to negotiate the deal, but once they ask for proof of where the funds are coming from...' Anna shrugged, glacing at her watch. 'I'd best get back. I've got an appointment this afternoon.'

They scaled the steps up to the coast path, where Kate was assailed by the recollection of her first meeting with Dev, hoping he might appear with Bayley, but the path was deserted. They paused by the gate to The Lookout for a moment.

'When's your brother back? It still seems odd to say that.'

Anna's eyes lit up. 'Tell me about it! I spent most of the first year we were in each other's lives stalling on the word every time I used it.'

Having been orphaned as small children and raised separately, the siblings had been unaware of each other's existence until a few years ago.

'He and Gemma will be back by Easter.'

'Ah, yes. His house-friend.'

'His what?'

With a laugh, Kate opened the gate. 'It's how they introduced themselves to me at the wedding.'

'Sounds about right. They hadn't quite found their way to each other at the time. Gemma's lovely, though, and has been so good for him. I can't wait until they're back.'

'It's beginning to feel like all roads lead to Polkerran Point,' Kate murmured. 'First you came here and stayed, then Lauren arrived and met Daniel, followed by your brother. It's as though, once here, the cove never quite lets go.'

Anna sent her friend a knowing look. 'Absolutely. You'd better look out.'

Kate merely smiled, saying goodbye and returning to the house. After all, it was down to Mollie. If she was happy, they'd stay. For herself, she had no interest beyond that.

Firmly extinguishing the little voice whispering 'liar' in the back of her head, Kate shed her coat and boots and headed upstairs. She'd have a long soak in the bath, start reading her latest book purchase and enjoy falling in love with a fictitious man.

Real ones had proven to be a waste of space.

Chapter Ten

The One Where Things Can Only Get Better

After her bath, Kate began preparing dinner, and soon the mince was simmering nicely. She checked her watch. She'd listen to the latest episode of her current favourite podcast until she needed to do the rest.

Leaning back in the armchair, her phone on her lap, adjusting her extremely unsexy Bose noise-cancelling headphones, Kate jumped when someone touched her arm.

'I'm sorry, Mum. Properly sorry. I promise I won't do it again.'

Kate sat up, removing the headphones.

'The screenshots or the being mean?'

Mollie had the grace to look chastised. 'Both. I didn't know it was wrong to...' Her voice tailed off, and she fidgeted from foot to foot. 'Leastways, it did feel a bit as though we were spying, but then, like, why is it there?'

Getting up, Kate walked back to the kitchen, Mollie in her wake.

'I told you, there are webcams all around the world, Molls. Some are at tourist spots like... oh, I don't know, up mountains or in city centres like Paris or Rome. This one is to see the beach, watch the waves when it's stormy. It's not recordable CCTV, like a lot of businesses or transport hubs have. Livestream webcams are purely for people's enjoyment.'

Mollie selected a plum from the fruit bowl on the island. 'I *was* enjoying it. It was sick.' She took a bite, raising her eyes to meet her mother's. Then, she swallowed. 'Okay. I get it. And I've promised.'

'It's the difference between right and wrong, Molls.'

'I know.' She sent Kate a culpable look, but her eyes were shining. 'But that's why it felt fun, like?'

Huffing out a breath, Kate gave the pan on the hob a stir. 'I suppose there are worse things you could do.'

'Oooh.' Mollie joined her. 'Like what? Joking!' she added at her mother's look.

'Truce?' Kate asked, awash with relief to have the incident dealt with, holding out her pinkie.

'Truce.' Mollie locked fingers with her. 'Is that chilli?'

'Yes. Do you want rice with yours?'

Selecting another plum, Mollie turned for the snug. 'Can I have chips?'

—

April was starting to look busy. Kate scrolled through the calendar of bookings, making a note of the events she needed to work and those she could safely leave the team at the hotel to oversee. She began to scroll backwards, stalling on the page showing the coming weekend: Ryther's eighty-fifth.

Much as she'd taken to the elderly gentleman — and hoped whatever his health issues had been he would be well enough to enjoy the family celebration — Kate really didn't want to be around said family.

She headed down to the kitchen to talk a few things through with the catering manager, and then spoke to the maitre'd and, satisfied they saw no need for Kate to linger once the guests had arrived, she headed for the staff room. The much-needed coffee would have to wait as her phone rang.

Dev.

'Hi.'

'What time do you finish today?'

'Five, if things go to plan. Why?'

There was no reply, and Kate held the phone away, frowning at it. 'Dev? Are you still there?'

'Yes. Sorry. I – er, can you spare a half hour? Could do with a quick meet-up to discuss something.'

'I've got to pick Mollie up as soon as I leave. Can we do it at mine about six?'

'If that's okay. Don't want to intrude on your evening.'

'Not a problem, it's just I leave her with other people so much, I don't want to take advantage.'

—

Kate called at Westerleigh to collect Mollie, regretfully turning down the offer of a cup of tea.

'Wish I could but I need to get home. Dev's on his way over.'

'Is he now?' Anna's amusement was obvious.

'Curb your thoughts,' Kate admonished. 'He didn't sound particularly enthusiastic.'

'I wonder what he wants to say that couldn't be done on the phone, though.'

Kate had pondered the very same, but a glance at her watch proved she wouldn't have long to wait to find out.

'Come on Molls. Thanks, Anna. I'll message you later.'

They exchanged a hug then she herded Mollie – still chomping on a brownie – out the door. It was twenty to six and as she followed her daughter up the hill, Kate tried to quash the small frisson of interest that arose every time Dev came to mind. Was she imagining it, or did it happen a little too often?

'Why is he coming here?' Mollie dropped her bag in the hallway and kicked off her shoes. 'I thought you didn't like him?' She grinned mischievously. 'Does he *know* you hate him?'

'Mollie!' Kate glared at her daughter. 'I never said that!'

A rolling of the eyes was the only response, and Kate sighed as Mollie shot up the stairs to get changed.

Ten minutes later, as Mollie raided the fridge, she persisted in questioning Kate about Dev.

'You did say he was annoying, Mum. But maybe it's because he's a man. You're off them anyway, aren't you?'

'Am I?'

'Dad did this to you. Why else aren't you interested in finding a new one?'

'I don't need one.'

'I didn't say you did. But Rick Devonshire's not bad looking for someone his age.'

'Mollie!' Kate spluttered. 'He can't be a day over forty, if that.'

'Like I said. And he dresses pretty neat for...' She grinned at her mum. 'He's got that nice choppy fringe you like too. Anyway, you and Dad split ages ago. You've been divorced, like, over a year. And,' she added, 'you spend too much time alone.'

With that, she vanished into the snug to continue her acquaintance with the Playstation, and Kate barely had a moment to take in her astute daughter's words before the doorbell rang.

Opening the door, Kate tried not to notice how eye-catching Dev was. She also tried not to take in his attire. Sadly, these endeavours merely led to her gaze fastening on his forehead, where the auburn hair flopped exactly as Mollie said it did.

'Er, is something wrong?'

Kate blinked. 'Sorry. No. Come in.' She led him into the main living area. 'Cup of tea? Coffee? I try to avoid it this time of day, but you're welcome to one?'

'Tea, please.'

'Take a seat.' Kate felt like she was at an interview, such was the formality in both their voices. The only question was, who was the interviewee?

Dev settled at the island as Kate made the tea, the conversation – such as it was – sporadic, and mainly concerned with milk and sugar, until she joined him, taking a stool on the opposite side of the granite counter.

As he looked around, she studied him covertly, this time trying not to notice how well his shirt fitted and – when his attention returned to Kate – how it complemented the blue-grey of his eyes.

'I've never been in here before. It's stunning.'

'I can't quite believe we live here. I'm so grateful to Daniel.'

Holding her gaze, Dev said nothing for a moment, but as warmth rose up her neck, he frowned.

'Are you sure nothing's wrong?'

Kate grasped her mug. 'All fine. What did you want to talk about?'

Dev looked uncomfortable. 'I'm out of my comfort zone here. This festival… it's nothing to do with me, other than I helped fund it before. That's all the involvement I want or need right now.'

Kate placed her mug on the counter. This was good news, right?

'I feel like there's a "but" coming.'

A faint smile touched his mouth, but it was brief. 'Look, this is the cove. Things operate… differently, here, I suspect, to what you're used to.'

'So I'm beginning to find out,' Kate interjected wryly.

'There's been a few… mutterings.'

It was Kate's turn to furrow her brow. 'By whom? About what?'

'From the committee. About you.'

Great.

'Go on then, hit me with it.'

Dev stirred in his seat, his finger running up and down the handle of his mug. 'They don't like—' He broke off and ran a hand through his hair instead, which meant the fringe bounced back onto his forehead, and Kate sat on both her hands to stop herself from reaching over to brush it from his eyes.

As this thought merely brought the colour rushing back into her cheeks, she was unsurprised at Dev's visible concern deepening.

'I'm sorry. Really, I am. I hate being the person asked to say this. I told them to speak to you but—'

'I'm also terrifying, I take it.' Kate was saddened.

'They aren't very good at being given tasks and they're even worse at being chased to find out if they've done them. You do know they live by the dreckly code?'

Despite herself, Kate laughed. 'Yes, I do.' She fixed him with her clear gaze. 'Is that it?'

'Well, no. In effect, they've resigned.'

Kate rolled her eyes. 'From doing nothing?'

Dev laughed, and as it was the first time she'd ever heard him do so, Kate's eyes widened.

No, he is absolutely not *even more appealing now.*

As he sobered, however, Dev's gaze held Kate's steadily and the heat – which had barely subsided – began to stir again. She really ought to break this look. Surely it was time she started dinner? Mollie had said she was starving. Why are his eyes creasing at the edges? And why is his mouth starting to curve upwards in that maddeningly attractive way?

'Hi, Mr Devonshire!' Mollie's shrill greeting broke the moment as she emerged from the snug. 'Mum, where's the charging lead? This is dying.' She waved the handset in the air.

Sliding off the stool with relief, Kate pulled open a drawer and handed the lead to Mollie, who shot over to the wall to plug it in.

'I'll head off. Sorry for—' Dev waved a hand as he stood. 'I'm sure you're doing a sterling job. They just aren't used to being… encouraged to move forward in such a way.'

'Nagged, you mean?' Kate gave a rueful smile. 'They must have preferred the way it was done in the past.'

'They weren't allowed to do anything.' Dev's scowl was telling as they reached the hall. 'Meetings were merely a chance for my— for Leigh to hold sway on all she'd achieved so she could sit back and accept the adoration that followed.'

'Oh, I forgot to ask. How's Theo?'

The transformation was instant, as though a heavy mantle had fallen from Dev's shoulders, and he sent Kate a warm smile.

'Coming to stay for the Easter break. He's so excited, bless him. He loves being in the cove.'

'And with his dad, too, I suspect.'

He drew in a short breath, then nodded. 'I hope so. This is tough on him.' The air of melancholy Kate had first noticed on him returned. 'Leigh… she keeps…' He shook his head. 'Well, I'd best go. Thanks for the tea,' he added as he opened the front door.

'No problem. Any time.'

Really?

Kate closed the door on him but peeped through the diamond-shaped pane of glass in the top as he walked down the drive, hands shoved in his coat pockets.

'Don't dislike him as much as you did, do you?' Mollie said as she caught Kate in the act.

'Shut it, Spud,' Kate said as she followed her daughter back into the kitchen, but as she headed to the fridge to inspect the contents for inspiration, she had to reflect that Dev was improving on further acquaintance.

Chapter Eleven

The One Where Kate Finds Something Missing

Anna and Oliver were due to come to The Lookout for dinner on the Friday night of Ryther's birthday meal at the hotel, and Kate was more thankful than ever she'd already agreed she didn't need to stay the entire evening. With Mollie stopping overnight with a school friend upriver in Polwelyn, it also meant she could enjoy an evening of purely adult company for a change.

Leigh had breezed in, looking stunning and slipping her arm through Dev's in a proprietary way as the guests arrived. Kate had greeted Ryther warmly and, to her surprise, he'd placed a kiss on her hand.

'Are you well?' she asked him as they walked along the corridor towards the private dining room.

'Quite fit for purpose, my dear.' He'd met her concerned look with a smile. 'Old age is quite the bugger, I'm afraid.'

'Are you here for long?'

'I'm staying with Dev, keen to spend some time with my great-grandson during the holidays. Theo wishes to go pony trekking.' His eyes twinkled as his gaze met Kate's. 'Exhilarating though I once found horseback riding, I shall not be joining him.'

With a laugh, Kate wished him an enjoyable celebration and watched as he joined his family inside the room. Then, her concern returned. Had he lost weight he could ill afford to lose?

She was also trying to dispel the feeling of disquiet she'd experienced when meeting Dev's unreadable gaze as she passed.

Unlike on her first encounter with Leigh, he hadn't extracted himself from her arm.

Pushing it aside, Kate welcomed her guests and they settled at the island for pre-dinner drinks, but when Anna asked how the festival planning was going, she decided it was time to regale them with the purpose of Dev's recent visit.

'They've all resigned. Apparently, the committee, such as they were, couldn't handle actually being asked to do anything.'

She watched Oliver pour the wine he'd brought with him.

'Seems par for the course since Leigh left.' He handed Kate a glass. 'Try it. It's one of Anna's favourites.'

Kate took a sip of the deliciously dry rosé. 'Yum! I think I might be ordering a caseload to get me through this. You're right, though, Oliver. It seems Leigh was the central cog and with her removal from the scene, the wheels have fallen off the wagon. Come on, let's sit more comfortably.'

'Why was Leigh there tonight?' Anna followed Kate over to the sitting area.

It was a question Kate had pondered. 'I'm not sure, but it doesn't look as if she's committed to detaching herself.'

And if you're honest, you'll admit it's how Dev feels about it that niggles...

Silently quashing the thought, Kate joined Anna on the sofa.

'Nothing surprises me where that woman's concerned,' Oliver intoned as he took an armchair opposite the ladies.

'I'm not sure she really wants to let go of the family.'

Anna bit her lip, looking from Kate to Oliver. 'Maybe she just hasn't had chance to prioritise her personal life? She must have huge responsibility, being so high up in her company.'

Kate sent Anna a kind smile. 'Your ability to always see good in people hasn't changed.'

The conversation drifted onto pleasanter things before they headed to the dining table to eat.

'I've cheated a bit,' Kate admitted to Anna as she placed a chicken and mushroom pie on the table. 'I made this earlier and I've just heated it up so I could enjoy the company and not be frazzled in the kitchen.'

'I don't blame you,' Anna said, leaning forward and inhaling deeply as Kate added a bowl of garlic and rosemary potatoes. 'Gosh, it smells yummy.'

'Here,' she handed around some bread rolls. 'Not homemade like yours, but from Shari's bakery, so should be good.'

'Shari's is my go-to when I've not had time to bake.' Anna passed the basket to Oliver. 'And I haven't lately.'

'Why's that?'

'My fault,' Oliver said, spooning peas onto his plate. 'I'm behind on researching the new book, so Anna's been trying to help.'

Throwing Kate a culpable look, Anna spread butter on her roll. 'I'm not a trained research assistant, sadly, much as I love history, so I'm not sure I'm much use, but the property company has been taking up so much of Oliver's time, and with Daniel now in the US it's become more hands-on for him.'

'I never expected, when I first came to Polkerran, to find everyone so busy with their lives,' Kate exclaimed as she tucked into the chicken. 'It looks like such a laid-back, calm place on the surface.'

'Just wait until the summer,' Oliver warned. 'It's mayhem.'

'Not that Oliver would know.' Anna sent him an indulgent smile. 'He barely emerges from his den once the main summer holidays are here.'

When the meal was over and Anna and Oliver left, Kate's thoughts turned to how the evening at the hotel was going.

The school holidays were almost upon them and some of those tourists would be pouring into Polkerran for a few weeks. Ryther had intimated Theo would be spending the school holidays with his dad. Did that mean Leigh would be in town too, so that the little boy got some time with both his parents?

Mollie may well be better off away from the toxic atmosphere that permeated the house when they lived with Hugo, but that wasn't the case for all separating families.

Kate truly hoped the little boy would get what he most wished for.

—

When Kate arrived at the hotel on Monday morning, Jean was already in the staff room and greeted her with a warm smile.

'I'll miss my shifts.' It was her last one before she returned to running the village ice cream shop full time for the season.

Kate made a coffee and joined Jean at the table.

'I envy you. I don't suppose you need an assistant, do you?'

With a frown, Jean stirred her coffee. 'I thought you loved organising things. There are so many events going on right now. You're such a natural.'

'I do.' Kate sighed. 'It's not work, it's the summer festival. I feel like I'm constantly taking one step forward and fifty back.'

'So why not do that?' Jean picked up her mug, clearly amused at Kate's confusion. 'Take it back in time, to its roots, when it was a traditional village fayre.'

Kate's imagination was caught, and her mind immediately kicked into gear. 'I like that idea. I've been unhappy with continuing Leigh's vision, especially as the locals don't get a chance to showcase their talents. Jean,' Kate smiled warmly across the table, 'you're a genius!'

Jean grinned. 'I've been known to have my moments.'

Pulling her laptop from her bag, Kate set it up on the table. 'You've given me inspiration. I'll just check in with my friend, Google, and see what she's got to say about it.'

'Talk to Anna, too. She's usually full of ideas.'

Jean left Kate to her investigations, but she wasn't too sure about asking Anna for assistance. From what they'd said the other night, she already had enough on her plate trying to help Oliver.

—

At the end of the week, the local schools finally broke up for the Easter holidays and Mollie went up to Bristol to spend the first week with her grandparents and to hang out with her cousins who lived in Bath.

With Mollie away, Kate extended her strolls after work. The nights were becoming lighter, and she enjoyed the longer circular route back to The Lookout, which involved walking down from the hotel to where the tidal beach below Harbourwatch met the coast path. She kept a change of clothes in her office and had taken to wearing her sturdy walk boots, as they had such a good grip on them, making her way along the broad rocks which stretched out a stony arm into the sea and provided a solid foundation for the small lighthouse perched on the end.

Although the forecast for the holidays was the usual mixed bag for the time of year, today was fine and clear, the water bore a glassy sheen, both out beyond the rocks protecting Polkerran from the sea and within the bay. It had grown milder too, and Kate noted the new arrival of hanging baskets on the many lampposts, several pleasure craft in the harbour and a noticeable number of strangers walking along the waterfront, many of whom were families.

Reflecting on her week, Kate was surprised how much she'd enjoyed it. Work was going well, with excellent feedback from the small events she continued to organise, and positive vibes for the upcoming clutch of weddings and family celebrations. She'd also just secured a business conference for early December, along with a twenty-first birthday party in the autumn.

Slightly less productive was her work on the festival – or fayre, as she now preferred to call it. She'd had a morning off in lieu of an evening event earlier that week and called at Anna's before the usual crowd descended, and as her friend finished her breakfast duties, she'd continued making notes on the proposed community event. Nicki had called in just as Anna joined Kate at the table, and they'd both been so enthusiastic about the idea of returning to the traditional fayre, Kate had begged them to garner some help. Promising to do what they could, she'd left feeling optimistic, and this evening her mind was busy with what exactly she needed help with.

'Well, you did say you didn't have enough to do,' Kate cautioned under her breath as she navigated her way along the uneven, rocky path. Smiling ruefully, she paused and raised her head to stare across the undulating water to where Westerleigh Cottage nestled, its lawned gardens sweeping down to the fencing separating it from a sheer drop into the waves caressing the rocks below.

Oliver and Anna's boat rocked from side to side as the waves dallied with it, tucked against its mooring in a sheltered inlet, and Kate's gaze drifted further back along the coastline towards the bridge, and then the harbour, before it travelled along the other side of the bay. Unable to help herself, her eyes landed on the outer walls of Harbourwatch, all that was visible of it from this position. She could see one side of the charming, square room where the wedding reception had been held, with its arched windows. Was Dev inside? What if he was at that very window, looking over to where Kate stood?

Frustrated with the direction of her thoughts, and conscious of the flaring interest triggered by any and every thought of the man lately, Kate mulled over why Dev intrigued her. There was no denying his physical attractiveness, but she knew his appeal lay more in how much he loved Theo. Having lived with Hugo's dismissive behaviour towards Mollie, her heart went out to Dev as he tried to navigate his diminished role as a parent.

Kate huffed out a breath and resumed her walk. It was none of her business, and their interactions to date had been sufficient to suggest he wouldn't appreciate her interest. Dusk would be falling in the next hour and if she wanted to complete her full circuit, she needed to press on.

A notification drew her attention to her phone and she paused to read it. Hugo, questioning the return of the jewellery again.

'Let it go, let it go,' Kate sang under her breath as she walked on, tapping in a quick reply. There, that would hopefully keep Hugo quiet for now whilst she put her plan in operation.

Barely had she tucked her phone away, however, when something caught her eye up by the lighthouse. Was it a bundle of something?

Kate emitted a slight gasp as the mound moved, proving itself to be a small figure in a green coat. Concerned, she increased her pace towards the lighthouse.

Chapter Twelve

The One With Daddy Cool

'Theo!'

A small head popped up as Kate neared the little boy, who sat on a rucksack. He leapt to his feet, wrapping his arms around his body, his expression wary and so reminiscent of his father.

Kate stopped a few paces away, smiling kindly. 'Are you on your own?'

A nod was the only response, but Theo averted his eyes, his gaze dropping to his feet, which were thankfully shod in sturdy trainers.

'I'm out for a walk after work,' Kate continued conversationally. She took a step closer. 'I like it out here, don't you?'

She wasn't sure why Theo was alone, but based on the first time she'd met him, she wouldn't be surprised if he'd taken it into his head to go adventuring again.

Another cautious step and Kate was in front of him. 'Theo?'

He looked up, his large blue eyes sad. 'Shall we sit for a bit? Not for long, because it's going to get dark, mind.'

Another nod, and Theo flopped down on his rucksack again, which emitted a sharp squeak.

Lips twitching, Kate settled on a smoothish rock beside him, and they both stared back towards Polkerran.

'I come here quite often,' Kate mused. 'I like the sound of the waves, it's soothing.'

A sound came from Theo, but again, he said nothing. She needed to encourage him to come with her, because if she had to leave him, by the time she came back with Dev – or anyone else who could help encourage Theo home – dusk would have fallen.

'Is that a friend of yours, in your bag?' Kate inclined her head towards the rucksack. 'I think I heard him ask to be let out.'

A reluctant smile formed on the little boy's features and he wriggled to one side, tugging the rucksack upright and opening it. Kate pretended not to notice the contents as Theo rummaged inside.

'This is Bungie.' Theo heaved on a pair of ears and held aloft a somewhat squashed teddy bear.

'Ah, how do you do, Bungie?' Kate said, shaking a paw. 'Pleased to meet you. My name is Kate and Theo is a friend of my Mollie. She's my daughter. Isn't that right, Theo?'

A vigorous nod followed.

'And how old is Bungie?'

'Like me. I was four, then I was five. At Christmas. So was Bungie.'

Gosh, he was tall for his age, then, bless him. And far too young to be out here alone.

'Where is your Mollie?'

'She's staying with her grandparents for a few days, but she'll be home soon. I'm sure she'd love to see you and meet Bungie.'

Theo's face fell. 'I'm going away.'

'Are you? Where are you going?'

'I…' he faltered, sending a regretful look at the lighthouse behind them. 'I… there's no door!' he exclaimed.

'Hmm.' Kate looked serious. 'You're right. I don't think anyone lives in this lighthouse, Theo.'

'But I read a book about one. A man lived in it. He put the light on to help the ships. He was lonely.'

'Did you want to visit him?'

Theo nodded.

'No one lives in this lighthouse because it's a remotely operated one. Do you know what that means?'

A shake of a head.

'The light is a bit like a battery one, so no one has to switch it on and off. Would you like me to find out if there's one that can be visited?'

'Yes, please!' Theo's countenance filled with delight.

'I'd need to ask your dad's permission, though. Shall we do that?'

A momentary hesitation, but then the little boy got to his feet, stuffing Bungie rather unceremoniously back into the bag and zipping it up.

'Can we go now? To the lighthouse with the man, I mean.'

'Probably not *right* now, but I promise I will find out for you. Anyway,' Kate glanced at her watch, 'it's teatime. I'm starving. Aren't you?'

A thoughtful expression settled on Theo's features as he hefted the backpack onto his shoulder. 'S'pose so.'

'Come on.' Kate held out her hand, unsure if it was the right thing to do. Theo seemed so reticent and wary of strangers, but to her relief – after a momentary hesitation – he placed his small hand in hers, and they made their way carefully back along the stretch of rocks to the relative safety of the root-strewn path through the trees to rejoin the coast path.

Kate chatted about Mollie and what she planned to do when she came back to Polkerran the following week, and Theo said nothing but seemed content walking by her side. As they reached the tall, wrought-iron gates outside Harbourwatch, Dev came flying out of the door.

'Theo! Where the *hell* have you been? Half the village is on the lookout. I was about to call the police!'

Theo's grasp on Kate's hand tightened for a second, but then he rushed into his dad's outstretched arms and a lump formed in her throat at Dev's anguished expression as his eyes closed, holding his son tightly.

'He's fine. He was off on an adventure to the lighthouse.'

Dev released a visible deep breath, then straightened, this time with Theo's hand clasped in his own. 'Thank you for bringing him home. I never thought to look out that way. He could have slipped, fallen into the water. I…'

Even in the falling light, Kate could see the emotion in Dev's eyes and how pale his skin had gone. Impulsively, she stepped forward, placing a comforting hand on his arm momentarily.

'But he didn't. He was very sensible and walked carefully. Now he's home, safe.' She turned to Theo with a kind smile. 'It was lovely to see you again. I won't forget my promise.'

Dev frowned as he looked between his son and Kate, but then Theo piped up.

'Kate must stay for tea, Daddy. She's very, very hungry.'

'Oh, no. That's very sweet of you, Theo, but—'

'Join us?' Dev spoke with a warmth that surprised Kate, and she hesitated.

'I think I'd better head back. I was doing a circular walk.' She gestured at her boots.

'Please come to tea.' Theo's plea was impossible to resist, and as he raced up the steps to the front door, Kate hesitated.

'If it helps, I'm starving too,' Dev added. 'I'd better make a few calls, let people know Theo's safe, but then we'll eat. There's always too much for the two of us and I hate throwing food away.'

A smile tugged at Kate's mouth as she followed Dev up the steps. 'Waste isn't good for the environment. If it will ease your conscience, I'll be happy to help out.'

To her surprise, Dev laughed, and Kate unfastened her boots, uncertain why it made her feel as though she'd won a medal.

–

Tea was eaten at the large, square kitchen table and consisted of hearty bowls of potato and leek soup, soft bread rolls and then a plate of sandwiches – sufficient to feed several people – and a bowl of crisps.

'Salt and vinegar, my favourite.' Kate popped a crisp in her mouth and Theo grinned at her.

'They're Daddy's fav too.'

Kate was finding it hard to look at Daddy. Dev's entire demeanour towards her had altered in an instant, and if this was the hidden man, he was having a powerful effect on her.

When the meal was over, Dev accompanied Theo to a snug off the far end of the hall, where the little boy happily settled down to play a game, Bungie tucked at his side.

'I'd better go. I'm—'

'Wait. Please.' Dev opened the door to a small but charming sitting room. 'I'd appreciate it if you'd let me know what happened.'

Kate walked into the room and Dev invited her to take a seat before walking over to a polished sideboard housing a well-stocked array of drinks.

'What's your tipple?'

'Gin, if you've got it?'

'Try the local one. Tonic?'

'Yes, please.'

Dev lifted the lid on an ice bucket and dropped some into a glass before adding the spirit and mixer.

'Try that.' He held out the glass and Kate took it, trying not to notice as his fingers brushed hers.

Taking a sip, she relished the cold liquid trickling down her throat, then nodded. 'Delicious.'

Dev poured himself a vodka and tonic and came to sit on the opposite sofa.

'So tell me, how did you find Theo? I looked high and low.' He ran a hand through his layered fringe, which flopped onto his forehead endearingly.

Endearingly? Really?

Kate cleared her throat. 'I was doing my usual walk to the lighthouse and back. He was just sitting there. I think he thought you could go inside.'

'Bloody hell. He's going to drive me to an early grave. I didn't even know he'd left the house until I went to the snug to tell him tea was ready. Stella – she's the daily who helps out here and does some of the cooking – didn't see him leave, either.'

'Is he unhappy? Not with you,' Kate added hastily. 'It's just I had a feeling – from glimpsing what was in his backpack – that he was… running away?'

Dev stalled, his glass suspended. Then, he lowered it slowly. 'What things?'

Kate shrugged. 'I only had a glimpse as he pulled Bungie out to show me, but I'm sure there were pyjamas and a toothbrush in there.'

'Damnit,' Dev muttered, taking a swig from his glass, then putting it aside. He leaned forward, resting his elbows on his knees, his blue-grey eyes fixed on Kate across the low table between them. 'I'm worried sick about him. He was supposed to come here for the full fortnight, but when Leigh dropped him off yesterday, she told him she'd be picking him up again on Thursday. Theo said nothing, but I could tell he was upset. He shot upstairs and wouldn't talk about it.'

Kate chewed her lip. 'He could be sad about the shorter stay, that's all.'

Dev shook his head. 'I think it's more than that. He keeps asking me why he can't live here. Leigh—' He stopped, running a hand through his hair again. 'She's often away, sometimes for weeks on end. Theo ends up being left with a succession of nannies – no one seems to work for Leigh for long.'

'Could he…' She hesitated. It really wasn't her business, and this was the first time they'd had a relatively friendly exchange.

'Go on.'

Dev's dark gaze held hers across the table, and Kate drew in a short breath.

'Could he not come and live with you permanently?'

His eyes flashed as he sank back in his seat. 'Do you think that's not occurred to me?'

Yes, of course it has. I'm not bloody stupid!

Kate drew in a short breath. 'That's why I'm asking. It's clear it's been decided he doesn't, but *could* he? Is there some way, now you can see how this is affecting him?'

Dev's expression closed in, reverting to the one she was sadly more familiar with.

'We're still finalising... things. It's holding up the Final Order. If Leigh would only make a decision on whether... never mind.' He drained his glass and sensing the conversation, such as it was, was over, Kate did likewise and got to her feet.

Probably better to leave before she was asked to.

She would have liked to say good night to Theo, but Dev led her back to the front door, and she shrugged into her coat and stepped outside, but as she passed him, a hand landed on her arm.

'Thank you for bringing Theo home.'

'No problem.' She waved an airy hand and set off down the steps. 'Say bye to him for me.'

With that, she strode out of the gates, not looking back, but very aware the door had not yet been closed.

Chapter Thirteen

The One With the New Order

The next day, Kate and Anna had lunch at Harbourmasters on the quayside.

'This used to be a souvenir shop,' Anna explained as they entered the new bar and restaurant, which had only opened in recent months. 'It used to be the village kids' go-to with their pocket money.'

Kate admired the stylish interior as they were shown to a table beside the window, which afforded a view of the water, the rocking masts of boats and the wooded hillside on the opposite side of the bay.

'Oh, my goodness. I'm loving this bit of being in Polkerran.' She grinned at Anna across the table. 'Reminds me of our girlie lunches in the Harrogate days. I missed you, and then Lauren!'

Once they'd placed their order, Anna fixed Kate with a compelling eye. 'So? Did you challenge Dev on what you overhead him say about you?'

Reflecting on the previous evening, Kate pulled a face. 'No. He was so relieved I'd brought Theo home, it wasn't really the time.'

A smile tugged at Anna's mouth. 'Mellow from too many glasses of gin?'

'Pillock,' Kate reposted. 'Actually, he had a really nice one. He said it was from a local distillery.'

'I'm not so much a gin drinker these days. Thank you.' Anna accepted her glass of wine and the friendly waitress placed one in front of Kate before leaving them to greet more arrivals.

'Cheers.' Kate clinked glasses with her friend, then noticed someone coming towards them. 'Oh, your brother's here.'

Anna spun around in her seat, then leapt to her feet to throw her arms around Matt, who hugged her back.

'I didn't expect you until tomorrow! Why didn't you say you'd be back early?' Anna embraced the young woman with him – Gemma, whom Kate recognised from the wedding.

She shook both their hands as a young man came up to them to see if they wanted to move to a larger table.

'No, thank you, we're not staying.' Matt smiled at him before turning back to Anna. 'Saw you by chance, so popped in to say hi. We managed to get an earlier flight. The taxi dropped our stuff with Jean at the shop but it's low tide, so we thought we'd mooch around the cove until we can take the boat back to Rivermills.'

'I'm so excited to see it again.' Gemma's green eyes sparkled as she looked from Anna to Kate. 'I left in the depths of winter, when the trees were bare.'

Gemma was related to the Lovelace family and had met Matt when working for him upriver at Rivermills House.

'Have you got the keys, then?' Anna turned to Kate. 'I think I mentioned Matty buying the house and studio on the tidal creek?'

Matt had been in a successful band some years ago and was now writing music, and the secluded nature of the property had been appealing.

'I'd love to see it sometime. I've heard so much about it.'

'Once we're settled, we'll have people over,' Matt assured her, then he took Gemma's hand in his. 'We'll leave you to it. I'll call you, Anna. Bye, Kate.'

With a warm smile for them both, Gemma allowed herself to be tugged towards the door and Anna settled back into her seat just as the food arrived.

'Mmm, this is delicious.' Kate dug her fork into the dressed crab, then added, 'Matt looked well.'

Anna gave a contented sigh as she speared a piece of calamari. 'He's much happier since Gemma came into his life, and although I've not seen them for nearly three months in person, we've chatted on video and his whole demeanour and outlook have turned full circle. They've been away to gather inspiration for new songs. Gemma's been learning to write lyrics to Matt's music. I'm so happy he's decided to make his home at Rivermills.'

They tucked into their food, talking about the challenges facing Oliver and about life at The Lookout.

As their plates were cleared and dessert arrived, the conversation turned to the summer fayre.

'At least the date is fixed now.' Kate huffed on a laugh, pouring espresso over her ice cream. 'I'm currently trying to find venues, but the indoor options are all booked up, and the quayside only has limited space.'

'They used to hold it at the village hall.'

Kate outlined the difficulties she'd already identified. 'I'm not giving up, though.'

'Well, I've found you some help, at any rate.'

'Excellent.' She scooped up the remains of the affogato. 'We'll just have to pray for dry weather. That's one thing I can't put in the planner.'

—

A few days later, Kate's gaze roamed over the motley crew assembled around the table at Westerleigh Cottage. She turned back to the kitchen island as Anna poured hot water into a teapot.

'Is this it?' She spoke quietly. 'The usual locals are the only offers of help?'

Anna sent the new arrivals a fond look. 'You won't fault their enthusiasm. It just requires... a little direction.'

Trailing after Anna, carrying a plate of freshly baked cakes and another of shortbread, Kate hoped that *was* all it needed.

She took the seat at the head of the table, conscious everyone was too focused on getting themselves something to eat and drink to pay her much attention. Allowing them the time, Kate skimmed the list she'd made earlier, grateful to Anna when she drew everyone's attention to why they were there.

As silence fell, aside from the occasional clink of a spoon against a mug or the munching of biscuits, Kate ran through the situation so far, namely the change of dates and the proposal to revert to a more traditional village fayre – for which she gave Jean full credit – the likes of which Polkerran had originally enjoyed some years ago.

This received a warm reception and Kate looked around the table at the faces showing varying levels of interest: Mrs Lovelace, Old Patrick and Mrs Clegg to her left, facing the window, and Jean, Nicki and Phoenix to her right.

Kate smiled in everyone's general direction. 'Who would like to do what?' She started to run through her list, and Mrs Lovelace soon piped up.

'Worked in an office, I did, backalong.' She waved a hand in the air. 'I'll not be minding a bit of paperwork. None of your ticksy computer stuff, mind. Retired, I did, once they machines took over from typewriters. People waving their floppy dicks at me.'

Nicki grinned. 'Blimey, Mrs L! Where the hellocks did you work?'

'Disks, mum,' Jean prompted kindly.

Mrs Lovelace rolled her eyes. 'Tha's what I says.'

'That would be lovely, Mrs Lovelace. Thank you.' Kate sent her a warm smile, and the elderly lady nodded, reaching for a slice of Victoria sponge.

'I can create a logo,' Phoenix suggested.

'Fantastic.' Kate scribbled on her pad as one by one, they made suggestions for the fayre, from a children's art trail – which Phoenix happily claimed, too – a story-telling tent, craft workshops, a possible guided history walk round the cove, if

Oliver could be persuaded to lead it, and stalls galore, including one for bric-a-brac (much to Patrick's disgust).

Then there was the performance aspect: poetry readings, folk music, the local Morris dancers doing a display, and so on.

There was a general murmur of approval as Kate thanked everyone for their suggestions and she scribbled into her notepad. Her to-do list was getting so long, they'd be lucky if Summy-Fessy didn't become Chrissy-Fessy instead.

Phoenix offered to rope in everyone from the studio in Mevagissey where she had a space and, slowly, people began to expand on their possible contributions.

Old Patrick did wood-turning, Mrs Clegg – though fairly house-bound now – was into crocheting, although for some reason most people looked sceptical about her offerings. Mrs Lovelace liked to knit, Jean had a successful online business making silver jewellery featuring sea glass from Cornish beaches, and so it continued. Phoenix produced local watercolours, her mum made homemade soaps and lotions and there were regional small businesses who set up pop-up stands of local food and drink at most events.

'Excellent.' More encouraged, Kate put her pen aside. 'So, the stalls themselves. You know, tables, chairs and so on. Where did you get them from?'

More silence, then Nicki piped up. 'I think they borrowed some from the hotel, but early June was pre the main Emmet season. I don't think they'll have them spare in August.'

Kate bit back on a sigh. 'Gazebos?'

'Bless you, my lovely,' Mrs Lovelace called, before taking another bite of sponge cake.

'I meant, what about if it rains?'

There was a general smattering of laughter. 'Bleddy hell.' Old Patrick glanced around at the faces. 'How long's this maid been in the cove?' He sent Kate a knowing look. ' 'Tis Cornwall, my lover. A good old Cornish mizzle is likely the only guarantee on a Bank Holiday.'

'The bistro has some, I think.'

'The finances look a bit tight, despite the valiant efforts at fund-raising at the Christmas fayre. We've got Dev's sponsorship, of course, but the more volunteers we can find, the better.'

'I'll be talkin' to me mates,' Old Patrick offered. 'Make a change, it will, from shove 'apenny and mending nets.'

It was a start, and although time was tight, and Kate knew she could probably handle it all on her own if she had to, it felt so much nicer to have a team of sorts around her.

The clock on the mantelpiece chimed the hour and, before she could ask anything else, there was a concerted movement to collect coats and bags and everyone headed for the door. From the snippets of conversation as they passed by Kate, it sounded like they had a lot to talk about and none of it fayre-related.

A few of them said goodbye, with Jean and Nicki sending her sympathetic looks as they filed into the boot room.

As Kate closed the door on their departing backs, Mrs Lovelace could be heard asking Old Patrick about a problem with her 'anti-septic tank', and Kate sank back against the wall, convinced she'd somehow stepped through a portal into a strange new land.

—

A few days later, Kate headed into the village after work. As she walked down the hill, she spotted a large Tremayne Estates for sale sign fastened to the row of charming alms-houses and another on a nearby gatehouse at the entrance to the manor house. It reminded her she needed to place a courtesy call to Mrs Tremayne.

Kate turned her steps towards the Spar, intent on picking up some milk, but paused by the ice cream shop.

'Hey, how's it going?'

Jean was unfurling a candy-striped canopy above the window, and she put her hands on her hips to survey it.

'Not bad. This needs a bit of work.' She gestured at the tell-tale signs where the winter damp had made its mark on the canvas. 'How're things with you?' She turned to Kate with a somewhat devilish grin. 'Managing to keep the helpers on track?'

Kate shook her head. 'Not a chance, and your mother's the ringleader, you do know?'

Picking up a cloth, Jean began to wipe down the outside sills. 'Yes, of course I do. If she gives you too much trouble, tell her she's fired.'

'I can't do that! I've already been hauled over the coals by Dev for trying to manage the unmanageable.'

A bit of an exaggeration…

Jean, however, nodded in sympathy. 'How's it going getting volunteers for the day?'

'About standard for Polkerran.' Kate grinned. 'Billy Two Feet has offered to man the overspill car park, but I've been warned he'll park the cars too close together, as "two-feet" seems to be the only measurement he lives by. Meanwhile, Charlie the Crab – who can't tell his right from his left – has put his name down to direct traffic, and Morwenna, who runs one of the teashops, took on running the dog show, but then confessed to being mega-allergic.'

Jean laughed. 'Sorry, I know it's not funny, but it's just—'

'The cove. So Anna keeps telling me.'

Kate's gaze drifted over towards the harbour. 'I can't fault everyone's eagerness but drawing it into a cohesive plan is like lining up a row of new-born chicks.'

'What about the food and drink stalls?'

'Anna's playing a blinder, as she always did. She was my wing-woman on so many events in Yorkshire. She's got a distillery coming along with their gin and vodka products, there's the people who make own-brand crisps from local potatoes, a honey stall, local jams and pickles and a large stand for the village bakeries.'

'I'll have my ice cream van by then.' Jean's striking eyes sparkled as her cheeks pinkened. 'I've always wanted one and my— a friend has sourced one for me. I've no idea what it looks like, but it should be here soon.'

'Brilliant. Can I book it for the festival? It would be perfect.'

'Of course. I always have extra staff during the main summer holidays, so I could man the van and leave them in charge of the shop.'

–

Kate had invited Nicki and her husband, Hamish, for dinner – a thank you for their help with Mollie – and as she busied herself preparing the meal, she did a quick video chat with her daughter, who was back with her grandparents after a few days in Bath.

As Kate hurriedly tidied herself later, her thoughts turned to Dev, whom she hadn't heard from or seen for a while. Unable to resist, she opened her laptop as she sat at the dressing table and, feeling like she was doing something she shouldn't, selected the web page for the livestream at the beach.

She pretended nonchalance as she applied fresh lip gloss and re-fastened her ponytail, glancing now and again at the screen. Dogs were only allowed on the beach at certain times of day now the season was upon them, but tonight she was disappointed, as there was no sign of Bayley.

'Idiot,' she muttered as she headed back downstairs, the heady spices of curry assailing her nostrils as she reached the kitchen. 'Own up to it. Bayley is not the reason, and you need to stop binge-watching that damn livestream as though it's the latest Netflix draw.'

Chapter Fourteen

The One Where Jean's an Ice, Ice Baby

Kate had missed Jean when she stopped working up at the hotel, but at least Nicki was around, doing her shifts in the beauty salon around school hours, so they managed the occasional catch-up lunch, and she stayed in contact with Phoenix, who – although remaining at the studio in Mevagissey – was keen to move back to the cove as soon as a suitable rental came up.

The three ladies were the only ones who were offering any practical help in the organisation of the festival, aside from Anna's attempts to line up takers for the food and drink stalls. Not that their contributions were balanced. Phoenix was full of enthusiasm, but it was fairly obvious she had her own agenda, which was to make sales and secure new commissions.

It was impossible to mind too much, though, and Kate understood that – with such a precarious source of income – events like this had to be maximised. Phoenix was grateful too, saying Leigh used to bat her away as though she were a persistent fly.

Nicki offered to do face-painting and hair-braiding for the children, and Dev had found the name of the company who'd produced the flyers and programme the previous year, leaving Kate to negotiate with them.

Getting the hotel to add the fayre dates and details – such as they were at present – to their upcoming local activities was easy, and Anna added a widget to her website for the bed and breakfast. Kate also had it posted as an event in the village Facebook page.

When Thursday rolled around, Kate took a day off as she'd be working the entire holiday weekend, and she decided to make the most of it.

She slid one of the vast doors aside and stepped out onto the terrace. The sun peered hopefully from behind a billowing cloud, its rays holding a hint of long overdue warmth as they caressed Kate's arms through the fabric of her dressing gown. A light breeze lifted the hair from her forehead, as though checking for lines, and Kate grimaced.

Nicki's colleague at the salon had thrust a leaflet into Kate's hand the previous day, offering laser treatment and fillers, saying they did a discount for staff, but Nicki had snatched it from her, balled it up and tossed it in the bin, declaring Kate had no need for it.

Something in the grass caught Kate's eye.

'Podge.' The cat's head popped up from chasing an imaginary fly. 'Here, baby.'

Emerging from the wildflowers beginning to bloom where the garden had been encouraged to take control, Podge trotted over to be fussed under the chin, then shot into the house and, with one last look at the view, Kate followed.

Half an hour later, she stepped out of the house in her walk boots and set off down the lane. Tempted to call on Anna, but knowing that would mean sitting with the locals rather than exercising, she turned towards the bridge and the main part of Polkerran.

Before she knew it, Kate was heading down the slope past Harbourwatch, trying with all her might not to think about Dev and what he was up to. She hoped he wasn't too low. Wasn't Theo due to leave today?

When she reached the charming tidal beach, Kate stopped to pick up a take-away coffee from the little cafe, stepping around a couple waving at someone via the webcam but as she resumed her walk, she was hailed from behind.

'Kate, it's me!'

Turning around, her heart warmed. 'Hello, Theo. How are you?'

'I'm staying!'

She was about to blurt out, 'For ever?' but thankfully Ryther appeared beside his great-grandson on the beach.

'For the holidays, at least,' he offered. 'Good morning, Kate. How are you?'

Kate felt she ought to be asking Ryther. Even had she not heard of his being unwell, she'd have noted the paler-than-usual complexion and her assumption from their previous encounter was right. He had lost weight.

'I am perfectly well, my dear,' the gentleman said quietly as he took a step closer.

Relieved, Kate smiled. 'I'm pleased to hear it. Now,' she turned to Theo and crouched down, 'let me see, what flavour do I think this is.'

Indicating the cone he held, she eyed the contents. 'Definitely some sort of chocolate... hmm... and are those bits of mini-egg I see?'

Theo nodded enthusiastically. 'It's yum. D'you want some?' He thrust the cone forward, almost touching Kate's nose and she laughed, raising her coffee cup.

'Thank you, but I'm thirsty rather than hungry.'

'Where are you going?' Theo asked as Kate straightened.

'Doing my usual walk.' She waved a hand. 'Out to the lighthouse and back. That reminds me, I looked into them for you. None of them are manned any more, I'm afraid, but there are ones you can visit. If your dad gives permission, would you like to come with me to see one?'

The delight in Theo's eyes was enough of an answer, but he unceremoniously shoved his half-finished ice cream at Ryther, who caught it deftly as the little boy threw himself at Kate, hugging her tightly around the top of her legs.

Laughing, she disentangled him just in time to see Dev come striding down the lane.

A strange sensation skittered over her skin and she took a stumbling step backwards, only to find herself backed up against the cliff that bordered the beach. Conscious of Ryther's keen eyes upon her, Kate fixed hers on Dev as he joined them.

'Kate.'

Correct.

'Hi. I've been admiring Theo's rather splendid ice cream.'

Dev ruffled his son's hair.

'Daaad.' Theo ducked away. 'That lady in the shop said this,' he waved what was left of his treat, 'is the bestest.'

'Let's hope she's got plenty of stock then, Teds.'

'Well, I'll leave you to it.' Conscious of her reluctance to do precisely that, Kate said a hurried goodbye and resumed her walk.

As she reached the top of the stone steps onto the path leading out to the lighthouse, however, she glanced back. Only the far side of the beach was visible from her raised vantage point. There were several families there, and Ryther, Dev and Theo were now over by the rock pools. The latter appeared to have finished his ice cream and wielded a small net, his dad holding a colourful bucket. Ryther's attention wasn't with them, however; it was on something in the distance, and Kate followed his gaze.

Unless she was mistaken, he was looking across the rippling water to where Westerleigh Cottage perched, nestled in its clifftop gardens.

—

Returning from the rocks sometime later, Kate could see no sign of the Devonshires, and she strode up the hill past the house as fast as she could. Once back in town, she glanced at her watch. Time for some lunch.

Toying with crossing the bridge to the Lugger, she looked around at the other options. The Three Fishes was more a drinking establishment. Both the bistro and the new restaurant looked busy, the latter having all its outdoor seating filled, which was great for business but not so much for someone as suddenly hungry as Kate was.

'Kate! Over here!'

Spinning around, Kate waved at Jean, who stood outside the ice cream shop, next to an ice cream van with a giant cone on the top.

Laughing, Kate skipped across the street between two passing cars, fetching up beside a beaming Jean.

'This is Greg.'

Kate sent her a puzzled look. It seemed an odd name for an ice cream van, but then she realised a man stood on the steps.

They exchanged greetings as Jean excitedly explained how Greg was an old friend and he'd made a rogue promise to her that, one day, he'd buy her a mobile ice cream shop. She hadn't really thought it would happen, but lo and behold, here it was!

Friend? Kate hid her amusement as she noted the looks being exchanged between Jean and Greg.

'Come and have a tour.'

Jean showed Kate the rather small interior and where the ice cream went and how to operate the machine which would produce the traditional swirls. Then they came back outside to admire the exterior, which had drawn quite a few onlookers made up of locals and holidaymakers alike.

Greg popped inside the van, appearing at the window, which he lowered. It was an old-fashioned vehicle in design, with a bulbous front and painted a warm russet, the same shade as the cone on the roof. When Greg pulled a lever, a candy-pink-and-white-striped canopy – similar to the one attached to the shop – unfurled itself, rippling in the breeze coming off the harbour, and Jean clapped her hands like a delighted child.

Grinning, Kate met Greg's amused look, which became decidedly affectionate when it moved to Jean.

'I think you're going to have quite the summer,' Kate whispered. 'I'll catch you both later.' Lifting a hand to Greg, who was helping Jean up the steps into the van, she eased her way through the throng of people, her stomach protesting at its continued neglect.

Perhaps the chippy was her only option today. It wasn't exactly a hardship, and Kate joined the fast-moving queue, soon emerging with a paper package emitting the delicious aroma of proper chips, liberally doused in salt and vinegar.

Looking around, she couldn't see a spare bench and was about to walk over to the harbour wall to lean on it when someone moving swiftly along the front caught her eye.

Kate turned back to the water, a frisson of something indiscernible fizzing somewhere within her core. Dev strode with some purpose, alone, and silently scolding her skin for warming so precipitously again, she approached the harbour wall with relief. Why, though? It wasn't as if he was looking for—

'Kate.'

With a start, she dropped her precious package, which thankfully didn't split open, but as she bent to retrieve it, Dev beat her to it, handing the chips over, his gaze raking her face.

'Sorry.'

'It's fine.' Kate willed the building warmth not to travel into her cheeks. The warmth was disobliging.

Dev, however, looked as uncomfortable as Kate felt. 'Could I have a quick word?'

Chapter Fifteen

The One Where Sweet Dreams are Made of This

It probably wasn't the best time to ask Dev if there was something wrong with his phone.

Kate nodded. 'Of course.' Then added, 'Where's Theo?'

'Busy rock pooling with Grandy.'

'Do you mind if I tuck in while it's hot?' Kate indicated the packet. If she didn't eat soon, her stomach would provide further embarrassment.

'Not at all but watch the seagulls. They are pretty evil.'

'So I've heard. Want one?' Kate offered the open packet to him, and Dev selected a chip. They both munched in silent contemplation of the harbour for a moment. A rather chubby gull had landed on the wall and gave them both the side-eye.

'Come on, you can't eat here. It'll end in carnage.' Dev led Kate across the street and down the side of the Three Fishes into a small beer garden she didn't know existed.

It had several wooden benches typical of pubs, mostly occupied, but Dev found a spare one at the back.

'This is safer,' he pronounced.

'Are we allowed to eat here? I didn't think they did food.'

'They don't.' He indicated a notice on the wall.

Safe haven for take-aways

House rule – buy a drink!

Kate laughed. 'Fair enough. What can I get you?'

'I'll go.'

Left alone, Kate studied a second notice, proclaiming 'Free WiFi'. Someone had crossed out 'free' and added 'crap'. Amused, her gaze drifted over the clever wire mesh creating a protective 'roof' over the garden, attached to sturdy wooden stakes. Open-air dining without the hazards. Perfect.

When Dev returned with a couple of bottles of beers and a glass for Kate's, she pointed to the open packet on the table.

'My eyes are bigger than my stomach. Feel free to finish them if you wish.'

She didn't like to push Dev on what he wanted to talk about, but assumed it was fayre related, and because she was enjoying the company – something she'd analyse later – she was in no hurry.

Dev did as he was bid, and Kate tried not to recall the grasp of his firm hands around her waist when he'd caught her from falling, but as she was fixated on them as he screwed up the wrapper and rolled it into a ball before disposing of it in a covered bin, it was a challenge.

'Look,' Dev began, shifting in his seat. 'I wanted to speak about Theo.'

Kate's heart softened at the anxiety filling his features. 'He seems so happy he can stay longer.'

'Yes. Thankfully, something came up in London more important to Leigh than her son… sorry.' He drew in a short breath. 'I shouldn't have said that.'

Unsure how to respond, Kate was saved the trouble as he continued.

'Theo's coming to stay again in May – he gets a fortnight for half term, but Leigh's off on another business trip – and he's so full of the lighthouse tour you… I mean…' He broke off, running a hand through his hair.

'My recent promise, you mean? When is he here? I had an email from tourist info the other day about an open day at the one near Trebutwith.'

She pulled out her phone to check the date. It was a match with the little boy's visit.

'Are you okay with me taking him?'

Dev stilled, and she was surprised by the vulnerability shrouding his frame.

'Is it okay if I come too? It's just… I don't get to see him as often as I'd like.'

Kate felt dreadful, and instinctively placed a reassuring hand on Dev's arm. 'I'm sorry! Presumptuous of me. I assumed it wasn't your thing. Or you hated heights.' She couldn't help but smile at Dev's reaction as he vehemently shook his head.

The movement reminded her she was holding onto his arm, however, and she whipped her hand away.

'Not at all.'

'Good. Then it's a date.' The words were out before Kate could stop them, and the tell-tale colour filled her cheeks. 'No. Well, it's *a* date. The open day date, I mean.'

Unsurprisingly, Dev had no response to this, and as soon as they'd finished their drinks, they parted ways, but Kate's thoughtful gaze remained on his broad shoulders as he walked back along the front.

What was it about that man that turned her into an imbecilic, waffling mess?

–

The second half of the Easter holidays sped by once Mollie returned. Having her parents to stay made things easier on Kate, as she was extremely busy at the hotel, and it meant Mollie had lots of days out. Evenings were fun, sitting around the kitchen island – or, on the couple of days when warm weather blessed the cove, sitting out under blankets on the terrace with the fire pit burning – and regaling each other with the day's antics.

With Oliver embroiled in some sort of dilemma over acquiring more local properties – and once again neglecting his writing – Anna had channelled her efforts into securing takers for the last two spaces for food and drink suppliers, and at last, Kate felt the fayre had a chance of success – if they could only find a venue large enough to replace the village hall.

They were soon back into the routine of work and school, and when Kate arrived at Westerleigh to collect Mollie one afternoon, she found her sitting beside Mrs Lovelace, nursing a mug of tea, Anna and Gemma standing at the head of the table, a laden chopping board in front of them.

'Come and join us,' Anna welcomed her, and Kate dropped her bag and coat on a chair and came to stand beside them.

'What are you making?'

'I'm showing Gemma how to put together a cucumber salad to go with grilled fish.'

Kate eyed the ingredients with interest. 'Looks delicious. Do you enjoy preparing meals?'

Gemma laughed. 'It's not my forte, but Anna's determined to bring me up to scratch.'

'She's better than she thinks she is,' Anna added, popping chunks of peeled cucumber and red onion into a chopper.

'What herb is that?' Kate pointed to the delicate leaves on the chopping board. 'I don't recognise it.'

'I asked that!' Mollie sent her mum a smug look. 'Chervil.'

'Oh, I loved they, back in the day,' chimed in Mrs Lovelace, beaming at Kate.

Anna exchanged a puzzled look with Kate.

'Who are you talking about, Auntie Dee?' Gemma looked up from squeezing a fresh lemon into a small jug.

'They dancing ice people,' Mrs Lovelace stated, which left none of them any the wiser. 'You know, won a medal for that bolero dance.' She pronounced it as though it was a shrug rather than a piece of music. 'That was the name, Chervil and something.'

'Ah.' Gemma smiled fondly at her great aunt. 'You mean *Torvil*, Auntie Dee.'

Mrs Lovelace appeared confused. 'What's a torvil?'

'Nothing for you to worry about, Mrs Lovelace. Can I top up your tea?'

The elderly lady handed her cup to Anna with a warm smile, then picked up a shortbread from the plate in the centre of the table. 'Can I take some of this for Cleggie? She misses your baking.'

'How's she getting along, Mrs Lovelace?' Kate asked.

'Fair to middlin', as they says.' She dipped her shortbread into her tea, then frowned as a piece broke off and sank. 'Says she's getting one of they nobility scooters.'

Mollie giggled, but Kate silenced her with a shake of the head.

'I'll put together a selection for you to take, Mrs L,' Anna said, as Gemma tipped the cucumber and onion into a bowl. 'Good. Now sprinkle the chervil on, drizzle the lemon juice and oil and add a dash of salt and pepper, give it a mix, and you're done!'

As Anna went to make more tea, Kate slid into the seat beside Mollie.

'How was today?'

Mollie shrugged. 'Okay. Old Hoppy, the media teacher, threw a hissy fit when no one had finished their projects on the power of movie posters 'cos we got distracted watching YouTube videos. Our house won again at netball and lunch was some sort of breaded thing. Blegh.' She stuck her tongue out. 'So I'm staaarving.'

Conscious she'd be having a word with her daughter later about incomplete homework, Kate spared a passing thought for Old Hoppy – Miss Hopkins was only in her thirties.

Then, she eyed the crumb-scattered plate in front of her daughter. 'Starving even after all those biscuits?'

Mrs Lovelace chuckled, patting Mollie on the arm. 'Young maid's been tucking in.' She leaned forward and selected a brownie from the plate and took a bite, encouraging Mollie to do the same, and Kate shook her head at her daughter's impish smile as she did so, returning to the kitchen island.

'How come Mrs Lovelace is here? I thought she called in the mornings with the other crew?'

'Jean wanted to go up country for a few days now the Easter madness has calmed down, but she worries about not being around for her mum, so Gemma offered to stay in the cove and keep an eye on her.'

Kate's eyes sparkled, wondering if Greg was the northern attraction, but said nothing. Jean seemed to want to keep things low key, after all.

—

May arrived and began to fly by, with Mollie enjoying the kayaking so much, she immediately asked if she could try the gig rowing taster session for juniors.

Walking to work most days was an absolute delight, as the village began to wake up for the season. More hanging baskets appeared on the lampposts that had sported strings of lights at New Year, and there was a vast bucket of flip flops outside the chandlery in place of the usual rack of wellies. Not that it didn't rain, of course. This was Cornwall, after all. But the days were noticeably warmer, the nights lighter, and the hillsides had also awoken, with the trees coming into full leaf as the month progressed.

As the May half term approached, however, Kate could feel her anticipation rising over the lighthouse visit with Theo… and his father. She'd not seen much of Dev lately, though they'd discussed the quotes for the flyers over the phone and agreed there was no need for a formal programme, but there was another meeting due with the so-called team, and this time it was to be at Harbourwatch instead of Westerleigh.

Kate woke on the Friday morning of the meeting to a myriad of sensations, mostly brought on by a rather unsettling dream, the wisps of which hung tantalisingly at the edges of her mind as she opened her eyes.

She blinked rapidly, conscious how warm her skin was, and kicked off the duvet. Taking a slug of water, she fell back against the pillows, fanning herself with her hand, then dissolving into giggles.

'You're an idiot,' Kate admonished. 'Why on earth you're acting like a swooning maiden in a Regency romance, I don't know.'

As she showered and dressed, however, she wavered between relief the dream had splintered into nothing, like so many do, and regret she couldn't recall more detail. From her tattered recollection, it had certainly been... *interesting*...

Skirting the harbour, Kate took in the pleasure craft bobbing up and down in the water of the bay as a furious amount of polishing, painting and general maintenance began. Sail lines rattled against the masts, the sea birds swooped and dived, their piercing calls echoing around the bay, and Kate relished the warm breeze encircling her bare legs. Hearing a tinkling bell, she looked over as Gemma emerged from Pen & Ink clutching a package.

'Hi, Kate! No work today?'

'Lieu day. We've got another meeting about the fayre. At Harbourwatch this time.' Kate gestured along the lane that ran parallel with the bay. 'I'm trying to tighten up the many loose ends, but the support team are a tad mercurial.'

'I hope Auntie Dee is behaving herself.'

'Bless her. She played a blinder typing up the draft flyer... well, aside from a few typos and listing Phee's offering as a "fart trail". I'm not convinced that was an accident.'

Gemma chuckled as they continued along the harbourfront.

'Talking of which, we sent out a batch, which Old Patrick and his friends were tasked with putting through letterboxes, but beyond that, I don't feel we'll be much further on than last time. Still, at least it's getting the date out there.'

'I haven't heard anyone talking about it.' She grinned at Kate. 'And they do like to talk, as you've probably noticed.'

Kate eyed her uncertainly. 'That's odd. I'll have to ask around. I didn't get one at The Lookout, but then it's way off the beaten track and they know I don't need one.'

'Ask Aunty Dee and Aunty Jay when you get there. They're in the thick of it down here in the cove. Maybe someone just got too lazy to go up any hills.'

Kate took her leave, walking briskly along the lane, her gaze on the water. As she neared Harbourwatch, however, her pace slowed. Was she anticipating Dev's company a tad too much? Was this why he'd popped up in her dream and in such a way?

'Idiot,' she cautioned in an undertone as she passed a group walking their dogs. 'It was simply a stupid dream. They happen. Park it.'

To take her mind off it, she did a mental run through of what she hoped to achieve from the meeting. Festival season was kicking off in several local towns, including the massively popular one in Fowey. It would be the perfect opportunity to promote the planned fayre later in the summer.

Ten minutes later, Kate walked through the tall, wrought-iron gates to Harbourwatch, her resolve to achieve *something* today hot on her (relatively low-key) heels. Her gaze drifted beyond the tall trees bordering the driveway to the sandy tidal cove below. Two people were holding coffee mugs from the small cafe and watching some of the swimming ladies.

Determining to go for a walk in the afternoon, she scaled the steps to the front door, but before she could knock, it swung open.

'Thank God you're here.'

Chapter Sixteen

The One Where Kate Realises Dev Does Something to Her

Kate tried not to laugh. If Dev's expression was anything to go by – emphasised by the disarray of his hair – the 'team' had already started doing their thing.

'Sorry. Am I late?'

'No.' He stood aside so she could enter. 'They were all early and are now on their second cups of tea. Stella says she can't keep up with the demand for biscuits.'

'I've brought seconds,' Kate reassured him as she made to remove her boots.

'It's fine. Leave them on. No danger of slipping on these stone floors,' he added.

Kate smiled faintly as they walked down the hall. 'The designer heels weren't a fit for today, either,' she quipped, and Dev flashed her a keen glance.

Before he could say anything, however, a sound of hammering came from behind the door on the right.

'Are you having work done in that gorgeous room?'

'Sadly.' Dev led her further along the hallway. 'Despite spending the earth on the renovations a few years ago, Grandy's desire that the period features remain intact hasn't solved a long-standing damp issue on the seaward-facing wall.'

He opened the door to a central room housing a vast old wooden table in the centre and a sitting area near the hearth. It was a stunning space, filled with light from an ornate glass hexagonal roof.

The sing-song of conversation was punctuated by cups clinking in saucers and plates being passed around. A Mad Hatter's tea party of sorts – with less hats and perhaps slightly more madness.

'Good morning,' Kate called over the buzz, placing her bag where Dev indicated at the end of the table. He moved over to the sideboard, and she eyed him covertly as she extracted her laptop and notepad, smiling when he placed a cup of coffee beside her, a biscuit balanced on the saucer.

'Thank you,' she mouthed as he inclined his head and walked off to resume his place at the opposite end of the table.

Kate had known Nicki couldn't make it today, due to her shift at the hotel salon, and she sent Jean a grateful smile as she cautioned her mum to silence. Once everyone had quietened down, there was an update on progress. It didn't take long, because there wasn't much.

She ran through the list of suggested activities, but was pretty sure Dev was the only person listening and made the only helpful suggestion, that perhaps they might be able to use the small village school and its playground as a venue. Determining to follow it up, Kate knew it was time to draw things to a close. She cleared her throat, and when that made no difference, tapped her cup with a teaspoon.

'And I says, didn't I Cleggie, I told her—'

Old Patrick rolled his eyes. 'Shut up, you old nag. Young maid wants a word.'

'Patrick,' Dev cautioned.

'I just wanted to ask you, Pat, about the flyer drop? Did you manage to get rid of them all?'

'By heck, we did!' Patrick nodded vigorously.

'Okaaaay.' Kate looked around the table. 'So you all got one, did you? Through your letterbox?'

There were a few furtive glances exchanged, but then Phoenix reached down and withdrew a handful of battered glossy pages and placed them on the table.

'I think when Pat says he and his mates got rid, he means they no longer have them. I found this batch stuffed into a bin in the Lugger.'

All eyes fastened on Patrick who glared around the table. 'Do'n you go looking at me, you cheeky beggars. We was asked to get rid of 'em all, an' we did. Good and proper, like.'

Kate's gaze shot down the table to Dev, her lips parted, but words failed her as he held her gaze, then gave a faint shake of his head, negating his financial contribution. She drew in a short breath, her mind spinning through the reprint costs and the waste of time they currently incurred.

Masking her shock as best she could, she directed a smile at the uncomfortable faces around the table.

'Never mind. I'll print a few batches on the home printer. They won't be as smart, but it will have the same information on.'

'I'll do it,' Jean offered, and Kate's heart warmed even further towards her. 'If you can guillotine them.'

Patrick sent a startled look in Jean's direction, and Kate hid her smile. She was a bit miffed, but the crime, such as it was, didn't warrant a personal punishment.

'Thank you.'

There wasn't really a lot more to be done or said, and they all filed out, Old Patrick wheeling Mrs Clegg in her chair, but as they passed Kate in the doorway, the elderly lady reached out a hand and clasped Kate's.

'Do'n mind Pat, my lovely. If he can see an easy way out of doin' anythin', he will. 'Tisn't personal.'

Kate leaned down and placed a kiss on Mrs Clegg's leathery cheek. 'Bless you. Thank you for coming again.'

Closing the door on the last of the team, Kate leaned against it, deflated.

'More coffee? Or something stronger?'

She looked over as Dev indicated the drinks trolley next to the sideboard housing the coffee.

'Tempting, but I'd better stick to caffeine, thanks.'

'So where do we stand? From what I can see, all you did was run through everything that needs to be done, and then give yourself the tasks.'

Kate followed Dev to the comfier seating area at the far end of the room, sinking onto a nicely worn-in leather sofa opposite an ornate hearth. She looked around with pleasure at the décor, a stylish mix of contemporary style against the period features.

'This is a beautiful room, even without the views of the water.'

'Or the damp,' Dev added, taking the armchair nearer the hearth.

'Is it serious?'

Dev pulled a face, which did nothing to detract from his attractiveness, and Kate dipped her head to stare into her cup.

This needs to stop, she silently chided.

'There seems to be a problem near the window, but they're not sure that's the root cause.'

Kate took a sip of coffee, relishing its bite and determining to fix her attention more firmly on the conversation rather than how snugly Dev's sweater fitted.

'I remember those gorgeous windows from the wedding.'

Releasing a small huff, Dev placed his mug on the coffee table. 'The maintenance bill isn't such a pretty sight.'

Kate's brow furrowed. Was it inappropriate to ask if—

'Not that it's about the money,' Dev added before she could speak. 'But they are all hand-made to specific measurements, as you can imagine with the arches. Anyway, they think the storms before Christmas which blew in off the sea have caused some water ingress by one of the chimneys. Someone's going up tomorrow to assess it. If so, it's an easier fix, more a decorating repair job, but it's caused a section of the shell frieze to protrude, so that will need replacing.'

Kate placed her mug on the table too. 'And that's a costly job too, I assume.'

'Grandy's incredibly protective of the frieze. He had it put in back when he used to stay here a lot, said he had it done for a friend. He's never struck me as sentimental, nor shown any interest in shells, so it must have been a very special one.'

With a laugh, Kate studied the man opposite. When had she decided he was nice? When had she realised she actually enjoyed chatting with him?

'Look.' Dev leaned forward suddenly in his seat, and Kate's heart did a small skip as he held her gaze with an intense look. 'I'm sorry. I had a feeling you'd overheard me. At the hotel, before you slipped…' His shoulders sank as he brushed his fringe aside. 'I kept wanting to say sorry, but —'

'It's okay,' Kate reassured him, realising it was. 'I didn't mean to eavesdrop but I was a bit stuck.'

'It's no excuse, but it's Leigh. She…' He huffed out a breath, falling back against the chair. 'She imagines things, and sometimes I just don't know how to shut her down.'

Kate wasn't sure what she could, or ought to, say but then a knock on the door came and a young man in work gear entered the room.

'All right, gaffer? Can you come dreckly? Jago's ready to show you the damage.'

Dev was already on his feet. 'Sorry, Kate. I'd best go. Feel free to finish your coffee. We'll catch up later on the fayre?'

'I'm done.' Kate waved a hand at her almost empty mug and followed the men from the room. 'I'll message you, see if we can set up a call in a day or so.'

With that, she left Dev to it and made her way back along the lane into town, her mind veering from the long list of things she ought to be concentrating on and the strange, unfamiliar, frisson of pleasure derived from being on the receiving end of one of Dev's genuine, warm smiles and finally understanding how much he'd wanted to say sorry.

-

A week later, as she worked through a proposal for a business in Truro for a two-day residential seminar in September, Kate took a call from Arabella Tremayne.

'I have been increasingly surprised not to have heard from you after my generous offer of assistance.'

Kate eyed the phone warily, then returned it to her ear. 'I'm so sorry, Mrs Tremayne. I did leave you a message the other week. To be honest, there isn't really a lot to report other than the date and the nature of the event changing from a full-blown festival to a more traditional village fayre.'

A bristling silence was the response, before…

'I see.' There was a further pause. 'And when do you propose having a programme ready? I have fulfilled my promise, you see. There were several of my prominent connections willing to advertise, though I'm not so sure they will be interested now the festival is to be such a low-key, community event.'

'That's lovely of you, Mrs Tremayne, but honestly, we have no need of a formal programme now, so do please thank your… connections but we do hope they will still come along to support us at the time. At least,' Kate hesitated, then went on to explain the lack of a suitably sized venue.

Kate fully expected the call to be over, along with the withdrawal of any further offer of help, but to her surprise, after another pause, Arabella Tremayne spoke.

'I would like to attend the next meeting. Will Oliver Seymour be there? If so, let me know the date.'

The call ended and Kate lowered her phone to the desk, wondering what the self-styled lady of the manor would make of the fayre 'team'. As for involving Oliver…

Kate shook her head. Madness. With zero expectation of help from such an unlikely source, she was soon engrossed in her work again.

Chapter Seventeen

The One With the Lighthouse Family

A few days later, Kate approached Harbourwatch again, this time with a mixture of excitement and dread, two extremes she could hardly account for. This was Dev, wasn't it? Just Dev, who'd sort of become... a friend, hadn't he?

If you say so...

'Be quiet.' Kate was unamused. 'It's an outing for Theo. Definitely nothing more.'

Kate could tell the easy colour had already started to creep into her cheeks as she stumbled on the steps to the front door, then hesitated, her hand raised to tug the old-fashioned bell pull.

Why was her heart pounding in her breast? How could she be feeling like some gauche schoolgirl with a mega crush when she was a mature adult?

Because you fancy him...

'Shut up,' she muttered more firmly as she grasped the brass handle and knocked.

'I do not fancy hi—*hi*!' Kate beamed at Theo, thankful he stood beside the man in question. She raised her eyes to his dad. 'Hi,' she repeated, conscious she'd produced a squeak good enough to rival any respectable mouse.

Dev said nothing for a moment, his gaze sweeping down to Kate's feet. 'Good call.'

Unsure how she was going to stop overheating like a faulty boiler during the car ride, sitting next to Dev and watching his tanned, firm hands gripping the wheel, the rolled up sleeve of his crisp white shirt constantly catching the corner of her eye, it was a relief as they left the village centre behind and began to ascend the hill.

Short-sleeved, formal shirts, not sexy. Long-sleeved, rolled up to the elbow...definitely sexy.

Thankfully, Theo's excitement spilled over and a stream of endless chatter came from the back seat, with only the occasional response needed from either Kate or Dev.

'Daddy says children must be... I can't be on my own.' There was a pause. 'Why can't Bayley come, Daddy?'

'I've told you, they don't allow dogs.'

The conversation continued along this vein, and Kate pushed aside her foolish thoughts to skim the details on the leaflet she'd been sent after confirming the booking.

'It says the views from the lantern house are breathtaking.' She threw Dev a brief glance. 'I wonder if that's more about the climb?'

Dev grinned, then addressed his son.

'Don't forget, Theo, to listen to our tour guide. It will help you do your school project.'

Kate rolled her eyes, knowing the reminder won't have appealed to Theo, who saw this outing as a great adventure.

'We'll buy a guidebook. It will all be in there for later.'

'How high can we climb?' Theo strained against his seat belt in the centre of the back seat, and Kate shifted so she could look at him.

'It says in this leaflet,' she waved it, 'that it's 31 metres tall and there are 113 steps to the top.'

Theo's eyes widened as if the number was simply too big to be imagined.

'Will we see ships?'

Kate made a moue with her mouth. 'Possibly. It's a busy waterway.'

Theo reached for the leaflet, and she handed it over even though Kate knew he couldn't read most of the words.

'It's a bit like our lighthouse at Polkerran, only ours is much smaller and no one ever lived in it. They are important for anything on the water to be able to navigate safely into the harbour.'

'It's also a marker for passing ships so they can identify various parts of the coast,' Dev added. Theo beamed at Kate and sank back in his seat.

She turned to the front again, thankful the weather hadn't forced them to postpone the trip and soon they left Trebutwith behind and turned down the lane to the headland.

Dev nodded towards the lighthouse as it came into view. 'Here we are, Theo.'

They waited by the Visitor Centre, as instructed, and Theo hopped from foot to foot, his hand secured in his father's while Kate read the board outlining the rules.

'This says how tall children must be to climb the steps.' She turned to Theo with a smile. 'You're fine. You've got your Daddy's height.'

'I've got his hair too,' Theo declared proudly, pointing to his dark auburn hair, and Kate's lips twitched as Dev ran a self-conscious hand through his own mop.

'A maximum of two children per responsible adult,' Kate continued to read aloud from the notice board. 'I wonder how they decide if we're responsible adults?'

'Doesn't bear thinking about,' Dev muttered so that Theo wouldn't hear.

'You're too hard on yourself,' Kate said quietly, then resumed her study of the board. 'Oh, look, Theo.'

The little boy dropped his dad's hand and grasped Kate's. 'What?'

The eagerness in his voice touched Kate's heart, and she leaned down to say in his ear, 'We get to wear hi-vis vests.'

Eyes sparkling with delight, Theo swung around and hugged Kate's legs, and she felt a lump rise in her throat at his sheer delight in something so simple. If it hadn't been for Hugo's great deception, perhaps—

'How's your heart?'

Kate all but gulped as Theo released her, throwing Dev a wary glance, but he gestured towards the lower part of the board.

'Those with heart or respiratory conditions are advised not to undertake the tour.'

For a second, Kate pondered what Dev might say if she said she had to forego on account of a heart bordering on the edge of a massive crush on him. Then, she pulled herself together as the guide arrived and started handing out the vests.

Probably best she kept that to herself.

—

The visit itself was more enlightening than Kate had anticipated, with the knowledgeable guide keen to share anecdotes about lighthouses, especially those on rocky outcrops surrounded by nothing but water, as they scaled the winding stone steps, one floor at a time.

'In the very early lighthouses, warning lights were provided by coal or even wood-fired burners, but eventually oil was used and now they are all automated and run on electric generators.'

'So no one *ever* goes to them now?' Theo looked crestfallen, and Kate placed a comforting hand on his shoulder.

'I'm afraid not,' the guide replied. 'There are periodic visits to maintain lamps and equipment, of course.'

She turned to answer a flood of questions about the living conditions when they were manned, about the changeover of the three-man crew – there to ensure someone was always on watch – known as the 'relief', and how a twenty-eight-day stint could last anything up to ten more if weather conditions prevented their exchange.

Eventually, they emerged onto the level housing the enormous, glass-enclosed lamps, a circular concrete platform surrounding it.

The strong breeze tore at Kate's hair, but despite the exposed situation, it wasn't cold, and she drew in a long breath as she looked out across the water.

The guide began to point out the locations of several shipwrecks, and Kate couldn't stop watching Theo's fascinated expression as his wide eyes followed the direction of the guide's hand as though half expecting a ghostly ship to emerge from the depths.

Conscious of Dev stood beside his son, she threw him a discreet look, expecting his gaze to also be on the water, but it wasn't.

'Thank you for this,' he said quietly, before leaning down to say something to Theo, and Kate swung back to look away too.

'I thought I told you to stop it,' she silently scolded her heart as it swelled like an inflating balloon.

'Look, seals!' One of the group members called, and they collectively moved to the front of the lighthouse.

'There, Teds.' Dev pointed out over the water.

Theo bounced up and down on his heels, beaming. 'Seals!'

Kate fished out her phone. 'Is it okay?'

Dev nodded, and she tapped away, trying to capture the delight on Theo's features as he watched the seals swimming and diving not far from the rocky outcrop supporting the lighthouse.

'Would you like a family photo?'

A young couple stood beside Kate, and the man gestured towards the phone as her gaze flew to meet Dev's.

'Oh, no. We're not—'

'Yes please!' Theo trilled, sliding his small hand into Kate's and tugging on his father's sleeve to pull him closer.

'I took a few,' the young man said, as he handed back the phone. 'There's always someone with their eyes closed, isn't there?'

Not knowing what to say, Kate pocketed the phone. Perhaps she ought to reassure Dev she'd delete them later?

Of course you won't. You'll probably crop one so it's just him.

It wasn't as if Leigh would ever see it, though, was it? She just didn't want the potential to cause trouble for him.

'Kate.'

She looked up at Dev as they all began to follow the guide back towards the steps.

'It's fine. Stop worrying about it.'

'Was I that obvious?'

Dev merely smiled, helping Theo navigate the step ladder down from the lamps, and Kate followed, conscious of them waiting for her at the bottom, her senses on full alert. It wasn't enough, however, to stop her losing her footing on the second to last step, and landing with an inelegant thump.

'Are you okay?' Aware of Dev's outstretched arm in an attempt to slow her precipitous descent, Kate nodded.

'I'm good.'

The remainder of the return to the ground floor went without incident, and they handed back the vests, Theo doing so with some reluctance.

'They might have mentioned that steep ladder at the top, that's in addition to those 113 stairs!' Kate exclaimed as they emerged once more into daylight.

There was a small souvenir kiosk, where Dev picked up a guidebook to take home and Kate – on his nod of approval – purchased a miniature model of the lighthouse, presenting it to Theo, who held tightly on to it as they returned to the car.

They stopped at a charming pub on the way back, where Theo studied the Children's Menu carefully, trying out the words he could read and letting his dad fill in the gaps – which was most of it.

'What's it to be, Teds? The nuggets, the burger or the pizza?'

'What's *that* one?' Theo pointed to the line at the bottom.

'All served with chips,' Kate recited, and Theo nodded.

'I'll have that one.' He frowned. 'What's "All"?'

Shaking his head, Dev set off to place an order, and Kate drew Theo's attention to another line at the top.

'It says all children's meals are served in a bucket with a spade. How cute is that?'

'Or harsh, depending on how you look at it,' interjected Dev as he returned armed with serviettes and a small wooden trug containing cutlery and condiments.

Theo opened the guidebook, sucking fiercely on the straw inside his bottle of pop, as Dev and Kate sipped on alcohol-free beer. She was struggling against how much she'd enjoyed the day, wishing Mollie had been there too. Her daughter's smug comment when she'd left to spend the day at a friend's house, about not crashing her mum's date, had left Kate floundering.

Once the food arrived, however, she relaxed a little more and Theo returned to studying the pictures in the book as she and Dev mused on the fayre venue dilemma.

'I'm wondering if we just give up for this year.' Kate pierced a piece of scampi with her fork and dipped it in the tartare sauce.

'Is that what you want?'

She popped the morsel in her mouth, chewing thoughtfully. Then, she shook her head. 'No. But I'm struggling to see a solution and time's ticking away.'

Dev picked up his burger, elbows resting on the wooden picnic table. 'You don't strike me as someone who walks away from things lightly.'

The words fell into a profound silence as Kate's mind shot straight back to her unhappy, loveless life with Hugo. Dev said nothing, merely holding her gaze with his own questioning look. Their eyes remained locked as the edges of his mouth curved and—

'What does *that* say?'

Kate blinked and drew in a short breath, then leaned over to look at where Theo pointed.

'It has a long maritime history.'

Theo's forehead scrunched up as he picked up a couple of French fries with his fingers and dipped them in ketchup. 'Marry time? Is that what mummies and daddies do?'

Unable to look at Dev, Kate chose to explain the nautical term before resuming her meal. Honestly, how could she look the man in the eye, when Theo sat so innocently beside her, yet all she wanted to do right now was toss her scampi in the bin and give 'daddy' a good old snog and ask him if he fancied some marry time?

If Kate had one abiding memory of the trip to the lighthouse though, it wasn't the stunning view from the top, the surprise at Dev awkwardly asking if she'd send him *all* the photos or the general warm fuzzy feeling she'd felt for the outing overall, it was Theo's innocent demand – after hugging Kate fiercely as they said goodbye – that his dad do the same.

Dev, to be fair, had immediately hugged Theo, who'd giggled, claiming 'Daddy was silly' before prodding him in Kate's direction. It had been an awkward affair, but as she prepared for bed, she reflected that although it would probably go on record as the briefest embrace in history, it had been a touching and precious moment.

And Kate had had far too few of those in recent years.

Having accompanied Mollie to her current bestie, Freya's, for the latter's birthday shopping day out in Truro, Kate walked back down the hill into the village, still wrapped in warm memories of the previous day.

It was a gorgeous morning and a long walk would probably clear her head best, but as she reached the junction with the lane running between the village and the headland where Anna's cottage perched on the cliff top, Kate hesitated. Did she want her head to be rid of such pleasant thoughts? Was there any point in pretending or denying it?

Kate wasn't stupid, but it was long, *long* time since she'd considered anyone in such a way. Lusting after Regé-Jean Page in *Bridgerton* surely didn't count… did it?

This was real, not pretend. What was more, it was someone who was as unavailable as an unavailable man could be.

Giving in to the inevitable, Kate fetched up by Anna's gate and checked her watch. She *had* promised she'd pop round, after all…

The moment Kate opened the door to the kitchen, she realised her error. It was nearing midday, and there they were – the barmy locals – gathered around Anna's scrubbed pine table in front of the window with the incredible view. A view they were all impervious to at present, yet it drew Kate's eye like no other, straight across the expanse of water to Harbourwatch. How on earth had Anna coped, when she'd fallen in love with Oliver and he lived over there, seemingly oblivious to her?

In love? *Where did that come from?*

Chapter Eighteen

The One With a Ruby Tuesday

'Hey, come in.'

Kate started as Anna came towards her, the habitual welcoming smile on her features.

'I thought you might come down earlier. It's okay,' she added, lowering her voice. 'They'll be off soon.'

Impulsively, Kate hugged her friend, and Anna eyed her keenly as they separated.

'You okay?'

With a nod, Kate squeezed Anna's arm and headed for the table.

'Morning, everyone.'

'Oh Lordy,' exclaimed Mrs Clegg. 'Did we forget, young'un? Was this to be one of them meetings?'

Kate laughed as she took a seat with her back to the view, in between Nicki and Phoenix. 'No need for alarm, Mrs Clegg. Mollie's out having fun and I've got a day off, so thought I'd call on Anna.'

'That's right,' Mrs Lovelace nodded, dislodging her specs from the top of her head so they landed on her nose. 'We like to call on our days off too.'

Nicki exchanged a grin with Kate as Anna brought a coffee over, and she let the chat roll over her for a moment, content to have company of any sort just now, and unsure what she'd have said to Anna if she'd been here alone. Perhaps it was best she kept her thoughts to herself?

She sipped her espresso, her gaze roaming over the happy, animated faces. It was hard to remain frustrated by them. They were all so well-intentioned.

'Where's your Jean today, Mrs Lovelace?' Kate smiled at the lady, who was brushing crumbs from her lips with a tissue.

The elderly lady picked up the last piece of shortbread on her plate. 'Off up country again, my lovely. That friend of hers – the one 'as gave her the van – he lives near Newcastle. There was this band playing Jeannie's been wanting to see as long as I remember, so he got tickets for them.' She held the piece of shortbread aloft. 'Now what was their name? Cleggie! Big band. Something to do with veggies.'

Kate exchanged a puzzled look with Phoenix, but Nicki essayed, 'Prefab Sprout?'

'Now don' go being silly, young'un.' Mrs Lovelace popped the biscuit in her mouth and munched as Mrs Clegg's brow furrowed.

'I've got it!' Mrs Lovelace pronounced through her biscuit. 'They'm going to see Coldslaw play.'

Nicki smothered her laugh as Anna began to clear the table.

Once they'd all gone on their way, with Nicki reminding Kate about the gig rowing taster session the following week and saying how much her boys were looking forward to hanging out with Mollie again, Kate helped ferry the last of the things to the kitchen and loaded the dishwasher as Anna wiped down the table.

'When's Oliver back?'

'Any time in the next half hour. Come on, let's go outside. It's too nice a day to stay inside.'

They took a comfy, cushioned wicker patio chair each, and Kate sank back into it, the sun caressing her skin as she stretched out her legs.

'So? How did it go?'

'Hmmm?' Kate's gaze was locked on Harbourwatch. Was that Dev out on the terrace? She leaned forward, then realised someone was waving a hand in front of her eyes.

'Oh dear.' Anna's amusement was barely concealed as Kate stirred in her seat. 'I know that look. I've been there.'

'I don't know what you mean,' Kate essayed, assuming nonchalance.

'As you wish. So, tell me about the lighthouse trip. Was it a success?'

Kate's mind fled with no respect for her inner caution back to the moment Dev had hugged her, her skin tingling as though the contact had been resumed, and her hands wrapped across her body, grasping an arm each. As the habitual warmth flowed upwards through her body, she sent Anna a culpable look, and her friend laughed.

'Oh my! You have to tell me! Come on, it's gone midday. I'll fetch wine.'

The wine helped. At least, something loosened the grip on Kate's tongue, and she related a summary of the day out and how it had ended.

For a moment, Anna said nothing, her gaze drifting out over the water, and Kate had no desire to resist the urge to do the same. It *was* Dev. Even at this distance, there was no mistaking his tall stature as he helped Theo down the steps hewn into the rocks to the small boat house tucked into an inlet.

'You're well suited.'

Kate blinked, holding a hand up to shield her eyes against the glare of sun as she turned to Anna. 'We can't be!'

'Why not? You're single parents and experiencing all the challenges that brings. You've each been burned by previous marriages. Both of you are intelligent, articulate adults with minds of your own.'

Kate strove to ignore the oh-so-familiar swirling in her midriff. 'Hugo bruised me, but I'm not blind. I know he's not the norm, but Dev... on paper, it might tick a few boxes, but emotionally, I suspect we're both off limits.'

'This isn't a project, Kate,' Anna warned. 'You can't assess it on strengths and weaknesses. You haven't been *emotionally* attached to Hugo for years, you said so yourself. You're just out of practice.'

Kate huffed out a breath, throwing Anna a resigned look. 'What sort of friend are you?'

'A good one who will only ever speak the truth.'

'It's such a contradictory building,' Kate said, steering the conversation away from Dev. 'Harbourwatch. So austere on the outside, yet the interiors are beautiful. Well, except perhaps the room where you had your reception. There's a bit of an issue in the plasterwork, according to Dev.'

Damnit. That was a fail!

Anna failed to conceal her amusement, but didn't comment. 'Aw, that's a shame. It's a gorgeous room and the shell frieze was so pretty. Aunt Meg loved shells.'

'Funnily enough,' Kate said, 'that's where the problem is. A piece of it is protruding. They think it's to do with water ingress.'

'Oliver says Aunt Meg used to go over when he lived there, said he felt she knew the place well. Something about that room seemed to unsettle her, though, even though she liked to sit there. Of course, that could just have been the early stages of the Alzheimer's.'

Anna's gaze turned towards the sea, Kate's returned to where Dev and Theo could be seen getting into a motorboat moored to a small jetty only visible because of the position of Westerleigh.

Was there any point in letting her feelings take free rein, when Dev was so obviously between the proverbial rock and hard place over Leigh's unpredictable behaviour and he'd made it patently obvious he would always put Theo's happiness before his own?

-

Kate raised the blinds in her bedroom at The Lookout on the Monday after half term, conscious of a sense of well-being.

Despite it raining all day on the Sunday, she and Mollie had enjoyed themselves, using the confinement to the house to scour the internet for ideas for a summer break. The gorgeous images of turquoise seas and pine-clad hillsides in Greece had met with their mutual approval, along with the vague plan to add a trip to Athens in at the end of the week so Mollie could indulge her love of history.

As Mollie headed into the snug later, Kate slowly lowered the lid of her laptop. So many of the resorts showed happy families, but even more had softly filtered images of couples walking hand-in-hand on golden beaches or smiling into each other's eyes as they dined by the waterside.

Perhaps one day she'd go somewhere romantic with a special someone?

The fact Dev was the first – the only, Kate begrudgingly owned – person to pop into her mind, she accepted. Surely her interest in him (which showed no sign of waning) was borne purely from his being the first man outside of work she'd interacted with in, well, years?

With Mollie back at school, and conscious time was flying by, Kate doubled her efforts to find a venue for the village fayre. Logistically, the harbourfront alone wouldn't work – although some use could be made of it – but she continued to explore other possibilities, from a community building on offer near Golant and the kind suggestion by one of the local fishermen to use the village hall at Polwelyn, under the management of his cousin. Sadly, as both were not actually in the cove, she eschewed the idea.

She left a message for the head of the PTA to see if she had any ideas. As Dev had mentioned, the school wouldn't be in use, as it would be the summer holidays.

Continuing to work some evenings or weekends because of events, whenever Kate had a day off in the week, she'd start the day with a brisk walk along the cliff path, she'd then pick up her laptop bag and head down into Polkerran.

On days when the weather hinted at the summer to come, she'd sit outside on the terrace at the new restaurant, Harbourmasters, where it was only a glance across the narrow road skirting the harbour to the water beyond and all its distracting activity.

With the laptop open and her trusty notebook to hand, she updated the details on the village website and community Facebook page, replied to emails and tried not to panic about what hadn't yet been resolved.

Ever present, however, in the back of her mind was Dev. Time to be honest with herself. She fancied him, but perhaps it was a good thing he was unattainable, wrapped up in the tendrils of a divorce that seemed to have stalled.

At the very least, it stopped her from taking any initiative. It was obvious from the little Dev had let slip that Leigh was possessive despite her flakiness over the commitment to the marriage. Both Dev and Theo needed a complication like that in their lives like a hole in the head, and Kate certainly wasn't going to be the one to do the damage.

It was a brutal reminder of the truth and, with resolve, she made efforts to banish her attraction and immersed herself in work, putting in more and more hours in her determination to think of nothing but that and Mollie.

Mollie, however, didn't seem to need half as much of Kate's attention as she used to. Thankful for her daughter's improved spirits and – as much as mercurial teens could be – happiness, it sadly left her with even more regrets over Hugo's great deception.

—

One blustery Tuesday, as June took hold, Kate took a seat inside Harbourmasters, warmly greeting Tyler, the friendly manager.

'I'll have a flat white for now,' Kate said, as he showed her to her favourite table by the window. For some reason, she'd not slept well and needed the caffeine kick. 'But I'll stay on for lunch, if that's okay.'

'We're not too busy today,' Tyler confirmed. 'Got some great specials on, mind.'

Kate immersed herself in emails, then pushed the laptop aside and opened her notebook to sketch out a rough idea of where each table would be if they managed to secure the school grounds.

Two flat whites later, she sat back in her seat, her eyes scratchy, as a WhatsApp came through from Mollie, asking if it was okay to go to Freya's house after school.

Tapping away in response, Kate was vaguely aware of someone being shown to a table by the other window. She put the phone aside and looked up.

Dev.

Kate silently warned her heart to behave itself and dipped her head, staring at her screen but not taking in any words.

'Kate.' Dev stood awkwardly by his chair across the room. 'Hi,' he raised a hesitant hand.

Smiling, Kate waved back. 'Are you having lunch?' He nodded, and it was so reminiscent of Theo, her heart melted. 'Care for some company? I'm bored of my own.'

It was true. Besides, she really did need to talk to Dev about the printer's quote for the banners, so why not do it now?

Because you've got a phone, numerous message apps, email or—

Kate silenced the voice firmly.

Dev looked uncertainly between Kate's table and his own, hands shoved self-consciously into his pockets.

'Could do with chatting through a couple of things, if you don't mind?'

That seemed to seal the deal, and Dev joined her.

One of Tyler's efficient team took their order, and left alone, Kate willed the easy colour to stay below her collar as Dev's eyes met hers across the table. He really did have ridiculously thick lashes for a man, and those blue-grey eyes were like a calm sea on a winter's day...

'So?'

Kate blinked.

'What did you want to chat about?'

'Oh! Yes. This.' Kate scrolled back through her emails, opening the one from the printer about the large banners and showing it to Dev, trying not to notice as his fingers brushed hers when he took the phone from her.

'It's a bit steeper than expected.' He handed the phone back, and in an attempt not to touch him again, Kate took it with two fingers, which resulted in her dropping it on the table with a clatter.

'Yes, it is, mainly because it needs to be in colour, but costs have gone up everywhere. At least there's a bit of discount because we'd like three of them.'

'Okay, that's fine. Anything else?'

'Just the nutty problem of a sizeable venue. I'm waiting on the head at the school, but she's been hectic with all the final term prep.'

They talked sundries as they ate and Kate, her tongue probably a little too loosened by the delicious wine, decided to take the risk of Dev leaving his meal behind and scarpering back to Harbourwatch by broaching the subject of his son.

'How's Theo?'

To her surprise, he smiled, such a gorgeous smile, it infused his entire countenance.

'Still full of the lighthouse trip, but even happier now it's been decided he's coming to live with me for a while.'

'That's fantastic! I'm so happy for you. And for Theo, too.'

'Leigh's chasing some big role – she won't say where – which means constantly being away for extended periods, but also she's finally accepted he's not happy in the prep school. She wanted him to board, but he's only little. He's going to attend the village school and stay for the duration of the summer. I'm hoping he'll be able to continue there when the new term starts in September.'

Filled with delight for the little boy, Kate couldn't stop smiling. 'When's he coming? It'd be lovely if you—' She hesitated. 'If you want – or Theo does – would you like to come over with him sometime? Mollie's very good with younger children.'

There, that was okay, wasn't it? It wasn't about Kate wanting to spend a bit more time with Dev, was it?

You're not deceiving anyone, least of all yourself...

Smiling even more brightly to squish the thought, Kate waited for the rebuttal.

Dev looked down at his plate, which he'd almost cleared. 'I – er...' He ran a hand through his hair and that damn fringe flopped down once more.

Kate sat on her hands as he raised his head to meet her wary gaze.

'That would be...'

Nice? A nightmare? The worst possible thing I can think of?

'Lovely. If you don't mind.' He picked up his fork and mindlessly moved the remaining pasta around, then looked up at Kate again. 'I don't... get out much.'

'Nor do I, to be honest. My only evenings out are when I'm working at an event.'

Oh no! Had she just hinted at him coming round one *evening*? Or even worse, taking her *out*?

Thankfully, Tyler's timing was impeccable, and as they ordered coffee, Kate's skin cooled.

The conversation became mundane after that, and Dev left Kate to finish as he had a meeting with one of his tenant farmers up near Trebutwith Bay.

Kate emerged from the restaurant into the same blustery day she'd left behind that morning, her mind a jumble of confusion over Dev, the feelings he'd begun to stir in her and why he'd paid her share of the bill too before he left.

Chapter Nineteen

The One Where Mrs Tremayne is a Wannabee

Kate worked flat-out for the next ten days, with events through the entire weekend. Anna had been begging her to call for a long overdue catch-up, so she sent Mollie a text to say where she'd be when she got back after school and made her way down the hill from the hotel into the centre of town.

It was a beautiful day for early summer. An array of geraniums, petunias and trailing lobelia had taken up residence on the metal hangers along the harbour front and a second rowing boat, which had clearly been repurposed, was crammed with late spring blooms in its new mooring outside the small aquarium.

She turned her steps towards the harbour itself, leaning for a few minutes on the wall to look around. It was an hour yet before the primary school children emerged, so it remained fairly quiet, but it was lovely to see Jean's ice cream shop open, the striped canopy which matched the one on her van unfurled, and outside Harbourmasters, the smart tables and chairs overlooking the water.

The restaurant reminded Kate of her impromptu lunch with Dev, and she cautioned her tummy when it did the strange dip that accompanied every thought of him lately.

She straightened, crossing the bridge to the quieter side of the village and wrinkling her nose as a whiff of engine oil drifted across from where a fishing boat idled near the harbour wall.

'Hey, stranger, come in!' Anna greeted Kate on her arrival, and she put her things on a chair and took a seat at the kitchen island.

They caught up quickly over tea and biscuits, and Kate watched Anna preparing dinner as she relayed the latest updates on the fayre.

'The head teacher met with the PTA, and it turns out we aren't covered by their insurance to hold the fayre in the building. They said we could use the playground, but it's so small and up the hill, away from the hub of the village.' Kate pulled a face, then she noted Anna's somewhat distant expression. 'Hey, are you okay?'

Anna summoned a smile, but it wasn't her usual happy one. 'Oh, I'm fine.'

'Hmm. We didn't work together for years without me knowing when you're decidedly *not* fine.'

Anna shook her head. 'It's Oliver. At least, it's not *him* exactly. It's work stuff.'

Kate glanced at her watch. 'Mollie will be here in about fifteen minutes. Do you want to share, or shall I keep my nose out?'

'I could do with your ear. Oliver's working on a new book. *Haunting History* was such a success, particularly in schools, they're keen for another of his non-fiction-that-reads-like-fiction books and they're dangling a three-book series for lower grades.'

'But that's not all?'

Anna shook her head again. 'It's this not-for-profit thing he set up.'

'Didn't you say Daniel became involved?'

'He runs the finance side. Even though they're now abroad, he can still do that up to an extent. When they do choose to sell, it's at a reasonable value and with a residency restriction in place. Daniel has been managing all of that, too. The thing is, it's becoming huge. When Oliver's dad died, he inherited a vast property portfolio, plus stocks and shares, which he's been liquidating over time to invest locally. Then, Matt sold up several properties he'd bought over the years and wants to give a chunk of the money to Oliver's scheme too.'

Kate eyed Anna with curiosity. 'Sounds fantastic. So come on, out with it. What's troubling you?'

For a moment, Anna said nothing. Then, a heavy sigh emanated from her friend.

'It's Alex.'

Kate's gaze narrowed. 'What the hell has he got to do with it?'

'I think I mentioned he wasn't fond of Oliver. He resented that he was everything Alex wasn't.' Anna sent Kate a rueful smile. 'That should have been my wake-up call, right there, but you know me, gullible as they come. Anyway, Alex continues to refuse to sell directly to Oliver – or rather, his charitable organisation.'

An unanticipated rush of affection for Polkerran wrapped itself around Kate. 'Isn't that counter-productive where the village is concerned? So long as the Tremaynes get the same price, with Oliver's scheme, the properties are lived in all year round, which brings trade to Polkerran and keeps it alive?'

'You'd think. Anyway, now Alex has put some more properties up for sale, and Oliver is letting the frustration of not being able to acquire them for the village's benefit get to him. It's taking his focus off his writing, so he's further away from meeting his deadline and hesitating over signing for a series he'd adore doing.'

'Wow.' Kate's mind was full, so she couldn't begin to imagine what Oliver's felt like. 'I saw the sign for the alms-houses and the gatehouse.'

'Oliver would love to get them for the community. I've told him to let it go, he's got enough on. Dev, bless him, offered a cliff-top cottage, but it's a bit remote, so instead has given a plot of land, so affordable housing can be developed with local occupancy restrictions. It's lovely, but now there's all the planning approvals to manage and the architect to engage and Oliver has Daniel and Matty, but one's remote and the other's in his studio half the time.'

Anna slumped in her seat, and Kate's heart went out to her.

'I wish I could help—'

The boot room door opened and Mollie came in, sporting a wide smile.

'Hi, Mollie,' Anna called. 'Would you like a cold drink?'

'Yes, please.' Mollie dropped her bag and blazer, then leaned down to extract a sheet of paper, which she held out to Kate before joining Anna, who had headed to the fridge.

Soon furnished with a glass of homemade lemonade and two biscuits, she took the sturdy armchair by the hearth, nudging Heathcliff over to make room. The cat opened one sleepy eye, then rolled on her back, and Mollie stroked her exposed belly as she nibbled on a biscuit.

'Can I go?'

Kate raised her head from reading the note, taking in Mollie's anxious expression. Despite her daughter's enjoyment of the local water sports, this was encouraging further interest in life at the new school.

'Are you sure?' Kate skimmed through the page again, then passed it to Anna, who had resumed her seat. 'It's for a whole week. I know you're off to London with the history residential, but this one's abroad, love.'

Foremost in Kate's mind was the wildly expensive skiing trip to Switzerland Mollie had begged to go on when at her equally expensive private school in Yorkshire. Having received tearful phone calls every evening, feeling the worst parent in the world when Mollie begged to be allowed to come home early and saying she needed to see the week out, she couldn't quite understand her daughter's desire to spend a week in southern France in September looking at Roman remains and receiving basic instruction on an archaeological dig.

'Don't show this to Oliver. He'll want to come too.' Anna smiled warmly at Mollie as she handed the paper back to her.

'I'm older now,' Mollie said, shaking her hair back over her shoulders and raising her chin.

Kate and Anna exchanged an amused glance.

'Let's talk about it later. I'm happy for you to go if you *really* want to, but I need to be sure.'

Satisfied with that, and tolerating a few questions about her day at school, Mollie drank her lemonade, polished off the second biscuit and, dropping a kiss on Heathcliff's furry head, took her glass to the kitchen sink.

'Can I go and see Oliver? He promised to lend me a book.'

Anna looked over at the clock on the mantelpiece. 'I'll make him a coffee, and you can take it up. He ought to take a break.'

Mollie seemed content with that and resumed her seat beside Heathcliff as Kate and Anna moved over to the kitchen. Eyeing her friend as she fired up the coffee machine, and aware she wouldn't want to continue their earlier discussion, Kate regaled her with her impromptu lunch with Dev at Harbourmaster's restaurant.

'Tyler said afterwards we looked like we were on an awkward first date.' Kate didn't see the look Anna exchanged with a curious Mollie.

A smile tugging at her mouth, Anna fetched milk, then faced Kate across the island.

'And was it?'

Kate frowned. 'What?'

'Like a date?'

Her lips parted, but nothing came out as a flicker of sensation rippled through her midriff. 'I – er, no!' She huffed on a laugh. 'Of course not! We were discussing the fayre. It's all we ever talk about. Well, except for Theo.'

Anna retrieved the coffee. 'It's ready, Molls.' She held it aloft, and Mollie came over to take it.

Unable to decipher the look Mollie sent her, Kate watched the door close behind her daughter deep in thought, then turned back to Anna.

'I did inadvertently invite him round one evening.'

Anna grinned as she dipped her hands in the soapy water in the sink.

'I suspect you're beginning to find your inner flirt again.'

–

Kate had popped down into the village when Nicki phoned to confirm her next hair appointment at the salon.

'How did this morning's meeting go?'

Kate hesitated, then said, 'It was… interesting.'

Nicki laughed. 'I'm sorry I couldn't be there. Were they being as helpful as usual?'

Quickly summarising – again, it didn't take long – Kate leaned against the harbour wall, admiring the flowers in the old rowing boat, which had now come into bloom.

'Mrs T turned up.'

'You're joking!' Nicki's amusement was blatant. 'Now I'm *really* sorry I wasn't there! How was she? As snooty as usual?'

Reflecting on the lady's unexpected arrival at Westerleigh, Kate had to laugh. 'She'd messaged to forewarn me, but only an hour before. I'm hoping she comes every time. It's certainly an effective way of curbing the locals, although they'd clearly warmed up by the time she left. Old Patrick told her he'd had what he called a "helluva" crush on her mother, back in the day. Poor Mrs T looked rather taken aback, especially when he'd added "solid legs, good farming stock".'

A giggle came down the phone, and Kate added, 'Although we did gain a point with her. Anna told me once she had a thing about Oliver. Contrary to her son, she's longed to become acquainted with him and never quite managed it, but he happened to come into the kitchen during the meeting.'

'Don't tell me he put on the charm?'

It was Kate's turn to chuckle. 'I did see Anna whispering to him by the coffee machine. I've never seen Oliver like that, but it was hilarious the effect it had on Mrs T. Anyway, she left soon after, and I'm not even sure why she came.'

'Perhaps she just wants to be part of something. Leigh rejected every overture from Lady T as well as anyone else,' Nicki added sagely before ending the call, and Kate pocketed her phone and crossed the street.

She needed to pick up some cards from Pen & Ink and intended to pop into the boutique too, where she'd seen a rather fetching shirt in the window. It was as she came out of the latter, carrier in hand, that she noticed the aforementioned lady getting up from a table outside Karma.

Kate turned about, heading for the Spar.

'Yoohoo! Kate!'

Mrs Tremayne hurried towards her, and Kate gave her a warm smile.

'Thank you for joining us this morning. It was lovely to have some fresh input.' To Kate's astonishment, the lady looked a little uneasy. 'Is everything okay?'

'Yes, yes.' The confident demeanour returned. 'I am impressed with how you have pulled something out of nothing. I like the idea of this more traditional fayre and the focus on the local community. I had not realised there were so many people in the village who had so much to offer.'

Not wanting to go down that road, bearing in mind Mrs Tremayne had played the role of a distant and disinterested lady of the manor all her married life, Kate said nothing.

'I wish to make a contribution.'

'That's very generous of you,' Kate began, but Mrs Tremayne shook her head.

'Not pecuniary. There's something I would like to offer. Perhaps you might care to use the grounds and stables at the manor house as the venue?'

Kate felt a sudden affinity with the idea of one's jaw dropping, but she pulled herself together, her heart lifting in delight.

'That would be fantastic! Are you absolutely sure? Is your… is Mr Tremayne okay with that?'

A wave of a dismissive hand told the story there. 'He is going on a golfing holiday for the entire month of August. He's hardly likely to notice.'

'I'm truly so grateful, Mrs Tremayne. The whole village will be.'

For the first time, the lady smiled. A genuine smile, which reached her eyes. 'Arabella. And It's nice to be part of something after all this time.'

With that, she walked off and Kate's thoughtful gaze remained on the lady as she walked along the street towards the lane leading up to Tremayne Manor. Thrilled to have secured a location at last, and such a fantastic one, she couldn't wait to tell Dev, but she felt sad for Mrs Tremayne. Her life's work seemed to have been treating the local community with disdain.

With her position in question following her husband's retirement, it looked like she'd finally realised what she'd missed out on and longed to find a purpose as part of the community.

—

'Mum, Heathcliff's out there again.'

'Where?'

There was no reply. Mollie, as usual, had her earbuds in, curled up on the sofa and resuming her giggles at animal reels.

Kate walked over to the expanse of glass. Podge looked unperturbed by the visitor, but Heathcliff – no doubt missing Anna, who'd accompanied Oliver on a trip to London for two days to see his agent – had her back arched and her black tail fuzzed up.

Retrieving a packet of Dreamies, Kate went outside, and once Heathcliff had finished her impromptu treat, she scooped her up.

'Come on, cutie. Let's take you home.'

Thankfully, Heathcliff wasn't averse to the invitation and nestled into Kate's shoulder as they headed down the hill, but just as she released the cat by the cat flap into the boot room at Westerleigh, the door swung open and Matt came out with Dougal at his heels.

'Oh, hi! Just returning something.' She pointed to the cat, who'd trotted along the path towards the terrace. 'Anna worries she'll get lost if she goes too far along the cliff path.'

'Thanks.' Matt locked the door. 'I'm just taking this one for a walk. Breakfasts are all done.'

'Oh! I didn't realise there were any guests.'

'Two lots of walkers. They were booked in before the trip was planned, so I said I'd stand in.'

'Gemma's still at the experimental stage, then?' Kate followed him round to the driveway.

'You could call it that. Still, she's far better at making beds and cleaning than me, so she'll be along later. She's got a growing brood to care for.' He laughed at Kate's puzzled look. 'A kitten, a puppy and soon some chickens. I'd better make this a quick walk. I need to get back while the tide's in, so Gem has time to get here to do her bit.'

'Do you mind if I walk with you? There's something I could do with talking to you about.'

'Sure, come on. Dougal!' Matt whistled and the dog came scuttling back to him, sitting patiently as he fastened the lead to his collar.

They were soon up on the open grassland near the top of the hill and, removing the lead, Matt threw a ball for Dougal to scamper after. Kate tried not to scour the dogs for Bayley but there was no sign of him or his owner.

'What's up?'

She started.

'Oh! I – we – really need your help, Matt. We don't have anyone with the know-how to manage the performance set-up. We've been offered the use of the grounds at Tremayne

Manor for the weekend, which is brilliant, but…' Kate's voice tapered off at the wary look crossing Matt's handsome features. 'I'm sorry. I shouldn't have mentioned it.'

'No, it's fine. I can help… happy to be the roadie, look into licences, and so on, it's just—' He whistled to Dougal, who came scampering across the field, the ball in his mouth. 'Look, I've got something going on right now.' His smile was tentative. 'I'd need to go up to Tremayne Manor, do some scouting around, work out the layout, etcetera. But I can't do it for a bit.'

'That's fine,' Kate said, hoping she sounded as though she meant it. Securing a venue had been a huge relief, but what she didn't need right now were any further delays – whatever the cause might be that prevented Matt from being proactive right now.

Chapter Twenty

The One With Nicki's Holiday

Opening the window the next morning, Kate drew in a contented breath. The sea, in a compliment to the sky, was a rich, cloudless blue. No white caps disturbed the surface, other than furrows of white foam flowing like whipped cream behind Hamish's fishing boat as it headed out to sea.

'Two days off,' Kate murmured under her breath, heading downstairs to make some coffee.

Sitting on the terrace a half hour later, on her second dose of caffeine and having eaten two slices of toast so heavily buttered they should have carried a health warning, Kate half-listened to the radio as she mulled on what to do with the time.

She looked around. The Lookout didn't have much in the way of a formal garden, with a sweeping gravel driveway at the front and some large pots housing small trees and evergreen shrubs. A terrace ran from there down both sides of the property and round to where Kate now sat – beautiful grey slate slabs, and beyond, a small area which had been sown with wild flowers which were emerging with abundant glee from their winter hibernation.

An hour later, Kate pulled into the car park of the local garden centre, where she spent a pleasant hour choosing several pots in various sizes, which she arranged for the garden centre to deliver as they were too heavy for her car, before browsing the selection of plants on offer. Once her boot was too full – even with the rear seats flat – to hold anything more, she set off for Lostwithiel.

It was as she was browsing the eclectic selection outside a large antiques emporium that she had the sensation she was being watched and, glancing over her shoulder, she saw a familiar figure turn away to enter the deli on the opposite side of the street.

'Stop it,' she cautioned the recalcitrant flutter as it woke up, trying to focus on deciding between an old iron folding chair or the wooden crates. The crates would surely not be as weather resistant?

A few minutes later, she returned to look between the iron chair and the crates. The sound of voices drew her attention and she saw Dev leaving the deli, a small packet in hand. Had he not looked over, she'd have given the fluttering a sharp slap, but he had and their eyes locked.

'Hey!' She waved a hand, expecting Dev to make his escape as fast as possible, but instead he crossed the road and, giving up the battle with the quivering, she smiled at him. 'Just the person. I need to make a decision, and I'm failing badly.'

Today, he wasn't wearing the khaki or brown ensemble she'd become accustomed to, but a light blue shirt tucked into narrow-leg jeans. He'd rolled the sleeves of the shirt up to his elbows but even so managed to look smart, despite the usual unruly hair flopping over his forehead.

'Err... might need a bit more background on that?'

'Oh!' Flustered, Kate turned to the two items by her feet. 'It's these. I'm putting together some pots, and so on for the back terrace, and I've seen these lovely displays. You know, on Pinterest. Anyway, you need things at different heights but I'm not sure the crates will be weatherproof. It's quite exposed up at The Lookout.'

'Seems to me the decision's already made. Happen to agree.'

'Thank you.'

They both stood awkwardly for a moment and Kate firmly quashed the little voice in the back of her head urging her to invite him for a coffee. Then, he cleared his throat.

'Look, it's handy seeing you. I was going to phone later. Now we have a venue, can we do a final run-through of the detail so I can sign-off on the sponsorship?'

Always about the fayre? Damnit!

'Right then, my lovely. What's it to be?' The owner of the reclamation yard had emerged from the doorway.

Kate did the deal over the iron chair, asking the man to hold onto it.

'My car's full, so I'll be back in about an hour?'

Dev stepped in front of her and scooped the folding chair up as though it was a piece of paper.

'I'm heading home now, I'll bring it for you.'

Kate was very aware of Dev's car behind her as she drove back to Polkerran, her attention not as much on the road as it should be and far too often with the rear-view mirror.

'Stop it,' she admonished as they crossed the bridge and took the lane running along the far side of the harbour. 'And *don't* offer him a drink he'll only refuse,' she further cautioned as they turned up the hill towards The Lookout. 'All you'll do for the rest of the day is obsess about why he said no.'

'You're going to be busy.' He nodded towards the bulging back of her car, with its trays and pots as he placed the chair against the shed.

'I can't wait. I love gardening. Well, thanks.' She waved a hand. 'Oh. That reminds me, how was Theo feeling about starting at the village school?'

'Excited. He's certainly happier than he was.' Dev's expression darkened, in contrast to his words, and Kate tilted her head.

'Are you sure about that?'

'What? Oh, sorry.' He ran a hand around the back of his neck. 'Theo assumes he's going to stay there – here – and that Leigh will come back to live in Polkerran. He's so used to her coming and going, and dragging him around with her, it's become almost… normal for him. That was fine until he started prep.' He sent Kate a rueful smile as he closed the boot of his car. 'He hated that London school.'

'Mollie hated her private one, too. She's so much happier here. I mean, she's always loved the learning side of things, but she didn't get on well with the… culture there. I'm stunned at how happy she's become, so quickly.'

'Perhaps Theo's right, then,' Dev mused as he fished the keys from his pocket.

Kate wasn't sure what to say to this, but she did her best to ignore a flash of dissatisfaction. This truly was nothing to do with her.

'See you at the next meeting. I think it's Anna's turn to host. Always draws a bigger turnout.'

'So I've noticed,' Kate added dryly. 'She bakes better than you or I.'

—

Kate's week sped by, with two evening events to supervise, meaning she had a free morning at home on the Friday.

Pouring a coffee, she then picked up a slice of toast and walked over to the full-length windows facing the sea. The aftermath of a storm earlier in the week was evident, with small twigs and the occasional branch scattered across the stone flags of the terrace but at least they looked dry now.

'I'm late!'

Kate turned around as Mollie breezed into the room, heading for the island and nabbing the last slice of toast. She took a huge bite, wiped her fingers on her skirt and then smirked as Kate rolled her eyes.

'What about your teeth? And don't forget your lunch!' She called as Mollie shrugged into her blazer, scooped up her bag and bent to stroke Podge.

Mollie headed for the fridge as Kate walked over to the island. 'And don't forget Anna's out this afternoon, so head to Nicki's after school, okay?'

'Muuum!' It was Mollie's turn to roll her eyes. 'You told me. Twice already.'

'And if you answered me, I'd know you'd heard,' Kate responded resignedly.

With a grin, Mollie merely waved a hand and shot out the door, and Kate drained her mug and headed upstairs to get into her gardening gear.

She passed an enjoyable morning with all the plants, arranging the pots into groupings as she'd seen on mood boards on Pinterest, standing back now and again to assess the look, then pulling something forward or swapping its place with another at a different height.

Sitting with a cup of tea when she'd finished, she flicked through her emails, occasionally watching Podge, who was parading up and down, tail aloft and pausing now and then to sniff a leaf, as though doing a royal inspection.

Friday afternoon went smoothly and, although she was still struggling to find back-up volunteers for the actual days of the fayre, Kate almost didn't mind. As she'd said to Anna only last week, she'd taken it on because she liked to feel pressured, so she could hardly complain.

In between doing her work the following week, she managed to have a meeting with Mrs Tremayne at the manor house to view the available space and the stables, which no longer housed horses but had been cleared and cleaned and lay empty. They would be excellent back-up in the event of any dodgy weather, but would also be perfect for stalls of perishables.

At least now, Phoenix could complete her beautiful artwork for the plan of the fayre. The local crafters were – according to Jean, who'd been put in charge of that aspect – beavering away at their various cottage industries. It was all very Polkerran Point, Kate reflected as she took her sandwich and a coffee out onto the patio at the hotel at lunch time.

'Hey!'

She looked up, smiling, as Nicki came over to join her, a lunch box clutched in her hands.

'What time do you finish?'

'Now. I've got a few errands to run before I meet the boys from school and will be back home in good time for Mollie if she decides to call on us.'

Nicki took a seat next to Kate and for a moment they both looked out over the manicured grounds of the Point Hotel to the gap in the rows of evergreens marking the border of the property, where the wide expanse of water could be seen in the distance.

The main part of Polkerran Point wasn't visible from here, being tucked below at the bottom of the steep hill, but the smaller side, where Anna, Nicki and now Kate lived, could be seen rising up its steeply wooded hill to the outcrop of cliffs where Westerleigh perched, and the rooftop of The Lookout was just visible above the surrounding woodland.

'It's so beautiful, isn't it?' Kate mused, picking up her wrap. 'I felt captivated from the first moment I came here, even though it was the depths of winter.'

Nicki made a small sound, then sent Kate an amused look. 'I was a bit more taken with the "wildlife" when I first came. The male of the species, that is.' She winked, then scooped up a forkful of salad and munched on it.

Kate laughed before taking a bite of her wrap as Nicki continued.

'It was, to be fair, more than ten years ago. God, that was a fun summer. Young, free and single.' She cast an impish smile in Kate's direction. 'That's you right now. I'm a bit jel!'

Almost choking on her next mouthful, Kate reached for a bottle of water. 'I'm not sure I'd call pushing forty "young", Nicki!'

'Don't be daft. Everyone's embracing the idea we're all ten years younger than it says on the tin.'

Kate picked up the last of her wrap. 'That explains a few things. Mollie acts like a three-year-old sometimes.'

They talked about their children as they finished lunch, but then curiosity got the better of Kate.

'So, how did you meet Hamish? I assume it was on that fateful visit?'

Nicki stretched out her legs, leaning back in the comfy patio chair, untying her blonde hair and running a well-manicured hand through it.

'I sort of got roped into it. My cousin, Ellie, had graduated uni, and she and her mates had booked a couple of caravans for the summer on a site up at Polwelyn.' Nicki waved a hand back towards where the river wound its way down into the bay. 'One of them dropped out at the last minute, so she asked me if I wanted to come. I wasn't too sure, to be honest. I knew her best mate, but none of the others. I'd only been on a beauty course at my local college.' She pulled a face. 'I wasn't quite degree material. But Ellie's the sister I never had so…' She shrugged.

'So how was it? Aside from the falling in love bit?'

With a smirk, Nicki nestled back against the cushion. 'Amazing. It's hard not to gel quickly when you're sharing a room with tiny twin beds and an even tinier bathroom! I met Hamish on the second day, fell for him in an instant. At the end of the summer, I chucked in my boring job as a receptionist in a salon and never looked back. My parents were horrified, but they're over it now they see how happy we are.' She sighed dreamily. 'Part of me wishes he had a steadier job, was around more in the evenings when I want some adult company, but I wouldn't change my life for the world.'

'I envy you,' Kate said. 'Marrying Hugo was the biggest mistake of my life, and I'd wish it never happened if it wasn't for the fact I wouldn't have Mollie. The sad thing is, we never had the companionship you have with Hamish, that close bond, yet I miss it so much it hurts. Why is that?'

Nicki said nothing for a moment, then leaned over and laid a comforting hand on Kate's arm. 'Maybe it's because it's what you now need.'

Kate huffed on a laugh as they stood and gathered their bits and pieces. 'Well, I hardly think I'm going to find the answer in a tiny place like Polkerran!'

What about the man who's more on your mind than off it?
'Ridiculous!'

'Sorry?' Nicki looked back over her shoulder as they reached the doors into the hotel.

'Nothing!' Kate smiled. 'Talking out loud when I should be talking to myself.'

'Hmph,' Nicki muttered as they walked down the corridor. 'That's because you spend too many evenings alone up at The Lookout. Think it's time you got out more. Leave it with me.'

Kate sent Nicki a warning look. 'Don't you dare start enrolling me in any clubs or quiz teams.'

With a grin and wave, Nicki left, and Kate returned to her office, deep in thought. Was she right, though? She was only thirty-nine. Wasn't it time she started living again?

Nicki clearly thought so, as did Anna. By the end of the week, they'd both sat Kate down at the table by the window in Westerleigh – where she'd deliberately put her back to the view out of the window – as they earnestly set out their idea for a blind date with a mutual friend.

'Think of it as practice,' Nicki had reassured Kate.

'It's just a date,' Anna added. 'It's not as though you're stuck sitting by the fire with him for eternity, arguing over the remote.'

'Or washing his undies,' Nicki added with a chuckle.

Kate had merely shaken her head at them both, but as her friends started to talk about their plans for the upcoming weekend with their husbands, she couldn't deny that she almost envied both couples.

Perhaps marital bliss was still on the cards for her. One day. With someone. Against her volition, Dev swept into her mind, and she ushered him on his way.

His life seemed an even bigger mess than hers had been.

Chapter Twenty-One

The One Where it's Raining Men

Monday wasn't the best of days. Mollie had thrown her toys out of the pram when Kate told her off for not finishing her homework again because she was too busy making loom bands, and she stormed off down the hill to the school bus without a backward glance. Podge had refused to come in when she called, so Kate left for work eyeing the grey skies and worrying about where he'd take shelter if the forecast storm arrived later in the day.

The impending date with Marcus – divorced, no children – who ran a small glamping business on Bodmin Moor loomed at the end of the week. Nicki seemed to think it was a match made in heaven, but Kate knew Anna had reservations, though she wouldn't be drawn on why. Having a sneaking suspicion it was because her deeply romantic friend continued to believe Dev the right man for Kate, she grasped the blind date firmly.

Out of necessity she'd had to take the car up to the hotel, but as she skirted the harbour, where the fishing boats, which had been out overnight, were now safely returning to the cove ahead of the storm, she could see the canopy of the ice cream shop rippling in the strong breeze coming in off the sea.

A busy morning had been followed by a lunch-time meeting which had left Kate heavy-eyed as the manager talked through a series of slides as though none of them had the ability to read.

With no appetite for the sandwiches and crisps on offer, Kate had dashed back to the ladies to freshen up, grab her coat and, with a wary eye on the black clouds now gathering overhead, got in her car and headed out of town.

Several hours later, with rain tumbling from bulging skies, Kate scurried from the warehouse where she'd been inspecting a stylish range of patio hire furniture, shivering as she slammed the car door and flicked open the visor mirror. An umbrella had been out of the question in such strong winds, but her hair now hung in raggedy tendrils around her face, and her shirt clung to her cold shoulders.

A hand went towards the heated seat button, but she hesitated. Was that a good idea when she was so wet?

Hopefully Mollie hadn't been soaked when walking up to Anna's after school and, with a bit of luck, Podge would have gone to sleep in a sheltered hole somewhere.

The rain continued to pelt down and the roads were awash with standing water, making progress slow at times as traffic backed up to allow room to avoid the deeper pools of water, but even with the windscreen wipers whipping away on the fastest setting, Kate's eye was still caught by a familiar figure huddled inside the bus shelter near the cemetery at the top of the hill above Polkerran.

Slowing the car, she reversed into the adjacent car park entrance and, pulling her jacket over her head, shot into the shelter.

'Ryther! What on earth are you doing here?' She eyed the elderly gentleman with astonishment, then concern. 'Are you okay? What's happened?'

Ryther did not look his usual dapper self. Aside from appearing to be as wet as Kate, his face was lined and pale.

'I am an old fool, when all is said and done.'

'Where is your car?'

'At Harbourwatch. I woke this morning and had a desire to be in the cove.'

Kate didn't miss his eyes darting towards the cemetery gates.

'Come on, I'll give you a lift. It'll be an hour before there's another bus.'

A further dousing of rain was hardly conducive to improving Kate's mood, but she was anxious about Ryther and keen to get him warm and dry.

'Shall I drop you back at Harbourwatch?'

The man at her side didn't answer at first, and she sent him a keen look, but Ryther slowly turned his head. 'You may. I shall wait in my car for Dev to come home.'

'Wasn't he expecting you?' Kate negotiated a small roundabout and continued down the hill into the village.

'No. I came on a whim, and there was no one home, so I called him but it went to voicemail. I… decided to go for a walk.'

Kate gave an exasperated huff. 'It's more than a mile to the cemetery from Harbourwatch, Ryther, and it's uphill for most of that!'

A faint laugh emanated from the gentleman and Kate's lips curved upwards reluctantly. 'And I am, as you no doubt are silently adding, eighty-five years old. My doctors have told me, however, that walking is the best exercise for someone of my years, and uphill is better for the heart.' He released a soft sigh. 'In more cases than one, as it happens.'

Not wanting to pry, Kate sent him a warm smile. 'I'm heading to Anna's. My daughter, Mollie, sometimes goes there after school if I'm working. Would you be okay waiting there until we can track your grandson down? Surely you aren't planning on driving all the way back to London tonight?'

'No, no. I'm afraid my days of driving for hours without feeling the strain are long gone, even with the Lady Margarethe to keep me company. That's my car,' he added, his usual smile returning, much to Kate's relief. 'My days of dalliance with delightful women are also long over.'

'I'm sure you were quite the charmer in your day, Ryther,' Kate said as she drove slowly along the narrow lane to Westerleigh Cottage. 'Here we are.'

She held the door open for Ryther and, as he emerged, she was struck anew by the paleness of his skin. It appeared as thin as paper, his normally alert gaze full of sorrow as it roamed over the house. He refused her offer of an arm and walked – perhaps a little more slowly than before – down the side of the house to the boot room.

'I'm here!' Kate called through the partially open door to the kitchen, as she helped Ryther out of his sodden raincoat, hanging it on a spare hook and adding her own jacket. She cast a resigned look at her bedraggled appearance in the mirror and pushed open the door. 'And I've brought a friend.'

Anna came towards them from the living area, a wide smile on her attractive features. It was so grimly dark outside, it was as though dusk had fallen ahead of its time, despite it now being June, but lamps threw out a welcoming light and a warm glow emanated from the log burner, which spat and crackled in a comforting way.

'Good grief!' Anna eyed Kate's appearance with a half-laugh. 'I won't state the obvious.' Her gaze moved to the gentleman who stood beside Kate, and she tilted her head. 'Have we met before?'

'This is Ryther, Dev's grandfather.'

'Oh!'

Kate didn't miss Anna's askance look towards the coffee table, covered in papers and photos, but her friend collected herself and shook Ryther's hand.

'I've seen you in the village from time to time. Lovely to meet you.' She eyed his equally damp clothes. 'Let me just tidy up, then you can sit by the fire. I don't normally light it at this time of year, but it's such a foul day.'

'I'll put the kettle on.' Kate set it to boil and opened a cupboard. 'Where's Mollie?'

Anna looked up from closing the lid on the wooden box Kate had seen before. 'Where do you think?'

Kate shook her head, walking over as Anna ushered Ryther into a chair beside the hearth.

'My daughter is obsessed with history. Tudor, in particular,' she imparted to him. 'Poor Oliver gets no peace when she comes over.'

The gentleman smiled faintly, accepting the throw which Kate had removed from the back of one of the sofas, tucking it over his legs. 'For me, it was music. I had no patience for that academic malarky.'

Kate smiled, returning to the kitchen to help Anna ferry the tea things over as the elderly gentleman tapped into his phone.

'I'm just asking my grandson to let me know when he's home. Thank you, my dear.' He accepted the cup and saucer from Anna, but refused her offer of a biscuit.

What with the hot drink and the fire, the urge to shiver had gone. Kate's bare feet had dried out and she glanced over at Ryther only to see he'd closed his eyes, leaning back in the sturdy armchair frequently used by Oliver, the almost empty cup resting in his grasp in his lap.

Lowering her voice, she nodded towards the box, which Anna had placed on the floor beside the sofa.

'Have you found anything fun?'

Speaking equally quietly, and casting a wary glance in Ryther's direction, Anna nodded. Bearing in mind their speculation before now on Aunt Meg's mystery man bearing a strong resemblance to the gentleman now resting by the fireplace, it wasn't really the time to speak in depth.

'I wanted to dig out one of those earlier photos of Aunt Meg. She was in her sixties when we first met, she'd recently retired from her role as head of the village school.' Anna took a sip of tea. 'I just felt the urge to see her. Today would have been her birthday.'

A faint sound emanated from Ryther, whose eyes remained closed, but then the door opened, and Kate looked over, expecting Mollie or Oliver.

It was Dev.

Heart thumping, Kate shot to her feet, then sent Anna a pleading look.

'Just popping to the loo.' It sounded like the mouse was back…

Ducking her head, and pretending she hadn't noticed Anna's knowing smirk, Kate barely glanced in Dev's direction as he crossed the room, and she shot out of the door into the hallway, then leaned back against the panelling.

Damn. She'd left her bag by the sofa!

Doing what she could to repair her appearance in the stylish cloakroom, she eyed herself in the mirror. Thankfully, she had dried out, but her shirt was creased and no amount of coaxing would persuade her hair to tie back neatly, so she gave up and left it hanging in wavy tendrils on her shoulders. Wiping away a stray smudge of mascara, she chewed on her lips to add some colour, then shook her head.

'Stop being ridiculous,' she murmured as she retraced her steps.

When she rejoined the others, Dev was questioning his grandfather on what had drawn him out to Cornwall on such an awful day, but Ryther merely said he'd woken with a desire to see the sea.

Dev grunted. 'You do know it would have been easier to get the train down to Brighton? Thank you for taking him in,' he addressed Anna as he helped his grandfather to his feet.

'It is Kate you should be thanking,' Ryther added, reaching out to grasp her hand and hold onto it. 'Thank you, my dear, for rescuing me.'

Leaning forward, Kate pressed a kiss on his cheek, disturbed to see how cold it remained. 'I'm glad I saw you. Now go with your grandson and get properly dry and warm.'

'Where's my great-grandson?' Ryther demanded as Dev led him towards the boot room.

'Behaving himself and staying in the dry, under Stella's motherly eye. Unlike you.'

Once Dev had retrieved Ryther's coat, he opened the back door, but Ryther turned to Anna, who placed her hand in his extended one.

'I am indebted to you, my dear.' His gaze dropped to the ring on Anna's finger.

She let out a small gasp. 'I remember you! You were here at Westerleigh, a few years ago now. You admired my engagement ring.'

Ryther sent Anna a culpable look, continuing to hold her hand. 'Forgive me. I wished to look at the beautiful view from the windows, one I had not seen in many years – back when, for the briefest moment in time – I was the happiest of men.' He raised Anna's hand and placed a kiss upon it. 'You will excuse me. I am weary now.'

He did indeed look drained, and Kate sent Dev a concerned look, which he met before giving a small incline of his head.

'Come on, old man. Let's get you home and fed.'

'Less of the old man, you young upstart,' Ryther countered, but his voice was less firm now and his gait still stooped.

'I think we've barely touched the surface of Meg's story,' Kate said as Anna returned from closing the door behind the departing men.

'I think you're right. Besides,' Anna chewed her bottom lip, 'it still doesn't explain who Neb is… I mean, surely Aunt Meg didn't have several on the go, did she?'

Kate and Anna stared at each other, then descended into amusement. 'Let's not go there. It's time I rounded up Mollie – who wasn't speaking to me when we left this morning – and rescued Podge from wherever he's been holed up.'

Chapter Twenty-Two

The One Where Kate Needs to Relax

'Mum, look! There's a touring of *Hamilton*. Can we go? It's at the Hall for Cornwall next month.'

'Let me have the dates and I'll see what works. Come on, we're late.'

It was Saturday, and Kate urged Mollie to pocket the phone and chivvied her out the door and down the lane to Nicki's, where they joined forces with Liam and Jason to head down to the slip near the harbourmaster's office where all the gigs were lined up ready for the taster session.

'Are you nervous?' Kate addressed her daughter's back as she donned her life jacket.

'Why would I be?' Mollie beamed at her as she refastened her hair tie and shot across the cobbles to join her school friends, and Kate felt a flood of happiness combined with dread, which almost made her feel sick.

Never had she seen her daughter so full of life, brimming with joy and delight.

And yet, she bore an ominous sense of foreboding over staying in Polkerran permanently. Had she truly gone beyond finding Dev attractive? Was she actually falling for him? That way madness... no, *sad*ness lay. And bizarrely, it brought a depth of despair that had never consumed her when life with Hugo had turned out to be a complete disaster. Perhaps she'd lived too long with disappointment, anything seemed better?

'I'd say penny for your thoughts, but I suspect they are worth far more.'

Thankful for the interruption, Kate turned to smile at Matt. 'You're far too kind.'

Matt shoved his hands into the pockets of his tailored shorts. 'Time will deliver a verdict on that one.'

'Oh. Should I ask?'

With a grin, he shook his head. 'Nothing too awful. I've just been spending too much time in the Big Smoke lately, obliged to deal with people I don't like. Glad to be back home.'

'I didn't expect you to be here.' Kate looked around at the children being watched over by nervous parents. 'I thought small animals were more your thing.'

Matt adjusted his designer sunglasses. 'More Gem's thing, you mean. She does love the water activities, but I'm told we're expecting the chickens today. It's the downside of too much time on her hands.'

With a smile, Kate scanned the gathering before spotting Mollie talking animatedly to Liam and Jason – who were still too young for the junior gig rowing.

'Oh, there's the big man. I'd best go update him on London.'

Kate followed Matt's gaze, then waved as she saw Oliver and Anna near the chandlery, who set off towards them, followed by someone else – Dev, with Theo clutching his hand.

Her heart dipped, then began pounding furiously in her chest, and an involuntary hand shot to it. She couldn't leave, it wasn't fair on Mollie, but looking around, there was nowhere to hide. Hopefully, the redness in her cheeks could be put down to the weather.

Ignoring Anna's knowing smile, Kate turned to Theo as Matt led Dev and Oliver aside.

'Have you come to watch?'

'Yes!' Theo held up a wooden toy gig. 'Dad says I can have a go in a real one, but not until I'm bigger.'

'Come on, let's watch them set off.'

Anna led the way to the railings overlooking the water and they squeezed in between Shari from the cafe and Tommy the Boat, so that Theo had a front-row view.

It was fun to watch, if a little haphazard, with such young crews, each gig bearing an experienced rower as helper, as well as a cox, and Kate cheered Mollie on, Theo doing the same at her side, his eyes shining and his cheeks flushed.

When the lesson was over, people surged to the slip to collect their charges and then dispersed towards the food hut on the quayside.

Anna took Theo to join the queue at Jean's ice cream van, and Kate handed over some cash to Mollie to get a burger and a drink. Wandering back over to the railings, Kate watched the gigs being tugged up the slipway to an assortment of trailers, as oars were fastened into place and life jackets stowed away.

Her date with Marcus was that evening, and never had she wanted to drop out of something more.

It would be different if it were with someone else...

'Would it?' she whispered, her heart jostling like the pleasure boats bobbing up and down, against a pontoon in the middle of the bay.

'Hey.'

She drew in a quick breath and turned around.

'Hey.'

Oh, my God, he looked so cute.

Today, Dev sported an open-necked white shirt, the long sleeves rolled up to the elbows. His eyes seemed more blue than grey, and the thick fringe of dark red hair lay on his forehead just waiting to be brushed aside and—

'Are you okay?'

With a start, Kate took an involuntary step backwards. 'Yes,' she croaked, then attempted to clear her throat. 'Never better.'

'Theo won't stop talking about the day at the lighthouse.'

'Oh, I'm sorry!'

'No, don't be. I've never seen him as happy as he's been recently.' Dev's handsome features darkened, and against her volition, Kate's hand shot out to rest on his arm.

'Is everything all right?'

'Leigh's visiting later. I never know her purpose.'

And no doubt she'd be staying in the family home…

'I… I hope it goes okay.'

Dev's gaze dropped to his arm, and Kate whipped her hand away.

'Sorry.'

He raised his eyes to meet hers, and despite her embarrassment, she held it, willing away any increased colour in her skin. 'Don't be. There's little enough kindness in the world.'

'Oh.' Inane, but there weren't any other words… was it even a word, or just a sound?

Their gazes remained locked, the call of the seabirds seeming to fade, along with the clatter of the trailers as they rolled away across the tarmac.

'Well,' Dev cleared his throat, shoving his hands into his pockets. 'I think I'd best find Theo.'

'Oh, yes! Of course. He *was* in the ice cream queue.'

They found the little boy sitting on a nearby bench tucking into his treat, Anna by his side. Her friend's eyes darted between Kate and Dev, before she got up to join Kate, Dev taking her place by his son.

'Well, at least you don't fancy each other. So that's okay.' Almost choking with laughter, Anna took Oliver's hand as the few stragglers remaining headed along the street towards the harbour.

Feeling like the worst mother in the world for forgetting about Mollie, Kate spotted her happily tucking into her burger, legs dangling over the water and hurried over, desperately hoping Dev couldn't see what her friend obviously could.

—

Heeding both Anna and Nicki's advice, Kate decided to leave her long, brunette tresses loose for the dinner date, using her GHDs to curl the ends so they hung in loose waves. Turning her head from side to side, she had to admit that Nicki's wonder crème had definitely delivered the shine she'd promised and, enjoying the weight of her hair on her shoulders, Kate slid open the doors to the dressing area.

'You look cool.'

The unexpected compliment from Mollie as she peered around the dressing room door surprised Kate.

'Really?' Was there a note of insecurity in her voice? Was it because she knew this date with Marcus was a waste of time, or because she still wished it was with someone else?

'Wear that one.' Mollie walked up to the wardrobe where Kate had hung three dresses, undecided on what look to settle for. This was, after all, a little Cornish fishing village, not a city night club.

'I wondered if it might be...'

'Too sexy?' Mollie smiled impishly, and Kate gently swatted her daughter's arm.

'That's not the look I was going for, to be honest.'

'Hmph,' Mollie muttered, but Kate didn't catch the rest of the comment.

'Do you really think it'll be okay?' The irony of being thirty-nine and asking a thirteen-year-old for reassurance passed Kate by, so unsure was she.

'It's a posh restaurant. Besides, it's the one that suits you best,' Mollie said, then left the room.

Kate slid the dress from the hanger and slipped it over her head, enjoying the feel of the silky fabric as it caressed her body. It was a designer dress she'd bought second-hand two years ago and never worn. The deep v-neck suited her bustline, and the soft fabric of the full skirt skimmed over her hips, falling in heavy folds beneath the cinched leather belt. It was a muted pattern of pale blues, grey, silver and dashes of violet. She'd impulse bought it because it reminded her of the Yorkshire moors on a benign late summer day when the heather was in bloom.

She glanced at her watch. Time to get a move on. Running her fingers through her loose curls, she picked up her clutch and nude high-heeled sandals and hurried down the stairs to put them on.

'What did you say, just now. Up there.' Kate gestured towards the staircase as she fastened the straps on the sandals. 'About the look I wanted.'

Mollie said nothing for a minute, passing her phone from hand to hand. Then, she shrugged. 'I said it would have been if it was a date with Dev. Wanting to look sexy. *He's* got rizz.'

'Mollie!' Kate's heart belted around in her chest like someone had just blown the start gun at the Olympics.

'Just sayin',' Mollie waved an airy hand. 'I'm off to Freya's. See you in the morning.'

Kate watched her daughter breeze out of the room, deep in thought, but then Mollie's head popped back around the door to the hall.

'Don't stay out too late. You'll get bags under your eyes for when you next see Dev.'

Chapter Twenty-Three

The One With Bucks Fizz

Marcus had been a lot of fun, and his job was fascinating, so the evening had sped by, but although Kate could feel her former self emerging, she wasn't remotely attracted to him.

Not that there was anything to not like about the personable man. He was probably the same height as Kate with her heels on, dressed very nicely and had warm, friendly eyes and a genuine smile. He wasn't pushy, but he did make it very clear he liked Kate. Was she being too wary? Should she leap in and have some fun?

The true measure of how she felt came on leaving the restaurant, however. As they walked, deep in conversation, towards the entrance, the doorman swept the doors aside to reveal Dev and Leigh.

Kate's heart, which had remained all night in its normal position in her chest, gave a swoop, the envy of any passing swallow, and she tripped over her own feet, instinctively grasping Marcus's arm. Deafened by the pounding in her ears and trembling from an inexplicable onrush of emotion, she stared at Dev as he all but froze.

Leigh flashed her beaming smile as they passed by, but Dev's expression was unreadable as he nodded in her direction, his sharp gaze flicking to Marcus and back before the moment was over. Realising she was still holding onto his arm, she'd summoned a smile and released him, scurrying head down through the doorway into the cooling night air.

Kate barely slept that night, her mind going to places she really didn't want to think about – had it been a romantic date? Was it at Dev's instigation, or Leigh's? And what about afterwards... at Harbourwatch...

'Stop it!' she snapped out loud, thumping her pillow before lying down again and trying – in vain – to curb her traitorous imagination.

At work on Monday morning, she was still on a short fuse and looked up in frustration when the office door swung open. She'd been trying to do a final proofread of a proposal, and this was her third interruption in the past ten minutes.

Chloe, the manager's PA, dragged in one of the elegant, brass-trimmed luggage carts.

'This just came from the printers?' She indicated the large, flat box resting on the base.

Coming round to inspect it, Kate summoned a smile. 'Thanks. It's the banners for the fayre. There didn't seem much point in having them sent to my house as they need to be put up on this side of the bay. There's three, one for the junction with the main road, one for the top of the hill by the cemetery and another one to go on the harbourside, near where the ferry stop is.'

A half hour later, the proposal on its way, Kate stood at the window overlooking the terrace. There were a few elderly couples drinking tea at some of the outdoor tables and another table with four young women on the prosecco. She couldn't hear anything but could tell they were having a good laugh about something, and a whisper of envy shot through Kate. She'd tied herself to Hugo at such a young age, she felt she'd missed out on so much of the adult girlfriend thing.

And the dating...

There it was again, that niggling reminder ever since Mollie had told her she was lonely and her friends had suggested she start seeing people. Find a person. Someone special. And she'd tried. She'd had a date, but pleasant as he was, she had no intention of seeing Marcus again.

Kate shuddered, despite the warm day, and turned away from the window, trying hard not to think about Dev.

Grateful when her mobile rang, Kate took the call.

'Hi, Nicki.'

'Hey. Just realised, with my boys off to the grandparents this weekend and your Mollie on her London school trip, we've got a window. You free for a girlie lunch on Saturday?'

Kate's mouth curved upwards, the offer coming so soon after her recent musings. 'Always.'

'Anna and I are heading to Harbourmasters for midday. Shall we get a table for three?'

'Please. I'll come to Anna's and walk down with you.'

―

The weekend soon came around and, relieved not to have had a call from Mollie within hours of reaching her destination – and trying not to worry too much as it was the first school trip involving staying away from home since the move – Kate had happily headed down to her much-anticipated girlie lunch with Nicki and Anna.

'So it's finally coming together?'

Kate wiped her fingers on her napkin as they finished their meals. 'Yes, thank God! Lots to sort out at the manor yet – layout for stands.' She waved an airy hand. 'Where's best for the pop-up pergola for the performers, bearing in mind the need for cabling, and so on, but compared to where we were…'

She rolled her eyes, and Anna and Nicki laughed.

'I just need to find a couple of available strong men now.'

Nicki waggled her eyebrows. 'If you find them, I'd love to meet them!'

The table was cleared amidst the laughter, but then Anna sent Nicki a concerned look.

'Are you okay? I mean, you know, you and Hamish?'

Having just taken a mouthful of her Bucks Fizz Nicki put a hand over her mouth, eyes sparkling, then swallowed quickly.

'Bloody hell,' she spluttered on a cough. 'Yes! We're fine. I was just joking, you daft bugger.'

'Sorry.' Anna looked mortified, but Nicki was still chuckling.

'Don't be silly. Besides,' she nudged Anna's arm and nodded towards Kate, who looked from one to the other, 'it's Kate who said she needed one. Well, two to be precise.'

'They need to come with cable ties, too. Industrial strength.'

This time, both Anna and Nicki dissolved into giggles, and Kate shook her head at them.

'Such children,' she chided, but amused, nonetheless. 'I'm not interested in finding a man for myself.'

Her friends exchanged a knowing look before Nicki fastened her gaze on Kate. 'But Marcus *lurrrrves* you. He can't wait to see you again.'

'Shut up,' Kate said, laughing. 'I'm not ready. It was… it was… too much like a date.'

Anna blinked. 'As opposed to?'

'It doesn't have to be serious, you know?' Nicki for once eyed Kate without humour. 'Men can be just for fun too.'

'Hah!' Kate almost snorted as she drained her wine glass. 'I'm not sure I'd know what to do with one these days.'

'I think you need more practice.' Nicki pointed at Anna's mocktail. 'I can't believe you have to drive later. We were supposed to be out on the lash too.'

Anna merely beamed. 'We're out to dinner tonight. One drink at lunch time and I'd be asleep for hours.'

In amongst Nicki's humorous asides, they turned down dessert, opting instead for coffee, and the conversation moved to Anna's recent trials.

'It's quite worrying. Oliver's been so stressed, but Matt's brimming with that confidence he has when he thinks he's on to a good thing.'

'You mean since he got together with Gemma?'

Anna laughed. 'Well, I don't have that many years to compare, but yes, you're right. Anyway, he's insisting on flying solo with whatever he's up to.' She looked around, lowering her voice. 'He's in London again, but he won't let on what he's doing. Gemma says that was par for the course when she was housekeeping for him last year.'

'Is Mollie becoming a nuisance for Oliver?'

'He loves anyone with the patience to listen to him talking history.' Anna chuckled. 'Though he's convinced her interest is more to do with whether he's a distant relation to Jane Seymour's family.'

After leaving the restaurant, they browsed the shops for a while, but as they walked over the bridge, with Anna on her way home, Nicki persuaded Kate to take a detour into the Lugger.

'Come on,' she pleaded as Kate showed some reluctance. 'How often is it we can do this?'

Caving to Nicki's pleading look, she laughed. 'Okay, okay.'

Kate and Nicki headed over to a booth away from the other drinkers, most of whom were locals, with whom they exchanged some banter.

'So what about Jago or Cobber?' Nicki inclined her head towards two of the men at the bar, wearing work gear as they downed a pint before heading home.

Kate stared at Nicki in disbelief. 'I'm not sure they'd be up for much fun.'

Nicki shook her head. 'Not for that, love. To help you get the banners in place.'

'Oh!' Kate grinned. 'Fair point.'

'So, it's a week since the date with Marcus. Wasn't there anything that stood out about the evening?'

Against her volition, Kate's mind immediately recalled locking eyes with Dev as he and Leigh entered the restaurant, and heat stole into her cheeks as the familiar quivering in her middle began its dance.

'Bleddy hell, as the locals say,' Nicki exclaimed. 'What on earth did he do?'

Kate sighed. 'Walked in with Leigh. He'd told me she was visiting but somehow, I didn't expect to see them out for dinner.'

Nicki's pretty eyes widened. 'I meant Marcus.'

The warmth in Kate's skin intensified as a hand shot to her cheek. 'Oh God. How embarrassing.'

A smirk was the only answer. Then, with a secretive smile, Nicki added, 'Or intriguing.'

'Or nothing. Not remotely interesting. Definitely not intriguing. Can we change the subject?' Was she pleading a little *too* much?

Nicki held out her hand for Kate's glass and got up. 'Of course. I'll get us a top up and then we can talk about you getting a bit more date practice.'

—

Nicki – with Anna's assistance – hadn't slacked, and on the evening before Mollie returned from her trip, Kate once again prepared for a blind date – this time with someone called Freddie, which was about as much information as either of them would share.

'You need to have things to talk about,' Nicki admonished as she worked on Kate's hair in her bedroom at The Lookout.

'Is that all he knows about me too, my name?'

'So far.'

She didn't feel remotely nervous, simply because… 'This is ridiculous.'

Anna chuckled. 'Not really. To be good at something, you must practice.'

'Although the results are better if your subject stays still,' Nicki advised with a grin as she wound another tress of Kate's hair around the curler.

Ten minutes later, Nicki had finished, and Kate had to admit she'd done a fabulous job of her hair, which lay in polished curls.

'It's so lovely to see your hair down instead of screwed back in that chignon, stylish as it is,' Anna exclaimed. 'It takes years off you.'

'It'll take more than a great hairdo to give me back the lost ones.'

Kate eyed herself in the mirror. There was a hint of her former self... wasn't there?

'Half an hour until you need to leave,' Nicki added, as they headed down the stairs.

All the nerves came whizzing back, and her anxiety must have been evident because Anna grasped her hand.

'It'll be fine. It's just a practice date. It's so much easier if you're not out to impress.'

Nicki laughed. 'Freddie is probably feeling the same.'

Ten minutes later, Anna and Nicki walked down the lane with Kate, waving her off like a lamb off to its first shearing before heading up the lane to their respective homes. Her steps faltered as she passed the ferry stop. What if he didn't turn up?

Kate chewed her lip, uncertain if this chap standing her up would feel like an escape or humiliation. Should she just head home now, ask Anna to send him apologies?

Her stomach let out a protest, and she grinned despite herself. Okay, perhaps she'd enjoy a nice meal first, *then* go home. Alone.

'Treat it like a business meeting,' she muttered as she passed the Lugger and crossed the bridge.

Pushing aside the whisper of Anna's parting words to *definitely* not do that, she turned her steps towards the harbour.

It was a quiet evening, being between school holidays, the lull before the next influx of visitors, and Kate passed few people as she walked along, thankful she'd opted for a more casual look, with wide-legged trousers that allowed for a chunkier heel.

A handful of stray tourists peered into the closed shop windows. Delicious aromas floated out of an air vent by Thai Dai's, and Kate's tummy rumbled in appreciation this time.

There were dogs taking their owners for a walk and a young couple in mud-caked boots outside the chippy when she turned for the waterfront.

How on earth did one recognise a 'Freddie' when that was the only information she had? The only Freddie she'd come across before now lived in Harrogate, had four legs and liked chasing rabbits.

Kate looked around. There were no noticeable men on their own. What if he hasn't come?

'So what?' she said softly, hefting her bag more firmly onto her shoulder. It'd be a relief. She could get a take-away and head straight home. To an empty house. And yet another lonely evening…

She fetched up outside the bistro. The tables by the windows were either empty or occupied by couples, as were the ones outside, other than a loud table of six at the far end. Kate checked her watch. She was early. Typical.

A strange sensation rippled through her, a sense of being watched, and she swung around. Dev stood by the harbour wall.

Chapter Twenty-Four

The One With a Little Madness

Suddenly short of breath, Kate raised a hesitant hand. There was no sign of Leigh and, with ten minutes to kill, she grabbed the moment, crossing the street to where he stood.

Willing the easy colour not to invade her skin, she noted Dev's swift sweep of her appearance, and she reciprocated, trying not to make her admiration too obvious.

'Hey.'

Kate smiled, despite her inner turmoil. 'Hey back. How's… things?'

Dev pulled a face. 'So-so. Theo's happy, that's the most important thing.'

Leigh must still be down. Kate glanced around, half expecting the vision of gorgeousness to materialise.

'I'm—' Dev cleared his throat as Kate turned back to meet his gaze. 'I'm on what I think the young folk call a date.'

'Oh!' So maybe Leigh *wasn't* still down… or was she babysitting Theo?

'I'd better go. Don't want to be late.' Dev gestured across the road.

Kate's gaze narrowed. 'At the bistro?' Hell, this was going to be fun, on yet another blind date with Dev across the room being all… *charming* with someone else.

'Yes, I—'

Kate's phone pinged and she glanced at it. Anna.

Oh, my God.

> Did we forget to tell you that Frederick is Dev's first name? xx

Her heart ricocheted off her ribs. She'd kill them both! Kate looked up at Dev in embarrassment. This was awkward.

'Do you mind telling me the name of your date?'

Dev took an understandable step backwards, a defensive look crossing his features, and Kate reached out a hand, then let it drop to her side.

'I'm not trying to intrude, it's just…' She huffed out a breath. 'Honestly. I'm on a date too. But I think it's with you.'

His eyes deepened in colour. 'I'm meeting someone called Rose. She's a friend of Oliver's… or so I was told.'

'Rose is my middle name.'

Dev turned his head to look out over the water, then faced Kate again. 'It would appear we've been set up.'

Kate pursed her lips. 'My friends, and my daughter, think I need to practice dating. Sadly for you, it seems you're the next victim.'

Expecting Dev to be unamused and take his leave as fast as dignity allowed, Kate was taken aback when he started to laugh.

He held her gaze for a second, then a hint of a smile tugged at his mouth. 'I thought you were looking particularly… nice. I like your hair like… that.' He gestured at the curls resting on her shoulders.

'Oh! Thank you, I think?' She glanced over the road at the bistro. 'Well, best head home. I need time to think about how to deal with a few people. Sorry, Dev.'

'Don't be. Look, it's seven. I don't suppose you fancy…'

You? Yep.

Kate waited.

'I mean.' He ran a hand around the back of his neck. 'People must eat.'

'It does seem pointless wasting the reservation.'

They set off across the street, Kate's mind racing. What on earth were they going to talk about? The only things they had in common were village fayres and failed marriages. As Nicki's parting shot had been 'don't spend all evening talking about kids!'… what else could they possibly find to discuss?

'This is madness, isn't it?'

A small sound escaped Dev. 'Probably. Just promise me, on this practice… date, you're not doing the role play thing, shake my hand and introduce yourself as if it was a meeting.'

No point in not being honest. 'It did cross my mind.'

To her surprise, Dev grinned at her, then gestured towards the door. 'Shall we?'

'Yes, please! I'm starving!'

They were led to a table near the full-length windows fronting onto the harbourside. A low wall concealed the water, but the tops of a mast were visible and the little passenger ferry could be seen as it bobbed along on its final run for the evening.

An awkward silence descended on them, masked by them both giving the menu far greater attention than was necessary, and Kate barely managed to conceal her relief when a smiling young girl came to tell them the specials and take their drinks order.

'So.'

'So,' Kate echoed as they were left alone again. 'How do we play this?'

Dev shrugged. 'Does it matter? It's not as if it was our choice.'

Ouch.

'Why did you accept the date?' There. Why not ask him?

His keen gaze held Kate's for a moment, until she stirred in her seat and looked away, nervously fiddling with her napkin, straightening cutlery that was perfectly in line.

'Grandy's on some sort of mission to move me on in life. I came out to forestall his nagging.'

Kate laughed, but then he continued.

'I was also asked to not let someone down.'

Touched, Kate was unsure how to respond, but thankfully, their drinks arrived, and they gave their food order, as Kate's mind swirled. It had to be either Anna or Nicki, but what had they meant?

'Cheers. Here's to being well and truly set up. By so-called friends, no less.'

There was a faint smile tugging at his mouth as he raised his glass, and Kate clinked hers against it, taking a sip of gin and wishing she'd asked for a double.

'What shall we talk about then? Not the fayre.'

Kate almost choked on her drink. 'Definitely not. And not the children,' she added, recalling Nicki's caution.

'I'm not sure that leaves us with much.'

'Are we also vetoing anything personal?' Kate knew she had so much curiosity about the Devonshires and their connections to Polkerran Point.

Dev's expression was speculative. 'It depends.'

'On?'

'How personal you want to get.'

'I don't want to pry into *your* life, if that's what you mean.' *Liar!* 'Nor do I want to talk about mine particularly.'

'Okay. Rules laid down. Off you go.'

'Would you mind telling me a bit more about your family roots – locally, that is? I'll admit to curiosity over your grandfather's connection to the cove. He seems very attached to it, but yet he doesn't live here.'

As they ate their way through their meal – fish and chips for Dev and a spicy pasta dish for Kate – Dev spoke matter-of-factly about his family and how they had been – and still were – extensive landowners in the region, to the apparent envy of the Tremaynes whose entire estate portfolio was tied up within the village. There had been a, mostly, friendly rivalry between Ryther's parents and those of the then incumbents of the manor house, until the Devonshires had outbid the Tremaynes on two prominent properties: Harbourwatch and Westerleigh.

'Wow.' Kate drained her glass and placed her napkin to her lips briefly before returning it to her lap. 'I've heard from Oliver how that rivalry, along with the desire to certainly reacquire the latter, has driven the present generation too. So did your grandfather live in one of the houses?'

Dev placed his knife and fork together. 'At first, then he went off to university and didn't return for many years, busy making a name for himself in the music industry. You know he was a bit of a giant in the music world some years ago? Has his own record label which he established in the eighties – the main rival to Stock, Aitken & Waterman?'

Kate nodded. 'Matt Locksley told me a little, because he and Gemma are writing songs for some of the label's artists.' Her brow furrowed. 'Surely Ryther isn't still working at… sorry. I was going to say his age, but he doesn't strike me as someone who wants to sit back.'

Dev let out a small grunt. 'No, he doesn't. Even these last few months, when he's not been well, he still insists on getting the low down on his companies. Secret Gem Records is the one he treasures most, though.'

'The locals said Harbourwatch fell into disrepair for many years. A few of them think you bought it and don't seem to realise it never left the family.'

Dev shifted in his seat, then began folding and refolding his napkin.

'I'm sorry. I didn't mean to touch on sensitive matters.'

He met Kate's anxious gaze. 'What people don't know for certain, they like to make up.'

They changed the subject, ordered coffee and it was Dev's turn to ask a few questions, but as Kate had banned any discussion of her life before Polkerran, there wasn't much to say beyond talking about the job and how much she loved The Lookout.

'Do you know Daniel and Lauren?'

'Not really. I haven't done much mixing in the village since we… *I* came back. That was Leigh's thing, getting involved.

I knew Oliver, obviously, because he was my tenant after I'd completed the renovations on the house, and we had a few dealings last year over property in the village.'

'And you allowed them to use your beautiful room for their wedding reception. That was a thoughtful gesture towards people you're not exactly calling friends.'

Was he *blushing*?

Concealing her smile, Kate waited, and her patience paid off.

'I like Oliver. I may not seem like a romantic, but when he explained how disappointed Anna was over the wedding becoming a local circus, it seemed the perfect solution. Especially as the house is where they first met each other.'

'You're a softie inside, really, aren't you?' Kate bit her lip, wondering if she was pushing it.

To her surprise, however, Dev laughed. 'That's what Grandy keeps telling me, though Lord knows why.'

He insisted on getting the bill, and when Kate offered to cover the tip, he refused.

'Isn't it right for the gentleman to settle when on a date?'

'I'd forgotten we were!'

Of course you had…

'Besides…' Flustered, Kate grasped for her bag as they stood, knocking the strap off her chair and it fell to the floor. 'Damn.'

She bent down to gather the contents, stuffing them unceremoniously into the bag.

'Thanks.' She took the pen Dev had retrieved from his hand, wishing the simple contact with his skin didn't impact on her own so fiercely.

Dev said nothing, holding the door ajar so she could emerge into the cool evening air, a crisp breeze blowing in off the river.

Kate fell into step with Dev as they left the quayside behind and made their way along the front, uncertain how to end a date which wasn't really a date. The man at her side must have been unsure too, because as they reached the harbour, he gestured over to the benches beside the wall.

'Sit for a minute?'

They settled on a bench facing across the harbour. Waves lapped gently against the stonework. Night had fallen and the water reflected the street lamps, glistening on the dark water, an owl hooting in the trees on the far side of the bay.

Kate was very aware of Dev at her side, his hand resting on the bench between them. The urge to cover it with her own was so strong, she had to clasp her own in her lap to prevent anything quite so stupid.

'Something happened. In Grandy's past.' Dev spoke softly.

'You don't have to tell me. I was prying a bit too much.'

'No. It's okay. I don't know the full story. I'm not sure anyone does. He and my father fell out over something. It seems to stem from when Dad was very young. They were estranged into adulthood for many years, but after my grandmother passed away, they made their way towards a reconciliation.'

'Do you know when this "something" happened?'

'Not really, except Grandy came to Polkerran for some reason in the seventies and took to spending a lot of time here. In Harbourwatch. The family still owned all the land, farms and the two houses in the cove, but the cottage was let out to a woman who taught in the village school. I've no idea who. Then, all of a sudden – according to my dad, who was a child at the time – Grandy stopped visiting Polkerran. Over time, Harbourwatch fell into disrepair from neglect and was boarded up.'

'What about the cottage?'

'The same lady lived there always, as far as I know.'

'Anna inherited Westerleigh from her aunt Meg, who was a teacher. It seems like she and your grandfather knew each other.'

She was prodding, but Dev didn't seem to mind.

'Interesting. Anyway, after my grandmother passed away, Grandy offered Harbourwatch to my dad, but he wasn't interested, so it was made over to me.'

'And you did it up.'

'It was a labour of love. It's such a beautiful house. I'd hoped to make a home there for Theo. For the family, but Leigh hated it here, took a post in the US, so we moved away. I thought once we were back in the UK, she might…' He lowered his head. 'She kept saying she'd had enough, left to take this job and that until last year, when she declared it was finally over and walked out, taking Theo with her.'

Dev's air of desolation as he pronounced these words was heartbreaking. Her heart going out to the man beside her, Kate got to her feet and held out her hand.

Dev stared at it, then up at Kate.

'Come on.'

He placed his hand in hers and she tried to suppress a sudden tremor as it shot through her body. Senses on high alert, she summoned a bright smile.

'Let's call at the Lugger for a nightcap. At least then we've fulfilled our practice date duties.'

As they headed out of the pub an hour later, Dev paused on the threshold and Kate almost ran into his back.

'Look,' he said, turning around. He hesitated, shoving his hands in his pockets. 'I'm sorry, Kate. I haven't been entirely honest with you.'

Her mind fizzing with all the things they'd talked about, Kate's senses were on high alert. What the hell did he mean?

'I knew you were Rose.'

Kate's lips parted but no words came to help her as she took in the implication.

'Oliver doesn't like subterfuge,' Dev explained. 'And nor do I.'

He leaned down and pressed a kiss to her cheek, and then he was gone, soon shrouded by the darkness outside the reach of the lamps on the bridge, and Kate fell back against the wall of the pub, a hand to her warm face.

Well, that was unexpected…

Chapter Twenty-Five

The One Where the Tide is High

Kate remained in a muddle of delighted confusion the following morning. It was a long time since she'd enjoyed a man's company in a way that left her keen for more.

With a late start pending, she headed down the hill, intent on calling in at Westerleigh on her way, but as she neared the end of the lane, she spotted a familiar figure.

'Hey, Matt!' Kate waved. 'No Gemma today?'

He waited for her to reach him. 'No, I've left her battling with some lyrics. I'm on my way to Anna's to sort out a birthday cake for Gem.'

Kate fell into step beside him.

'Oh, when's her birthday?'

'Next month. I've never seen a grown adult so excited.' He paused, then added, 'Except Gemma at Christmas.'

Kate laughed, then raised the envelope she held. 'I'm just dropping off more fayre leaflets for the B&B.'

'How's it going?' Matt held open the gate for Kate to walk through.

She huffed a breath. 'Hard to say, to be honest. But – as my old boss used to tell me – it is what it is!'

'Que sera, sera?' Matt essayed as they filed down the side of Westerleigh Cottage.

'Yep. A bit like that. I've had to learn to roll with the punches since I took it on.'

It was obvious the usual proceedings were in place at Westerleigh, with the locals around the table in the window, Oliver making himself a coffee at the machine and Anna preparing a meal at the island.

'Morning!' Anna called, putting aside her rolling pin and wiping floury hands on her apron as Matt went over to drop a kiss on her cheek, then walked up to Oliver and pretended to do the same, only to have his brother-in-law swat him away before clapping him affectionately on the back.

'Just the person,' Oliver said. 'Got time for a caffeine fix?'

Anna rolled her eyes at Kate, who had come to join her at the island.

'Shall I pop these in the dining room?' She held up the envelope, but Anna shook her head.

'I've only one room in use at the moment, so I'm sending them out to my mailing list. Can you put them on the desk in the study?'

Kate did as she was bid, but as she placed the envelope on the old-fashioned blotter, she noticed the photos propped up against one of the drawers in the antique wooden desk – one of Meg and the other of the handsome man.

Picking up the latter, she studied it in more detail. It was from the tea caddy that Anna had been looking through a few months ago, and Kate was more certain than ever this was a younger Ryther.

There was nothing on the back in this instance, but his resemblance to Dev was marked, and Kate suspected Ryther had been a similar age when it was taken. It had the look of a photo that had been held many a time, judging by its condition.

Placing it back on the desk, Kate returned to the main room, accompanied once again by the memory of those precious hours with Dev after their meal and the feelings they incited.

'Are you okay?' Anna's concern was evident as she fetched up beside her.

'It's nothing.' *You wish*. 'Although I think I need to have words with you and Nicki.' Anna just laughed, and Kate shook her head. 'I'll go and catch up with everyone.'

She could see Matt and Oliver, each clutching a cup of coffee as they stood, deep in discussion, at the railings overlooking the gardens and the water, which was as smooth as glass this morning.

'Morning, everyone,' Kate chimed as she took a seat beside Phoenix. 'How are we?'

'Well now.' Mrs Lovelace eyed her in her usual beady fashion before a warm smile broke over her wizened features. 'Don't you look a proper maid jus' now? Be you going on another of they dates?'

Kate blinked and Nicki winked at her across the table. 'Word soon gets around.'

'About what?' Kate looked around at the avidly curious faces, for once more interested in her than how full their cups were.

'You and young Mr Devonshire, back along,' Mrs Clegg added, slapping Old Patrick's hand as it crept towards the half-eaten shortbread on her plate.

Kate sent Nicki an imploring look.

Nicki spoke gently to the lady at her side. 'Kate and Dev are both working hard on the fayre, as you know. They were simply... having a meal, weren't you?'

'Yes,' Kate said firmly. It didn't matter what they called it. The evening had been enough for her to accept the supposed juvenile crush on the man was in danger of becoming much more.

'Of course you were,' Jean said smugly.

'As it happens,' Kate pressed on. 'We need to discuss the performers. Patrick, are you okay with taking the opening slot, and can you let me know what you'll be singing? It's for the schedule on the day, which we want to put up on socials and on a board by the pergola.'

Old Patrick, who'd managed to successfully steal the remainder of Mrs Clegg's shortbread and was busy munching on it, brushed crumbs from his mouth and mumbled, 'Aye.'

As this was all she was likely to get right now, Kate gave up, letting the general chat wash over her as her gaze – despite a sound inner talking-to – drifted out of the window and over to Harbourwatch. From her seated position, she could only see the upper floors, rooftops and chimneys, but it didn't stop her wondering what Dev was doing today.

A faint smile touched her lips.

'He's coming for dinner tonight.' Anna spoke softly in Kate's ear as she leaned over her to place some fresh cakes on the table. 'Care to join us?'

Kate sent a frantic look around the table, and although Jean had, she was certain, just averted her gaze, amusement tugging at her mouth, Nicki was less subtle and gave yet another exaggerated wink.

'Oh, I... no, sorry. I can't.' Flustered, Kate got up and followed Anna back to the island.

'Can't? Or won't?' Anna sent her a knowing look and Kate tried to suppress the frisson of anticipation.

She was saved from answering by the return of Matt and Oliver, the latter placing their cups in the dishwasher, the former tugging his phone from his pocket.

'Everything all right?' Anna asked, glancing over at her husband, who was likewise studying his phone screen.

'Yes. We've finally secured the sale. Tremayne never clicked.'

'That's fantastic!' Anna's eyes shone with pride, and she hugged her brother. 'Thank you for doing that.'

Matt sent Kate a sheepish look. 'Not sure I'd be up for it again. Subterfuge isn't my artifice of choice.'

'Is this the alms-houses project?' Kate had addressed Matt, but it was Oliver who answered as he joined them.

'Yes. Thanks to Matt operating from his London address *and* having a different surname to Anna's maiden name, it meant the deal could be done without the connection being discovered. Tremayne has been bragging about sealing the sale to a celebrity, but isn't going to be too happy when he finds out the truth.'

Anna looked up from trimming the edge of the pie she was making. 'Can he do anything about it?'

'Not now. It's a done deal. Signed, sealed and paid for.' Matt held his hand out and Oliver shook it.

'Matt's playing a blinder today. He's just put me in touch with someone who can help with the book research.'

It was true, Oliver did look far less stressed than he had of late, and Kate was pleased to see its effect on Anna, who reached up to kiss him.

'Then we can celebrate this evening. Can you join us, Matt? You and Gemma?'

'Would love to, it's likely to be much more appetising than anything we're likely to conjure up at home.'

'Dev and Kate will be here,' Anna added, ignoring Kate's frantic gesturing.

'Excellent.' Matt turned to Oliver. 'Was Bella any help?'

Oliver raised his phone. 'She came straight back. Sounds hopeful. We're talking on Monday.'

There was commotion over by the table as everyone began to gather their belongings and get to their feet, and with a swift look at his wife, Oliver scarpered back to his den.

Matt turned back to Anna. 'I came to show you my latest results.'

'Oh!' Anna picked up the finished pie. 'Let me just get this in.'

Matt sent Kate a slightly embarrassed look. 'I'm trying to make up for lost years, doing an A level online.'

'Good for you,' Kate said, still too caught up in how she could wriggle out of the dinner invite and what she could wear when she changed her mind later.

As she said goodbye to Anna, already distracted by what Matt was showing her on his phone, and followed the locals out of the door, she refused to listen to the voice telling her she was only making things worse.

Of course she wasn't. Dev had no idea she liked him.

Like that.

Did he?

The evening at Westerleigh passed without incident, if you ignored Kate's jitters getting the best of her and her clumsiness coming to the fore, dropping not only her dinner fork but later her dessert spoon on the floor, spilling the dregs of her wine when she knocked over her glass and stumbling over her own feet in her hurry to help Anna in the kitchen.

'Did you have to seat me opposite him?' she'd hissed at her so-called friend as they made coffee.

Anna had merely sent her a secretive smile, but there was a distraction when Mrs Clegg phoned in a blind panic. She was outside the Spar but she couldn't get her mobility scooter to start and how was she to get home without her sticks and carrying her late-night shopping?

Oliver didn't need asking, heading out the door to walk down into the village to help. Once they'd raised a toast to Matt for doing the impossible, it was time for him and Gemma to leave to catch the high tide before it turned – Rivermills was only accessible by boat – and, ignoring Anna's blatant satisfaction, Kate left with Dev on her heels, hoping she could at least manage it to where the lane from The Lookout met the one into the village without stepping on either her or Dev's toes.

'I'll walk you back up the hill. It's growing dark.'

Kate's tummy quivered in anticipation, but before she could do anything so stupid as to ask him in for a nightcap, common sense prevailed.

'There's no need, but thank you.' They'd already reached the aforementioned junction, and paused beside a lamppost just flickering into action. 'I love these long, lighter evenings, don't you?'

Dev faced towards where the sea entered the cove, and Kate covertly admired his profile, then swiftly moved her gaze to the water as his head turned.

'When I'm here, I almost don't care what season it is.' Dev's voice was low, throbbing with unexplained emotion, and Kate edged a little nearer.

'Has the cove worked its magic, then? I've heard of so many people now who came here for all sorts of reasons and stayed.' Kate huffed lightly. 'Anna thinks I'm next in line.'

I'd stay for you, Dev, her mind whispered, but she shook the thought away.

Dev, however, swung around and leaned against the low stone wall bordering the lane. There was a gap in the run of water-facing cottages there, hence being able to view the sea beyond the cove's protective arms of land. In an attempt not to get lost in Dev's grey-blue gaze, Kate forced her own to drift aside, only to land upon the lighthouse on the stretch of rocks beyond the tidal beach.

'I've been meaning to say, there are several family activity days coming up at the hotel over the summer holidays. I wondered if Theo might enjoy some of them? I'd be happy to go with him if they clash with your work…' Kate's gaze remained on the lighthouse, lost in the memories of their day out. Then, she added quickly, 'But I know you love to do things with him as much as you can. I'm not trying to intrude or anything, I promise.'

There was no reply, and Kate's shoulders stiffened in embarrassment. Had she let the freedom with which they'd chatted on their so-called date lead her into a familiarity Dev wasn't up for in his present complicated circumstances?

'I'm sorry. I shouldn't have suggested it. I—'

'No. I'm the one who should apologise. It's not you or the lovely suggestion.' Dev's expression was harder to read as the light continued to fade from the evening, but Kate's eyes hungrily devoured it as he shrugged.

'I'm not used to… there's seems to be no hidden agenda with you, and I…'

He sounded as though he was testing the words, only half believing them, and Kate held her tongue, hoping for more.

'I like it… you… I mean, your company, Kate. Somehow, you help me feel differently about… things.'

'Does it help if I say ditto? About the company,' she added hastily.

Dev didn't speak again for a moment, but then the edges of his mouth curved, and he gave a short nod.

'Look, I'd best go. Stella's looking after Theo and I promised I wouldn't be late back.'

He headed along the lane towards the bridge, and Kate held back, watching his tall form disappear into the falling darkness before turning her steps for home, her mind a jumble of hopes and dreams.

Chapter Twenty-Six

The One Where Someone's Reunited

Anna had suggested they go to the tidal beach on Saturday – something she'd also roped Nicki and her boys into, as Hamish had done something to his back when unloading his catch and planned to go up to the urgent treatment centre in Port Wenneth – and Kate kicked off the covers and headed for the shower, mulling over what to wear.

'You're going to a beach, idiot,' she muttered as she padded across the room.

Directly below the house of the man you can't stop thinking about… who likes your company.

'Who's also in relationship hell. The last thing I want is to make it worse for him,' Kate scolded as she shed her dressing gown, turning the shower to cold.

To emphasise the point, she began singing the chorus to 'I'm gonna wash that man right outa my hair'. It was from her mum's favourite musical and although not entirely apt, it helped.

The warm breeze flowing in from the window steered Kate towards her favourite soft shorts and a finely layered strappy top, and soon she was outside the gate to Nicki's cottage, pleased with the light tan already building on her limbs and enjoying the glimpse of the glimmering water, dancing in the bright sunlight as though someone had cast a handful of stars over it.

There was a steady flow of pleasure craft moving in rhythm across the undulating surface of the harbour, happy voices floating across the balmy air and, being the weekend, families with young children were already making their way along the lane towards the bridge, carrying buckets and spades, towels and bags of sustenance.

'It's the calm before the storm,' Nicki said sagely as she stuffed a towel into the bag on the kitchen table.

'We don't like to knock it, mind,' Hamish added. 'Those emmets, they want to come, and we need them, but there's no denying we're glad to see the end of 'em when they head back up country in the autumn.'

Kate laughed, lifting the cool box and adding it to the laden trolley. 'Right, let's go. Judging by the bouncing heads outside, there's a bit of impatience to get there.'

Pulling the trolley down the lane, Kate's gaze – yet again – fixed on Harbourwatch, perched on its sheer cliffs across the water. Was Dev at home? It had been more clear than ever last night how happy he was to have Theo living at Harbourwatch, but she could sense the undercurrents, as though he half expected Leigh to turn up. Would she stay this time, or snatch his son away again?

'Hey, Kate!'

Rousing herself, Kate speeded up, aware the little passenger ferry had docked on the jetty, and she stepped aboard as Hamish waved them off before heading to collect their car from its parking space.

Mollie, Liam and Jason sat together, giggling about something or other, and Kate exchanged a look with Nicki.

'Plotting some mischief, no doubt.'

As they approached the beach, Kate forced herself not to peer through the open gates into Harbourwatch, hidden mostly behind its high walls, chattering inanely to Nicki about nothing in particular and oblivious to her friend's amused glance.

'There's Anna.'

They steered the trolley down the ramp onto the firm sand, heading to the rocks bordering the right-hand side of the secluded cove.

'Can we have an ice cream?' Jason's gaze was fixed on a family as they passed, all enjoying some of the delicious wares from the small cafe.

'In a minute,' Nicki warned. 'Let's get sorted first.'

Several families had settled in for a long stay, with little pop-up tents, rugs spread out with picnic fare and various beach toys scattered around.

'It'll be rammed in a few weeks' time,' Anna said, as they laid out their own towels to temporarily claim their bit of beach, unloading the cool box and two bags for life stuffed with buckets, spades and inflatables.

Having already donned their swimwear under their shorts and T-shirts, Liam and Jason whipped them off and tossed them at Nicki, who caught them, laughing.

'Be careful, boys! Put your beach shoes on, please, before you go into the water.'

Mollie stripped off too, and they headed down to where the shallow, gentle waves lapped the wet sand, and were soon kicking water at each other.

Anna had also brought a cool box along and she dug into it, handing around chilled homemade lemonade and shortbread, and the three of them sat on the towels, leaning against the smooth rocks behind them.

Kate adjusted her position a little to avoid a protrusion of rock, but found by doing so, she was looking straight up at Harbourwatch, whose upper floors and rooftops were just visible in their embrace of tall trees.

'Wondering where a certain person is, are we?' Nicki nudged Kate's arm.

'I was thinking about Theo, actually,' she responded primly.

Anna chuckled, stretching out her long legs. 'Of course you were.'

'I was simply mulling on how lovely it must be as a child to grow up somewhere like this. Idyllic.' She sent a wry smile towards the others. 'Until teenage, perhaps.'

'My mum thought I was mad, giving everything up to move here and marry a fisherman. Mind you, I was only in my early twenties. She probably thought I hadn't shopped around enough.' Nicki gave a splutter of laughter. 'Trouble is, there weren't that many good shops where I lived ten years ago and there are even less now.'

Kate rolled up a shawl and lay her head on it, enjoying the strength of the sun on her bare limbs, and bent her legs to dig her toes into the soft sand.

'What was your upbringing like, Kate?'

Staring up at the sky, which was cloudless today, Kate mulled on life back at home.

'I have lovely but slightly pushy parents.' She turned her head to the side, then met Anna's gaze where she sat on the other side of Nicki. 'Oh, God, Anna. I'm sorry. We're so thoughtless, chuntering on here negatively about parents.'

A small smile touched Anna's lips as she shook her head. 'You don't have to worry about me. My whole perspective has changed in recent years, firstly from having Oliver in my life, then discovering my brother. And now...' She hesitated, then rested a hand on her tummy, and Nicki sat forward with an audible gasp as Kate scrabbled upright.

'You're not!' she exclaimed in delight, and as happiness flooded Anna's face and a tear slid down her cheek, she almost crawled over Nicki's legs to hug her friend.

'I'm so happy for you!'

Nicki wrapped her arms around them both as best she could for someone so petite. 'Me too!'

With a watery giggle, Anna met their avid expressions as they released her.

'It's twins.'

'Wow!' Nicki's eyes fastened on Anna's middle.

'In at the deep end for Oliver, then,' Kate added as she crawled back to her towel.

'Let's raise our lemonades to the Babies Seymour!'

Kate and Nicki bombarded Anna with questions, who admitted she'd been struggling with tiredness – hence her only having one room in use at the B&B recently. She was four months along, didn't yet know the genders and the babies were due in December.

'The perfect little Christmas gifts,' Kate said mistily.

Anna, however, rolled her eyes as she dug into the cool box for more refreshments. 'Gemma is in her element. Matt's warned me she'll probably buy the babies little elf costumes.' She smiled wistfully. 'If we can only get some help for Oliver, things will be perfect.'

'I thought Matt had found someone?'

'She's a bit reluctant to commit to spending six months here. Maybe some people just don't like Cornwall.'

They all exchanged a look, then burst out laughing, but conversation was at an end for a while, as the boys and Mollie returned begging for treats. Mollie took some cash from Kate and led Liam and Jason over to get ice creams, which they tucked into with relish, perched on a flat bed of rock nearby.

The boys were noisily debating whether spending some of their pocket money on a fishing net or a crabbing line would deliver the best results, with Mollie acting as umpire, as the ladies resumed their conversation from earlier.

'So how did you meet Hugo? Is it indelicate to ask?' Nicki squinted over at Kate, who shrugged. Funny how any mention of him in recent months left her… not so much cold, as numb.

'He was presented to me. Or rather, my parents shoved me at him. They wanted me to go to St Andrew's, you know?'

'Ooh, were you trying to catch a prince?' Nicki teased.

'My mum hoped so. Imagine, me with my lower-middle roots. I knew for a fact I'd be way out of my comfort zone, and I can't tell you how happy I am the other Kate got him.'

'So where did you study?'

Kate leaned back against the rock again, conscious of its warmth seeping through the sheer fabric of her top.

'Bath. I didn't meet anyone special, but I headed home afterwards and Dad – who'd recently joined the local golf club – brought Hugo home one day.' She rolled her eyes at Nicki and Anna. 'He was everything they considered a suitable match – Oxford educated, career-focused and loaded. I was too naïve to see beyond the idea of falling in love. Hugo seemed more than happy, but I don't think my parents ever knew he for ever derided the inferiority of my upbringing and lack of valuable connections.'

'Like Mr Darcy, but without the character improvement,' Anna intoned.

Mollie, who'd – unbeknownst to the ladies – come over to collect a book from her bag, interrupted them.

'Hey,' she said plaintively, holding aloft a battered copy of *Pride & Prejudice*. 'Anna only lent me this last week. No spoilers, please.'

Exchanging amused looks, the ladies changed the subject and, Kate reflected, as Nicki got up to join her boys in the water and Anna lay down to close her eyes, that although she may have been an idiot to marry Hugo in the first place, she wouldn't change things, even if she could. She had Mollie as compensation for the loveless, often miserable marriage, and she had hope. Hope that there was another future out there, somewhere.

At Harbourwatch, she refused to look.

–

The hot weather continued into July and Kate continued to enjoy the walk to the hotel. As she crossed the bridge on a Thursday lunch time – having a later start due to needing to work the evening – she could see the build-up of visitors steadily increasing.

She took a short cut, then spotted Mrs Lovelace outside her cottage and diverted to say hello.

'Everything okay, Mrs L?' Kate smiled at the elderly lady. 'Is that Cleggie's?' She pointed to the mobility scooter parked by the gate.

'Nay, my lovely,' Mrs Lovelace beamed up at her, a hand resting on the nifty little basket attached to the front. 'Aways wanted one, so I treated m'self.'

'Of course. Well, drive carefully. These hills are steep.'

By the time she reached the hotel, Kate heeded her own words. Thankfully, she'd learned to walk in her Converse trainers and don her more favoured heels once at work.

It was a busy afternoon, especially as it was also prime wedding season, with a couple of weekends coming up when the whole hotel would operate as a private hire venue for two such events.

Studying the online schedule of the one coming up soon, she made a few notes, then looked up in relief at the interruption as Nicki's head peered around the door.

'Got time for a cuppa? I've just finished.'

Kate glanced at her phone. Three o'clock. It was going to be a long evening. 'Always.'

They settled in a shaded area of the large terrace, which was busy with people indulging in afternoon tea or early cocktails.

A heat haze hovered over the sea where it met the bay, shimmering like glass, and the sun shone from a rich blue sky.

'Oh, look. There's Oliver and Matt.'

Kate turned to follow the direction of Nicki's gaze, to see the two men in conversation with a woman whose back was to them.

Nicki sipped her tea. 'Gosh, I needed this.' She kicked off her sandals and wriggled her toes. 'If town wasn't so rammed, I'd go down to the harbour and dip my toes.'

Kate laughed. 'You'll have to watch they don't catch you. No swimming allowed, remember?'

Nicki chuckled. 'Jem's a bit jobs-worth, isn't he?' Then, her eyes widened. 'Oh my God!'

'What?' Kate frowned. 'Did you forget something?'

Nicki, however, had leapt to her feet and shot across the terrace.

Oliver, Matt and their companion were heading across the patio towards the doors into the hotel, but Nicki had flown towards the woman, arms outstretched.

'Bella!' She exclaimed, and the woman did a double-take, then hugged Nicki as she all but threw herself at her.

'Hey! I forgot you lived down this way now.'

'Kate, come here.'

Nicki beckoned her over. 'This is my cousin Ellie's mate, we met on our post-graduation holiday all those years ago.'

'Hi, I'm Bella. I used to tutor Matt when he was trying his hand at a History A Level last year.'

Kate shook hands with the striking woman. She had pale gold hair, flowing over her tanned shoulders, a prominent nose and the most startling pair of amber, almost hawk-like eyes, which Kate felt didn't miss a trick.

Nicki nudged Bella's arm. 'So, what *are* you doing here?'

'Matt put me in touch with Oliver. I'm going to be his research assistant for the next six months.'

'Fabulous.' Nicki's eyes danced with delight. 'We'll have to get Ellie down too and have a proper reunion.'

Bella sent Oliver an apologetic look. 'I'll be here to work, Nicki, not party like the last time.' A shadow crossed her face, but it was gone so fast, Kate wasn't sure if she'd imagined it.

'But you'll be living here? Will you stay at the B&B?'

'Oliver has one of his cottages free from next month, so I'll be taking that.'

With that, the three of them left, and Kate parted with Nicki at the door to the salon and returned to her office.

She tried to focus on work, making phone calls to double-check delivery times for the cake, balloon displays and flowers, and chasing the champagne order. Then, Kate turned her attention to the impending evening, but after a few moments, she pushed back in her chair and went over to look out of the window.

Kate's mind swiftly returned, as it so often did throughout the day, to Dev. Surrounded as she was with people getting hitched, people having babies, people celebrating the big moments in life, it was hard not to reflect on both their present situations. Did Dev have regrets? He was hard to read, despite his obvious thawing.

She had a suspicion he wasn't necessarily in love with his almost-ex-wife any more, but that he would do anything – quite rightly – for Theo's happiness, even if meant compromising his own.

As this not only emphasised Dev's goodness over Hugo – and her ex-husband's dismissive attitude towards their daughter – but also brought back the weight of culpability Kate still struggled with at times, she hugged her arms across her middle, shivering despite the pleasant weather.

Mollie's current happiness must surely mean she'd done the right thing?

'Well, it's too late now,' Kate admonished softly, turning away from the view and the temptation to go for a long walk.

Kate closed the lid of her laptop with a snap.

That should curb any urge to check the livestream at the beach. Dev had enough on his plate, without being served the added complication of an anonymous stalker.

Chapter Twenty-Seven

The One Where Kate Realises Why They Call it the Blues

The manic weekend flew by, and Kate was grateful for a day off on the Monday to recharge. After a light lunch at the kitchen island, she chased up some loose ends in relation to the supply of electrical equipment for the fayre's performance stand, then put her laptop aside.

It was a beautiful, if slightly cool, day but a walk beckoned. She fed Podge, who had just stirred from dozing on the sofa, then donned a light jacket, pocketed her phone and headed out across the terrace to the gate leading on to the coastal path.

Checking her watch, Kate eyed the steps down to the sands below The Lookout. It would be hours before Mollie came home, as she was having tea with her 'girlie bestie' after school and then heading down to youth club.

Turning on her heel, Kate followed the path back towards Polkerran, down to the bridge and then picked up the lane that would take her upriver to Polwelyn. It would make a change from walking to the lighthouse.

It's also not taking you past Harbourwatch, or the tidal beach...

'Quite right,' she muttered, striding along with her hands in her pockets, pleased with her will power and oblivious to the contrariness of her thoughts, which had no respect for her intentions.

Since the date-that-wasn't-a-date with Dev, she hadn't been able to get him out of her mind... With a self-deprecating laugh, she left the lane behind and clambered over a stile into a field bordered by a grassy path.

Who was she trying to kid? She hadn't exactly tried. She was attracted to him. Big time. Getting to know the man behind the reticent demeanour had been like peeling back layers, yet the more she discovered, the deeper she wanted to dig.

Foolish indulgence, she cautioned silently as the path descended downhill into the woodland.

As soon as she crossed the wooden bridge near the gate to Rivermills House, nestled on its tidal creek, and resumed the route to Polwelyn, however, her thoughts immediately reverted to Dev.

What was it that she found so... *endearing* about him? Everything about that man drew her towards him. She didn't just love how Dev looked, she *liked* him, wanted to spend time in his company.

He's a kind man; a generous one, her mind whispered, not for the first time. *And not afraid for the world to see his affection for his child.*

But still the questions remained over Dev's intentions with regard to Leigh. Was he truly going to let her call all the shots, and, if he did, how likely was it she might change her mind again and come back for good?

Her mood immediately nose-diving, Kate blew out a frustrated breath as she emerged from the path onto a tarmacked lane, and soon she was at the bottom of the hill by the waterside.

A breeze whipped through a gap in the high bank opposite, beyond which the river flowed down to Polkerran, and Kate tucked a stray strand of hair behind her ear.

'Am I interrupting?'

With a start, Kate swung around.

'I thought you were on the phone for a minute.' Dev gestured at Kate's hand as she lowered it. 'Then realised it must be invisible.'

'Oh!' Kate stammered, unsure where to look. 'Hi, no. I was... well...' She stopped, meeting Dev's understandably confused look with a rueful smile. 'Miles away. As you can probably tell.'

'I shouldn't have disturbed you. Come, Bayley.' He whistled and the lab lifted his nose out of the hole he currently inspected and trotted obediently to Dev's side, where he received a rub of the ears for doing so.

Come on, Kate, seize the day! You did everything you could to avoid this, Fate must have other plans!

'No! No, it's fine. Really. I came for a walk to try to think through a few things, but to be honest, I'm done with it. The thinking.' She gestured back up the hill. 'I don't suppose you're ready to walk back?'

Kate all but held her breath. If he rebuffed her, she'd feel a right idiot, but she desperately needed some company – *adult* company.

'I'm ready.'

The tide was on its way back in as they walked back along the front to regain the lane up to the coast path. Some of the small boats that had been lying almost on their sides were gradually perking up as the water lapped around their hulls and slowly roused them from their sandy beds.

Once on the path, they walked out of necessity in single file, Bayley charging ahead, but where the path broadened, they fell into step side by side.

Kate, having wracked her brain for an easy topic and desperate to avoid any awkward silences, spoke up.

'Are you happy the school holidays are almost here?'

'Yes. Theo has quite a few plans.'

'So has Mollie. How will it mesh with your work?'

'I do most of it from home, and Theo can come with me when I call on the various farms. There are always fencing repairs to oversee, tree surveys to organise, and so on. He loves being in the country, meeting the animals. The farmers know him now and let him help with feeds and the odd bit of digging.'

'It sounds idyllic. I sometimes wonder if I made a mistake, settling for office work and being stuck inside all the time.' She laughed. 'I had a date recently, and he's set up a glamping business. It sounded so much fun, a real mix of admin and the outdoors.'

She glanced at Dev as they made their way along the root-strewn path, but the air of melancholy she'd noticed on him that day he'd been in the restaurant had returned.

Before she could speculate further, however, the path became single file again, and Dev led the way down the slope beside the isolated tidal inlet. They paused on the little wooden bridge over the tumbling stream which fed into the creek.

'That's where Matt and Gemma live, isn't it?' Kate pointed to the whitewashed building on the right-hand bank. There were two kittens curled up in a wooden box lined with a blanket by the picnic table, and chickens could be heard clucking somewhere behind the building.

'I could do with popping over to see if Matt's home.'

'Oh. I'll leave you to it.' Disappointed, Kate stepped down from the bridge and turned for the steep hill rising up to the right through the woods, but a hand landed on her arm.

'Can you wait a minute? I won't be long.'

Kate smiled, relieved. 'Yes, of course.'

She was about to return to the bridge, but then footsteps came towards them and Gemma appeared at the wooden gate proclaiming the property 'private'.

'Hey! Come on in! I've just put the kettle on.'

'Is Matt home?'

'In the studio but he won't mind being disturbed. I think he's had enough of it for today.'

Gemma led Kate into the house as Dev made his way across the lawn.

'Wow, this is lovely!'

They'd entered a large room with white-painted stone walls and a vaulted ceiling, half of which was a homely-looking sitting room with squashy leather sofas, soft throws and a vast log burner in an inglenook fireplace. Windows, one of which was circular, drew light into the room, which glowed with welcome. The other half was a state-of-the-art kitchen with every conceivable appliance.

'Wasted on me,' Gemma laughed as she made tea. 'Matt's taken control of the cooking. I just deal with cleaning up the aftermath.'

Kate followed her out into an equally light-filled conservatory with floor-to-ceiling windows and a large table surrounded by a dozen chairs.

'It feels as though you're right in the middle of the creek.' Kate admired the outlook as she took a seat.

'I know.' Gemma beamed. 'I love it so much.'

They chatted about life in Polkerran, the upcoming fayre and how Mrs Lovelace was managing with her scooter.

'I saw one parked outside the bookshop yesterday,' Kate mused. 'I assumed it was Mrs Clegg's as it had crochet tassles on the handles. Good to see Oliver managed to get it going again.'

Gemma chuckled. 'Didn't you hear? He arrived at the Spar, cavalry to the rescue, only to quickly establish there was nothing wrong with the battery. The key wouldn't turn because she was sitting on someone else's. She'd forgotten hers was outside the Three Fishes.'

'Oh no! How funny. And how's your auntie Dee coping with hers?'

'She'll be getting a speeding ticket if she's not careful.'

With a laugh, Kate picked up her mug. 'Matt says you're looking forward to your birthday.'

Eyes sparkling, Gemma nodded enthusiastically. 'We're going to have a barbecue here. It's a Sunday. You and Mollie must come. It'll just be us, Anna and Oliver, Dev and Theo. It's when Nicki and Hamish are away with the boys, though, so sadly they'll miss it.'

'What about your aunts?'

'Auntie Dee's not so agile these days at getting in and out of a small boat, so Auntie Jay is hosting an afternoon tea for us the day before.'

'How lovely.'

By the time they'd finished their tea, Dev and Matt had emerged from the studio and when Gemma led Kate out onto the decking from the conservatory, they were stood by the water, which was steadily filling the creek.

She and Dev resumed their walk back to Polkerran, but conversation was impossible on the steep climb up through the woods, apart from a mumbled 'thank you' when Kate stumbled over a protruding root, emitting a loud yelp which immediately had Dev spinning around and helping her up.

She didn't like to tell him she'd been too busy fastening her eyes on his back to look where she was putting her feet and was too out of breath at the top of the slope to utter a single word.

They talked about the fayre as they rejoined the lane back to the cove, though, and apart from still needing Matt to visit the manor for a site assessment, and then to come and look at her proposed layout, it seemed everything was ready to roll.

By the time they reached the bridge over the river, the village school was churning out its young charges, and Dev said a hurried goodbye to go and meet Theo, but Kate lingered, leaning on the parapet as he strode along the waterfront, then turned down the lane to the school.

She stared out across the water as it flowed beneath the bridge into the bay, her mind a jumble of delight at having been in Dev's company once more and sadness it couldn't continue indefinitely.

Kate started at the noise emanating from the harbour and looked over. The crab boat had come in and plastic crates clattered as they skidded across the stones into the waiting hands of those loading them onto vans to ferry them to the nearest fish market.

Heading back along the lane skirting the quieter side of the harbour, Kate studied the skies, veiled today in a thin layer of pale grey cloud, an ethereal light bathing the rippling waters outside the bay's entrance, and her eyes drifted from the small lighthouse perched on the rocks stretching out to sea, and then to the small beach just visible beneath the rocks.

Harbourwatch brooded above them, silent and watchful, and Kate sighed as she continued on her way, head bowed now.

Why was it she wished she was heading home with Dev and Theo and not returning yet again to an empty, lonely house?

Chapter Twenty-Eight

The One Where Kate is Walking on the Moon

The rest of the school term sped by, with sports days and awards ceremonies, culminating in a lively performance of Annie in the village hall, featuring many of the pupils from Polkerran's school, but directed, choreographed and produced by those studying drama at Mollie's school in Fowey.

Kate barely saw Dev other than in passing, and their email and message exchanges had dwindled to almost non-existent. With the fayre the only mutual connection, she had no excuse to contact him, especially as there was little left to do, but how she longed to simply hear his voice.

Phoenix and her fellow artists from the studio had come up with a fabulous art trail for the children around the cove, and Matt had been up to Tremayne Manor to assess the cabling needs for the musical performances. Meanwhile, Bella had moved into her cottage and was busy researching specific aspects of history for Oliver's book.

Pleasure craft jostled for space on the temporary pontoons and the village was crammed with visitors as every holiday let and hotel room filled with those bent on seaside pleasures. The beach below Harbourside heaved from dawn until dusk on the warmer days – regardless of whether the sun showed itself – and Kate scanned the crowds in vain but saw no sign of Dev or Theo.

Berating her heart for finally caving in, Kate didn't know how to handle the conflicting emotions. Never had she felt like this in all her life. The attraction she'd had to Hugo all those years ago paled into insignificance. Dev was becoming all she could think of; yet he was entirely out of reach.

Frustrated and desperate for distraction, Kate took Mollie away for their week in Greece, where they soaked up the sun as she pretended to read book after book, lounging by the pool but imagining the lapping of water to be that of Polkerran harbour.

The distance solved nothing. Kate missed Dev so much it hurt, and knowing there was no chance of a sighting, she'd taken to opening her laptop as soon as she woke, lying on her side in the vast bed, a warm breeze stirring the voile panel covering the window, and staring at the livestream, willing him to take Bayley for his early morning walk.

When he did, she watched him throwing a stick into the waves for Bayley to fetch. Then he'd stand, hands shoved in his pockets, staring out to sea. What was he thinking? Did he – at any moment – ever wonder about Kate? The pain would always intensify as he returned up the beach, the happy dog at his heels, carrying the stick proudly, and tears would prick her eyes.

Worse, however, were those mornings when Dev didn't appear – she assumed due to the unpredictable weather, which was typical of a British summer, being fair one day and foul the next. Kate did her best, though, to give Mollie a great holiday, and they enjoyed some fun boat trips, ending the week with three days in Athens so they could explore the Acropolis and visit the museums.

It was the end of the first week of August when they returned home and the next day was Gemma's birthday gathering. Kate knew Dev and Theo were on the invite list for the barbecue, she only hoped nothing had changed to prevent them going.

The following morning, having barely slept from a combination of anxiety over Dev not going to Rivermills at all and how she could possibly conceal her feelings if he did, Kate rose early and took a cold shower in the hopes it would wake her up.

A notification pinged as she fastened her hair into a ponytail, and Kate walked to the window, the better to appreciate the gorgeous day as she viewed the screen.

> Come to us for two o'clock, we'll go upriver together. A xx

Kate shot a message back and headed to the dressing room to choose what to wear.

At one thirty – having changed several times – she tapped on Mollie's door.

'You ready, love? Anna wants us at Westerleigh soon.'

'I'm down here!'

Kate looked over the banister. Mollie was at the foot of the stairs, dressed and with her bag already on her shoulder.

'Keen, aren't we?' Kate teased as she reached the ground floor.

They reached Westerleigh in good time and were soon down at the small jetty where Oliver's boat was moored.

Kate eyed the bags lined up in the cabin. 'Did you do enough food, Anna?'

She laughed as she took a seat. 'Gemma was in a blind panic, so I said I'd help out.'

'Or do it all,' Oliver muttered, but he sent his wife an indulgent smile before shooing Dougal – who was joining them on the trip – away from the bags.

'We've brought some,' Mollie piped up, stowing the bag next to Anna's, and Oliver started the engine, and they set off across the bay.

'When does Nicki get back?'

'Tomorrow. I think their flight was due into Bristol around six in the evening.'

They'd reached the bridge now, and as the boat emerged on the other side into the calmer, deep green waters of the river, Kate relaxed.

'I had no idea how busy it would be in the cove at this time of year. The beach was rammed yesterday, when I went to get a coffee at the little shop.'

Anna smirked, flicking a glance at Mollie, who was occupied learning to steer the boat under Oliver's direction.

'You seem to spend rather a lot of time down that end of town lately. Hoping to bump into someone?'

Heat flooded Kate's cheeks, and she put a hand to one of them. 'Stop it!'

'Sorry.'

'You don't look it!'

Anna scooted a bit nearer. 'He can't keep his eyes off you, Kate.' She spoke softly. 'Surely even you have noticed.'

Of course she had. It was just that she didn't want to believe it, in case it was all her own imagination messing with her, encouraging her to dream. Besides, she hadn't seen or heard from Dev in what felt like for ever.

'He's never given any indication of... anything.'

Anna patted her on the arm and turned to look upriver.

'There's Theo! Hey, Theo!!!' Mollie waved frantically as she dashed to the side of the boat, and conscious her heart had done a fast lap around her chest, Kate avoided Anna's eye as she oh-so-casually turned her head to look behind them.

Dev's boat was a sleeker, speedier model than Oliver's but with the six knots limit, he was unlikely to catch them up, and she tried to ease the combination of trepidation and excitement gripping her throat. That gave her approximately seven minutes to get her act together.

Grateful Dougal had taken a seat beside her, Kate put an arm around his comforting body, tongue lolling as he faced the front of the boat, the breeze caressing his ear tips and ruffling his golden coat.

They had almost unloaded everything by the time Dev's boat drifted slowly up against the mooring and Kate – whose preference would have been for watching him secure the ropes – concentrated instead on ferrying bags to the picnic tables by the water's edge.

It wasn't yet high tide, but the clear water lapped against the lawn. The sun was fully on the sheltered creek, and a soft breeze teased the treetops, barely stirring the long grasses at the end of the inlet by the little bridge.

The distant chug of boats drifted over as they passed by, heading up and down river, and the sea birds' cries as they soared overhead mingled with the clucking of chickens from somewhere behind the house and the sound of laughter filtering out through the open windows of the conservatory.

'Hey.'

Kate willed her heart to stop its foolish pattering and turned a warm smile on Dev. 'Hey. You made it, then.'

He said nothing for a moment, his eyes raking her features, and she almost held her breath. He'd opted for a fitted polo shirt and tailored shorts today which, with his lightly tanned skin, looked rather fetching.

'You look…' He cleared his throat. 'Well. Good holiday?'

'Yes, thanks. Lots of sun and chillout time. How've you been?'

Dev didn't reply, his gaze locked with hers, and Kate clasped her hands to prevent them from reaching out to straighten his collar, which was tucked under on one side.

'Dev?'

He gave a visible start. 'Sorry. There was a minor crisis up on one of the farms near Lerryn yesterday. It looked like it would be a whole day job today, but we managed to sort it quickly.'

'Dad!' Theo dashed over, grabbing Dev's hand and tugging. 'Come look at the pretty kittens. Can we get one, Dad? Can we?'

Kate drew in a slow breath as they walked over to a basket on the lawn, turning her attention to emptying one of the bags. It held far less distraction than standing close to Dev, listening to the now familiar growl of his voice, which no longer sounded grumpy but warm instead, but oh how filled with delight she was to finally see him again!

The afternoon passed in leisurely pleasure, with Mollie and Theo paddling in the sandy-floored shallows, the former towing a small dinghy for a while, with Theo attempting to use the paddles to steer. Matt had fired up a vast barbecue outside the studio, and before long he and Anna had placed a feast on a trestle table which, along with the salads, fries and crusty rolls brought over by Kate, were soon devoured.

Gemma had done her best to fry some onions for the hot dogs, and some of them were close to edible. Mollie and Theo tucked into theirs with relish regardless, and once the meal was over, the ladies took a lounger each as the men declared they had 'business' to discuss and disappeared inside the house.

'Watching the Test results, more like,' Gemma murmured, eyes closed.

—

'Gemma's very interested in your grandfather's well-being,' Kate said with a smile as she followed Dev out onto the deck later.

Dusk had begun to fall, and Oliver and Matt were busy lighting lamps hanging from hooks outside the studio. There were strings of white lights suspended between the deck uprights too, and it all cast a warm glow over the tranquil scene, moths fluttering to and fro and the occasional hoot of owls in the treetops.

Mollie and Theo were sitting on the jetty, their legs dangling over the water, which had slowly begun to recede. Every now and then the little boy's piping voice or Mollie's giggles would drift upwards on the still night air.

'They met when she came to Polkerran last year and have formed quite a bond.' He sent Kate an amused look in the fading light. 'The ladies have always seemed drawn to him for some reason.'

It didn't seem the right moment to point out how drawn this *particular* lady was to Ryther's grandson, and Kate turned back to the wooden railing, her hands resting where the residual warmth from the sun's rays lingered.

'Kate,' the word was almost a whisper, but with her senses on high alert, her skin tingled as she became aware of Dev moving closer, his arm almost touching hers. His gaze remained on the children, and she drew in a short breath and focused on Mollie. Surely it would help her be less aware of Dev's proximity…

'Kate,' he said again.

'Yes?' she murmured in response.

'I missed you. Missed talking to you.'

There was silence for a moment as Kate's heart swelled with delight.

Then, he continued, speaking softly. 'It's said the Devonshire men only have one grand passion in their lives, one eternal love.'

Kate held her breath.

'Sadly, there's a family history of it not being the person they marry.'

A laugh rose up and caught in Kate's throat.

'Will you – I mean, would you…' Dev broke off, and Kate turned swiftly around, eyes scanning his face, shadowed in the dim light.

He ran a hand around the back of his neck, as she'd become accustomed to seeing him do, but she waited.

'Would you like – I mean you and Mollie, of course—'

'Yes, of course,' she interjected, then bit her lip. 'Sorry. You were saying?'

He edged slightly closer, casting a quick look at the jetty, then fastening his blue-grey gaze on her. 'I mean, we don't *need* to eat. We've been eating all day. I don't suppose you're hungry at all, but…' He stopped and swallowed visibly, and Kate summoned all her will power not to speak.

It failed her.

'Kids are always hungry. Molls and Theo are bound to want something.'

'Yes, yes,' Dev nodded firmly. 'Good point. Well made. So, would you—'

'Time to light the candles!'

Matt appeared at the top of the steps from the lawn, Oliver on his heels, as Dev took a step back, shoving his hands into his pockets.

Glancing over the railing, she saw Mollie herding Theo towards the steps, and although her heart refused to stop pounding, she felt strangely elated, as Matt and Oliver disappeared inside the house, smiling warmly at Dev as they waited for the youngsters to appear.

'It looks like they're about to prove us right.'

Kate fled to the bathroom once inside, staring at her wide-eyed reflection, then rubbing at a smudge on the side of her nose. When would this colour ever fade from her skin? Then, she puffed on a breath. Had Dev been about to invite her to dinner? At Harbourwatch, she assumed? This evening? She couldn't eat another thing, but she wasn't averse to feasting on his features…

Returning to the main living area, feeling no calmer, her eyes found Dev instantly, sitting on the arm of one of the sofas, Theo on his lap as they watched Matt light the candles on Gemma's cake.

Once the song was over, the cake cut and those who still had room were tucking in, she took a glass of champagne from Oliver as he moved around the room with the bottle, then found Anna at her side.

'I think you've caught a bit too much sun,' she murmured, but Kate could hear the humour in her voice.

'Stop it,' she said quietly, putting a hand to her warm cheek.

'Or perhaps I mean caught someone's *grand*son?' With a chuckle, Anna gave Kate a one-armed hug and headed over to sit beside Gemma, who rested a hand on the growing mound of the twins.

Should she go over to Dev? Theo was happily tucking into his cake, seated now between Oliver and Matt.

Her phone pinged and she fished it out of her pocket. Arabella Tremayne.

Opening the message, she sipped the champagne, but then she coughed, putting the glass aside and re-reading the words. She slipped out of the room into the conservatory, the phone to her ear, her mind racing as the call connected.

'Arabella, hi. What's so urgent—'

Two minutes later, Kate pocketed the phone, turning slowly and retracing her steps. Her mind had screeched to an unceremonious halt. What the hell was she going to do *now*?

Chapter Twenty-Nine

The One With Dire Straits

Kate's eyes sought Dev as she hovered in the doorway and she beckoned him over, ignoring Anna's amused look as she closed the door to the conservatory.

'We've got a problem.'

Dev frowned. 'What's wrong?'

'I just took a call from Arabella Tremayne. The manor house is no longer at our disposal. Non-negotiable.' She stared up at Dev, conscious of the wobble in her voice. 'We're just a few weeks away, and we've lost the fayre's only possible venue.'

'Sit down,' Dev pulled out a chair and Kate flopped onto it, putting her head in her hands on the table.

'I could weep,' she said in a strangled voice before raising her head. 'But I won't.'

'What exactly did she say?' Dev sat beside Kate, which wasn't helping her think straight at all.

'She was a bit odd, to be honest. She's usually quite condescending, you know? But she seemed... embarrassed, almost.'

'So she should be. How could she do this at such short notice? More to the point, why?'

'She did come to that.' Kate sighed. 'She – or rather – they, Tremayne Estates, have found out who now has ownership of the alms-houses. Alex has rescinded her offer, overruled it, which he can do, I'm afraid.'

'Pity,' Dev snapped. 'And petty by way of a reaction.'

There wasn't anything further to be said or done this late on a weekend, so Dev suggested they keep it to themselves for now and Kate agreed.

Thankfully, with Theo becoming tired and the tide not prepared to change its habit for them, it brought about the natural end to the day.

The boats eased away from the jetty, and Gemma and Matt, who held the puppy, waved its paw at them until they became mere shadows on the lawn as the boats drifted out through the gap into the river and turned for Polkerran Point.

Dev had said no more about dinner and, much as she'd have loved to spend more time with him, Kate was partly relieved. Her head was struggling to cope with everything she had organised and how on earth she was going to extract the fayre from its present mess.

As the boats neared Polkerran and Dev's headed to the opposite side of the bay, he put up a hand to them all, and Mollie called out to Theo before all went silent again, aside from the lapping of the water against the boat and the humming of the motor.

—

A restless night had been no aid to Kate's frame of mind, but although the disaster on her plate ought to have been paramount, it was Dev who filled her thoughts as she lay awake through the early hours and to whose memory she opened her eyes after falling asleep just before the alarm.

Opening her emails as she sipped coffee at her desk in the hotel, Kate found one from Arabella Tremayne and read it through before sitting back in her seat. What could she possibly say? The lady, to be fair, was mortified by her son's actions and had probably never had – or at least, had the inclination – to apologise for much in her life, but even she seemed to be aware of the impact on so many people.

Alex had been bragging to all his associates about the coup, full of glee at not only outwitting Oliver's organisation but also selling the properties to a man as rich and famous as Matt.

When his mother, on the phone to Alex after Matt's visit to the manor to assess the cabling needs, was full of having just met a well-known musician – a former band member of BorderLine Beat, no less, Matt Locksley – and brother to a Polkerran resident, Anna Seymour – the penny dropped.

Speechless with rage at discovering he'd sold to Oliver's brother-in-law, and powerless to do anything about it legally, Alex lashed out the only way he knew how: by hurting the people around them.

It was his attitude towards *her*, however, which had upset Arabella most – a mother who had always championed her 'golden boy'. Telling her she was both stupid for allowing it in the first place but that she'd redeemed said stupidity by not getting anything signed, because it meant they could cancel without any repercussions, he immediately withdrew the estate's offer to use the manor's grounds.

Kate worked her way through emails and quickly closed any relating to the fayre. Questions about a variety of last-minute topics could wait – at least for the forty-eight hours she'd agreed with Dev it must be kept secret while they tried to mitigate the situation.

Poor Matt, she mused as she closed her eyes, inhaling the comforting aroma emanating from her mug. He'd feel dreadful when he knew.

A notification dropped on her phone.

Dev.

Snatching it up, Kate read the message, then glanced at the clock, tapping a reply, then hitting refresh on her Inbox what felt like a hundred times before his email landed.

Opening it, she skim-read, then leaned back in her seat.

Matt already knew what had happened. Alex had sent him a vitriolic message, gloating over the chaos he'd been able to create for something so precious to the stupid cove and its 'imbecilic community'.

Later, having been to the kitchens to discuss an upcoming party with the chef, Kate emerged into the elegant hallway, intent on getting back to her desk and ploughing through more emails, when her heart started to skip in pace with her steps.

Dev stood by the reception desk.

'I'm in the car, just dashing off to Truro, so thought I'd drop in. How are you?'

Touched by the concern on his face, Kate summoned a smile. 'Not too bad. My brain is in overdrive, though, trying to think of a way round this.'

'Matt suggests we meet after work. Can you do that?'

For you, I'm available any day, every day…

'That'd be great.' Kate walked with Dev towards the main doors.

'Send me a message. Your place or mine?' She spoke quietly, conscious of a couple of guests walking past as the doors opened to reveal a delivery driver balancing several parcels. 'Mollie's at a friend's this evening until about eight.'

'I'll let Matt know and come to you, then. Theo will be fine with Stella for an hour or so.'

—

It took every ounce of will power for Kate not to throw herself at Dev once he'd arrived at The Lookout. She desperately needed his arms around her. It might not solve anything with regard to the fayre, but it would bring a vast amount of comfort and – to put it bluntly – would certainly shove the whole damn mess straight out of her head!

As it was, she led him into the kitchen and once he'd been furnished with a bottle of beer and she had a glass of wine, they walked out onto the terrace.

It had been a warm day, and she'd changed into shorts and a top, shoving her feet into flip-flops. Dev was equally casually attired this evening, and as they took a seat at the patio table, Kate reflected on how much more relaxed he seemed than when she'd first met him in the winter.

'Cheers.' She held out the glass and he clinked the bottle to it.

'Not sure what we're cheering.'

Kate sent him a resigned look. 'Me neither, but there has to be *something* we can do. I can't let all these people down.'

'You won't. It's not in you to do that.'

Touched by his faith in her, she nevertheless shook her head. 'But I went down every possible avenue before the manor came up. How can I tell these lovely people, who've been working so hard and depending on it to make some income?'

'Hey.' Dev put his bottle on the table and stood. 'Come here.'

Kate didn't need a second bidding as he held out his arms, and she shot into his embrace before he changed his mind.

As his strong arms folded around her, she laid her head against his chest, hoping he wouldn't mind. She could feel his heart beating through his thin shirt, and she closed her eyes, an unbearable ache gripping her throat. God, she loved this man. If only he was free…

'There has to be an answer. We just have to hope no one gets wind of what's gone on until we can offer a solution.'

Dev's voice reverberated as Kate remained tucked into his embrace, her senses on high alert. She could happily have stayed there for ever, but the doorbell had other ideas, and she shot out of Dev's arms as fast as she'd gone into them.

'It'll be Matt.'

Although part of her regretted the disturbance, Kate knew full well it was a blessing in disguise. She had very little restraint where her feelings for Dev were concerned, and who knew what stupidity she might have been tempted to try had their innocent embrace not been brought to an end?

Matt followed Kate and Dev onto the terrace. If they were going to have a round table to brainstorm ideas across, it may as well be one with a view.

'Gem says we need a boat – a big one – so we could moor it off the jetty by the harbourmaster's office.'

'That's an inspired idea!'

'It is – except getting a large enough one at such short notice in high season is proving nigh on impossible. She's been on the case since I found out but hadn't had any joy when I left earlier.'

'Oh, bless her.' Kate had a real fondness for Gemma. 'Well, if we survive this and there's a fayre next summer, let's bear it in mind!'

—

Kate had yet another bad night, lying awake with every possible scenario running through her head on how to miraculously pull a large enough space in the small location that was Polkerran Point out of a non-existent hat.

Despite their best efforts the previous evening, no solution had presented itself – not that any of them thought it would, but Kate reflected that Matt and Dev were certainly more coherent than the previous support network she'd been left with.

Kate had an evening event to work later, so had a few hours to spare in the morning, and she walked down to Westerleigh to find Anna busy with breakfasts for her two guests. Making herself a coffee, she settled at the table, laptop open as she searched on Google, yet again, in the hope some inspiration would present itself.

She looked up when the door opened, fearing the locals were early, but Bella entered.

'Morning,' she said cheerfully as she headed for the coffee machine. 'Oliver's in need of a caffeine shot.'

Kate closed the laptop on the disobliging Google and joined her in the kitchen. 'How's it going?'

'Good. I'm really enjoying it, to be honest. Research like this is a refreshing change after running nothing but online courses. Not that I'm deserting my students per se. I'm still fitting that in.'

Anna came in, bearing an empty tray.

'I've never known people consume as much toast as this pair!' She hurried over to the bread board and began slicing the bread she'd made on the previous day. 'Would you like some, Bella?'

Bella shook her head. 'I'm fine.' She picked up the mug. 'I'll take this to Oliver and come back to make some tea, if that's okay?'

'Feel free,' Anna mumbled, having popped a stray bit of crust in her mouth.

Once she'd ferried the toast and more butter into the dining room, Anna returned to clear up the breakfast things. Kate lent a hand, but then her phone pinged, and she glanced at it, expecting Mollie.

'Unknown number.' She scanned the text message, then swore under her breath.

'What is it?' Anna wiped her hands on a tea towel and came to join her at the island.

'Hold on, I need to make a call.'

Kate headed out onto the terrace through the open doors in the sitting room and waited for the call to connect. Five minutes later, her pounding heart reverberating in her ears, she walked to the railings bordering the terrace.

How could the sea be so still, quietly undulating as though it hadn't a care in the world? How could the sky be this clear, devoid of cloud, a glorious backdrop for the seagulls, wheeling mindlessly above?

Returning to the kitchen, Kate found Bella setting the kettle to boil and Anna stacking the dishwasher.

'What's up?' Anna's concern was evident. 'It's not Mollie?'

Shaking her head, Kate's grip on her phone tightened. 'It's this damn fayre. Look, there's something I need to tell you.'

'I can come back later.' Bella headed for the door, but Kate shook her head again.

'No, stay, Bella. This might need the vision of someone on the outside looking in.' She bit her lip. 'Sorry if that sounded a bit rude.'

Bella laughed as she returned to the kettle. 'Not at all. I'll be with you… dreckly!'

Two minutes later, the three women settled at the pine table, mugs of tea on the table, and Kate revealed the Tremaynes withdrawal of the use of the manor and grounds for the fayre, and the urgent need to find a solution while keeping the situation quiet.

Anna was full of questions, and neither lady noticed how still Bella had become, until Kate glanced at her.

'Are you okay? You've gone white.'

Her mouth a thin line, rigid with some sort of emotion, Bella's eyes flashed.

'That bloody Tremayne family!'

Kate exchanged a lightning look with Anna. 'You know them?'

'Sadly, yes.'

'Well, they've well and truly dropped us in it,' Kate continued. 'It's bad enough we've lost the venue and have yet to find a workable alternative. Now, the local press has found out.' She raised her phone from the table. 'A journalist just called, wanting a quote from me for the next edition of the paper.'

Chapter Thirty

The One When the Going Gets Tough

Anna exchanged a puzzled look with Bella. 'How on earth did that happen?'

'Anonymous tip-off, they said.' Kate blew out a breath. 'But that's it. We've run out of road.'

Some colour had returned to Bella's pale skin. 'Do you know why the Tremaynes changed their mind? I don't have a high opinion of them, but it seems a bit odd at such short notice.'

Kate hesitated, unwilling to cast shade on anyone.

'Kate?' Anna prodded.

With a sigh, she pushed back in her seat, clasping her hands in her lap. 'Retaliation.'

Anna's mouth opened slightly, then closed with a snap as understanding dawned. 'That latest deal. The one Matty did.'

'I'm sorry, but yes. A good deed that led to a foul one.'

Bella's amber eyes flashed again. 'This sounds like the hallmark of *Alex* Tremayne.'

Anna explained to Bella as succinctly as possible Oliver's not-for-profit organisation and its purpose, and Alex's refusal to sell any Tremayne properties to it, hence Matt – unknown to Alex as a connection – going in to seal the deal.

'To be fair to Mr and Mrs Tremayne, they had little choice. Since the retirement, Alex has full control of all decision-making, even though he never comes here.'

'Thank God for small mercies,' Bella muttered. 'Bastard.'

Kate and Anna exchanged another look, and the latter eyed Bella with curiosity. 'You know him *well*, don't you?'

'I thought I did, once.'

'Is it any consolation if I say I went there too, for a while?' Anna pulled a face.

'I suspect we are two of many.'

Something had been niggling at Kate's memories, and realisation suddenly came. 'Was this when you came down for the caravan holiday, about ten years ago?'

Bella didn't speak for a moment, then nodded. 'It was.'

'Nicki told me about it when explaining how she met Hamish.' Kate tried to recall the detail. 'She never mentioned Alex, talked more about her cousin – Ellie, was it?'

Bella nodded. 'Ellie's one of my best friends. We met at uni, and when we finished eight of us booked a couple of vans for the sumner. One of the girls dropped out, so Ellie invited Nicki. God, it was a laugh!' Then, she sobered. 'The aftermath, not so much. At least, it was great for Nicki. The rest of us… well, it's ancient history, for Ellie and I especially.'

'Have you never been back since?' Kate picked up her phone. She really needed to message Dev to give him the heads-up on the journalist.

'Nope.' Bella finished her tea and stood. 'I resisted Oliver's offer for weeks, trying to gauge if git-face was ever at home. Back when I met him, he worked for the family in the estate agent office in the village. When it was clear he never visited, I took a gamble, especially as it's summer. He made it very obvious when we were together he couldn't stand Polkerran in tourist season. Look, I'd best get back to work.'

'I'm so sorry,' Anna said after Bella left the room. 'Matty will feel terrible when he finds out.'

'He already knows,' Kate reassured her. 'He's okay – feels bad but ultimately, there's nothing any of us can do about it.'

The postman called as Kate prepared to leave for work, and Anna's giddiness was heartwarming when she opened the packages of baby clothes.

'I'd better get all this upstairs to the nursery before Oliver catches me. He already thinks we've bought enough to last the babies until they start school.'

'I'll give you a hand.'

'We're going to move down from the top floor once the babies move into their own room,' Anna advised as she nudged a door on the first floor open with her knee.

It was the room Mollie had stayed in when they'd first come to Polkerran Point, and Kate placed her boxes on the already-built changing unit and walked over to the window, trying her hardest not to look over at Harbourwatch. She failed. Miserably.

Clamping down on her emotions, Kate turned away, walking over to admire the cute baby clothes in Anna's hands.

'I can't believe I get to have two babies at once.' Anna's eyes shone with delight and, impulsively, Kate hugged her.

'You deserve it. You waited long enough.'

Unanticipated emotion gripped Kate's throat as she spoke the last word and she ducked her head, placing a hand on the soft fabric of the little Babygro.

'Hey,' Anna spoke softly, resting her own hand on Kate's arm. 'You okay?'

Kate sniffed back unbidden tears, dredging up a weak smile. 'Yes, sorry. No idea where that came from.'

Liar.

The thing was, she desperately wanted to confide in someone about Hugo's great deception. But Anna wasn't the right person... at least, not right now.

—

On Wednesday, Mollie went on the village youth club's annual jaunt – this year, a day trip to Bodmin Moor to visit Jamaica Inn, incorporating a talk about Daphne du Maurier and the local inspiration for her works followed by a ramble around Cardinham Woods.

Kate had been in early for a breakfast meeting, so she packed up her desk after lunch, with plans to do a couple of hours work at home. It was a beautiful summer day. She'd go home, enjoy a cuppa on the terrace and then get on with a few emails before tackling the much neglected housework. Perhaps the physical exercise would help her think about something – anything – but her current dilemma.

'I don't know who you think you're fooling,' she admonished as she walked up the lane to The Lookout. 'It's not the fayre consuming your every thought. Drop the wishful thinking and channel some positive energy!'

It might well have worked, had there not been a packet on the floor in the hall when she walked in – re-directed from her parents' house, but clearly addressed in Hugo's flamboyant hand.

Curious, Kate tore the seal and pulled out the contents, then sank onto a sofa, hand trembling as she read the typed note: 'You left these behind', followed by a crying-with-laughter emoji.

Bitterness towards Hugo – the lies he'd spun, the deliberate false path he'd led her down – rose into Kate's throat, and she dashed to the kitchen and hastily downed a glass of cold water, wishing she could wash away the memory of him so easily.

Pacing in the living room, her mind whirled in a cocktail of anger, despair and frustration. She needed to do something physical, find somewhere to channel her emotions before Mollie came home.

Snatching up the envelope and its contents, she shoved them into a drawer and hurried up the stairs to change into an old pair of shorts and a T-shirt that had seen better days. Fastening her hair with a clip, she stared at the hollow-eyed woman in the mirror. Where had the light tan gone? Kate placed a hand against her cheek, pale as a winter frost. Her skin was cold too, belying the white-hot anger simmering inside and, with a growl, she grabbed her sunglasses and fled the room.

A half hour of vigorous digging around the edges of the decking, and Kate had planted out several of the peony plants she'd picked up from the farm shop. They would create a beautiful border in late spring... if she – they – were still in Polkerran...

Normally able to compartmentalise problems she couldn't immediately solve, Kate huffed out a breath as she stretched her aching back, removing her soil-covered gloves and walking to the edge of the deck. The burst of anger had subsided. She'd become conditioned to what Hugo had done during the last two difficult years. After all, what could she do about it? Absolutely nothing.

She breathed in deeply, then exhaled, welcoming a sense of calm and peace that she'd somehow found becoming part of daily life since the move.

Polkerran had taken a hold. Kate could feel it, and she pressed a hand against her chest. It was in her very core, her soul, she was certain, and unbidden, Dev's face came into her mind. Hugging her arms around her waist, Kate turned into the breeze, closing her eyes and, for a nano-second, imagined being with Dev, of feeling those strong arms around her.

The squeal of a gull overhead banished the image, along with the growing heat in her arms, and Kate's momentary happiness dissipated as fast as soft wavelets absorbed into fine sand.

What was she going to do? He was all she could think of and wanted to – if it wouldn't be the most embarrassing of giveaways – talk about. The depth of her feelings for Dev had grown over time, subtly, quietly, softly, yet now they threatened to consume her. There was no future there, no life lying ahead of them... her... but she couldn't stop hoping, dreaming. Yet remaining in the cove, should Leigh decide to come back, was unimaginable.

'Enough!' Kate exclaimed, sadness and despair mingling in her tired mind. She walked over to the edge of the wildflower garden, where there was a pile of discarded rocks, left over from the landscaping at the front of the property.

She needed to wear herself out. That way, she might find some sort of repose at night instead of tossing and turning like a boat freed of its moorings, failing to find safe harbour.

Forcibly ignoring the ache within her breast, Kate walked over to retrieve her gloves, picking up the shovel, but a faint sound forewarned her of someone's approach.

'Hey, I rang the bell, but no one answered.'

Oh no! Not now!

Kate sniffed, though she wasn't sure why, adjusting the sunglasses on her nose, which had slid a little from the sweat she'd worked up, conscious of her untidy appearance, tattered brain and the direction of her thoughts.

Dev had been smiling, but now he looked uncertain and, despite the agitation, Kate summoned a weak smile.

'Sorry. I didn't hear.'

'Your car was there…' He gestured back around the side of the house. 'So I took a punt…'

'Of course.' Kate couldn't bear to look at him, her heart knocking against her ribs as though desperate to be let loose. 'I… er, I've been gardening.'

Inane comment, you blethering idiot.

Looking down at her scruffy attire, the gloves and spade, Kate all but shrugged.

'Can I help?'

She glanced up, but Dev had already taken the shovel from her listless grasp and walked over to the pile of rocks.

'What look are you aiming for?'

Kate cleared her throat. 'Oh, er, I was going to make a rock garden. Pile them in a bit more order, but not too much.'

She took a step back, stumbling in her anxiety to distance herself, but as she righted herself, her sunglasses flew off, landing with a clatter on the decking.

Dev picked them up and stepped over to hand them back, but then he stilled as his gaze raked her face.

'You've been crying.'

The concern in his voice almost had Kate undone. She put a hand to her face, surprised to find wetness on her cheeks. When had that happened?

'Oh!' She sniffed again, then dug into her pocket for a tissue.

'Can I help? Do you want to talk about it?'

She blew her nose as discreetly as possible. 'It's nothing.'

Dev sent her a quizzical look. 'Forgive me for disagreeing.'

Kate chewed on her lip. She desperately needed to open up to someone. Aside from it being the wrong timing for Anna, and Mollie being too young, she knew instantly that there was no one else she'd rather talk to… and in that moment, the depth and undisputable solidity of her affection for him hit home. She was deeply in love with Dev, wholeheartedly. Passionately so.

And she would never be able to tell him.

Chapter Thirty-One

The One Where Kate is Not Alone

'Come on.' Dev set off across the decking towards the open glass doors.

Awash with her sudden realisation, Kate's legs ignored her instruction not to move and before she knew it, she found herself doing as Dev said, taking a seat at the island as he opened the fridge.

'Sorry for pushing in,' he said over his shoulder. 'But I can tell when someone needs to talk. Do you want a cup of tea or something stronger?'

I want you, her mind whispered.

Kate cleared her throat again. Sod it. Dev knew she needed to talk. *She* knew she did. They'd become friends. She'd bottled it up for years. Maybe speaking about it would help?

'If you'll have something with me, I'd like a glass of rosé, please.' She gestured towards the open fridge. 'There's some in the door. What would you like?'

'I'll have one of these if that's okay?' Dev waved a bottle of beer as he extracted both from the fridge, then took the stool opposite Kate at the island.

'Cheers.' He clinked the bottle to Kate's glass, but she returned it to the island.

Dev took a swig, and she watched his throat convulse as he swallowed. As he lowered his hand, however, he caught her fixed gaze, his brow furrowing.

'Kate? This isn't what we call talking?'

Embarrassing.

'No. Sorry. It's hard to know where to begin. Ancient history, really.' She eased off the stool and walked over to the drawer, extracting the envelope and its contents before resuming her seat.

'This came in the post this morning.' She pushed the basal thermometer and notebook across the island, and Dev put his beer aside.

'Hugo – my ex – sent them, along with this.' She pulled the piece of paper from the envelope and handed it over.

Had his fingers deliberately stroked hers as he took it?

'It won't make any sense, but it stems back to something that happened a few years ago… or rather, not so much *happened*, but came out.'

Stumbling over her words, her head bowed most of the time, but occasionally taking surreptitious glances at Dev – silent across the island, his expression impassive – Kate revealed the great deception.

She'd always wanted a big family… three, maybe even four children. It wasn't like they couldn't afford it. When Mollie was a toddler, she decided it was time to go for a baby sister or brother for their first born, and although there were already cracks in the façade of their marriage, she put it down to Hugo's stress at work – he was young and upcoming and desperate to make his mark, achieve a directorship by thirty.

When nothing happened after several months, she told Hugo of her concerns, but he brushed it aside. Doctors appointments, medical checks and all everyone kept saying was, you're trying too hard. Worrying about it is part of the problem. Relax. You know you can get pregnant, Mollie is the evidence. Give it time.

So she did. Another year. She begged Hugo to get checked, in case something – she couldn't imagine what – had gone wrong, but he refused, citing the same line as the doctors: Mollie was proof they could conceive.

IVF? Hugo had laughed in her face, refusing to fork out what he deemed a waste of money, again quoting the obvious. And how could she not accept the logic? Yet why wasn't she falling pregnant?

And then she found out.

'Two years ago, we moved into this vast mausoleum of a show house – a status symbol Hugo had been aspiring to all his life. It was an awful time. I was working full time and trying to manage Mollie's distress at being removed from a school where she was happy and put into a private one that said more about status than care for a child's well-being.'

Bowing her head, Kate fought to control her voice as the memory of that dreadful time intruded.

She swallowed hard on rising emotion. 'That's when I found out how pointless this had been.' Kate pointed to the thermometer, the notebook of her optimum ovulation times, returned to her that morning by Hugo. 'Clearing out cupboards and drawers, I came across the paperwork. Hugo had gone for the snip to ensure there would be no more children.' She gulped on a breath, hand to the sharp pain in her breast. 'The same week I was in hospital for Mollie's birth.'

A small sound escaped Dev as Kate raised sorrowful eyes to his, unsure how he'd take the revelation.

'My *God*. I'm so *so* sorry, Kate.'

He reached across the table with both hands, and she placed hers in his with no hesitation, cherishing the firm clasp as he held onto her, giving them a light squeeze.

'The bastard! And to send you those.' He glared at the thermometer and notebook. 'What did you… How did you…'

'I couldn't believe it at first. I've been through every possible emotion: shock, anger, disbelief and then grief.' Something had a grip on Kate's throat now. 'I grieved for the children I'd never had, that I foolishly kept thinking would come along.'

Kate sighed as Dev released her hands. 'I'd thought about leaving so many times over the years, but I worried it wasn't the right thing to do for Mollie. Finding those papers was it, though. I finally discovered the courage to walk away, for both mine and Mollie's sakes. When I told Hugo why, he laughed. Thought it hilarious. Even thanked me for the constant coupling.' Kate threw the thermometer a look of distaste, then shuddered. 'It makes me feel unclean now.'

'Don't let it,' Dev cautioned, easing off his stool. 'This is his fault, not yours.'

'Sorry to lay this on you.' Kate's heart was aching, weeping on her behalf, but not for the past now. It was breaking over the loss of a future with Dev, who probably shouldn't even be there...

Then, she frowned. 'Why did you call?'

'It's not important. Look, I'd best go. Theo will be coming out of school shortly.'

They walked into the hallway, and Kate shuffled from foot to foot as he opened the door, discomfited now by her grubby T-shirt and tear-stained cheeks.

Dev turned around. 'Will you call Anna, get her to come over?'

'No. It's not fair. She'll feel awful for me, and she shouldn't have any downside to her current joy. I'm so glad we've become... friends, Dev. I don't want Molls to ever know about this, but talking has helped.'

'I don't like leaving you. Are you sure you'll be okay?'

To Kate's surprise, he took a step towards her, and she held her breath for a second as he reached out and tucked a loose piece of hair behind her ear, then rested the back of his hand against her cheek which, unlike the earlier chill, felt as though it was suddenly on fire.

Eyes wide, Kate kept them fastened on Dev's face. His eyes – so often the steely grey-blue of a winter sky – seemed deeper in colour. How had she never noticed those tiny flecks of silver?

His gaze dropped to her mouth, then flicked up. Was she imagining it, or was he leaning towards her—

'Bus broke down on the way to the woods, so they sent us home in a replacement.'

Mollie came bounding up the steps and breezed past them as they both took a swift step backwards, Kate's heart pounding fit to burst.

'Hi, Mr Devonshire.'

As Mollie disappeared through the door, Kate wrapped her arms around her waist, feeling gauche and embarrassed, but Dev clearly hadn't attended the same school of mortification.

He leaned down and placed a lingering kiss on her cheek.

'Call me if I can do anything to help,' he said softly, the hand once more against her now rather warm cheek, and then he was gone, and Kate's hungry eyes followed him as he disappeared out of the driveway, before closing the door and leaning back against it.

Mollie's head popped around the doorway. 'I might only be thirteen, but even I know *that* was sexy.'

—

Kate slept surprisingly well, blinking in confusion when she awoke, peering at the alarm and then sinking back into her pillow. She'd come to a tumultuous realisation yesterday. Why wasn't she a wailing and pitiful mess after realising how deeply in love she was with Dev, with little hope of him reciprocating?

But he kissed your cheek… if Mollie hadn't come home when she had, might he have…

'Stop it!'

Kate tutted as she swung her legs out of bed, then stretched languorously, flipping her hair over her shoulders. Was there any chance Dev — despite the complexity of his situation — more than liked her company?

'Idiot,' she muttered as she headed for the bathroom. 'You're channelling your inner teen again. Time to grow up.'

It was as she rapped on Mollie's door to make sure she was awake, as she was off to another junior gig taster day with her friends, and made her way downstairs that it came to her.

For all the nastiness behind Hugo's gesture, finally telling someone what had happened, having a *friend* listen to her, be there for her, had been the balm she hadn't realised she needed. Yes, her heart was veering from the giddiness of anticipation to constricting with sadness, but something had been set free by her confession. However things stood between her and Dev – and maybe she'd never know – she would always cherish how he had been with her and she knew without a shadow of doubt that he had been the one person, the right person, to share it with.

As for her ex-husband... little did he know, but he'd done her a favour on more than one count, and soon he'd know about it.

The usual breakfast rush ensued once Mollie arrived downstairs, but Kate's mind wasn't really on anything her daughter was saying as she chattered away over her cereal.

'You've missed your chance.'

'Sorry?' Kate looked over from the sink.

Mollie placed her bowl in the dishwasher and pointed to the small leather box on the counter, containing the infamous rings. 'Yesterday was recycle bin day.'

With a faint smile, Kate resumed scrubbing the pan from the previous night's dinner. She'd left it to soak but it was stubbornly holding onto the residue of chicken kiev.

'I'm off. See you later.'

'Don't forget your packed lunch,' Kate called, but Mollie had already whisked through the door so, drying her hands on a tea towel, she scooped up the box and caught her in the driveway.

Shaking her head as she returned to the kitchen, Kate mulled – not for the first time – on the wasted time. All those years, hanging on in the marriage for Mollie's sake, convinced it was wrong to break up the home, remove her from one of her parents, had done them both more damage than good. If only one had the benefit of forward vision…

Half an hour later, Kate grabbed the ring box and headed out to the car. She had a date at lunch time, and not with an unpredictable Cornish wind. No. This time, there would be no return for the rings.

A small smile touched the edges of her mouth as she reversed the car and set off down the hill. Hugo had been triumphant the night before, when she'd messaged to say she'd received his package, and it was only fair she reciprocated. She'd sell the rings and send him whatever she got for them. His snide remark, telling her not to think about hiding the true proceeds and keeping some of it herself, she'd laughed off. She had no desire to have anything more to do with the bloody things.

All she needed now was the final closure.

Chapter Thirty-Two

The One With the Lady in Red

Kate headed to Westerleigh when she finished work, surprised to find Dev there, talking to Matt and Anna. Before she had time to work herself into a state over the very sight of him, Oliver joined them, bringing Bella too.

Anna urged everyone over to the table, but despite her protests, Oliver wouldn't let her carry the tray over, insisting there were plenty of hands to do that.

Matt steered his sister into a chair and sat beside her, as if half expecting her to leap out of her seat, and Kate grinned as Bella placed a plate of biscuits on the table.

'This is killing you, isn't it?'

Anna slumped back in her seat, a hand on her growing bump. 'I've got months to go yet. I can't stop doing things!'

'No, but you don't have to do everything,' Matt cautioned as Oliver carried over a tray of coffee and some mugs, followed by Dev with the sugar and milk.

'I still don't get who dobbed us in to the newspaper.' Kate helped herself to coffee from the pot.

'You say only you and Dev knew what had happened – other than the Tremaynes? Surely it was one of them?'

'We think it was probably Alex.' Kate glanced at Dev, then away before she fell into the trap of simply staring at him.

'I can't believe he's still up to his old tricks,' Bella added, stirring sugar into her tea.

'I forget you knew him.' Anna grimaced.

Bella pulled a face. 'Wish I could!'

They mulled over possible ways to mitigate the crisis, but there really was only one option. With barely a fortnight to go, there was no choice but to shut the fayre down. Kate had exhausted every possible venue before the manor had been offered.

'All the banners state where it will be held too.'

Bella's amber eyes were on fire, her hands gripping the table, and she muttered an expletive. 'Sorry, Kate, truly. I wish there was something I could do other than offer platitudes.'

'We all do,' Oliver added. 'I take full responsibility, Kate.'

'You'll have to share it with me, then,' Matt chipped in, dunking a biscuit in his tea.

Kate shook her head. 'No, none of you are to blame. This is down to one person only.' She sank back in her seat, conscious of Dev's sympathetic look as he studied her across the table. 'I need to work out the best way to tell those involved before the next edition of the paper comes out on Tuesday.'

Friday morning was spent – in amongst Kate's daily tasks – doing as she'd said, notifying people, apologising profusely and being vague about the loss of the venue. This wasn't Arabella Tremayne's fault either, and she didn't deserve to take the flack for her horrid son.

Kate ended the call with Phoenix, who'd taken on the job of contacting all the artists who'd expected to exhibit at the fayre. She'd been full of sympathy and adamant the art trail could still take place, as it was along the lines of a treasure hunt around the cove, not confined to one place.

Scrolling down her list, Kate ticked off the food and drink vendors, which Anna had taken responsibility for contacting. She was about to call the chap who organised the Morris dancing group, who'd also volunteered to man the barbecue, when her mobile rang.

It was her contact at the charity shop. Ten minutes later, the call ended, and as soon as lunch time came around, she drove over to Port Wenneth to complete matters.

The next morning, she stood in the queue at the post office inside the Spar, waiting to send off a parcel, when Old Patrick came in.

'Wasson, my lovely?' he greeted her, and Kate smiled, hugging the parcel to her chest as she waited in line.

'I'm okay, Pat, thank you. How's things with you?'

'Nay so bad, young'un.' Pat picked up a newspaper, folding it and tucking it under his arm, but then something caught his eye outside, and he headed for the till. 'Best be gettin' on. Cleggie's out there on that scooter agin. Be the death of her, silly old mare.'

Kate hid her smile as she shuffled closer to the post office counter. Mrs Clegg was indeed rolling along the harbour front with gay abandon on her wheels, visitors leaping out of the way as she brandished one of her sticks as though a participant in the two-thirty race at Epsom Downs. And there, thundering along behind her, was Mrs Lovelace.

—

On Saturday afternoon, there was an open day at the private yacht club, which took place annually to raise funds for the RNLI. There would be games for the kids and food and drink on offer, and as Kate had promised Anna she'd come along with Mollie, she got ready, desperately trying not to think about whether Dev would be there with Theo.

'Molls? Are you ready?'

Kate checked her large tote and, satisfied she had everything, slung it over her shoulder, walking over to close the doors overlooking the terrace.

It was a stunning August day and a bright sun shone down on the pots Kate had so carefully planted out and tended. Their blooms were spilling over now in abundant trails. She'd need to water them later.

Returning to the island, she scooped up her keys.

'Molls!' she called up the stairs.

'Okay, okay. Geez!'

Skipping down the stairs, Mollie rolled her eyes at Kate. 'Anyone would think you were keen to see someone.'

Not even trying to hide her smirk, she headed for the hall, and Kate huffed on a breath. It was pointless trying not to think about Dev, so she wasn't even going to attempt it.

'I just hate being late, that's all,' she admonished as she followed Mollie down the driveway.

'Hard to turn up late when it's an open house.'

Quashing the urge to snap back with a very juvenile, 'what*ever*,' Kate hurried to catch up with Mollie's quick pace.

Polkerran continued to heave with visitors, and the long spell of dry weather seemed to bring more people by the day. The shops and businesses were booming and making the most of it. They needed to earn as much as they could at times like this to balance the dead winter months.

Once they'd arrived at the juniors sailing club, Mollie headed off to join her school mates on one of the jetties, munching on sweets or crisps, and Kate willed herself not to look around for Dev.

As it was, the initial moment of peace was soon over. It was surprising how many people now knew Kate, considering the short time she'd lived in the cove, as she gave out the same evasive answer on the fate of the fayre again and again.

'There you are!'

Kate swung around to greet Anna, giving her a hug and admiring her noticeable bump. 'Gosh, for five months…'

'I know,' Anna shook her head. 'Goodness knows what size I'll be by December!'

'Is Bella coming over?'

'No. We did ask her, but she said she had to go up to London this weekend, so left yesterday morning.' Uncertainty filled Anna's features.

'What's up? You don't think she's had enough of the cove? She did seem wound up by the mention of Alex the other day.'

'I hope not. It's taken so much pressure off Oliver.'

Kate didn't have chance to say any more, as Nicki came over.

'Anna, you look more blooming every day, and Kate, you look stunning.'

'Oh, er, thanks.' Kate glanced down at her tailored pin-stripe shorts and Skechers. 'Not my most glam look.'

Nicki chuckled, tucking her arm through Anna's as they made their way across the grass to the refreshment tables set up opposite the water.

'I meant overall. Nice to see you sticking with the less formal hair.'

'And this…' Anna briefly touched the linen of Kate's sleeveless top. 'I'm not used to seeing you in dark red. Is it because it reminds you of someone?'

Kate's mouth opened to protest, well aware of Anna and Nicki's amusement, but then she spotted Dev by the water. He must have been crouched down by Theo, but had now straightened and he turned and his gaze met hers over the heads of the people spilling across the lawn.

Closing her mouth with a snap, she swallowed fast on rising emotion, and Anna looked over her shoulder.

'Ah. Talk of the devil. Let's go and say hi.'

'No! I mean, I can't…'

Anna ignored her, tugging Kate by the hand as they navigated their way to where Dev remained standing, Theo sitting at a long table with several other little ones.

'Hey.' Dev's smile was warm, and Kate's heart smiled back, much to her consternation.

'Hi, and hi, Theo. How are you?'

The little boy glanced over his shoulder, rapt with attention as he turned back to watch Tommy the Boat's demonstration. 'We're making knots.'

'He's been talking for days about having a go. I think I'm surplus to requirements.'

'I know the feeling. I didn't see Molls for dust the moment we got here. Oh.' Kate looked to her left. 'Where did Anna go?'

'Was she here?' Dev's brow furrowed as they both scanned the growing throng. 'I spy Oliver, but then he's never hard to miss over a crowd.'

Nor are you, you're almost as tall…

'How's it going with the cancellations.'

Kate pulled a face. 'Well, in the circumstances. Most people are understanding, even if they're disappointed. There have been a few complaints, but…' She shrugged. 'I hate giving up on it. I feel such a failure, that I've let everyone down.'

'Kate.' Dev's grey-blue eyes held a warmth she longed for, voice lowered. 'You could never let anyone down. This isn't your fault, or mine. It's not even Matt's or Oliver's. We all know who's to blame for the whole debacle. You,' he added, placing a firm hand on her bare arm to give it a gentle squeeze before releasing her, 'are amazing.'

Words had all but fled Kate's brain, but Dev seemed perfectly at ease, turning back to answer Theo's sudden call. And why wouldn't he? *He* wasn't madly in love.

What she'd said the other day, about never having truly experienced the condition, could hardly have been more evidenced. The crush, the lust that often runs through the veins when young had beguiled her into believing herself in love. Finally, she comprehended its fickle sensations, and the total discordancy with how she now felt.

Flustered, Kate made her escape, joining Nicki and Hamish at the gin stand.

'Where are Liam and Jason?'

'Queuing up for the kayaks.' Nicki pointed to where there was a line of children of various ages, unsurprised to see Mollie and her friend, Freya, also hovering.

Tommy the Boat and Peggy, who lived in Polwelyn, were doing their best to keep them in order, the latter walking along and handing over suitably sized life jackets.

'Kate.'

Heart pummelling her chest again, she turned around.

Dev didn't look quite so content as earlier, his phone gripped in his hand.

'Can I have a quick word?'

'I... er, yes, of course.'

She ignored Nicki's knowing look as they walked away.

'What's up?'

'Just had a call,' Dev spoke quietly, fetching up at the far end of the lawn, near to the entrance, 'from Arabella Tremayne. Said she tried your phone, but it went to voicemail.'

Kate's forehead furrowed. 'Well, she can't have anything else bad to tell us. Can she?' Her troubled gaze met Dev's.

'She wants to meet. Now. Says it's urgent. At least,' Dev shrugged, 'will you come? She asked for both of us.'

'Oh. But what about—'

'I saw Anna on the way to find you. She's keeping an eye on Theo for me. I'm sure Nicki will watch out for Mollie.'

'Yes, of course. Where does she want to meet?'

'At Tremayne Manor.'

Chapter Thirty-Three

The One With the Manic Monday

A half hour later, a stunned Kate followed Dev out of Tremayne Manor. She cast a stern look at the 'sold' banners on the adjacent gatehouse and the run of alms-houses on their way down the hill into the centre of Polkerran.

Much as she admired Oliver's purpose, those property acquisitions had caused no small amount of stress!

'You're very quiet.'

Ultra conscious of the man walking along the street beside her, Kate made an effort to harness her cartwheeling thoughts.

'Well, I was definitely not expecting *that*!'

A faint laugh came from Dev as they reached the entrance to the sailing club. 'Nor was I, but we're back on, whatever the reasons. Tremayne Manor is reinstated.'

'It makes me a bit edgy – might it happen again?'

'Try not to think about it.' Dev pushed the gate aside, but as Kate made to step inside, he stayed her with his hand.

'Now isn't really the time, with so many people around, but can you spare some time later to run through what we do next?'

Gladly. Want to come round, stay the night?

The intrusive thought popped into Kate's mind unbidden, and a hot sensation shot through her body, and – judging by Dev's slightly taken aback expression – into her face.

She cleared her throat. 'Yes, of course. Do you and Theo... I mean, would you like to... it would be nice...'

'Yes.' Dev's mouth twitched. 'Whatever it is. We can come round later on, or just walk back with you?'

For a nano-second, Kate almost went for the former. It would give her time to shower, change into something simple but elegant, put on some make-up...

'Let's just go back from here. I'm sure I can cobble us some supper together.'

'We may not need any,' Dev said as he pushed open the gate. 'If the smell from the barbecue is anything to go by.'

Dev had been right. Neither Mollie nor Theo wanted anything else to eat once they'd returned to The Lookout and happily took their cans of Dr Pepper into the snug to play a game. Kate pushed aside the glass doors to the terrace and turned on the lamps. It wasn't even dusk, but hopefully, Dev wasn't in any hurry to leave.

The man himself stepped out onto the terrace. The only sounds were the distant echoes of waves rolling onto the beach below the cliffs and the ever-present call of the seabirds, drifting on the thermals above the undulating dark blue blanket of sea.

'Here you go.'

'Thank you.' Kate took the glass of wine from Dev and gestured towards the table and chairs. 'Take a seat.'

Once they were settled, side by side, Kate raised her glass to his. 'Here's to Arabella Tremayne.'

Dev pulled a face, and Kate sent him a quizzical look. 'So you don't think *she*'s the reason the venue has been reinstated?'

'Not the reason, no, although don't get me wrong. I'm grateful to her for putting things right as fast as she has. But she's clearly been given permission, and we know where that's come from.'

Kate confusion merely deepened. 'Why would Alex do that, though?'

'As Grandy is fond of quoting, "*Cherchez la femme*".'

Kate sipped her drink, enjoying the sourness of the dry wine on her tongue.

'You suspect Bella is the missing link? But she hates Alex.'

'And isn't hatred akin to love?'

Dev held her gaze, but Kate broke it, heart racing.

'Maybe...'

'Anyway, let's hope everyone's happy to return to the original plan.'

Kate nodded, unable to speak for a moment. Then, she sighed. 'I think I'm going to have a very busy time on the phone again tomorrow.'

—

No truer words had been spoken, but at least Sunday whizzed by, and on Monday, Kate called the journalist at the local newspaper first to explain that there had simply been a miscommunication somewhere, and the Polkerran Village Fayre would proceed as planned.

Conscious the publication was going to print, Kate laughed at the relief in the junior reporter's voice.

'Thank goodness,' she gushed. 'They'd already dropped the piece because they've uncovered a scandal at a fishmonger's in Port Wenneth. I can't say any more, but it'll be all over the paper tomorrow.'

Shaking her head, Kate sent Dev a message to let him know, then headed to work, her feet barely touching the ground as she dealt with the preparations for the two upcoming weddings at the hotel, both of which thankfully had full-time wedding planners attached to them, which would leave her free to be on hand at the fayre throughout the Bank Holiday weekend.

With Anna dealing with reinstating the food and drink vendors and the local produce purveyors, and Phoenix contacting all the creatives, it only left Kate to put in calls to the performers, and they were back on track.

Feeling as though she'd done a week's work by Monday evening, Kate was relieved to arrive home, and as soon as she'd changed into shorts and a T-shirt, she headed for the fridge and poured a glass of wine.

'How did you get on at Jean's today?'

Mollie was lying on one of the sofas, continuing her read of *Pride & Prejudice*.

'It was mint.' She tossed the book aside. 'Lydia's dumb. And so's this Wickham. He gives me the ick.'

Kate spotted the linen basket by the larder. Damn, she'd left it there this morning and forgotten to put the washing on.

'Dad's as bad. What's up with *him*?'

She assumed innocence. 'Why?'

'He messaged me. Which he *never* does. Says you've blocked his WhatsApps.'

'He's not wrong. The only matter outstanding between us, as far as I'm concerned, has been resolved.'

Kate picked up the laundry basket and headed for the utility, but Mollie followed her.

'He's pretty pissed off.'

'Molls! I've asked you not to—'

'Soz.' Mollie held up her hands. 'It slipped out.'

'Well don't let it!'

Placing the basket on the floor, Kate lifted the lid. It was somewhat ironic that the item on the top was the T-shirt she'd picked up in the charity shop the other day, and her lips twitched.

'What did you do? He says you conned him over the rings. Not that I care,' Mollie added airily. 'He had no right to them, they were gifts to *you*.'

Kate shoved several items into the washing machine. 'I got rid of them. Sold them, after a fashion.'

'What do you mean?'

Kate said nothing until she'd finished loading the machine, but then she straightened. Confession time.

'I told him I'd send him what I got for them.'

'*Mum!* You could always have given the money to me!' Mollie grinned, and Kate couldn't help but laugh as she set the machine in motion.

'True, but then he'd have kept asking for it.'

'So?' Mollie persisted, as they went back into the kitchen.

'I gave them to a charity, to auction.'

'Sweet!' Mollie selected a handful of grapes from the bowl on the island. 'Not that Dad deserves anything. You gave the charity something from the proceeds?'

'On the contrary,' Kate said succinctly.

She took a seat at the island, opening her laptop. She needed to get on with some emails. Mollie, however, lingered, popping a grape in her mouth and chewing.

'I don't get it.'

Kate fired up the laptop. 'When I donated the rings and said they could keep one hundred per cent of whatever they could raise at auction, they insisted I accept something from the shop, the one in Port Wenneth?'

Mollie's eyes were round with rapt attention. 'And that's what you sent Dad?' Going off into peals of laughter, she walked around the island to hug Kate. 'So proud of you, Mum!' She stepped back. 'What did you get? He's got it, right?'

Kate turned to the laptop. 'In exchange for the rings, I received – or rather, selected – a couple of… unique 1970s ash trays. They were particularly hideous, especially the one shaped like a swan.'

'But he has a phobia about birds! And he doesn't smoke!'

'No, he doesn't, does he?' Kate said and, with a delighted chuckle, Mollie left the room.

Although he's probably fuming right now.

–

The following morning, Kate settled at her desk, doing her utmost to concentrate on a proposal for a recruitment company based in Plymouth, who wanted to secure a state-of-the-art business centre with spa facilities for a series of mini-residentials for their management team.

Barely had she opened the file, however, when the urge to check the webcam at the beach came over her, and she opened it up, feeling horribly voyeuristic but also fizzing with hopes of a glimpse of Dev walking Bayley before the daily dog ban came into force.

There were two dog walkers on the beach, but neither had Dev's tall form. As she watched, however, a familiar figure did walk over to one of the benches: Ryther.

A soft smile touched Kate's lips. His step was sprightlier than when she'd last seen him, and she hoped he was fully on the mend. Then, recalling she should be working, she closed the page and forced her mind back onto the proposal.

After a long day, however, with back-to-back meetings most of the afternoon and last-minute checks to do on this evening's silver wedding party, Kate stopped around six to drink a hastily made cup of tea. She had ten minutes before she needed to go along to check everything was ready in the private dining room. Five minutes to enjoy the brew, she mulled, casually opening the beach livestream, and then five to tidy her appearance.

As her gaze drifted over the scene, taking in the familiar and now comforting view, watching the waves roll rhythmically onto the sands – free of families today because of the weather – she noticed some of the ladies who enjoyed swimming in the sheltered cove emerging from the water and chattering to each other.

They passed by the webcam on their way out of sight, around the corner of the coffee shop to the shelter where they tended to don their dry robes before grabbing a hot drink, but all of a sudden, Kate's attention was caught as a very familiar figure darted past. A small figure, that flashed a quick look up at the camera, before disappearing out of sight to where the swimming ladies had just gone.

Mollie!

The tea forgotten, Kate walked on auto-pilot to the cloakroom, made a perfunctory effort to tidy her hair and remove the shine from her nose, her mind spinning over her daughter's purpose.

Arriving home later that evening, she found Mollie in the snug.

'Hey, Mum,' she said, without taking her gaze from the vast screen, across which characters leapt and fought.

Kate reached over and removed the controller from Mollie's grasp, and she scowled at her mum.

'I was on my last life!'

'Tough.' Kate came to stand between Mollie and the screen. 'What did you do after leaving Freya's?'

'Came home.' Mollie folded her arms across her chest, her expression mutinous.

Weary now, Kate sank onto the adjacent leather recliner. 'Before that, Molls. I saw you on the beach.'

Mollie looked momentarily dumbstruck before she giggled. 'You've been on the livestream! I wonder who you were looking for?' She pretended contemplation, a hand stroking her chin, then grinned.

'Fine.' Kate sighed. 'But I did see you there. After what happened a few months ago, I'd really appreciate the truth, Molls.'

'Nice to have your mother's trust. I made some more of these.' She indicated the clay bracelets on her wrist. 'I liked using the watery colours, you know, the greens and blues. I added the words "beach" or "waves" to them and wanted to give a few away.'

A combination of relief and guilt swept through Kate. 'I'm sorry, Molls, for suspecting you of something... are you saying you made bracelets for the swimming ladies?'

The colour that so easily stained Kate's cheeks flew into her daughter's. 'Might have done.' She lowered her head for a moment, then looked up at Kate. 'I didn't know what to do, but I felt bad. I mean, they didn't know I'd been rude, like. But...' She waved her hand vaguely.

With a small laugh, Kate leaned right over and hugged Mollie, who wriggled fiercely.

'Aww, gerroff, Mum!'

'So proud of you, Molls.' Kate got up. 'What d'you fancy for tea?'

'Can I have cheesy nachos?'

Handing back the controller, Kate mentally sifted through the contents of the fridge and larder. 'Probably. Leave it with me.'

Her phone pinged as she closed the snug door and she picked it up, kicking off her heels and wriggling her toes as she sank onto the nearest sofa.

Dev.

'For heaven's sake,' she admonished her trembling midriff. 'Calm down.'

'How did it go?'

Kate's eyes closed. God, she loved his voice!

'Kate? Can you hear me?'

'Yes! Sorry. All fine. Matt's sorting the cabling and Gemma's coming over to help too. Anna is overseeing Jago and Cobber, who've agreed to put up the bunting along the harbour. Everyone's lined up for Friday morning, so we can get tables set up ready for when people arrive to prepare their stalls, and so on. Arabella Tremayne's arranging to have the lawns cut before then and has even offered cups of tea on tap.'

In fine bone china cups, of course, and served by her housekeeping team, but it was a kind gesture all the same.

'Oh, and Dickie the Chippy has made a couple of fantastic wooden direction posts with signage to things like the loos, story-telling tent, the performance area, and more.'

'Excellent. The forecast is looking good too.'

Such inane conversation, when all Kate wanted to do was sit and talk to Dev about anything but the fayre. As it was, he ended the call and she was left with nothing to do but pull together some cheesy nachos and something a little healthier for herself and then spend the rest of the evening staring out of window at the distant sea, her head full of unrealistic dreams.

Chapter Thirty-Four

The One Where Karma isn't a Chameleon

By Thursday evening, Kate had finished work, confident the events over the weekend would pretty much run themselves, with the individual wedding planners in charge and the efficient team at the hotel well-versed in their roles. She remained on-call, but in effect she was now off until Tuesday.

After dinner, with the fair weather continuing, she persuaded Mollie to walk down into the village. She'd had confirmation the tables, chairs and electrical equipment had been delivered to the manor earlier that day, but Kate was keen to check everything was in place on the harbour too.

Polkerran was bustling with visitors, sitting outside the restaurants and pubs or leaning on the harbour wall, tucking into their take-aways. The queue for the chippy snaked around the corner, children sat crabbing on the steps down to the water and the gulls dipped and soared, beady eyes watching for any discarded morsel.

There was a flashy red sports car parked outside Harbourmasters, with several people admiring it. The air was warm, a light breeze wafting across the bay and caressing Kate's bare arms as they walked along the front, her eyes scanning every group of people in hopes of a sight of Dev.

'Look, Mum.'

Mollie pointed to where Dickie the Chippy stood beside another of his excellent signposts, which had been inserted firmly into the hole which supported the harbourfront Christmas tree in winter.

'It looks fantastic,' Kate greeted Dickie warmly as they joined him. 'I didn't know you were making one for down here too.'

'Well now, my lovely, off-cuts there'll always be. What better use to put 'em to.'

There were three direction pointers sporting black lettering, one of which bore the words 'Village Fayre', another 'Parking' and a third pointing at the harbour, making it clear it was the perfect destination for 'Gurt Tossers'.

'Er, Dickie, do you think that's quite—'

'Kate!'

Anna waved at her from across the street as she and Oliver emerged from the bistro, Matt and Gemma in their wake, and they came over to join Kate and Mollie.

Oliver's eyes narrowed as he read the sign, the edges of his mouth twitching on the last one, but before Kate could request Dickie replace it with something slightly less offensive, there was a commotion further along the harbour.

'Come on,' Matt urged them as he took Gemma's hand and they hurried to the scene.

'Bella! Wait.'

Six pairs of fascinated eyes watched as Bella swung around to face Alex Tremayne.

'Wait? For what?'

'I can explain. It's all a misunderstanding.'

Bella put her hands on her hips as Alex fetched up in front of her, out of breath. 'How… original. And just who was it that did this *misunderstanding*?'

'Not you or I. That's all that matters. I was underestimated, don't you see?'

'Oh yes, I do see.'

'Oh dear,' Anna muttered to Kate. 'Alex thinks he's regained the upper hand.'

It was true, his expression had morphed from one of genuine desperation to assurance.

'That's better.'

Kate exchanged a swift glance with Oliver. Wasn't he being a bit too patronising?

'No, Alex. It's not better.'

'But I gave Mother permission to offer the manor back to that lot,' he gestured towards where Kate and co stood. 'When you came to see me in London the other day, I couldn't believe it. You must know I did it for you, Bella.'

'Aww.' She tilted her head to one side. 'You did it for *me*? That is so… ten years too late.'

Bella spoke clearly and precisely, inadvertently drawing the attention of a few people who were sitting on the benches or strolling along the harbourfront. 'Let's be honest. You did it to make yourself look better, because you thought – mistakenly – it would seem selfless. But you've never done anything for anyone else in your life. You're a moron, Alex Tremayne, who doesn't care about anyone but himself.'

Bella turned away again, but as she neared the jetty where the ferry normally docked, Alex grabbed her arm, swinging her around.

'I'm changed. I mean, I *am* changing. For you.'

'Poppycock,' Bella retorted.

Kate glanced at Mollie to see how she was taking this, but her daughter was busy videoing the whole thing.

Placing her hand on the phone, Kate shook her head at Mollie, who scowled but stopped filming. In the meantime, Alex had resorted to putting on the charm, speaking rapidly but quietly.

'Wish I could hear what he's saying,' Gemma whispered.

'I can't believe she's even listening.'

A faint sound escaped Anna and they all drew in a collective breath as – her expression unfathomable – Bella took a step closer to Alex, then placed her hands on his chest.

'Surely she's not going to fall for— Oh!'

With a sudden shove, Bella pushed Alex full in the chest with both hands, and he toppled backwards, arms flailing, into the water with an almighty splash, accompanied by a spontaneous round of applause from those watching.

'Oh, my God!' Gemma threw Anna a panicked look. 'Can he swim?'

'Let's hope not,' Oliver drawled.

'You've got to feel some sympathy for the fish, though,' Matt added.

To Kate's relief, Alex was striking out for the steps in a flashy crawl, somewhat impeded by his clothing but much to the amusement of everyone gathered round the harbour.

Bella, however, was already striding away.

Alex ran up the steps past the astonished faces of the crabbing children, his clothes clinging to his body, hair plastered to his head, but before he could chase after Bella, a hand landed on his shoulder.

'Not so fast, young'un,' proclaimed Jem, the harbourmaster. 'Having trouble reading, are we?'

He pointed at the notice pinned to the wall:

No Swimming – fines payable

Alex brushed sopping hair from his forehead, glaring at the man. 'Do you know who I am?' he bit out.

Jem leaned back a little, hands stuffed into his pockets, his gaze roaming over Alex's damp features. He turned around, his gaze taking in the holidaymakers and locals watching with interest.

Then, he pulled out a walkie talkie. 'Kevern, lad? You there? Call the doc. Got a teasy incomer 'ere, don' know his own name.'

'And that,' Oliver said succinctly, urging the others on, 'is how the cove deals with Gurt Tossers.'

By Friday afternoon, everything was ready for Polkerran Point's traditional summer fayre, and as Kate emerged from the stables at Tremayne Manor, she looked around with delight.

The festoons of fabric bunting supplied by the hotel danced enticingly in the light breeze, hanging between the trees and across the arched entrance to the manor's forecourt.

Dickie's wooden signs were in place, and the manor gardeners had positioned some large pots bearing summer blooms at the bases.

The local food and drink purveyors were busy setting up their stands inside the stables, their happy, chattering voices drifting out of the massive wooden doors and rebounding off the ancient stone walls in the courtyard.

Across on the expansive lawns, which afforded stunning views of the water beyond, were various pergolas and small marquees, all housing the various offerings pulled together by Kate over the past few months. Again, there was a plethora of activity, and she smiled faintly as she crossed the flagstones and headed for the gates into the lane beyond. It was such a warm evening, and Arabella could be seen instructing her staff to offer drinks to those still setting up.

Jean's ice cream van was parked near the entrance, the chrome shining and the windows glossy from a vigorous polishing and the barbecue in place opposite.

Half a dozen members of the senior gig crew had volunteered to help out with the myriad of things that needed doing over the weekend, such as manning the car parks – armed with tins of change for those who preferred not to pay by App or card – carrying out stewarding duties and running the bar. The hotel had offered its own mobile prosecco cabin and agreed to staff it.

As she walked down into the centre of the village, Kate admired the floral displays. It was as though Polkerran was determined to shine in all its glory for the influx of visitors for their special celebration of all things local.

She passed Mrs Clegg's mobility scooter, parked outside the Spar and sporting a short run of mini bunting between the handlebars and something that vaguely resembled a large crochet ice cream cone on the back, bobbing up and down as the wind caught it. There was no danger she'd get on the wrong one now.

Glancing at her watch, Kate headed over to the railing bordering the harbour. The squeals of happy children could be heard alongside the cawing of the seabirds, and as she watched, Tommy the Boat moored up with his last trip of the day, smiling customers spilling out on to the jetty, some heading straight for the ice cream shop, which remained open despite the evening's approach. Unless she was mistaken, Kate was sure she saw Greg behind the counter with Jean, too.

She ought to head home, but the thought of the empty house – with Mollie staying over at Freya's again – didn't appeal, especially on such a beautiful evening.

The temptation to walk along the lane parallel with the water and past Harbourwatch was great however, and, after a moment's inner debate, she gave in. Just to look at the house where Dev lived would increase her heart-rate tenfold. Didn't it realise there was a six-knot speed limit in the cove?

Amused despite her inner sadness, Kate headed that way anyway. She would walk on the beach she'd grown so fond of, sit on one of the benches for a while and simply... be.

The weekend was going to be manic in a way she'd always enjoyed; she may as well savour this moment of calm.

When Kate reached the beach, it was still buzzing with holidaymakers enjoying the exceptionally warm evening. The cafe had stayed open too, serving a constant stream of ice creams, pasties and drinks. There wasn't space on any of the benches either, but Kate found a piece of rock to perch on and tried with all her might not to crane her neck upwards to stare at Harbourwatch.

After a while, however, her bum became numb, and with the crowd not thinning at all, she set off back up the lane, but as she drew level with the tall, wrought-iron gates to Harbourwatch – propped open today – a car came towards her, and she stepped to one side, only to realise it was Ryther. She gave him a quick wave as the vintage green jag pulled into the driveway before continuing on her way, but barely had she gone a few paces when she was hailed from behind.

Ryther stood in the lane, beckoning her, and Kate reluctantly retraced her steps. He'd better not be about to—

'Come on in! I haven't seen you in a while, my dear.'

Desperately seeking an excuse, but not wanting to lie by pretending Mollie was waiting for her, Kate floundered.

'Precisely,' Ryther intoned, steering her through the gates and up the steps to the front door before she could summon a genuine protest or – more importantly – check her hair and make-up.

Chapter Thirty-Five

The One With the Power of Love

Kate's senses were heightened, her skin alternating between hot and cold. Maybe she was going down with something? She clasped her arms around her middle as they entered the house, aware she was creasing her top by grasping it so tightly, unsure why she was in such bits.

Get a grip!

Kate chewed her lip as Ryther shed his lightweight coat and opened a closet to hang it up, desperately searching for small talk to take her mind off Dev and what he might think of her uninvited appearance in his home.

'Ryther's an usual name. Do you mind me asking where it came from?'

The gentleman indicated they head down the hallway, and she fell into step beside him.

'It was my grandmother's nickname for me and somehow it stuck.' He sent Kate a mischievous smile. 'I was a demon on a pony, you know. My maternal ancestors stem from Germany, where the name means horseback rider or knight. I rather liked the inference.'

Kate grinned at the boyish delight suffusing his features as they reached a set of double doors.

'Here we are.' He pushed open one of the doors to the central room with the ornate glass roof Kate had seen before, and she summoned a smile to mask the trepidation that had returned with a vengeance.

Dev's surprise was evident when he looked up from the vast table, where he sat beside Theo, working on a jigsaw puzzle, but he didn't look displeased.

'Kate!' Theo had far less reservation and he discarded the colourful piece he held and shot around to hug her.

Laughing, Kate laid a gentle hand on the little boy's head as he released her.

'Have you come for supper?'

'Oh! No, I—'

'Kate was passing by,' Ryther said as Theo turned to hug his great grandfather before resuming his seat beside his dad. 'So I invited her in. I hope that was okay?'

He looked to Dev, who seemed amused.

'Kate's always welcome here, Grandy, but on past experience, I'd say you'd have invited her anyway.'

Despite her inner tumult, Kate couldn't help but laugh at the pretend afront on Ryther's face, before he winked and gestured towards the sofas by the hearth.

'Come and entertain an old man for a while, my dear, while these two finish their jigsaw.'

Kate hesitated, but as Dev and Theo's had returned to the puzzle, the former guiding his son in finding the next piece, she acquiesced.

'Would you care for a tipple?' He indicated the decanter on the coffee table between the sofas and his own glass. Then, on seeing Kate's gaze flit to the clock on the mantelpiece, added, 'It's well over the yard arm.'

Perhaps it might calm her jitters?

'Yes, please.'

He poured her a small sherry, and Kate took it, refraining from saying she hadn't drunk it in years. At least it looked like a dry one. She took a cautious sip, then smiled at Ryther, the sherry easing the constricted throat that seemed to be part and parcel of being in Dev's company these last few weeks.

'Dev tells me everything looks quite splendid up at the manor. Are you looking forward to the weekend?'

Kate pulled an amused face. 'I'm part excited and part terrified. There's an… unpredictability about the cove that means you never know what to expect.'

'Having heard from my grandson about your support team, I'm not surprised. I've known Pat most of my life, and the late Arthur Clegg.'

'Is Mrs Clegg a local too, then? Her accent isn't pronounced like the others'.'

Shaking his head, Ryther placed his glass on the table. 'Cleggie moved here from London when she married her Artie. They're all partners in crime, though. I've seen them in action before.'

Kate laughed, then drew in a short breath when Dev looked up. She fixed her gaze on the man opposite.

Focus on the mundane…

'So,' she cleared her throat. 'Dev told me a little about the Devonshire connection to Polkerran. You grew up here, Ryther?'

'Indeed.' For a moment, he stared into the empty hearth, then turned his keen gaze on Kate. 'You are familiar with some of the house's history?'

'Be warned,' Dev's voice sent a tremor through Kate, and she assumed nonchalance as she turned her head to where he now stood by the table. 'Grandy will wax lyrical for hours about the cove if you let him. Come on, Teds. Time for your supper.'

He ushered Theo from the room, and Kate's taut shoulders relaxed their grip as she sank back against the cushions to listen to Ryther's tale.

Kate wasn't blind to the emotion behind his eyes or the slight inflection to Ryther's voice, despite speaking fairly matter-of-factly about both stunning properties perched on their respective outcrops. Yet something had happened here, in the past, surely?

'Is that when…' Kate hesitated.

'Harbourwatch fell into a bit of a state?' Ryther emitted a faint laugh, though he looked unamused. 'The poor house.

Neglected, unloved, abandoned.' He glanced around the now charming room. 'They say buildings cannot mirror the emotions of the human state. How wrong they are.'

Emboldened, Kate leaned forward. 'Would you tell me? What happened all those years ago? What drove you away from somewhere you loved so much?'

For a moment, Ryther didn't speak, and Kate suspected she'd gone too far. Perhaps she ought to go, leave the family in peace?

She made to get up, but Ryther reached out a hand, and she took it. He had a firm grasp, despite his age, and he squeezed her own hand lightly before releasing it.

'Do not mind me, my dear. Memories come thick and fast sometimes. Why is it they are so clear, so vivid, so fresh, yet I will be blowed if I can recall what I even had for lunch yesterday?'

Kate shook her head.

'I wish I knew. My biggest failing is stairs. I swear there's a portal on them so that you repeatedly forget why you went up them in the first place.'

Ryther looked over as Dev returned to the room.

'Theo's having something to eat with Stella. He'll come and say good night shortly.'

'Join us, my boy. We're discussing this house.'

'As you were when I left the room. There can't be much more to say.'

Kate was uncertain whether she was thankful Dev had taken a seat on the same sofa – albeit at the opposite end – or not. Every nerve was standing to attention, yet surely this was easier to handle than if he were sitting opposite, beside Ryther, those blue-grey eyes drawing her hungry gaze?

'I am addressing the most recent years. The house was boarded up, I'm afraid, and left—'

'To rot,' Dev added succinctly. 'I should know. This house and I are now intimately acquainted.'

Kate's gaze dropped to her lap, and she clasped her hands together.

Was it weird to envy a house?

'You have done a wonderful job, Dev, in restoring its beauty.'

'Thanks to your financial support.'

Ryther waved a dismissive hand and continued. 'My Dev was kind enough to preserve some of the things I treasured.'

'Oh! Like the shell frieze in the gorgeous square room?'

The stillness of the figure opposite was in stark contrast to his normal animation, and Kate was alarmed by the sudden paleness in Ryther's papery thin skin.

'Are you okay, Ryther?'

Was he feeling unwell? Kate made to move forward, but Dev was quicker, reaching for the decanter and adding a splash of sherry to his grandfather's glass.

'Here, Grandy, take it.'

Dev flashed a glance at Kate, his expression reflective of his concern, but he resumed his seat, and having done as he was bid, she was relieved to see colour returning to Ryther's cheeks.

He coughed slightly as he placed the now empty glass to the table. 'Forgive me. Some memories may fade but the wounds do not.' His gaze drifted to his grandson. 'The care you have taken in restoring this house warms my heart, Dev. That you have made it your home brings me great peace.'

'You've never explained why you left, Grandy. Or why you and Dad fell out when he was young.'

Ryther said nothing for a moment, his gaze flitting between his grandson and Kate, who could detect the conflict passing over his elderly features. Then, he released a long sigh.

'I have not spoken of this before, but I feel it is pertinent just now and, Dev, my boy, I would caution you to listen. It is quite simple. I adored the most incredible woman, as beautiful inside as she was to observe.' His gaze became distant, as though lost in the mists of time. 'Unfortunately, she was not my wife, whom I had loved once. It is a hard path, is it not, when it is a one-way street with no U-turn at the end?'

Her heart saddened, Kate wished she could reach across and take Ryther's hand. She cast a discreet look at Dev, whose eyes were fastened on his grandfather.

'This lady lived here in Polkerran. At Westerleigh, which she rented from my company. We fell deeply in love one beautiful summer. I had a ring made for her. A promise ring, for how could I suggest more in my situation?'

'She had no idea about your life away from here?' Kate asked tentatively.

Ryther shook his head. 'Not then. I wished for a divorce from my wife, but I had a young son.' He looked over at Dev. 'Your father. And he needed me, so although your grandmother knew I had someone else, that I wished to marry them, she held it over me. I decided to leave anyway, but then—'

His voice caught, and Dev fetched water from the carafe on the sideboard.

'Thank you.' Ryther took a gulp, then another. 'I felt honour-bound to confess my secret.'

'To Meg.' Kate's voice was a mere whisper, but Ryther held her gaze, then inclined his head.

'Of course. I told her the truth, of which she had known nothing. That I was married and had a son, but much as I loved my child, I was leaving them to be with her. She was upset, which I anticipated, but what I did not was the devastation, or the depth of her subsequent anger. She told me in no uncertain terms to go away and never contact her again. Be the father I ought to be. That no child should be without their parent. I couldn't reason with her on any level, and our precious time in the cove was over.'

He drew in a shuddering breath before continuing. 'It did not stop me loving Meg, or thinking about her... us. It was a love the like of which I'd never known, or ever did again.' He bowed his head, and when he raised it, his eyes damp, he continued, his voice creaking with emotion. 'My heart shrivelled and died, and so did Harbourwatch.'

Chapter Thirty-Six

The One With the Bitter Sweet Symphony

Kate was awash with sorrow, for both Ryther and Meg. She drew in a short breath. She should never have asked him to explain. She cast a quick look across at Dev, expecting to see disapproval, but although he frowned, he addressed his grandfather.

'What about Westerleigh?'

Ryther cleared his throat. 'I made it over to Meg, through the holding company. She did not wish to take it, and the negotiations went on for some time through solicitors, but eventually, she acceded. She and Westerleigh were emotionally bound. I could sense it, and I had to do everything I could to ensure they were not parted.'

'So what stirred you to return to the cove, Grandy?'

Ryther said nothing for a moment, but his shoulders sagged as he rested against the cushions. Weariness consumed his features, and Kate's heart went out to him. Not knowing if it was right or not, she got up and sat beside him, taking his hand, and he squeezed hers lightly, his gaze fixed on his grandson.

'I discovered Meg was in a hospice, suffering from that evil disease, Alzheimer's.' Ryther drew in a long breath. 'I took a risk, ventured back to Cornwall. To Bodmin. I tried three times to walk through the door to her room, but failed. I came back here,' he waved a hand in the air, 'to the cove. Stood on the beach below this house for ages, staring across at the cottage, remembering the happiest days of my life. So short, so intense, but never forgotten. They... *Meg* left an indelible mark.'

He pressed a hand to his chest, then cleared his throat.

'The next day, I visited her. They warned me she wouldn't know me, but little did they comprehend it was to my advantage. I sat there for hours, staring at our clasped hands, marked by the passage of time. And I talked. I told her how much I still loved her, that I'd never stopped and wished she could have forgiven me. She drifted in and out of slumber, but then all of a sudden, she roused up and fixed me with a stare. I swear,' his voice wobbled, 'I am certain she knew me, for the brief moment in time, but then she became agitated. I called a nurse, and they advised me to leave, but as I reached the door, Meg spoke. "Follow the shells," she said, holding one out to me. I took it from her as her eyes closed. She said no more, and I left.'

'Oh, my goodness.' Emotion gripped Kate's throat and she fought to hold back tears. 'Ryther, I'm so very sorry.'

His head drooped as a faint sound came from the other sofa, and Kate glanced over at Dev. His mouth was taut with restraint as, shoulders rigid, he clasped his hands tightly in his lap.

'You never mentioned this to me before, Grandy.' His voice crackled with emotion, and Kate sent him a sympathetic look, wishing she could hold both their hands at the same time.

Ryther's eyes had closed, but he still held firmly to Kate's hand, and she rested her other one on top.

'And then, Meg passed away, and there was nothing to prevent me returning to Polkerran. I attended her funeral – not that anyone knew – and a few weeks later, I summoned the courage to visit the grave. It broke my heart anew, that we were never reconciled, but I was able to return the shell she gave me, pressing it into the fresh soil there. Now I go every year on her birthday.' He opened his eyes to meet Kate's, which were damp with unshed tears. 'As I suspect you discovered recently.'

'But I don't understand. Did she not explain her intransience over her rigid belief in a child being with its parents? She didn't have children of her own, as far as I know. It seems at variance with the gentle, kind woman Anna knew her to be.'

Ryther shrugged. 'It is a mystery I will never have an answer to. And Meg *was* kind and gentle. That much I can confirm.' He sat forward, then straightened his shoulders. 'It feels good to have spoken of it after all this time. Thank you both for bearing with an old man's waffling.'

'Not at all,' Kate reassured him.

'I wish you'd felt you could talk about it to me sooner, Grandy. I hate to think of you weighed down by such a sad secret.'

'Well, it is between the three of us, and there let it remain.'

'Would you—' Kate hesitated, glancing briefly at Dev. 'Would you allow me to share this with Anna? Meg treated her as the child she never had. She may know more.'

Ryther drew in a slow, meditative breath before his keen gaze moved between his grandson and Kate. Then, he inclined his head.

'If you wish, though I will not raise my hopes. Now,' he picked up his glass and topped it up with sherry, 'enough on the past. Cheer me up with something more encouraging. What brought *you* to the cove, my dear?'

With both Devonshire men's keen eyes on her, Kate fidgeted in her seat.

'A fresh start.' She hesitated, then decided to address the elder gentleman, as he had asked the question. So what if Dev had heard it before. 'There's a strange almost symmetry. I had stuck with a very unhappy marriage for far too long, mainly for my daughter's sake, thinking it was the right thing to do. The *only* thing to do. That escape would come once she was grown up.' For a second, the former sadness consumed Kate, but she shook it off. 'When I see how happy Mollie now is, I regret not doing it sooner.'

'And you, Kate?' Ryther probed. 'Are *you* happy?'

Using every possible restraint, Kate managed not to instinctively look across at Dev. 'Let's just say, I'm getting there. It took me some time to realise I've been alone most of my married life.'

'So have I,' Dev interjected, then blinked as though he'd surprised himself in saying it.

Kate sat back in her seat, hands in her lap again.

Ryther nodded slowly. 'I see that is all you are prepared to say. For now.'

'Look, I'd best go.' Kate got up, desperate for air.

Ryther got to his feet slowly, and she placed a kiss on his cheek.

'Thank you for inviting me in.'

To her surprise, however, Ryther gripped both her hands in his, his eyes raking her face, then fastening on her own curious gaze.

'I gave up something so precious because I did not have your courage, Kate. I should have fought harder.'

Reflecting that she hadn't felt particularly brave, Kate merely squeezed his hands gently and he released her.

'Good night, Ryther. I'll see you tomorrow?'

'You most certainly will, my dear.'

'I'll see you out,' Dev offered, but Kate paled.

The last thing she needed was a moment alone with him!

'I'm fine,' she waved a hand and shot towards the door. 'Say good night to Theo for me.'

Tugging open the heavy door, Kate inhaled deeply. Dusk had begun its gentle enveloping of all in its path, and the breeze from earlier had stilled. Not a breath of air moved, and for a second, she hesitated on the top step, then froze as she heard footsteps behind her.

The traitorous thing in her chest bounced around as though going for gold in the trampoline, and she looked round as Dev joined her.

'That was intense.'

Kate couldn't help but laugh gently at his perplexed expression.

'I must admit, I wasn't expecting it, but I feel so sad for them both.' Kate became thoughtful. 'I'm sure Anna will know more. She's been digging through a box of letters and photos belonging to Meg. I wonder if she'd be willing to part with one, for your grandad. I suspect he'd love to have a picture of Meg from back then?'

Dev didn't respond and Kate turned away, ready to escape, but then he stirred.

'It's a good idea. Thank you, Kate, for being so... kind towards him. Not judging him.'

She stared up at Dev in the light streaming in through the doorway. 'None of us can help falling in love. Sometimes, Fate isn't as kind as we'd like.'

Okay, now she *did* need to leave, before she said something stupid!

Dev, however, stayed her with his hand.

'It was so manic earlier, I didn't get chance to say what a superb job you've done. Everywhere looks fantastic up at the manor. I'm sure it's going to be a roaring success.'

'Thank you,' she said, though it came out as a whisper, as though love had stolen her voice, holding it hostage.

'I think it's I – or the whole cove – who should thank *you*, Kate. If not for your vision, tenacity and drive...' He shrugged endearingly, shoving his hands into his pockets, and emotion caught in her throat.

Great. That will really help the vocal expression.

Kate essayed clearing it. 'Team effort,' she managed to croak, but before she turned to take the steps down to the driveway, she impulsively reached up to press a kiss on Dev's cheek.

Except Dev – for whatever reason – chose at that very moment, to turn his head.

As his lips brushed against hers, Kate drew in a sharp breath, but then the pressure of his mouth became firmer, albeit briefly, before he stepped back.

'I'm not going to say I'm sorry.'

Kate's eyes scanned his in the fading light.

'Good,' she spoke softly.

Then, as Theo could be heard calling along the hallway to his dad, she shot down the steps with no regard for her natural clumsiness and scooted out of the driveway without looking back, pressing two fingers to her mouth as she walked as fast as she could up the lane.

'You're too old to be feeling all this... *stuff*!' she exclaimed breathlessly as she reached the top of the slope where the lane levelled out.

Except deep down, Kate knew that she wasn't, and the slightest hint at Dev possibly having feelings in return was almost too much to cope with.

Think about the fayre, think about the fayre, her mind scolded as she headed along the lane into the village.

In any other direction, even more heartbreak lay.

—

Kate woke early to another beautiful morning, and walking out onto the terrace in her nightclothes, she could feel the warmth building already. The sky and sea were an intense blue and merged on the horizon, seeming as one.

Two trawlers headed out over gentle crests of waves towards the distant fishing grounds, trailing flurries of white behind them. A scattering of diamonds glittered over the surface of the undulating water, and Kate's gaze moved to the right.

Although she couldn't see Harbourwatch from the terrace, she knew its exact location by direction, and as her thoughts on falling asleep and on waking were immediately with one of its occupants, she had no difficulty now in picturing Dev, having breakfast with Theo and Ryther, and wishing she was there too.

'Perhaps not dressed like this,' she mused, heading inside to shower. Then she'd give Mollie a prod and get ready, with every intention of being up at the manor long before anyone else arrived.

Forty-five minutes later, having changed her mind three times on how to wear her hair and leaving behind a jumble of discarded clothing, Kate hurried down the stairs.

'I'm off, Molls. Send me a message when you're on your way.'

Mollie waved a hand, her gaze not moving from her iPad as she tucked into cereal, and Kate shot down the lane, checking her phone. No messages. That was something.

Or was it? It was a relief nothing relating to today had come in, but wasn't she hoping to hear from Dev? What about that brief kiss? Was she overthinking what, in reality, was pure coincidence, accidental, a happenstance?

'Or serendipity…' she murmured on reaching the bridge, but then a message pinged and she studied her phone. It was Anna, with whom she'd had a long chat the previous night about Meg.

> I've had a word with Oliver. I'll see if I can catch Ryther today. There's something he needs to know.

Puzzled, Kate leaned on the parapet for a moment. What could this possibly have to do with Oliver? Then, she put it aside to take in the view, letting the scene wash over her as she mentally reviewed her to-do list for the day.

It was a peaceful scene this early, with very few people about beyond some activity on the harbour. The little red-and-white passenger ferry bobbed by its mooring, several seagulls sat on the railings in a line, as though waiting for the next bus, and a small electric truck pulled up by the chippy to empty the bins ready for another busy day in the cove.

Layers of heat embraced the village, even the birds seemed to wheel more slowly overhead, their cries strangely muted, and relieved she'd opted for tying up her hair, Kate adjusted her sunglasses and set off for the manor.

By nine o'clock, the stalls were brimming with goods and the vendors were exhausted, fanning themselves with anything that came to hand and forming a constant queue at the water coolers. Kate made her way around, chatting to everyone and taking photos of the displays ready to share on socials later.

She checked there were plenty of cushions in the story-telling tent, then joined a wilting Mrs Tremayne for a cup of tea, before heading back to wait for Mollie.

Soon, people were pouring through the gate. Kate went to provide back-up on the entrance stand, greeting and directing and hugging Anna when she arrived with Oliver in tow.

'Who's that?' Anna nodded back over at Chloe, busy selling raffle tickets. 'She looks sort of familiar.'

'She's the manager's PA at the hotel. I—'

'Kate, Kate, we're here!' Theo's piping voice could be heard, but Kate couldn't see him beyond the people closer in the queue until her gaze met Dev's across the jostling heads.

'I'll catch you later.' Anna moved away with a smile, and breath catching in her throat, Kate dragged her eyes away and tried to focus on smiling as she handed out Phoenix's maps, and pointed out where the loos were and the meeting point for lost children.

Then, they were at the front, and as Dev bought some raffle tickets, Theo came to hug her.

'I'm so 'cited. I was awake *all* night.'

'Some of the night, Teds.' Dev ruffled Theo's hair as they moved along the line.

She held out a map to him. 'Not sure you need this,' she managed to say. Then, she looked around. 'Where's your grandfather?'

'He'll be down later.'

'Grandy's waiting for Mummy's train!' Theo beamed at Kate as her heart sank.

'Last-minute thing.' Dev glanced over his shoulder. 'We're holding up the queue. Look, I really need to tell you something. Catch you later?'

Kate nodded, feckless strands of hope sneaking around her heart.

With that, they were gone, Theo charging across the lawn to where a young man dressed as a puffin sat, making balloon animals, Dev in his wake.

Chapter Thirty-Seven

The One With Tears for Fears

The stables had become the sanctuary of choice as the mugginess continued to build. There wasn't a breath of breeze inside the walled grounds at Tremayne Manor, but the thickness of the walls ensured the former block housing all manner of perishables remained comparatively cool. Kate browsed the stalls once Mollie arrived – quickly deserting her for her school mates.

Filling her bag with local cheese, a bottle of gin, a delicious relish and a box of oat crumble biscuits, she emerged back into the fierce sunlight, removing her sunglasses from on top of her head. A steady line had formed now by the barbecue, enticed, no doubt, by the delicious aroma of grilled burgers and hot dogs.

There had only been one emergency call from the hotel, too – a small hitch in the delivery of some of the flowers, now rectified – and Kate had done her best to keep herself occupied, veering away every time her steps led her towards Dev and whatever activity Theo was engaged in.

The craft workshops seemed to be running to time, with Old Patrick's wood-turning demos and both Mrs Lovelace's and Mrs Clegg's knitting and crochet sessions popular, especially with the older contingent.

Matt was busy overseeing the equipment as the various performers did their bit, with Gemma on hand to help with the changeover between acts, there was a steady stream of people browsing the many tables, and Kate was delighted to see the stock reducing as visitors stowed purchases into their bags.

Sneezing could be heard from the front lawn, which played host to the dog show, and Kate hoped Morwenna had dosed up on her allergy tablets. Jean and Greg were doing a roaring trade from the ice cream van, and an attentive group were making their way in Oliver's footsteps out of the arched gate on the first guided history walk.

'It's fabulous, Kate!'

She smiled as Anna joined her, carrying a wicker basket filled with all manner of things.

'I can't pass a stall without buying something, but this is getting heavy and Oliver's told me to stop!'

'You can store it with mine if you like?'

Kate led her to a door protected by a keypad, into a small room where stallholders could leave their valuables while they were busy.

'We're starving.' Anna patted her belly. 'Have you eaten?'

Kate's tummy felt like a tumultuous sea right now. 'I'll get something later, but I think you need to sit down. This heat is draining.'

Anna did look rather flushed, damp tendrils on her forehead, and she followed Kate to a shady area where patio tables and chairs were scattered but the oppressive intensity remained. Grabbing some water from one of the coolers, Kate brought it over, but then she spotted Ryther and waved him over.

Anna patted the chair opposite. 'Have you got time for a chat?'

Ryther's keen gaze darted to Kate, and she sent him an encouraging smile. 'I'll leave you to it.'

She made to turn away, but Ryther reached out and stayed her.

'I'd prefer you to be here, Kate. Please.'

Hearing the anxiety in Ryther's voice, she sat beside him, and he took her hand and clasped it.

'I explained a little to Anna about your history with Meg.' Kate spoke softly, conscious of the rigidity of Ryther's frame as he stared at Anna.

He didn't respond beyond a squeeze of Kate's hand, and Anna's smile became gentle.

'I believe I can shed some light on why Meg felt as she did about children and their need for a parent.'

Speaking quickly, Anna related what she'd understood all the time she'd known her aunt Meg: that she'd never married or had a family, but that she bore a great sadness which was connected to the loss of a much younger sister who'd died in infancy.

What Anna had not known at the time, and was later revealed by a letter Aunt Meg left her to find by following a trail of shells, was that the infant was not her sister but her daughter, and she didn't die. She was taken from a teenage Meg and adopted, and she'd never seen or heard of her again.

It had also come out that Meg tried to contact her daughter later in life, and failed. Then some years later, Oliver had arrived in Polkerran in search of his maternal grandmother. His mother – Meg's daughter – had never revealed her adoption to him, he only found out when going through papers after her death.

Such was Meg's shame over having fallen pregnant at fifteen to a man who, unbeknownst to her, was already married with a family, she begged Oliver not to reveal his connection to her.

He honoured her request. No one in the cove other than Anna (and, later, Lauren) knew of the relationship to this day.

'As far as anyone here understands it, Oliver befriended Meg. He helped maintain her home and gardens, they spent a great deal of time together in the few years before she became ill. We've only just been piecing together the rest of the story. We didn't know about you, Ryther, until recently when we found more of her papers and photos.' Anna's expression saddened further, and Kate gave Ryther's hand a reassuring squeeze. 'Meg never got over the loss of her daughter, we think it may be what led to her insistence on your staying with your son.'

Anna broke off to rummage in her bag, and Kate cast a wary glance at Ryther, who'd gone incredibly pale and clung to her hand with a grip that belied his age.

'Oliver thought you might like to have these.'

Ryther reached a shaking hand to take the photos from Anna, dashing his other across his eyes.

'I—' He attempted to clear his throat. 'I have no words just now, my dear. Will you forgive me if I take a moment?'

Kate got to her feet with Ryther. 'Will you be okay?' she asked, eyeing him with concern.

'Better than I ought,' he responded, turning to Anna and taking her hand and pressing a kiss on the back of it.

'I am indebted to you, dear Anna. And please pass on my heartfelt thanks to that handsome husband of yours for sharing such personal information with me.'

He walked away, his attention on the photos, and Kate released a slow breath.

'Gosh. I must tell Dev, and oh!'

'Kate?' Anna tugged on her hand and pulled her down into Ryther's vacated chair. 'Why are you looking like that?'

'Like what?'

'As though it's the end of the world.' Anna's gaze followed the direction of Kate's frantic look. 'Oh.'

Ryther had been making his slow but steady way back across the lawn to where Theo could be seen, having his face painted by Nicki, his father watching on, when a vision in lavender skipped past him – something Kate could never have mastered in stilettos on grass – and rushed up to Dev to throw her arms around him.

Expecting him to release himself, as he had done the first time she'd met Leigh, Kate almost choked on the tautness of her throat as – with Leigh now holding onto his other arm – he gestured towards a far bank of trees, his head cocked as he listened intently to whatever she was saying.

Emitting a small gasp at the pain lancing her side, Kate shot out of the seat.

'I-I'll be...' She waved a futile hand and headed down the lawn towards the gates, unsure of her purpose or destination, even forgetful of Mollie, when an elderly man stepped out of the shadows.

'Please don't leave.'

Conscious of the wetness on her lashes behind her sunglasses, Kate drew in a sharp breath.

'Sorry, Ryther,' she all but croaked. 'I must.'

'No, my dear. Some things are worth fighting for, but one should not have to go to war alone.'

Bemused, Kate stared at Ryther. He looked more himself, calm and confident – unlike Kate. What should she do? She couldn't bear watching Leigh clinging to Dev's arm like a limpet for the rest of the afternoon. Was she staying over?

Then, she frowned. 'Where did Theo go?'

'Ah. I saw the lovely Gemma just now; she promised to wait with him until he fully resembles a tiger.'

A faint smile touched Kate's mouth, and it was the reminder of the little boy and how much she wished him to be happy that pulled her from the self-focused spiral that had threatened to consume her.

'I must go and find Mollie. She'll make her own way home when she's ready, but I'd better let her know I'm leaving.'

'Before you go, I have a confession. I fear this is my fault.'

Kate blinked. 'How can it be?'

'I called Leigh after you left yesterday. Told her it was time she let Dev go, stopped playing games. That he had the right to be happy. I forgot with whom I was speaking.' He sighed, shaking his head slowly. 'She insisted on speaking to him, and when he came back into the room, Dev said she was coming over today, claimed she wanted to talk to him about the future, that it was very important. He tried to put her off to next week but... well, this is Leigh.'

Ryther left her then to wait for Theo, and Kate ventured warily around the grounds. It didn't seem to be thinning out at all, nor did the heat abate. People were using their maps as fans and some of the manor's staff could be seen restocking the cups by the water coolers and changing the cannisters.

Of the other Devonshires there was no sign.

'They left.' Anna spoke softly by Kate's side, and her sadness, if at all possible, deepened.

'Good.'

'I'm so sorry.' Anna's voice wobbled.

'There was nothing... it wasn't even...' There were no words, really, and they hugged each other briefly. 'I'll find Molls, then I need a breather for an hour before coming back to help with the clean-up and re-set.'

There was a brief distraction when Jason and Liam came running over, almost breathless with glee.

'That Mrs Lovelady,' Jason, the younger, gasped, hands on his hips. 'Hahahaha.'

'She had a bite of a burger,' Liam gurgled with joy. 'But her teeth came out with it, and it fell to the ground.'

'And one of the dogs from the show ran off with them!' Jason went into peals of laughter, and Kate managed a faint smile. It was all too short a distraction from her present gloom, however.

Barely five minutes later, Kate headed to the storeroom to retrieve her bags, but as she closed the door she came face to face with Leigh.

'We've met before, I think.' The melodious voice belied the less-than-friendly expression on Leigh's stunning features. 'You work at the hotel.' Her tone was dismissive and Kate bristled, the momentary lurch of discomfort swept away.

'We may have, and I may do.'

Kate moved to go past her, unsure why she was there.

'Stay away from my husband.'

Stopping in her tracks, Kate swung around. Leigh may well have a voice of steel when dealing with business, but she wouldn't get far using it on her.

'Like *you* do?' Kate drew in a breath, conscious of those within her vision, relishing the late afternoon shade, the happy chirruping of children mingling with the singing, the chimes from the nearby church and the occasional toot of the horn attached to the ice cream van. 'Look, I have no idea why you are even speaking to me. Dev and I are just friends.'

'So he claims.' Leigh sent Kate an assessing look. 'Women always fall for him. He's too kind, especially when they are so *needy*. Well, you won't be seeing him in any capacity much longer.'

Her tentative hopes collapsing like books tumbling off a badly fitted shelf, Kate suppressed a sob as it rose unbidden.

'But we both live in Polkerran,' she choked out.

To her surprise, Leigh began to laugh. 'You are so naïve, you small-town people.'

Rude!

'You think you know Dev, but clearly you don't. He will do anything for his son's happiness.' She turned away, and Kate made one last attempt.

'So why don't you help? Let Theo stay here with his father.'

Leigh turned about, eyes ablaze with triumph.

'I can do better than that. I've just taken a role in Singapore. For three years, even more prominent than the one I had in the States. We're all leaving – together – and I doubt you'll see any of us for a very long time.'

Chapter Thirty-Eight

The One Where Kate Keeps on Movin'

When she returned to the fayre grounds after the visitors had all left, Kate threw herself into helping with the clean-up, carting sacks of rubbish to the large bins by the garages, wiping down tables and chairs, and ferrying boxes of artwork, books, jewellery, pottery, and so on from the backs of people's cars so they could replenish their stock for the morning.

Throughout it all, Dev and his leaving Polkerran, going so far away, hovered menacingly in the back of her mind, and with piercing clarity, she realised why he'd wanted to talk to her.

Mollie knew something was wrong, but instead of sniping as she usually did when Kate was in a bad mood, she said nothing, volunteering to help with the clear-up.

Kate stretched her back as she walked into the grounds after dumping yet another bag in the bin, her eyes scanning the hive of activity. Anna had gone home, as had Nicki and her boys, but Matt was busy – with the help of Gemma and Bella – at the performance marquee, and Oliver, who had been carting stacks of chairs around as though they weighed no more than Heathcliff, could be seen at one of the bric-a-brac stalls, browsing through what looked like a very old book.

'How did it go?' Kate asked Jean, who was currently stacking cones in the holder by the van's window.

'Brilliant.' Jean's eyes shone. 'So much fun, too. We've run out of three flavours, so Greg's gone to the shop to check on stock for tomorrow.'

Walking on, Kate chatted with a few of the vendors from inside the stables, fiercely trying to prevent her mind travelling along the lane to Harbourwatch. She didn't want to think about Leigh being there with three people who had become dear to her: not just Dev, but Theo and Ryther too.

'Idiot,' she scolded under her breath, as she fetched her bag again from the store. 'You stupid, *stupid* idiot.'

Dev was beyond dear to her. He had become in danger of being her entire life, if fate had only let him.

How she got through the evening, Kate wasn't sure, though the empty bottle of wine on the counter the next morning might have had something to do with it.

Mollie had even brought her a cup of tea in bed, but the unexpected gesture and the silent hug from her daughter had been enough for emotion to surface, and as she stepped into the shower, Kate could feel the hot tears streaming down her face.

It was quite the repair job, but eventually, she dug out her largest pair of sunglasses and was ready. The air already felt oppressive, a heat haze shimmering on the vast open sea, but there was talk of a storm later, and she tucked a brolly into her bag before heading out.

Hopefully, Leigh would ensure Dev didn't come anywhere near the fayre today. There'd been no word from him, but why should there be?

There was nothing left to say.

—

Sunday was pretty much a repeat of Saturday, with throngs of people enjoying the traditional fayre, clapping to accompany the Morris dancers, tucking into popcorn or ice cream and singing along with the performers, from the fishermen's choir to Old Patrick with his incredibly haunting ballads.

Children ran here and there, sporting painted faces and braids in their hair, some waving balloon animals, others their windmills or candy-striped bags stuffed with treats from the old-fashioned sweet cart, selling confectionary Kate recalled from her own childhood. People passed to and fro, carriers bulging with food and drink, knick-knacks from the bric-a-brac stall or prizes they'd won in the raffle.

If Kate's heart hadn't been torn to shreds overnight, it would have been full on perceiving the delight on everyone's faces, the happy atmosphere and the constant requests from those attending and those manning the stalls to do it all again next year.

If only Dev had been here to share it with… but he wouldn't be here next year, would he? He'd be thousands of miles away, living a life that had nothing to do with Kate. Living with Leigh.

An ominous rumble came from above and several people looked upwards, but aside from a couple of small white clouds bubbling up on the horizon, the sky remained a rich cerulean blue.

Kate kept herself busy, refusing to think about what might be happening up at Harbourwatch, willing her mind not to dwell on the emptiness of the upcoming months, and before long it was nearly four o'clock and time to wind things down.

Mollie had eschewed a second day at the fayre, saying she'd maxed out her inner child. Freya's parents were heading to a water park up near Newquay and had invited Mollie along, with a view to her staying the night at her friend's later.

Anna had been ordered by Oliver to rest because of the weather conditions, but Matt had still manned the equipment for the performances, and as the afternoon waned, he was beginning to dismantle the pergola now, with help from a couple of locals.

Nicki had continued her face-painting and hair-braiding, but Hamish – despite his aching back – had gone out early in his boat, keen to avoid the storm if it arrived and, looking upwards, Kate wondered if their luck was about to run out.

Kate popped down into the village with Bella for some packs of water, as the water coolers had been drunk dry, but as they walked back along the front, hopping on and off the crowded pavements, a car sped by, taking the turn for the hill out of the village: Dev's.

The ache in Kate's chest intensified and her pace stalled.

'You okay? Give it to me, I can carry both packs.'

Kate shook her head at Bella.

'I'm fine,' she reassured her. 'Just having a breather.'

They set off again, but Kate's mind spun relentlessly. Leigh had been in the passenger seat. Where were they going? Surely they weren't leaving immediately? It had been impossible to see if Theo was in the back seat.

Kate left her pack of water with Bella, who began handing them out to drooping stall holders.

The skies had darkened, a strange greyness overlying the blue, which had softened almost to lilac, and another rumble rolled in across the top of the cliffs. An eerie silence followed, as though all the birds had been sucked from the sky.

Before long, the big clean-up was over, and with all the volunteers and stall holders chipping in, along with the Tremayne Manor staff, the grounds were soon empty, the equipment all stored in the garages again, ready for collection, and Jean was easing the ice cream van through the gates.

Functioning on some sort of auto-pilot, Kate had a quick word with Mrs Tremayne, expressing copious thanks and a promise to stay in touch, and she was free to go. She headed down the lane into the village, knowing full well her bereft feelings were nothing to do with the event being over.

What was it Ryther had said? 'A love the like of which I'd never known, or ever did again…'

Was that to be her fate? Would this gut-wrenching pain stay with her for ever, an ache that could never be assuaged?

Pressure built in Kate's chest as she strode on, with no idea where she was going, other than she had no desire to go home alone.

Menacing, swollen clouds covered the sun now, but the stickiness seemed more intense. Kate's skin felt clammy, and she lifted the hair off her shoulders, but no comforting breeze stroked her neck.

There was a long queue outside the ice cream shop. The tables outside Harbourmasters, the bistro and the Three Fishes were spilling over with people, and the sound of voices and laughter pounded Kate's senses.

Her throat felt dry and she shot into the Spar, but as she emerged into the street with a bottle of water, a furious growl emanated from the leaden skies followed by a loud clap, and the heavens opened.

People dived for cover, shuffling inside the pub and restaurants, huddling under the awnings, pulling clothes over their heads, some finding it hilarious, such was the relief from the unprecedented week of extreme heat.

Rain pounded the ground, quickly forming pools of water and soaking a group of young people who refused to take cover and were holding out their arms to embrace the outdoor shower, splashing in the puddles in a way they probably hadn't done since they were kids.

Kate walked out into the downpour, uncaring of the soaking, letting the droplets mingle with the tears running down her cheeks. Who cared, anyway?

She *would* go home. Run a hot bath. Open some wine, and pretend this wasn't happening to her. Kate turned her steps in the direction of the bridge, but as she passed Jean's ice cream van, neatly parked opposite the shop again, a hand shot out and grabbed her arm.

Kate stared up at Dev as the rain continued to pour. How he came to be there, she couldn't fathom, but wasn't it irrelevant? He was lost to her. Emotion gripped her so fiercely, she let out a murmur of pain and spun away, oblivious to how slippery the cobbles now were and, in her haste, her foot slipped from under her.

Two arms caught her, wrapped firmly around her waist and – heart pounding fiercely – Kate allowed herself to be drawn upright.

Dev didn't release her for a moment, his voice close to her ear. 'We must stop meeting like this.'

A laugh rose unbidden, morphing into a sob, and Kate tried to wrench herself from his grasp, but Dev merely turned her around.

'We need to talk.'

Kate's breath was coming in shallow bursts.

No, we don't, Dev! It will make things even harder...

Dev scanned the sheltering crowds. Jean, as it happened, had unfurled the ice cream van's canopy, and stood chatting with some passersby who'd taken advantage of her offer of shelter, and he suddenly grasped Kate's hand and urged her up the steps at the back of the van.

'Stay there a minute. Please.'

Brushing damp tendrils of hair off her forehead, Kate ran a finger under each eye, certain her mascara had long been washed away, her heart pounding madly in her breast. Where on earth had her sunglasses gone?

She wasn't ready to hear Dev tell her he was doing what he'd always intimated he would: giving the marriage another try for Theo's sake, going away. Far, far away... making his own fresh start.

The rain was pounding so hard on the roof, at least it would prevent Dev hearing her heart doing the same. Then, Kate puffed out a breath. This was ridiculous. Whatever he had to say, she couldn't handle it right now. It would have to wait.

Chapter Thirty-Nine

The One Where They Stay Another Day

Kate made for the opening, but Dev was back, his height filling her only escape route, and she sank back against the driver's seat, grasping the leather backrest tightly as he closed the door.

He said nothing for a moment, remaining at the other end of the van by the built-in freezer, and slowly, the sounds on the rooftop eased to a constant patter. Then, he ran a hand round the back of his neck in the endearing fashion Kate had become used to, and her heart – which had huddled into a bruised corner – swelled a little against her volition.

'Look, Kate, I've been wanting to talk to you for a while, but I just didn't know what I could say. And now, there's been some developments overnight.'

I know.

'I'm going to be able to be with Theo *all* the time.'

I know that too.

Despite her despair, however, Kate was deeply moved by the delight infusing Dev's features. She *had* to be happy for him; she loved him too much not to be.

'That's wonderful.' To her surprise, her voice was steady, but she cleared her throat nonetheless. 'I'm so pleased for you, for Theo too.'

He took a step towards her, then stopped. 'I wanted to tell you, but—'

Kate's heart went out to him. 'There's no need. I understand, truly I do.' Her eyes ached from holding back further emotion.

Time to embrace reality, to give up on pointless dreams. To go home and drink wine. Lots of it.

'It seems your grandfather's confession was somewhat prophetic. I hope this will bring you…' Something had a grip on her throat now, and the words weren't coming out quite so easily. 'I wish you…' She gulped in a breath as she completed the trite phrase. 'Every possible happiness.'

Dev stilled, saying nothing for a moment, but then he locked eyes with her across the small space.

'Do you, Kate?' he whispered, so softly she strained to hear the words. 'Do you wish me every possible happiness?'

Still struggling to form words, Kate nodded.

Oh, no. Don't smile like that, she begged him silently, as his eyes shone with blatant delight.

Kate made a dash for the door, but Dev easily stalled her, pulling her gently in front of him.

'I am in love with you, Kate.' Dev spoke quietly but firmly and she held back a small gulp, her eyes frantically searching his.

Then, she slowly nodded as, throat aching with suppressed emotion, she tried to savour this one last moment with him. He might well love her. She'd half suspected the attraction had become mutual, but he would do the right thing and stand by the marriage for the sake of Theo – just as his grandfather had done before him. She couldn't fault him for it. Damn it, she even admired his loyalty, his fierce determination to do the best for his child.

'If this is our moment for honesty, then I'll confess. I've fallen in love with you too.' Kate drew a shaking breath. 'I know it can't go anywhere, and I'd never want to come between you and… what you want. But it feels important to say it.'

She didn't know where to look, or what to do, uncertain whether her heart or head were in the most tatters. She needed to leave, but Dev was effectively blocking her escape simply by staying where he was. There wasn't, after all, much room inside an ice cream van.

'Look at me, Kate.'

How she loved his voice, especially when he spoke in such a loving way…

Slowly, she raised her despondent gaze from where it had fixed on a box of waffle cones. She paused. Dev didn't look at all troubled or distraught, especially for someone who'd just admitted to being in love with the person he wasn't technically still married to.

'I didn't know you loved me back.' Dev reached out to wipe a stray tear from Kate's cheek, and heat seared through her skin at the touch. 'I hoped… but I tried not to.'

She grabbed his hand as he withdrew it and pressed a kiss on his palm.

'I've been falling for you for months, but it doesn't feel right talking like this, now you're starting afresh with your…' She couldn't say the name, recalling the woman's expression from the previous day.

'I'm not.'

'But she told me… I thought…' Mind fizzing, Kate all but held her breath as Dev reached out for her hand, and the memory of their first meeting, of his touch as he curled her fingers over the rings, skidded into focus.

'Grandy did me a favour with his interference. Leigh was on the first train down this morning, full of her plans now she's got this dream job.' His expression wry, Dev tugged on Kate's hand and she stepped closer. 'It's been a theme of the marriage, chasing the so-called dream role. Little did I realise it would be what finally set us free.'

'I don't understand…'

'I've spent the last year convinced the best thing would be to try again, if only Leigh would stop gadding about the country and give it a go. For Theo's sake, not mine, I might add.' He shook his head ruefully. 'I've watched your example, taking the opposite route, seen it working. And Friday night, I did a lot of thinking about Grandy's confession, the decision you'd made. It brought so much into focus. I wanted to tell you, before Leigh even appeared… when I arrived at the fayre. I'd realised what really mattered. And it wasn't just Theo.'

'But I thought you were leaving, going away.' Kate's bewildered gaze scanned Dev's face.

'Leigh is moving to Singapore. Alone. Theo's staying with me. It's taken time, but she's finally acceded full custody. She failed to consider, in all her scheming, that she can't legally take Theo out of the country without my consent, and she now knows I won't be persuaded to give it. When it came down to the perfect job or her child, she picked the former. As for me,' he raised his free hand to cup Kate's cheek, 'I'd already come to my own decision. I'm… Theo, and I, are not going anywhere.'

Kate's mind whirled, her heart spinning in her chest like the multi-coloured beach ball of death when Word crashed on her. What did this mean? Was there a chance for them after all?

'But I just saw you both in the car, I thought you were leaving.'

'I drove her to Par for the next train back to London.' Dev shook his head. 'She'd insisted on coming down so she could tell me all about her new plans. When I refused to give in over Theo last night, she said I'd regret it. I had no idea she'd spoken to you. I was furious. She agreed to sign the Final Order and send it to her solicitor immediately, said she hoped we'd rot in hell.' A mischievous look, one Kate had never seen, crossed Dev's features. 'I said thanks, but we'd rather stay in the cove for the foreseeable.'

A trickle of hope filtered through Kate's veins and, as Dev closed the gap between them and pulled her fully into his arms, she allowed it to flow freely. There was a pause while grey-blue eyes held brown, but their lids lowered when their lips met, the kiss soon picking up in intensity as she finally allowed herself the freedom to express her feelings.

Dev's mouth moved sensuously over hers as Kate's hands crept along his shoulders and up into his hair, and it was a few moments before they became aware of a tapping noise and reluctantly parted.

'Open up, lovebirds!'

Kate bit her lip, but Dev merely smiled and reached over and flicked the handle and the door swung open to reveal Jean.

'I hate to interrupt,' she began, barely concealing her amusement, 'but the storm's passing over, there's blue sky on its way and the queue outside is, I'm pretty certain, for a whippy ice cream and not an interview.'

'Sorry, Jean. But thanks.' Dev grinned and reached for Kate's hand, which she willingly slipped into his as they stepped down onto the harbourside.

'I'm soaked through. I'd better go home and change.' Kate didn't want to end things like this, even though she was brimming with happiness inside.

'Me too,' Dev said quietly, squeezing her hand, but as they were in public, that was all he did. 'Do you... can I come over when I've changed? There's more to explain, things to say, time we did some more,' his gaze drifted briefly to Kate's mouth, 'talking.'

With a laugh, she reciprocated the squeeze before dropping Dev's hand and scooting along the harbour, heedless of the remnants of the storm, splashing through puddles and uncaring of her damp clothes clinging to her body.

A quick shower later, and feeling as though she was genuinely preparing for a first date, Kate's tummy kept dancing a jig. Every moment she thought of Dev, of the pressure of his mouth against hers, the feel of his arms around her, knowing now that he was in love with her...

There it went again, this time with a full-on reel.

'Calm down,' she cautioned, gripping her middle through the towel as she unwound a second one from her hair. 'I'll never have a steady enough hand to do my make-up if this carries on.'

Dev hadn't said how long he'd be, but—

Her phone rang.

Dev.

'Hi.'

'Hey. Is there any chance you could come over here instead? It's Grandy, he's… well, I don't like to leave him just now.'

'Oh, I'm so sorry. Yes, of course.' Kate eyed her appearance. 'I'll be there as quick as I can.'

Hoping Ryther hadn't had a delayed reaction to all he'd heard the previous day, Kate performed the fastest ever hair dry, twisting her brown waves into a casual up-do. Her Greek tan, topped up nicely in the recent prolonged spell of good weather, would have to suffice. She added a flick of mascara and a pale lip gloss and headed out.

Although the roads were still wet, the pavements were drying out. People had returned to the outside seating at the venues in the village as she passed by, and before long Kate had reached Harbourwatch, infused with happy expectation.

Dev had the door open before Kate had chance to ring the bell, and once it closed behind her, they both stood a little awkwardly for a second, before making a sudden mutual move towards each other, his mouth descending on hers as she clung once more to his shoulders, losing herself in the delight of finally being able to express how she felt.

For someone so reticent, Dev certainly didn't seem to have any problems conveying his own feelings, the kiss becoming more intense as he drew Kate closer, and she willingly pressed her body against his, only for them both to dissolve in amusement as his hand caught her clip and it fell to the floor with a clatter, her hair cascading onto her shoulders.

'I love you so much,' she said brokenly, conscious her eyes ached anew, but with inexplicable delight instead of sadness now. 'And I thought you were lost to me.'

Dev dropped a lingering kiss on her lips, then the tip of her nose, before wrapping his arms around her, and she relaxed into his hold, savouring the steady beating of his heart beneath her ear.

'I wasn't sure if you'd be able to come alone,' Dev spoke softly, his chin resting on top of her head.

There was a strange, comfortable familiarity, as though it had always been this way, and Kate nuzzled even more closely into Dev's shirt, inhaling his cologne and closing her eyes.

'Molls is away overnight.'

There was a movement in Dev's chest, and she raised her head to look at him.

'Damn,' he whispered, tucking a loose strand of hair behind Kate's ear. 'I mean, that would have been…'

Rather than find the words, he made his feelings clear with a short but sensuous kiss, and Kate melted against him. Seriously, if she wasn't gripping his shoulders she might well have dissolved into a pool at his feet.

'What would it have been?' she asked softly, their gazes locked on each other.

'Nice,' he replied. 'Very, very nice.'

He was about to repeat the action, but the sound of running footsteps and a call of 'Daaaddy' was sufficient to return them to reality, and Kate shot out of Dev's arms, tugging her top straight and striving to calm her heightened senses as Theo came scampering along the hall towards them.

Chapter Forty

The One Where Love is All Around

'Kate! Yay. Did Daddy tell you I'm staying?' He puffed out his chest. 'I'm going to live in the cove for *ever*.'

He turned to his father. 'Great-Grandy has gone to lie down for a bit. Can I read him a story?'

'Not just now, Teds, though that's a lovely idea. I think he's tired and needs a bit of rest. Let's go into the drawing room.'

He led the way along the hall to the beautiful, square reception room Kate recalled so well from Anna's wedding, and she walked over to admire the stunning views from the windows, which were triple aspect, facing the village, the sea and in between, across the water, Westerleigh Cottage perched on its rocky promontory.

Recalling Ryther's recounting of his love affair with Meg and its heart-breaking denouement, a fleeting sorrow crossed Kate's features.

A small hand slipped into hers, and she dragged her gaze away to look down at Theo, her heart melting at his sweet face peering up at her.

'Don't be sad. This is the happy room.'

'Is it?' Kate allowed Theo to lead her over to a sofa, where he perched, patting the other seat, and she sank into it.

'Great-Grandy said so when he felt better. He says it…' The little boy's brow creased. 'What did he say, Daddy?'

Dev had taken the seat opposite, and he leaned forward, elbows on his knees. 'He said it answered his dreams many years ago, and today it fulfilled its final destiny.'

Theo nodded fervently. 'He said it made him happy again, so don't be sad, Kate.'

'I'm not, I promise.' She sent Dev a slightly self-conscious smile, and he returned it warmly, so much so, as he held her gaze with his grey-blue stare, she could feel warmth travelling along her skin, and she swallowed on rising emotion.

How could this be? It was almost too wonderful for words, although judging by Dev's expression, conversation wasn't exactly what was on his mind.

'Stop it,' she mouthed, turning her attention to Theo, who wanted to show her his latest puzzle, and she followed him from the room willingly, with a backward glance at Dev, who hadn't moved but was now grinning at her obvious embarrassment.

Ryther didn't return downstairs during the evening, although Dev checked in on him, and once Theo had gone to bed – insisting both Dev and Kate took turns in reading to him from his favourite book – they finally had a moment alone and wasted no time in continuing their earlier... discourse.

'God, I've wanted to do that for months,' Dev mumbled into Kate's neck after drawing a dreamy, sensual kiss to a close.

Kate leaned back in his arms. 'You hid it well.'

Dev drew her over to the sofa and they sank down beside each other, fingers entwined.

'I was fighting the attraction, constantly. On the one hand, I felt like I couldn't stay away, didn't *want* to, but with the divorce stalled after the Conditional Order, I was hardly in a position to act like a completely free man. Telling someone you've fallen for them when you're still technically married to someone else was never on my bucket list.'

'I tried so hard not to want you, Dev,' Kate responded. 'You had so much to deal with, what with things not being finalised and being desperate to do the best thing for Theo.'

This notion brought Ryther's recent confession to mind, and Kate shifted in her seat so she could see Dev's face.

'What happened earlier, for your grandfather to be unwell, and then so happy?'

'Ah. Well, I'm sure he won't mind my telling you, but needless to say I think he's found some much-needed closure.' Releasing her, Dev pulled Kate to her feet, leading her over to one of the arched windows. 'Do you remember the problems with the shell frieze?'

'Yes, of course.'

'This section,' Dev pointed to a corner piece, clearly newly restored, 'had begun to protrude some months ago. It seemed connected to the water damage but it wasn't. Someone, at some point in time, had forced this piece aside to tuck something behind it, and the frieze finally chose to give up its secret.'

Kate moved past Dev to stare across the water at Westerleigh Cottage. 'This has to do with Meg.'

'Yes.' Dev came to stand beside her, his gaze also on the property opposite. 'There was a slim envelope, yellowed with age, the hand barely legible, but Grandy knew it instantly as Meg's. It was addressed to someone called Neb, and—'

'Oh!' Kate exclaimed, and Dev turned to look at her.

'You know the name?'

'Anna found photos with it on, and said Meg had kept letters from a Neb.'

'Grandy's little in-joke with her. His real name is Benedict. Ben, or Neb if you reverse it. Just as Meg became Gem, which led to him naming his much-loved record label Secret Gem Records.'

Eyes wide, Kate scanned Dev's face. 'Wow. And... sorry. I interrupted you.'

'You can interrupt me any time you like. So long as I get a kiss by return.'

Kate duly obliged, but then she rested her head against Dev's shoulder as he turned them both towards the window again.

'There was a brief letter in the envelope and, thankfully, having been a little more protected, it was still legible. Grandy almost fainted as he read it, shed a great many tears, hence my asking you to come over, but given a moment to recover, he spoke. Meg had written it when Oliver was renting the house. She'd apparently taken to coming over, sitting in this very room because here she felt close to Grandy. She never got over losing him, but she did finally forgive him, wanted him to know that… somehow, one day. He'd installed the frieze for her, knowing of her love of shells, so she decided that's where she would hide it. If he was meant to find it in time, then he would.' Dev sighed. 'As it happened, it seems the letter found him instead.'

'That's sad, but so romantic. Poor Ryther, and poor Meg. Did the letter hint to him as to why she rejected him so forcefully?'

'She did imply there was something in her past – a secret she couldn't bear to impart – and she begged for his forgiveness too in being unable to share it with him.'

'Thank goodness Anna – and Oliver – were able to help.'

'Indeed. Grandy's found a closure he never anticipated after all these years.'

'Bless him. And bless Meg for writing those words, although it would have been a lot easier if she'd simply posted the letter!'

Dev laughed. 'True, but she probably didn't have any other address for him, and there would be no guarantee the right eyes would land on it. And she did tell him, in her one lucid moment, to follow the shells.'

—

Kate awoke the following morning filled with a delicious sense of anticipation. Saying good night to Dev had been incredibly hard, but they both agreed that they ought to take things at a steadier pace than perhaps they wished for Theo and Mollie's sake. All the same, it hadn't stopped Dev from leaving Kate with a good night kiss passionate enough to keep her warm all the way home!

Invited to join the family for lunch, she headed to Harbourwatch, having collected Mollie from her friend's house, and was pleased to see Ryther very much himself.

Soon after the meal had concluded, Mollie having headed down to the beach with Theo, they stood in the lane outside Harbourwatch as the gentleman steered the stately green Jaguar up the lane, and as it faded from view, Dev slipped his hand into hers.

'I'm glad Grandy found some peace at last. I'm not condoning what he did, but if ever there was proof of undying love, then surely he and Meg were it?'

Kate sighed softly, squeezing Dev's hand. 'You could see how much it affected him – her forgiveness. Who'd have thought it was there all the time, tucked inside that frieze? And "follow the shells"… Anna once said she and Oliver had been the only ones Meg told about that in the midst of her illness, and yet look how the story continues.'

Dev put an arm around Kate's shoulders, and she slipped her own around his waist as they made their way down the lane towards the beach. The closeness of Dev's body was stirring all manner of sensations, and Kate couldn't help but anticipate the intimacy they might soon be able to enjoy, the easy colour washing over her cheeks.

'What is it?' Dev was half laughing, half concerned as they reached the edges of the sands, outside the little cafe.

'Nothing. You. Us.' Kate quivered as Dev ran a finger down her cheek. 'Stop it,' she admonished gently, a smile negating the words.

She flicked a glance towards the cafe. 'There's a webcam up there, we could be on view to half the country.'

'And two significant children,' Dev added as he took her hand and tugged her along behind him onto the beach, waving at Mollie and Theo, who had thrown their towels on a couple of rocks and were currently paddling in the shallows, hand in hand.

'Bayley did put a bit of a sulk on at not being able to join us,' Kate added, glancing at the sign which declared the times of day when dogs were allowed.

'Okay, *three* children.'

Dev opened the beach bag they'd brought down earlier and spread a tartan rug on the sands, and soon he had settled with his back to the cliff, Kate nestled in front of him, their legs stretched out together. She leaned back against him, so content she felt her heart – which had been much bruised of late – might burst with sheer, unbridled happiness.

'Are you comfortable?'

'More than you'll ever know,' Dev replied close to her ear, blowing softly on her neck.

Kate giggled. 'That tickles. I meant with your back against the rocks.'

'I'll let you know. Now, we have more important things to talk about. You suggested last night we continue our dating, but with the children to start with?'

With a gentle sigh, Kate picked up one of Dev's hands and dropped a kiss on it. 'I-I mean, *we*, need to be feeling our way—'

Dev's chest heaved, and she sat up and craned her neck to look at him. 'What's so funny?'

He lowered his mouth to her ear. 'I'm not going to object.'

Laughing, Kate nestled back against him. 'Feel our way with Mollie… and Theo, of course.'

'And Bayley. Don't forget him.'

'Or Podge.' Kate sat up again, this time shuffling round on her knees, then sitting back to address Dev. 'Do you think they'll get on?'

Dev took Kate's hand. 'How about our dating alternates between The Lookout and here? I'll bring Bayley when I come to you with Theo.'

'I like that idea.'

'Daddy!'

They looked over to see Theo jumping up and down, waving them over. Dev got to his feet and Kate followed him across the wet sand to the shoreline, where Theo excitedly showed them two small crabs in his bucket, then thrust his colourful net at Dev.

'These are the best pools,' Mollie called from where she stood on the flat rocks exposed at low tide, and for a moment, Kate watched Theo, clinging tightly to his dad's hand as they made their way to join her, then turned to look around.

Settling on a nearby patch of sand, she dug her bare toes into the soft grains, raising her head, eyes closed, as the sun kissed her skin. She had no fears for the future, only a glowing happiness that filled her entire body with joy. Recalling the sensations of the previous evening as she and Dev began the delightful expression of their mutual affection, something pulsated through Kate's body, but sensing someone's presence, her eyes flew open.

'Damn,' Dev said quietly, as he sat beside her, stretching out his long legs. 'I was going to steal a kiss.'

'You can't,' whispered Kate, as she watched Mollie and Theo abandon their nets and buckets to go paddling in the shallows, 'steal something that's willingly given.'

He leaned over and pressed his mouth to her cheek. 'That will have to do for now.'

They sat in silence for a moment, their mutual gazes on Theo and Mollie, then Dev spoke softly.

'I didn't expect this… you… my life to feel so complete.'

Moved, Kate could feel emotion welling behind her eyes, and she lifted his hand to press a firm kiss into his palm.

'Nor did I.'

Although I think it was on a list somewhere…

They returned their gaze to the children, and Kate rested her head on Dev's shoulder.

'I've been thinking. Mollie goes on her archaeological trip to France in a fortnight. Isn't that when the two-day camp for the early years pupils is taking place on Exmoor? I'm sure I heard Nicki talking about it.'

'It is. Theo is desperate to go, but I wasn't sure if he was too young.'

Kate lifted her head to look at him. 'Did you know Nicki's going along as one of the chaperones? I'm sure she'd be happy to keep an eye on him.'

He held her hopeful gaze for a moment, then the edges of his mouth twitched.

'And what was it you were thinking?'

'Weeell...' From the way Dev was now looking at her, she was pretty sure he had a good idea what was coming. 'I might get lonely up there at The Lookout... on my own... at night. I wondered if you'd like to... you know.'

'Yes, please.'

Laughing, he put a finger under her chin and raised it for a quick kiss.

'I'd more than like to.'

With that, Kate had to be content, and she relaxed into him as he placed his arms around her, almost overcome with gratitude for her present life.

Kate closed her eyes again, conscious of the steady beat of Dev's heart, of his solidity, his strength. She could hear the shouts of children playing, the distant chug of a boat coming into the bay, the waves sliding onto the sands and the caw-caw of the gulls overhead.

Polkerran Point had, after all, become the perfect fresh start and a new beginning, filled with hope for the future.

For Kate, for Dev, Mollie and Theo... and not forgetting Bayley and Podge. It seemed the cove had worked its magic once more, and healed them all.

Acknowledgements

So, here we are at the end of the fourth book in the Little Cornish Cove series and my list of thank-yous grows ever longer.

I must start at the beginning, with Emily Bedford, my amazing editor at Canelo. She has been with me through thick and thin during the writing of this series, and without her, I'm not sure this particular book would ever have been finished! Thank you, Emily, for yet again being patient, encouraging, insightful and full of enthusiasm for Kate and Dev's story even when I wavered. Your faith in it kept me going, and I'm already missing the characters dreadfully, even after leaving them to their happy ever after.

With regard to the actual writing of the book, I needed – as always – to do some research before I started, and my thanks go out to these lovely people:

Lin Rogers, who is part of the Penzance Literary Festival team. Lin and I had a fun video call, followed up by several messages, whereby she helped me understand the process and some of the challenges in running a festival of this nature, along with an insight into the personal elements that can help or hinder;

Dee Groocock and her lovely daughter, Tilly. Thank you both for the chats and the heads-up on being a bright young teen in today's world. Tilly, you are the inspiration behind Mollie's love of musicals and history;

In the same vein, thank you to all the lovely authors who responded to my cry for help in the Savvy Writers' Snug on

Facebook. You shared so many wonderful snippets, anecdotes and more on living with a young teen these days, which I hope make Mollie's behaviour credible.

I'd also like to thank my daughter, Rachel, for once being a thirteen-year-old girl, and likewise my son, Tom, for being a very cute five-year-old boy, albeit these moments in time were both spread across the nineties. I'm sure at the time you didn't expect anything you did to be chronicled in such a way but thank you anyway for the inspiration and to Tom especially for occasionally putting words into Theo's mouth.

Victoria Clark and her fabulous boutique takeaway cafe/shop at Readymoney Cove in Fowey inspired the one at the tidal beach in Polkerran Point, where Kate spends quite a lot of her time, and the livestream webcam there – which keeps me company at home all the time I'm writing – also had its moment to shine. Thanks to Victoria for giving me some background on rules around livestreams!

Being a writer can be a lonely job day-to-day, and I'm grateful to be part of a lovely local writers' group, The Beverley Novelists, who meet up monthly to discuss all aspects of writing. Thank you, ladies, for some great get-togethers over the past year, and a special shout-out to the fabulous Sharon Booth and Jessica Redland, who helped me find my characters when they refused to play ball. Your advice gave me hope and direction and ultimately the missing link to getting where I needed to be.

Thank you to all the readers who've embarked on this journey with me and badger me, in the gentlest way, on whose story will be next. Some of you are getting extremely good at picking up the hints scattered through each book, too! If the cove really was a place, I'm sure we'd all end up meeting around Anna's table for a good old natter.

I must also express my deepest thanks again to all the bloggers who diligently support authors by taking the time to read and review their books. I am in awe of your commitment to reading so many books and of the time and dedication you put into the reviewing craft.

On that note, heartfelt thanks also go out to Kelly Lacey of Love Books Tours and Rachel Gilbey of Rachel's Random Resources, for organising such brilliant blog tours.

It wouldn't be right if I didn't end as I always do by thanking the person who makes everything possible: my husband, Julian. He continues to be supportive, encouraging and hilarious when I really need to lighten up. There is nothing he won't do for me to help me have the time, space and freedom to write, but he's always around for a brainstorm or two if I need him. Having said that, he's *very* glad there's only one more book to go in the series!